LUXURIA

SHADES OF SIN

LUXURIA

SHADES OF SIN

COLETTE RHODES

ILLUSTRATED CHARACTER COVER BY:
MYA SARACHO (@A.LOVEUNLACED)

DISCREET COVER BY:
COLETTE

LUXURIA IS A MONSTER ROMANCE BETWEEN A HUMAN AND HER NOT-QUITE-HUMAN HUSBAND, SUITABLE FOR READERS OVER 18. CW: BREEDING KINK, PRIMAL PLAY.

"WHEN IS A MONSTER NOT A MONSTER?
OH, WHEN YOU LOVE IT."
- CAITLYN SIEHL

OPHELIA

PROLOGUE

I wonder if any of my colleagues will be monster food tonight, I thought idly, smiling and nodding at whatever they were saying while tracing lines in the condensation on my glass. The sun set early at this time of year, and there was nothing a monster liked more than a drunk human in a dark alley.

"We should take a trip!" Marina announced, her voice slurred from one too many strawberry daiquiris. Happy hour was ending in fifteen minutes though, and we were all trying to cram in as many drinks as possible before prices doubled like the fiscally responsible degenerates we were.

"Where?" Carl asked in a bored voice, his arm draped over the back of my chair, fingers toying absently with the ends of my hair. He must be *really* drunk. Usually, the austere software developer with the secret kinky side didn't show me any kind of affection outside of the bedroom under the cover of complete darkness, where we both pretended it never happened immediately afterward.

It had been a while, though, so his itch probably needed scratching. *Was I feeling it tonight?* Maybe not as much as usual. It'd be a nice change to fuck someone who didn't have trouble looking me in the eye the next day. Maybe even someone I didn't have to run into in the tiny kitchen at work whenever I wanted a cup of coffee.

"Mexico," Marina said decisively. "We'll drink tequila on the beach, swim naked, fuck strangers. Well, you guys will, I'll have the hubby with me. But still! I'll watch."

I was the youngest entrant to our inappropriate little crew of colleagues, having joined the software development company we worked at three years ago straight out of college. Since almost everyone there, including our boss, was more interested in computers and computer-related activities than human interaction, our group had bonded out of necessity after long-haul flights together and more than a few late nights at trade shows.

"You're such a creeper," Amanda laughed. She and Marina were both sales reps and by far the most outgoing of our after-work drinks crew. Marina had married her high school sweetheart and was fairly miserable about it, so she was the driving force behind these get-togethers—anything to avoid going home.

I just had nowhere else to be, and while the idea of spending time back in my cramped apartment with my three roommates held zero appeal, there was already an itch under my skin to get the fuck out of here.

There was only so much pretending I could do that I was just a regular human with a regular human life who did regular human things. And while I'd been ostracized from the Hunters years ago, I still had to request permission from them every time I wanted to go out of state in order to avoid a huge drama with both the Council and my family. There was no drunken stranger-fucking trip to Mexico in my future.

3

"Are you thinking about work again?" Amanda asked with a dramatic sigh, poking me in the ribs. "I can practically see your brain making a to-do list for the next show. You have brochure designs flashing behind your eyes. We just got back from Boston, relax a little!"

I laughed along with everyone else, even though, no, that wasn't what I had been thinking about at all. I didn't know when everyone had decided I was a workaholic, but one person had said it and the identity was apparently going to follow me around forever now.

"Do you think you could drag yourself away from the office for a couple of days for a trip to Cancún, Ophelia?" Marina asked, giving me her best puppy dog eyes.

"I don't have a passport."

"So get one," Carl replied, his voice closer than expected to my ear. Usually, he smelled pretty good—the man was a cologne connoisseur—but tonight he'd been drinking rum and coke, and the scent of it on his breath was doing nothing for my libido.

Rum was really the kind of thing you only needed to puke your guts up on once to never want to look at it again.

"Mm, I'll look into it," I said absently, grateful my phone started buzzing on the table at that moment so I had an excuse to dip out of the conversation.

Astrid.

I frowned, holding the phone up in front of me with my thumb hovering over the answer icon. My older sister *never* called me. She was the golden child, an accomplished Hunter who had more kills under her belt than I could even fathom, and our parents had strongly discouraged any communication between us since I'd been kicked out to preserve her immaculate Shade-killing reputation.

Her call went to voicemail before I could make a decision, but almost immediately, she was calling back.

"I think I should get this," I said apologetically, swiping my purse from the seat next to me and sliding out of the booth.

"We'll order you another drink!" Marina called after me as I escaped to the relative quiet of the corridor that led to the bathrooms.

"Hello?" I answered hesitantly, wrapping one arm around my middle and leaning back against the exposed brick wall. "Is everything okay? Are Mom and Dad okay?"

I couldn't think of any other reason she'd call me. Our grandparents were all dead, and the Hunters Council had assigned our extended family to different regions when I was a kid. I barely knew them. It was easier for them to control us if we looked to the Council as our only support network.

"They're fine," Astrid replied stiffly. *"How are you?"*

The question sounded so uncomfortably awkward I wondered if she was reading off a script.

"I'm fine," I said slowly.

"Good. That's good." She sighed heavily and dread balled in my stomach. Someone must have died—why else would she call me? Except the Hunters had all turned their back on me when I'd been kicked out, so I didn't know why she sounded so concerned about telling me. As harsh as it was, I doubted I'd lose any sleep over the people who'd so readily abandoned me.

"Oh my god, is it you? Are you sick?" I asked suddenly.

"What? No. No one is sick."

"Then why are you calling me?"

Astrid laughed—a short, hollow sound. *"You know, I wish I could say this was a social call. I know I haven't been the best sister to you, especially since you left—"* Kicked out, but whatever. Semantics. *"—but unfortunately, it's not. I guess on the plus side, I'll probably be seeing a lot more of you soon."*

"What? Why? Astrid, what the hell is going on?"

"The Council has a job for you."

5

ALLERICK

CHAPTER 1

My crown dug into my skull, feeling tighter and heavier than usual. It was an enormous iron monstrosity, an elaborate combination of loops and spikes designed to fit around my horns, and I only wore it on special occasions.

Like my wedding day.

The crown was uncomfortable on the best of days, but today it was suffocating. A weighty reminder of what it was to be a king. Soon I'd have a queen of my own to suffer alongside me.

"Brother," Damen called from his seat in the front row, "do you think you should perhaps work on looking a little less objectionable before your bride makes her way down the aisle? I'm sure she'll be suitably alarmed without the posturing."

Soren, my stoic Captain of the Guard, elbowed my loudmouthed younger brother and heir. "You should refer to him as 'your majesty' when there are so many others around," he hissed. "Or better yet, say nothing."

I snorted at Damen's arrogant grin, the tips of his fangs glinting in the low, silvery orb light. Damen would sooner rip those fangs out of his mouth than give up an opportunity to antagonize me. Perhaps I should put him in his place in front of so many others—all the highborns of the shadow realm had turned out for their king's wedding—but, then again, no. Let them see that Damen, and Damen alone, was immune from my wrath.

He wasn't going to earn their respect any other way.

It was a mostly still evening, but even the faintest gust of wind made the ancient stones of this temple groan ominously. The high arched ceilings always seemed one storm away from collapsing, and long strands of black grass had sprouted between the cracks in the fractured cobblestone floor. The gray stained-glass windows on the outer wall were holding on by sheer luck, and the whole structure was probably only standing because it was connected to the better-maintained palace.

I should fix it, I thought to myself. The plain wooden bench seats we'd dragged in specifically for the occasion looked too nice for the crumbling place. There were so few devout left that maintaining this wing of the palace seemed pointless.

"She has arrived," Garren, the priest overseeing our ceremony, whispered. He was particularly horrifying looking with his mottled gray skin and the three strands of hair his scalp was desperately clinging to, and that was precisely why I'd picked him to officiate. I didn't want my new queen to get too comfortable.

This marriage was not of my choosing. The Hunters Council, the ones with all the power, had said they would send *a woman* to be my bride, one of their choosing. My Council, the Council of Shades, had promised *me*. The marriage was meant to be security—a Hunter living in the shadow realm under my protection—but *my* Council hadn't been specific enough in requesting a bride. My future wife was probably one of the highest-ranking huntresses, with hundreds of kills under her belt, sent to be a constant reminder that if the treaty was broken, the lives of my subjects would once again be in danger every time they traveled to the human realm to feed.

"How many with her?" I asked in a low voice, my hands clasped so tightly in front of me that my claws were almost savaging one of them. How would my new bride feel about that? Our pitch-black, claw-tipped fingers didn't appear on the non-corporeal Shade forms she would be used to seeing in the human realm.

"None, your majesty," Garren stuttered, looking back at one of his acolytes at the edge of the dais who was relaying information to him. "She came alone. As she should, of course. Not that it was required in the treaty, but as a sign of respect to her new husband."

Garren was a sniveling little cretin who thought very highly of himself, and I struggled to keep the disdain off my face every time he spoke.

I frowned for a moment before smoothing out my expression. And the Hunters called *us* monsters. I wouldn't send my worst enemy to get married in the human realm *alone*. Either my bride was a lethal force to be reckoned with all on her own, or the Hunters were making it clear that they weren't taking this union seriously. This *treaty* seriously.

It was easy for them *not* to take it seriously. Their people weren't dying. Times were tough for Shades. Feeding off fear was a lot harder when our prey was too desensitized from special effects and prank shows to know when to be afraid, the idiots. Not to mention all the recording devices that made our lives a nightmare.

"Selene is taking her luggage to search now," Garren whispered, relaying more information from outside. "Your bride is on her way to the entryway."

Soren tapped his foot impatiently—it had been difficult for both of us to entrust his second to greet my bride at the portal outside the palace, but I selfishly wanted Soren to be here. Shades did not make for good subjects, and the peace treaty had been a hard sell, even though it was literally to save their lives. The marriage that the Council had decreed would guarantee it had been an even harder sell, and I couldn't be sure some wouldn't try to cause trouble because some in the regions already were.

The relationship between the Crown and the Council was symbiotic, but not always seamless, and I only truly trusted my brother and the captain who was like a brother to me.

I straightened, angling myself towards the aisle as the choir began a haunting dirge to welcome my future wife to her miserable end. If I was going to be unhappy in this marriage, so was she.

"I give it a day," Damen whispered conspiratorially, not making much of an effort to lower his voice. "She'll be throwing herself at the portal, begging for those savages to come back for her. Or for the sweet release of death," he added dramatically.

"Shut up," Soren growled, elbowing Damen. He was silent for a moment before adding, "I give her an hour."

I gave her until she saw my face for the first time. Any moment now. Perhaps she was an accomplished Shade-killing assassin in the human realm, but this was the shadow realm. This was *our* world. Unless she was on the delegation of Hunters who had come to negotiate with us, she'd never seen a Shade in our true form before.

You should be embracing this arrangement, not trying to scare her off.

Fuck it, if she was going to run from the sight of my face, that hardly seemed like my problem.

The heavy wooden doors creaked open, drawing the attention of the hundred-strong crowd. An intimidating prospect for any bride, let alone one in an entirely different realm, surrounded by Shades. Bogeymen. Nightmares.

And these were the cream of the crop—only the Court and the Council were in attendance. They'd decked themselves out in their most elaborate shadow coverings and accessorized with their most expensive jewels. Shades in every variation of black and gray stood at attention, the orbs of silver light along the walls catching on the elaborate onyx decorations most had twined around their horns for the occasion. Their glowing eyes were the only spot of color in the entire room. In the entire realm.

Until *she* appeared.

A slight figure dressed in white appeared on the threshold, and my lips twitched at the stubborn tilt of her chin.

"Maybe two hours," Soren conceded in a quiet voice, standing along with the rest of the room, twisting back to look at her.

My bride started down the aisle, and I made no attempt to hide my perusal of her body. Let her see the monster she was marrying in his true form and everything I could do to her soft human form written on my face.

Her silk dress was more silver than white on closer inspection, and although it covered her from her collarbone to her toes, including full length sleeves, it was far tighter than I expected from the usually unglamorous, practical Hunters.

And her *face*. Oh, her people had certainly chosen one to tempt me. Maybe they wanted this alliance to hold after all. She was... bright. Once upon a time, we were told there had been life and color in the shadow realm, but it was so long ago that it was basically a myth. With the exception of our eyes, this world was all shades of gray, or it had been until my new bride walked into it.

Big brown eyes that would cry so pretty, smooth pinkish ivory skin with sharp angular cheekbones and a tight set jaw, and silky reddish-brown hair hanging straight down her back. How soft would it feel running through my claws?

Where the fuck had *that* thought come from? I'd gone to the human realm to feed since I was an adolescent, and never once was I attracted to my meals. Granted, Hunters were different, but I'd had an even more visceral reaction to their kind.

Still... how beautiful would her hair look, whipping in the wind as I hunted her through the forest?

Perhaps I could have fun with my little human huntress of a wife, while I had her. She was no match for me in my own domain with my solid form and teeth and claws that could tear her apart.

At least she wasn't hideous to look at.

Her approach was painfully slow, each step timed with the drawn-out dirge, and her inferior eyesight probably couldn't make out my features yet, especially in the low light. No sun shone in the shadow realm.

She could see the crowd as she passed, if she chose to. She chose not to, her eyes determinedly trained towards the end of the aisle where I waited.

Smart, I thought with begrudging approval. No queen could be seen gawping at her subjects if she wanted to be taken seriously. How long she would be queen remained to be seen, but she seemed to be making a show of doing it properly for now.

I knew the precise moment my delicate little bride spotted me. The most delicious, mouth-watering scent filled the air, making the eyes of every Shade in the room glow hungrily.

Fear. Human fear always smelled so sweet, like the most sumptuous cake, inviting us to take a bite. Hunters knew better than to show us any fear, and I had never scented the emotion on them before.

It was far more potent than a regular human's.

Addictive, even.

Was this a trap? An elaborate ploy to make me let down my guard?

Brown eyes perused me as boldly as I'd perused her as my bride stopped in front of me, both of us turning to face each other, ignoring the rest of the room. I smiled—not kindly—letting her see my fangs, running my long black tongue over my teeth with a flourish. My brother chuckled obnoxiously from the front row.

"What is your name, little huntress?" I purred. A fresh wave of fear perfumed the air, making me salivate, but her face hid her emotions admirably.

She didn't *look* afraid at all.

She must be well trained, I reminded myself. Even if she couldn't quite suppress her body's natural instincts, she was accomplished enough to disguise them on her face.

"Ophelia."

There was no tremble in her voice, and although she had to tip her head back to meet my eyes, her gaze was unnaturally defiant. How interesting.

"I am Allerick, but you may call me 'your majesty.' "

It galled me slightly to admit that *Queen Ophelia* was an impressively regal sounding name for an accidental monarch.

Damen laughed again, some of the court tittering along with him.

"As you wish, your majesty," Ophelia replied, inclining her head. The movement drew my attention to her smooth, pale neck. *Pretty.*

"Shall I begin the proceedings?" Garren asked, his tongue flicking out towards Ophelia as though he would have a taste of her terror for himself. My hand shot out before he could move back, gripping Garren's chin and slamming it up so both rows of fanged teeth pierced that lecherous tongue which had no business being near my bride.

He howled in pain as black blood seeped from the puncture wounds, his snake-like eyes widening in terror as he attempted to hiss an apology while his tongue was still thoroughly impaled.

"I require another priest," I called out mildly without taking my eyes off Garren, my claws digging into the flesh of his cheeks as I maintained my hold on his chin. "One who does not seek to taste that which does not belong to him."

Garren mumbled incoherent apologies as I threw him back on the stone floor, knocking into a plinth and sending a vase of black flowers to the ground with a crash. Soren was there before I could blink, gripping the bleeding priest by the neck and dragging him across the stones before flinging him easily out the window.

Unsurprisingly, Ophelia's scent sweetened, her eyes trained diligently on me through the entire interaction. Soren retook his seat, and both he and Damen leaned forward, inhaling deeply.

They were lucky I didn't like them less.

"Your majesty," Weylin, a priest I liked even less than Garren, murmured, appearing behind us in hastily pulled on ceremonial robes.

"Get on with it," I drawled. "I require a drink."

Of spiced wine. And perhaps my new bride's pussy, since we were supposed to consummate this damn arrangement for it to be valid.

Not necessarily in that order.

Weylin cleared his throat. Weddings were uncommon in our world now, but when they happened, the vows emphasized choice. Choosing to forsake all others. Choosing to love one another.

Not even the Council in their pushiness to make this marriage happen had suggested we use those traditional vows here. Nothing about this was a choice.

"Ophelia, huntress and human, do you take Allerick, King of the Shades, to be your husband in a union recognized by both of our kinds?"

She blinked for a moment, those oddly expressive human eyes giving away her confusion. She'd expected more.

"I do."

Such a pretty voice. So breathless. Another fear response she couldn't quite hide.

"Allerick, King of the Shades, do you take the human and huntress Ophelia to be your wife in a union recognized by both of our kinds?"

I paused for a moment, just long enough to make her nervous, watching her face carefully for that moment where one pretty tear escaped, or that angelic face crumpled with horror. I couldn't decide if I admired her stoicism or hated it. I wasn't particularly old, yet it had been a while since anything interested me.

Her scent couldn't lie though. That delicious fear was all mine.

"I do."

And with that, it was done. I was married. The king had taken a queen, albeit not a crowned one. The Council could force me to rush the other aspects of this cursed union, but I'd crown her when I was good and ready.

My hand in marriage was more than enough power to be giving the little huntress.

"Come along, little wife," I purred, wrapping my claws around her slim arm and guiding her towards the aisle. "You smell like a meal, and it's time for the feast."

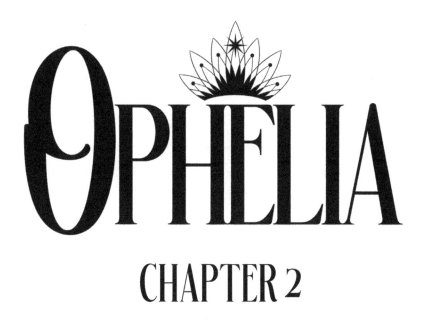

OPHELIA

CHAPTER 2

A clawed hand as black as pitch kept a firm grip on me as we made our way back down the aisle. Honestly, it was more of a frog march than a romantic post-ceremony stroll, but the joke was on him because I was into being manhandled.

Seriously, I was one muttered complaint about how slow my human legs moved away from whispering, 'sorry, Monster Daddy,' and dropping to my knees to ask for forgiveness.

That's not very queen-like, I reminded myself. *Fuck it, they shouldn't have sent a failed-Hunter–slash-marketing-coordinator to do this job.*

If you pick the last resort option, you get last resort results, and all of those results sounded like a very fucking good time to me.

That was *if* my new husband was into me, which was... debatable, at best. He sort of looked like he wanted to eat me, but I couldn't decide if it was in a good way or not. He'd gone *nuts* on that priest guy for sniffing me, but I could be reading romantic intentions into that display of violence that weren't there. It didn't help that I couldn't read his expressions, or any of theirs. I'd never seen a Shade in their corporeal form before—in the human realm, they appeared as hooded wraiths or reapers with cloaks made of shadow, floating above the ground.

The clothing was still made of shadows here—which would take a while to get my head around—but the bodies were all very much solid. And without the oversized hoods covering their faces, I was getting a close up look at a Shade's face for the first time, and *me likey*.

My fingers itched to sketch the features of everyone around me, and I scoffed silently at the raunchy monster fantasies I'd drawn before and how wrong I'd gotten the details.

Unlike in my imagination, their faces weren't blurry and undefined. They were surprisingly humanoid—two eyes, a nose, and a mouth—but everything was far more angular and their cheekbones jutted out like they'd been carved from stone. There was *nothing* human about the rows of pointed teeth on display when they smiled, and even less human about their bright, jewel-colored eyes. They had no pupils, no sclera, no iris. Just a whole eyeball of almost glowing color. The kind that if you saw peeking out from under a shadowed hood in the middle of the night would make you pee your pants in fright.

My husband's eyes were an icy blue so pale it was almost silver, but the colors seemed to range, as did all the other features. Allerick's thick, leathery skin was the darkest shade of black, but as I discreetly took in those around us as we passed the rows of Shades at our ceremony, there were paler shades of gray too.

I stumbled on the cracked cobblestones in my stupidly long dress as we passed through the wooden doors into the hall, grateful I'd opted for sensible footwear. The Hunters Council had provided this dress, as well as the rest of the wardrobe I'd brought with me. Fortunately, the gown was long enough that they hadn't noticed I'd slipped on comfy nude-colored flats underneath. I'd assumed that a pair of glittery stilettos would look weird and out of place here, and considering the Shades didn't even wear shoes, I'd been absolutely right.

Only Allerick's unyielding grip on my arm kept me from faceplanting on the floor. He barely broke his stride, all but dragging me along as he twisted to give me a *look* over his shoulder. I hadn't appreciated how much information I yielded from eyes before now. Allerick's blank blue stare gave me nothing, and he didn't so much have eyebrows as thick ridges over his eyes instead. How would I know if he was frowning or not?

He'd probably been frowning this entire time. I needed to see a smile for contrast.

It was a shame that he seemed to be such an asshole because I'd definitely come into this feeling sorry for him. The Hunters had a whole list of candidates they'd run down before I'd finally agreed to come here and marry the King of the Shades as a show of good faith in the treaty. There had been no such option for Allerick—the deal was for the king, and the king alone.

I could understand why he was pissed about it, but I was disappointed that he seemed to be pissed at *me*. I wasn't on the Council. I hadn't negotiated the stupid terms.

The crowd was a noisy mass behind us, slowly filing out of the decrepit-looking temple, but we mostly had the corridors to ourselves with the exception of the silent bodyguard-looking Shades trailing us. *Say something. Make small talk.*

"So, uh, nice palace. Your majesty," I hurriedly tacked on the end. It was lucky for me that the Shades seemed to know most human languages, probably as a safety measure so they could understand the Hunters who hounded them. It gave them an unusually super-polished accent, something I'd noticed when the priest was speaking.

Allerick threw me an impressively judgmental look over his shoulder for someone who couldn't raise their eyebrows or roll their eyes.

"A lot bigger than my apartment," I continued, because if there was one thing I was good at, it was filling silence with inane chatter. "You could probably fit my whole place in this corridor. Or my old place, I should say. This section of the palace looks a lot newer. Have you been renovating?"

"No."

Cool, cool, cool.

It did look less derelict around here—there were no cracks in the floor threatening to upend me, and the dark gray stone walls were solid, the black sconces shining under the flames within them. I'd been warned that everything in this realm was in tones of black and gray except the eyes of the Shades, but that couldn't have prepared me for seeing it in person. The entire palace was made of dark gray stone, the furniture all looked to be blackened wood, and the glowing orbs gave off a silvery light rather than a golden glow. Was there even a flame in there? It didn't look like it, but they didn't have electricity here either.

It was all surreal enough that I didn't necessarily feel like I'd gone back to medieval times, even if that's where the level of technology was at in the shadow realm. It felt too much like being in a different world entirely to care about the lack of power or internet access.

I'd have plenty of time to mope about that later when I was bored and couldn't scroll through pictures of people I didn't care about.

Allerick had said something about a feast, so I was expecting it when he led—or rather dragged—me into an enormous stone hall lined with long tables, and a dais at the front set up for two.

18

Romantic.

"You don't have to drag me, you know," I pointed out. "I am here entirely willingly."

He made a noise of disbelief but released my arm all the same. The physical contact had been surprisingly reassuring, and I felt the absence of it as soon as he released me. However, I wasn't a fan of being dragged around like a prisoner in front of all these Shades.

Attempting to recover some dignity, I straightened my shoulders and pulled up the hem of my dress so I could get up the steps of the dais without falling on my ass. There were staff there to pull out our chairs, and I smiled at the one who did mine. He flinched back like I'd hit him, and I felt my face heat as I looked down at the floor instead, attempting to gracefully climb into a chair that was definitely designed for someone bigger than me.

"His mother was killed by a Hunter," Allerick said conversationally the moment they were out of earshot.

"I'm sorry to hear that," I said quietly, meaning it. Just because I hadn't been involved with the Hunters beyond being born one of them didn't mean that everyone here wasn't going to view me as one. The Hunters Council hadn't really prepared me for that, and I felt suddenly embarrassed that I hadn't thought of it myself.

We sat in uncomfortable silence as the court filed in, taking their seats automatically, like they all knew exactly where to go. I did my best to seem as bland and unthreatening as possible, which *should* have been easy because I *was* bland and unthreatening. By age sixteen, the Hunters Council had already told me I wasn't suitable Hunter material.

Allerick stood as the last of the Shades were seated, and I debated whether or not I was supposed to stand as well. My darling husband wasn't extending an invitation to join him, so I folded my hands in my lap instead, pasting the most pleasant smile on my face like this was all normal.

I also really didn't want to get in and out of the oversized chair with everyone staring at me.

"My fellow Shades," Allerick boomed, spreading his arms in welcome. The sleeves made of shadow moved along them, flickering just enough to showcase his bulging upper arms before they were covered again.

Well, damn. I'd always had a weakness for arms.

Allerick's nose twitched, and he glanced down at me, mouth twisted into what I *thought* was a frown. He turned back to face the crowd before I could truly analyze it.

"Thank you for attending my wedding, securing the treaty between the Shades and the Hunters. This is the dawn of a new era for us. An era in which we can visit the human realm without fear of execution. This *marriage* is a symbol of the peace between our kinds, a commitment and a sacrifice on both sides."

Who said romance was dead? It hadn't escaped my attention that he'd said 'marriage' like it was a curse word, but whatever. He didn't have to *love* me, he just had to be married to me. And consummate that marriage to make it valid.

I was hoping he'd be as into that idea as I was, but it wasn't looking likely.

"For now, let us eat, drink and celebrate," Allerick finished with a flourish as the side doors flew open and servers appeared heaving platters of food on their shoulders.

The crowd cheered, shouting and stomping, and I forced my smile a little wider as Allerick took his seat next to me, pouring himself a goblet of wine from the carafe on the table before sliding it towards me.

Was it wine? I wondered, eyeing it nervously as I poured it into the silver cup. It was *gray*. I wasn't the most cultured woman out there, and honestly most of my alcohol had come in canned form when I wasn't getting a happy hour deal, but I was pretty sure wine wasn't usually gray.

"Regretting your decision yet?" Allerick asked in a disinterested voice, drumming his claws against his goblet.

"Nope," I replied with more confidence than I felt, shooting him a smile over the rim of my cup before taking a small sip.

Huh. It tasted like Christmas mulled wine. It just *looked* like particularly runny sludge. Delightful.

"Strange little thing, aren't you?" he asked, spreading those enormous legs wide and eating up my personal space. The casual way he entirely dominated the room around him *did* things to me.

"So I've been told," I murmured, attempting again to smile at the servers who set a platter of... *something* in front of us. They also backed away like I was about to whip out a silver dagger and plunge it into their chests.

"They'll never like you," Allerick told me, lazily picking through the items on the platter and adding them to his plate. *Meat*, I decided. It was different kinds of meat, devoid of all color like everything else here. "The court won't fear you—they're the strongest of us—but the staff are not. A trip into the human realm has been an exercise in terror for them, and it's necessary in order to get the sustenance we need to survive. *They're* the ones who benefit from the treaty."

"I know," I said gently, letting my mask of pleasant calmness drop for a moment so he could see the honesty in my face. I'd never been on Team Kill All The Shades. I *wanted* this treaty to work.

Allerick grunted in acknowledgment before giving his full attention to his food. *Huh, no cutlery.* Pretending I was not at all thrown off by that, I followed his lead, using my fingers to put a little of everything on my plate and sampling small bites.

The first one tasted like chicken. Not in a 'tastes like chicken' way either, in a 'this is actually chicken but gray.' It was cool and weird at the same time. My sister had heard a rumor that Shades didn't eat vegetables, and we'd packed a few in my bag just in case, but I was going to need more. Everywhere I looked was platter after platter of meat in *grayscale*.

I almost didn't want to explore it too closely. I kept glancing down at my own hands, making sure the pinkish undertone of my skin hadn't leached out from being in this strange gray world.

You'll get used to it, I reminded myself. *And you don't have to worry about student loan repayments or next month's rent. So there's that.*

I'd agreed to this hoping that it would improve my situation in life, with the guarantee from the Hunters Council that it was safe and I wouldn't be killed for my efforts. Maybe I'd also hoped it would earn me some kind of place among the community I'd been kicked out of so many years ago. They hadn't been asking that much of me really—I could go home whenever I wanted, though I had to live here and travel home via the Hunters Council portal. The Hunters had paid off all my debt, and I no longer had living costs to worry about. They'd outfitted me with a swanky new queen wardrobe in muted colors, enough to stand out without being a beacon. If I got to fulfill some specific fantasies in the process, that would be an added bonus, though it wasn't looking like that was going to happen.

It's going to be fine. You are going to make the best of this. You are Ophelia Bishop, failed huntress and moderately talented marketing coordinator.

You can do this.

Wedding feasts were apparently as torturously long in the shadow realm as they were in the human one. There were no speeches, no dancing, no cake, but there were several courses of meat and a seemingly unlimited supply of wine. The Shades moved around the room eventually, switching seats with each other and laughing together. Allerick seemed content to eat and brood in silence. That was mostly fine since it gave me an opportunity to observe, but it also meant—combined with the wine—that my overactive imagination was getting wildly carried away without conversation to focus on.

Could Allerick make those shadows pin me down on the bed? Could he make them into shadow ropes and tie me up? Did the shadow clothing act as a physical barrier, or could I just reach right through it?

If my new husband didn't get this wedding consummation on the road soon, I was going to hike up this absurdly tight dress and do it myself, right in front of all his subjects.

No more wine for you, I scolded internally, twisting my fingers together to stop myself reaching for the goblet just for something to do.

I glanced over at Allerick, finding him half sprawled on his enormous chair having finished eating, legs spread invitingly wide only a few feet away from me as he surveyed the dining hall below us. Why wasn't he accosting me yet? Freeing me from the confines of all this damn fabric?

I'd been promised monster fucking, and I wasn't getting any damn monster fucking.

"Your scent," Allerick growled, leaning in to inhale me again. *Yes,* my scent. *Quite.* Surely that was enough of an invitation? I'd always been told that Shades had an acute sense of smell.

In my week of awkward and uncomfortable prep with Astrid, she'd led me to believe that Shades were insatiable, that they found us irresistible and only their incorporeal forms in the human realm kept us safe, but apparently *that* was a lie.

Allerick looked plenty corporeal to me here in the shadow realm, and the most amount of physical touch I'd gotten was a clawed hand around my forearm.

My new husband helped himself to another goblet of wine, showcasing a stretch of roped forearm beneath his pitch black leathery skin, and I sighed quietly to myself, surveying my surroundings instead since apparently I wasn't going to get railed in my wedding dress any time soon.

His two curved horns were so impressive, he didn't even need the elaborate crown that somehow nestled between and draped decoratively over them to show them off. Was that a sign? The bigger the horns, the bigger the dick? I covertly scanned the room, deciding my husband for sure had the biggest horns here. Allerick inhaled sharply.

"Am I displeasing to you, *your majesty*?" I asked, excessively chatty from the wine. I couldn't quite keep the disdain out of my voice at the title he insisted I use. *I didn't need to like my husband,* I reminded myself. This was an arrangement, a truce between enemies. All I had to do was *be* married to him.

Allerick looked lazily over my body again, the most shameless arrogant man or monster I'd ever come across. "You are pleasing enough, wife."

Well, high praise indeed.

As desperately as I craved the stretch and burn of what I was sure was an impressive cock hidden under the robe of shadows, I still had *some* pride.

Back in the human realm, I'd had my pick of lovers. I wasn't about to beg and whimper for a male who found me *pleasing enough* even if he did have a big monster dick hiding under those shadows.

With a tight smile at my husband, I reached for my goblet, forgetting my earlier promise to myself not to drink anymore and taking a swig of the spiced wine. The burn as it went down my throat helped distract my lust-addled mind.

He probably wants an open marriage. You can work with that. There are plenty of other good-looking monsters. Probably ones without royal egos.

Except I didn't particularly like that idea. Those marriage vows had *meant* something to me.

Allerick inhaled again, something that may have been confusion crossing his inhuman features.

"How does that *soothe* you?" he mumbled with disgust.

Soothe me? We had very different ideas of what was going on here.

Before I could correct him—was that wise? He was still the king, and he'd insisted on the 'your majesty' nonsense—two imposing figures rose from their seats and made their way in front of our table.

At first glance, they looked almost identical to my husband except for the fact that Allerick wore a crown and his eyes were icy blue, but there were other differences too. One had the prettiest purple eyes and was *grinning* at me, displaying a row of vicious-looking teeth. He looked a lot like Allerick, but with a slighter build and a simple crown sitting between his horns.

The other one had eyes the orangey color of a sunset, and his mouth was turned down in what I was pretty confident was a frown, his posture defensive. He wore no crown, though his shadowy clothing was arranged in a crisscrossed way over his chest before continuing down sort of like a tunic, reminding me of armor.

While the orange-eyed one wore no crown, they were both important, that much was obvious. They were nearly as big and impressive as Allerick was.

Nearly.

Just my luck that I should get the most attractive husband in the monster realm, a king no less, and he'd be a colossal asshole.

"My younger brother and heir, Prince Damen," Allerick drawled, lazily gesturing at the one with the purple eyes and the crown. "And Captain Soren, head of the guard."

Damen smirked, all trouble and spoiled princeliness, while Soren looked at me with a mixture of curiosity and suspicion.

I held my head up, giving them a bland smile that I hoped looked queenly.

"How is our new *queen* faring?" Damen asked, giving me a sly smile that was all pointed teeth as he gestured for two chairs to be brought over.

"I'm faring well, thank you," I replied politely, shredding a piece of roasted meat with my fingers. I knew that Shades needed fear to survive, but it seemed the meat was for sustenance. Did they eat three meals a day? How often did they go to the human realm to suck up some poor person's fear?

They could still go with the treaty in place, they were just restricted to certain areas on rotation. It was meant to stop any one area from being over targeted, though it sounded to me like a ploy by the Hunters to make it easier for them to monitor Shades.

The Hunters would ban feeding altogether if they could, but we all knew that some degree of fear was essential. Balance had to be maintained.

"Really? You're faring *well?*" Damen asked doubtfully.

"You sound disappointed, your highness," I said mildly, popping some shredded beef—gray beef?—in my mouth and arching an eyebrow at him.

"I made a bet," he replied unrepentantly, smiling wider in a blatant attempt to intimidate me. Pity for him that he didn't know my brain was wired wrong. Whenever I saw pointed teeth, I imagined them pressing against the delicate skin of my neck, pinning me in place while my monstrous lover fucked me ruthlessly into the mattress. Or the ground. Or the wall. Basically anywhere he could have me.

"Ah, that's more like it," Allerick sighed, inhaling deeply. "Never forget where you are, little huntress."

So... he wanted me to be horny? He seemed to like when he could smell my arousal, but he spoke as if he wanted me to leave.

Maybe it was a game? I wasn't opposed to being hunted through the palace halls and consensually ravished, but I wanted to know him a little better before we played *that* way.

"Will you stay long here, your majesty?" Soren asked awkwardly.

Allerick waved his hand dismissively. "You may call me 'Allerick' in front of her as you normally would in private. Only *she* cannot."

Charming.

"We will not stay long. Enough not to offend our guests. Then I will take my new wife back to her quarters. Perhaps we'll see if her dainty little human body can accommodate the King of the Shades."

"I'm glad you find me pleasing enough for that," I replied coolly, making sure I inclined my head deferentially as I did so to soften my words.

Despite the taunt, I was fairly confident he was all talk. Allerick didn't seem to struggle to keep his hands off me, and he spoke with such disdain that it seemed more likely that I outright repulsed him.

Damen snorted. "Everyone in this room finds you plenty pleasing for that, Queen Ophelia. You smell like a Shade's wet dream."

Did Shades have wet dreams? Did they come more than humans? In my drawings, there was always a lot of cum.

"Watch your tongue, brother," Allerick chided, his eyes flashing dangerously. "That's my wife you're talking about. Only I can tell her about how every Shade in this room wants to get their hands on her," he growled, leaning right into my personal space so I felt his hot breath on my neck. "Those pretty trembles belong to me."

My thighs were trembling aplenty.

"I'd rather not have a riot on my hands, if we can possibly avoid it," Soren said in a bored voice, his nostrils flaring. Everyone was weirdly casual about smelling how wet I was. Maybe it was normal around here? Maybe everyone walked around horny all the time and my senses were just too dull to pick it up?

"And Meridia already looks ready to commit murder," Damen noted, glancing back at a female in the crowd. She was *stunning* and terrifying all at once. Tall and lithe, with only the scantest shadows covering the important bits, the swell of her breasts and curve of her hips almost entirely on display. She had long black hair that hung all the way down her back, parted by silvery curved horns that protruded from her head. Her eyes were a crimson red, a borderline demonic color. I'd hate to come across her in a dark alley, but regardless, she was exquisite. No wonder my husband only found me 'pleasing enough.'

Soren grimaced, angling himself in front of where she sat in the crowd. "My sister won't cause any problems."

That was a blatant lie and we all knew it. The Shades had eyes that were difficult for me to read, but there was no mistaking the *hatred* in Meridia's as she leaned around her brother, gaze firmly affixed on me. Her long black claws gouged into the wooden table with such ferocity that I heard the sound from all the way up on the dais over the sound of clinking utensils and laughter.

She continued to stare at me as she raked her claws through the table like it was my face, teeth bared in a vicious snarl.

Holy shit.

Allerick tilted his head to the side, watching her performance with the exact same disdain he'd shown me so maybe it wasn't entirely personal. "I admire your optimism, Soren. Come, wife. Before the captain's sister guts you at your own wedding feast."

I stood as Allerick did, and a spike of fear—pure, unadulterated fear—made my breath hitch. I hadn't come here expecting my life to be *pleasant* necessarily, but I had expected to be safe. That was a fundamental aspect of the agreement between our peoples. Perhaps I'd been too blinded by the appeal of being ravished by my future husband to consider that he may not be able to control his subjects.

Maybe I'd been a little naive about how the Shades would actually feel about having a Hunter for a queen. Even if I was a Hunter who'd never *hunted*.

Allerick, Soren, and Damen all paused, their noses wrinkling like they smelled something sour. With no warning, Allerick's enormous hand wrapped around my forearm, his claws running snags through the silk fabric of my dress as he all but dragged me from the room. The crowd behind us cheered, jumping up from their seats and stamping their feet on the stone floor until I felt like my bones were vibrating even as we moved down a hallway, away from the others.

Away from the murderous sister of the captain. Would she follow? She undoubtedly knew these halls better than I did.

"Make it stop," Allerick hissed, releasing me abruptly. I stumbled on the train of my dress, catching myself with a hand on the rough stone wall, my palm stinging on impact.

"Make what stop?" I asked, baffled.

"That smell, however you're making it. It's repulsive," Damen replied on his brother's behalf, gagging slightly.

"She's bleeding now too," Soren said in a grim voice, tipping his chin at my palm. I held it up in front of me, finding a few scratches. It would need to be cleaned, but there were only the faintest lines of red showing where my skin had broken. They really did have sensitive noses.

"Great, she'll probably die now, and I'll be on the hook for a dead wife," Allerick muttered, his claws scratching at his temple in a comically human gesture.

"Or I could clean and dress the minor scrape, then bathe to get whatever the repellent smell is off me," I said wryly, growing impatient. Who knew Shades were so dramatic?

I was the one that had just been silently threatened.

"And you won't die," Allerick confirmed, narrowing his eyes as though he wasn't sure if I was telling the truth.

"You're not really what I expected from the King of Shades," I said with a frown, forgetting to censor myself.

"Well, you're not what I expected from a Hunter bride," he retorted, sounding mightily offended. "Follow me, we will bring you to your chambers where your attendant is waiting. That disgusting scent *lingers*," he added under his breath irritably.

Damen held a hand in front of his nose as he strode after his brother, but Soren hung back, his glowing eyes narrowed slightly as he stared at me. "How strange, that this repulsive scent surfaced in relation to Meridia. If you hurt my sister, we are going to have problems, my *queen*." He stomped off after the other two while I shuffled behind them in a daze, clutching my hand to my chest. How was it he thought *I* was the dangerous one here?

ALLERICK

CHAPTER 3

That *smell*. I could admit I'd been seriously considering getting my new wife into bed, if only to see what that delicious fear tasted like on my tongue, but not now. Not when she was putting out that revolting scent that seemed to cling to her, overriding the tantalizing sweetness that had been there a moment before.

She smelled *off*. Maybe she was ill? Maybe the meat hadn't agreed with her? It was nothing that couldn't be found in the human world, just in different colors.

Perhaps it was the wine?

The Council had assured me she'd be fine with our food and drink. I'd be beyond irritated if I ended up with a dead queen on day *one*.

"How long does it take to consummate a marriage? Longer than you can hold your breath?" Damen teased quietly, sidling up next to me as we made our way through the brightly lit halls that led to the royal couple's wing of the palace. I shot him a glare out of the corner of my eye that didn't perturb him in the least.

What to do about the consummation clause? I rarely devoted my time to thinking about sex—fucking one of my subjects was not a decision I took lightly—but for hours it had been all I could think about.

I wouldn't have taken Ophelia by force—I wasn't *that* kind of monster—but my new wife had looked at me with enough coyness in her gaze to make me think she was open to the idea of coming to my bed—either because she was sent here to kill me and thought I'd stop paying attention when I buried my cock in her, or she was a pretty little idiot who would have changed her mind the moment reality set in.

The Council of Shades wouldn't consider the marriage valid until we'd both sworn an oath that we'd taken that step, but I didn't see why I should be forced into bed with anyone because of some Council or another telling me so. Was I the damn king or not? I'd fuck my wife when I was good and ready to.

"What *is* that?" Damen muttered, his nose twitching. We both nodded to the guards who stood either side of the archway that led the royal couple's private quarters. The Queen's Chambers were opposite my own, and the Council had deemed that the most respectful place to put my bride.

With that strange grotesque stench clinging to her, I was questioning how wise that decision was. Perhaps I should put her in the dungeon where she couldn't make us all ill with her reek.

"Anger?" I suggested, keeping my voice quiet enough that Ophelia wouldn't overhear. Soren was still walking a step behind her, undoubtedly watching her like a hawk. "It surfaced after we mentioned Meridia."

Shades who came into contact with Hunters often didn't live to tell the tale. I'd never faced one in battle, nor had Damen or Soren. If it was a warning sign that she was about to attack, none of us would know about it.

"A pity," Damen said lightly. "Her fear is potent. I'm impressed you didn't indulge while sitting so close to her at the feast. Unless you were saving it as a special wedding night treat for yourself," he added with a mischievous grin.

"Mind your manners," I warned my insolent brother.

"I mean no harm," he replied, holding his hands up innocently. "You know we're all very curious about our new queen. How do you even, you know, consummate with a human? Does it actually feel good? They're very dainty looking—"

"These are your rooms," I told Ophelia loudly, ignoring my obnoxious younger brother. Before I could open the door, Soren was there, entering before me and checking the room for any security threats.

This wing of the palace was only accessible by brightly lit halls, and the entrance to the entire wing was guarded at all hours. She'd be safe here. I was more concerned about my own safety now, in case that smell was a sign of impending attack.

"Affra!" I called, striding in behind Soren with Ophelia at my back. She wasn't producing the reek any longer, but it clung to her skin and clothes.

"Here, your majesty," Affra squeaked, scurrying into the room from the corridor. She bowed low to the ground, the gesture looking uncomfortable for her. She was ancient—too old to go out and hunt on her own. She was reliant on being fed from the communal stores in exchange for her labor like most of the other elderly in our realm.

"*Queen* Ophelia, this is your attendant, Affra. She has a room next to you and you can use the bell to call her whenever you require something. Affra, draw the queen a bath," I ordered, before glancing at the hand Ophelia was still cradling.

There was an uncomfortable feeling in my chest as I noted the way she clutched her wounded hand to her chest, the faint metallic tang of blood present underneath the other unfortunate smell. It was a feeling I disliked and couldn't easily place.

Perhaps I had eaten too quickly.

"I can deal with the hand," Ophelia said confidently, giving Affra a kind smile as she hurried past. "Where would you like me after I have bathed, your majesty?"

33

Damen made a strangled sound at the blunt question. What a strange creature. Not nearly blushing and virginal, nor coolly confident, ready to plunge a silver dagger into my heart at the first moment either. Between the near-constant rush of fear she'd been experiencing, followed by that strange, repulsive smell, I wasn't sure what to do with this new wife of mine.

I hesitated, hoping she hadn't picked up enough of my tells yet to notice.

"Here," I clipped, turning on my heel and striding out, my cloak of shadows whipping the air behind me. There was a pause where Damen and Soren probably bowed, hopefully taking their new queen seriously since she was here to stay for the meantime. I wasn't going to be the one to break the treaty. While I found the entire arranged marriage concept distasteful, I could recognize that our current methods weren't working.

I didn't want my people to starve.

I crossed the hallway into my own chambers, leaving the door open for Damen and Soren to follow.

"Leave us," I instructed my attendant, Cyr, who immediately disappeared into the servant's entry, having worked for me enough to know when not to bother with bowing and scraping.

"What an odd wife you have," Damen chuckled as he entered, heading for the bar in the corner.

I grunted in agreement, turning to face Soren. "Do you think she'll run now that she's alone?"

"Before your ceremony, I would have assumed so. Now, after that strange reaction to Meridia, I'm less certain," he admitted.

"That *smell*," Damen agreed, pouring himself a glass of wine without bothering to offer anyone else one. "After she'd been so deliciously tempting in her fear all through the ceremony and the feast."

A whip of my shadows flicked out, catching Damen's cheek hard enough to sting. He grinned, unrepentant.

34

"Possibly it was some kind of attack reflex," Soren warned, his thoughts mirroring my own. "I'll talk to some of the elders, see if they've heard of such a thing. At least Meridia can hold her own, I suppose."

She could *more* than hold her own, which was what had me worried. After a few too many wines at dinner, Meridia hadn't been able to conceal her hatred when she looked at Ophelia. She hadn't even *tried*.

"Tell Meridia that if she kills the queen, I'll send her bound and gagged into the Pit without second thought," I said coolly, catching Soren by surprise. "Aside from the fact that there is a treaty relying on this union, it would be the height of disrespect to me to attack my wife."

"And you would have ripped off your own horns before marrying Meridia," Damen snorted, toasting his drink towards me.

Soren bowed his head, immediately acquiescing. Meridia had been shameless in her desire to be crowned queen, and I knew that he'd been worried her overtures would put his own position in jeopardy.

It was an unnecessary concern. Soren was too good of a captain for me to dismiss him just because of his ghastly sister.

"Of course, I'll make it clear to Meridia," he assured me.

"Good. As for Ophelia..." I mused, elbowing my brother out of the way to pour my own goblet of wine and swirling it slowly around the cup. "She didn't *look* afraid. She smelled so tempting, but there was no trace of fear in her face or posture."

"Perhaps the Hunters sent their most accomplished actress?" Soren suggested mildly.

It *would* make sense for them to send someone who was more than she appeared. That she would spy on us and report back to her people was a given, but it was whether she was *more* than that. It would void the treaty if she killed me, but I'd already be dead by that point and perhaps that mattered more to them?

The whole situation was infuriating. I'd given my Councilors leave to negotiate the finer points of the treaty on behalf of the realm, and it had been them who'd pushed the marriage point, wanting a Hunter here as a guarantee. *A hostage*, a quiet voice in the back of mind that I tried to ignore pointed out.

How easy it must have been for my Councilors to arrange this when they hadn't been the ones forced to give anything up.

"Perhaps she's an evil, vicious wench, sent here to destroy us all under the pretense of peace. Or perhaps not. Truly, we don't know as much about Hunters as we should," I pointed out before taking a swig of my wine. "The unidentifiable scent only proves that point."

Soren opened his mouth to object before closing it again. He had scores of books on Hunter weaponry, the way they fought in groups, and their less-than-human attributes. We knew they could see us when regular humans couldn't, and we knew from the treaty negotiation process that they could travel between realms using portals, a practice that we believed used to happen with more frequency but had stopped hundreds of years ago. Probably because in our realm, we were a far bigger threat to the Hunters than they were to us.

Perhaps there was more that separated the Hunters from their purely human counterparts. More knowledge that had been lost over hundreds of years of pure survival on our parts.

"Does no one smell their fear when they fight them?" Damen asked. "Surely, we would know that it is an addictive scent. Someone would mention that."

"Not many live to tell the tale of those encounters," Soren reminded Damen. My brother could be the smartest of all three of us, but he lacked direction. Perhaps one day he'd find something productive that captured his attention, but until then, he seemed content to spend his days drinking and getting into mischief. *I must find something to occupy him.* "Those who survive the silver throwing knives tend not to speak of the encounters."

I pursed my lips, pacing back and forth in front of the bed. "I don't think the little huntress was afraid when she smelled so tempting."

"What else would she be? In a room full of monsters, binding herself to the biggest one?" Damen scoffed. "That she didn't piss herself when you made Garren eat his own tongue was a small miracle, but the scent grew stronger then. It *had* to be fear."

Idiot baby prince or not, I was inclined to agree with him.

"You're probably right," I sighed, tapping my claws against the black goblet in my hand. "But until we know more, perhaps consummating the union would be... unwise."

If Ophelia *was* dangerous and sent here to kill me, then getting in bed with her would be the height of stupidity. Plus, *not* consummating the marriage would give me an escape clause if I needed it...

Damen made a strangled noise. "But what if she lets you feed on her fear while you're—"

"Enough," I growled. "The treaty explicitly forbids feeding on her fear, and I don't need you rubbing it in. I'm as eager as anyone to know what it tastes like. But my prudence is why I am king, and you are not."

"I disagree," Damen replied with a mischievous grin. "It is because you're bigger than me. Were the crown determined by brains—"

"You would still be second best," Soren interjected drily. "I should return to the feast, try to catch Meridia before she does something regrettable."

"Too late for that, many times over," Damen laughed, while Soren shifted his weight awkwardly, trying to hide his embarrassment.

While Soren tried to avoid the details of his sister's attempts at seduction wherever possible, everyone knew that after a particularly public rejection from me, Meridia had made a fool of herself in front of Damen instead out of spite. Or perhaps desperation.

I'm sure it was a piece of information Soren desperately wished he could unlearn.

Knowing that I hated formality when it was just the three of us, Soren quickly excused himself without bowing, making his way back into the hall. Hopefully, he'd check the guards were still in place and at attention on his way past. They were to keep others out, not to keep Ophelia in, and my new queen would be safe from Meridia's spite if she was in her room at least.

"Shall I send someone to your room to entertain you if you're not going to bed your wife?" Damen asked. "Who was it that was begging and crying last night for you to fuck them before you were a married Shade?"

"Shut up," I grumbled without any real heat. "That was mortifying."

"Yes, how you suffer," Damen agreed gravely, eyes twinkling with mischief.

"And no, don't send anyone. I'm not spending my wedding night with someone else."

I'd be spending it with my wife, she just didn't know it.

If she was an assassin, she was a terrible one, I thought wryly as I slipped into Ophelia's rooms before Affra could shut the door behind her, carrying the silky wedding dress in her arms as she left, presumably for laundering. All of the orbs of silvery light within the palace walls were under my control, and I'd deliberately left the ones around the furthest corners of the room unlit so I could slip into the darkness and watch her if I needed to.

For security purposes.

But given that she was a huntress and had grown up knowing that light was one of our greatest weaknesses, I'd expected her to have brought candles and matches as her first line of defense to keep herself safe. Affra had to know I was here—the palace was kept brightly lit at all times specifically so no Shade could hide in the darkness within these walls.

I watched silently as Ophelia arranged some of the things she'd unpacked atop the vanity, wondering what all the strange colorful potions she'd brought with her from the human world were. She was arranging them with great care, and it was clear that she was fidgeting. How curious. With a long look at the closed door over her shoulder, Ophelia sighed and unbelted the knee-length dark robe she'd been wearing, pulling it off slowly and hanging it over the back of the chair.

The shadows only cloaked me, they didn't *mute* me. I almost gave myself away with a groan like I'd never seen a woman's naked thighs before.

I'd never seen naked thighs like *that*. Not that I found women of my own kind unattractive, but I was attracted to my wife to an inconvenient degree.

Was she wearing that for me?

Of course. I had told her to wait for me here. That's why she'd dressed in a tiny, pale pink scrap of fabric that barely brushed the top of her thighs and dipped low on her chest, revealing the swell of breasts. The revolting scent from earlier had vanished, and she was back to smelling like the most mouthwatering buffet of fear I'd ever encountered.

How terrified she must be, to be emitting that scent so strongly when she was alone in her room. That she could hide her feelings so easily on her face was a little unsettling, though I had to wonder why she even bothered? Surely, she knew how sensitive our noses were. Hunters hadn't gotten so good at killing Shades by accident.

A shiver of unease ran down my spine at the idea of her lying here filled with fear. I wasn't the kind of monster who accosted unwilling women in their beds, and it bothered me that she thought I was.

Had I been too hard on her? There had been moments at dinner where she'd seemed almost compassionate, but I couldn't let myself be fooled by that. We all had our roles to play in this marriage, this treaty, this entire *arrangement* going forward.

With another sigh that seemed to border on impatience, she padded over to the dresser, pulling open the top drawer and taking out a few items that definitely weren't clothing. I tensed as she made her way back to the bed, climbing into the center of the luxurious gray and black silk bed, and settling back against the cushions. She unrolled some kind of fabric holder, and I held my breath, expecting silver daggers or something worse, exhaling silently when I realized they were just... drawing supplies? She carefully unbound a leather sketchbook, bending her knees so she could rest it against her thighs before picking through her pencils.

I couldn't see what she was drawing from where I was sitting, but I *could* see the smooth backs of her thighs and the slight curve of her ass.

My mouth watered with the need to feed, and I almost released the shadows cloaking me and dove onto her. She was waiting for *me*, why shouldn't I? Why shouldn't I see if she tasted as good as she smelled? If her delicate little body could accommodate me.

Because she's a Hunter.

Because once you consummate it, you're stuck.

Because she's an unknown quantity. Because she smelled repulsive just an hour ago.

Because she's dangerous and addictive and temptation incarnate, and you're fucking married to her.

OPHELIA

CHAPTER 4

There was a quiet shuffling sound, and it was interrupting my delightful sleep. I wanted to open my eyes and investigate, but my alarm hadn't gone off yet and I had moral objections to even pretending to wake up before my alarm forced me to.

I rolled over with a groan, silky sheets sliding over my legs as I moved.

Silky sheets.

Not microfiber ones that had seen better days.

My eyes flew open as it hit me where I was. In the Queen's Chambers in a goddamn *palace* in the shadow realm. Newly married, and alone in my bed.

I pulled the gray silk sheet up as I slowly worked my way into a sitting position, leaning back against the cushions while Affra quietly set a tray of food and what looked like a steaming pot of tea on the small cafe table next to the wall.

"Good morning, your majesty," she said, bowing low. "I apologize if I woke you."

"No apology necessary," I yawned. "I don't suppose we can drop the 'your majesty' stuff?"

She chuckled quietly. "How about 'Queen Ophelia'? Is that more to your taste?"

"It feels arrogant to say 'yes,' but I have gone my whole life feeling like someone should call me a queen, so I'm going to roll with it," I sighed, flopping back against the pillows.

"You're not what I expected for a Hunter queen," Affra remarked mildly.

"That's what my husband said," I quipped. *Ugh*, my husband. Fuck that guy.

He'd just stood me up! On our *wedding night*. Even if consummating our marriage hadn't been a necessity for validating the treaty, being stood up by my own husband on my wedding night was a kick in the teeth. We may not have chosen each other, but I had hoped we could at least be civil. I'd been attempting civility, and *I* was the one who had to leave my home and everything I knew behind.

Because I'd been quietly shuffled out of the Hunters, they hadn't paid for my college education the way they did for regular Hunter youths. I'd been drowning in student debt from the marketing degree I'd gotten from SU, and my coordinator job had barely made a dent in it, yet it still left me barely able to afford rent in a shitty apartment with three other people that maybe got five minutes of sunlight on a good day.

When Astrid had called me a week ago with the Council's offer—including wiping out my debt—it had seemed like such an exciting adventure and a chance to fulfill the fantasies that had long haunted my dreams that I gave little thought to agreeing. Maybe even a chance to win back a little approval from the people who'd taken it away all those years ago, like my parents and my sister. I'd spent more time with Astrid in the past week getting things ready than I had in *years*, and it was weird to realize that I was missing her already.

My parents, not so much.

They'd found my sketchbook when I was sixteen and still in the training that all Hunter children had to go through. After some truly terrifying yelling from my dad and distraught sobs from my mom, they'd reported me to the Council who'd declared me unfit to continue training and shipped me off to a human boarding school until I was old enough to be responsible for myself. It had been a lonely existence, trying to fit in amongst regular humans who had no idea what kind of creatures emerged in the darkness.

Once you know what the things that go bump in the night are, it's hard to pretend otherwise.

I'd gotten a little better at pretending like I wasn't miserable and alone in a world where I didn't quite fit in the past couple of years, but I'd naively hoped this would be the opportunity I'd been longing for my entire life.

"Bacon, your majesty?" Affra asked quietly, standing back to show me the tray she'd arranged on the table and dragging me out of my thoughts. I gave her a tight smile as I climbed out of bed in the sexy little getup I'd idiotically worn to seduce my husband, hastily grabbing the robe I'd discarded last night and shrugging it on. A crate of fresh fruit and vegetables sat in the corner where my things had been left, and I picked through it, selecting an apple for my breakfast.

There was only so much meat I could stomach. I was glad Astrid had thought to pack vegetables for me, while also wondering how she even knew to do that. She probably had inside information—at age twenty-six, Astrid was shaping up to be the youngest member of the Hunters Council ever if she secured a spot at the next election. Aside from the fact that she'd received the full extent of Hunter training, she'd probably been given extra instruction to prepare her for leadership.

Not that she'd seemed overly excited about the prospect while I'd been staying with her. Astrid had changed the subject instantly every time I'd mentioned her future on the Hunters Council.

"Shall I take that to the kitchens?" Affra suggested while peering into the crate of healthy goodness, wrinkling her nose slightly. Despite semi-loving being called a queen, it was beyond weird to be waited on, but I didn't want to offend her by dismissing her. "The cook can learn how to prepare them for you."

I took a seat at the small table. "I don't mind going to the kitchens and preparing them myself. Will I take all my meals here?" *Alone?*

"Dinner is served in the dining hall each evening," Affra replied, her voice softening slightly. Had she been expecting the king here this morning? Or at least some mussed sheets or evidence of his presence?

I snatched up the bacon a little more aggressively than necessary, nibbling on one end and dreaming of cutlery as bacon grease clung to my fingers. "And in the meantime? Am I expected anywhere during the day?"

Affra hesitated, pausing as she straightened the sheets on the bed. "Not that I'm aware of."

On the one hand, I wasn't qualified to lead a flock of pigeons, let alone a realm of Shades, so that tracked. On the other, what was I supposed to do with my time? I wasn't even a real queen, not really. Our marriage wasn't yet valid, and I hadn't been crowned.

Was that the point of him staying away last night? Did he not want this treaty?

That didn't seem right, not after what he'd said at dinner about the Shades standing to gain more from the treaty than the Hunters did.

Maybe he just doesn't want you.

Considering this was an arranged marriage, that thought hurt more than it had any right to.

I finished my breakfast, tasting nothing, before excusing myself to the bathroom to wash up. By the time I emerged, Affra was waiting next to the vanity with a brush in hand, ready to do my hair. It felt a little excessive since I had nowhere to go and no one to see, but I sat down at the vanity regardless. She took her time brushing out my hair, humming thoughtfully as she separated the strands with her claws before running the brush through it. I briefly worried she was going to scalp me by accident, but on closer inspection, Shade claws were like black fingernails except longer and sharper, and they still had soft pads under their fingers, so I didn't think I was at serious risk of losing either a chunk of hair or skin by accident.

Not that I'd had the opportunity to touch my husband's hair to compare, but mine seemed softer than their almost leathery hair appeared, and Affra seemed as interested in me as I was in all of them.

Besides, it was *colorful.* I was a natural brunette with an addiction to red hair dye, and never had I been more grateful for my vain ways. Auburn hair in the shadow realm was badass.

Affra reached past me, tugging open one of the many drawers on the elaborate vanity and procuring a surprisingly large black box. Too big to be jewelry, that was for sure.

Maybe my husband didn't like me, but I wasn't about to say no to presents.

"A gift from the Crown Prince," Affra murmured, carefully opening it with her claws and presenting it to me.

"Prince Damen?" I asked in surprise. A welcome-to-the-family gift then. I tried not to be disappointed.

Though on closer examination... maybe it was less a welcome than a threat. Or at the very least a reminder. Inside the box was the most enormous, elaborate hair pin I'd ever seen.

It was a black metal raven—the symbol of the Hunters—with its wings outstretched, head proudly tilted up, beak protruding. The silvery pin was long and thick enough to double as a weapon, with a curved hook at one end to slide it in.

Right through the raven's outstretched wings.

The symbolism was not lost on me.

"You are the Queen of Shades now," Affra reminded me in a soft voice. "A queen of monsters, and a part of this world."

Was I? I'd certainly be making a statement with this. Forsaking my kind even if I'd never been truly a part of that group, but it was a risk when our marriage was even entirely valid yet.

A test. This must be a test.

"I'll wear it," I said, blowing out a breath. I knew what I was leaving behind when I handed over the keys to my old apartment and changed into my wedding dress in a communal bathroom at the Council headquarters.

Just like I'd always dreamed of when I was a little girl, I thought sarcastically. Who didn't want to spend their wedding day traveling through a terrifyingly dark portal all alone in a dress that was a tripping hazard, whilst wheeling their suitcase behind them? *Bride Goals.*

Affra hummed in approval, her claws scraping my scalp gently as she twisted and piled my hair into a bun, leaving a few strands at the front loose. Once it was up, she held the huge raven behind it, securing it with the ominous-looking pin which she held carefully by the loop.

The pointed pin was shinier than the raven, but I knew it wouldn't be silver. Silver was the one material that could kill Shades, and while they seemed to make jewelry out of it, I'd already been checked for weapons on arrival.

I took a moment to put on light makeup before carefully doing winged eyeliner as sharp as the pin stabbing the raven on the back of my head. Affra seemed at a loss when it came to my clothes, which made sense since they just whipped up some shadows to cover the important bits.

How convenient would it be to never need to do laundry? I was jealous.

Not wanting to stick out any more than I already did, I ignored all the colored dresses and pulled out a floor-length black dress that wrapped tightly around my waist but had drapey sleeves and a flowing skirt. It wasn't quite clothes-made-of-shadows, but it was the closest I had.

Despite it being a lot more formal and fancy than the clothes I'd worn in the human realm, I kind of liked the way they made me feel. I was dressing for the job I was underqualified for.

Affra gave me a nod of approval, clearing up my breakfast dishes while I slipped my feet into simple black flats. I was dressed. I was presentable. I'd eaten.

Now what?

Not that I was missing where I used to work with the cubicle right in the center of the floor as far away from the windows as possible, but at least I'd had some kind of purpose.

Even if that purpose had been counting down the minutes until I could leave, so I could get back to my tiny room with the mold on the ceiling and binge watch old episodes of *Kitchen Nightmares*.

"I'm going to go out and explore," I told Affra with as much confidence as I could muster. *Queen shit, right there.* She nodded absently, pausing to give me a quick bow.

So... I could explore, then? At least I wasn't a prisoner in my rooms.

The corridor was silent as I pushed it open, the door opposite mine firmly shut. Was that Allerick's room? Was he inside, still asleep? As tempted as I was to barge in and demand answers, I had a severe case of Wounded Pride that I needed to deal with before I attempted that.

Instead, I turned right, walking down the brightly lit corridor like I was totally at ease being there. I wasn't afraid necessarily, just not as *confident* as I'd like to be. That feeling only increased when I passed through a stone archway flanked by two guards, and one immediately fell into step behind me.

I paused, turning to look at her, and she bowed quickly, keeping her eyes trained at the floor.

"Hello."

She glanced nervously up at me with dark blue glowing eyes. Strange to see a Shade nervous, though I guessed I was the unknown in these walls, not them.

"Er, hello. Your majesty," she tacked on quickly, flicking her short black hair out of her face. Like everyone else I'd seen, she was draped in a cloak of shadows, and I wondered if they wore any armor underneath them.

"That is... very unnecessary," I assured her. "Just Ophelia is fine."

"Queen Ophelia," she replied instantly. "My name is Levana. I've been assigned to accompany you today."

"Anywhere in particular?" I asked drily, unable to keep the snark out of my voice. Would it be too much for my *husband* to swing by and mention any of this to me?

And fuck my brains out so I could tick off some legal requirements and a few bucket list items?

"Um, well nowhere in particular," Levana answered after a small pause. She seemed uncomfortable, so I didn't push it—it wasn't her fault that Allerick was a dick, or that the Council of Shades had negotiated a Hunter wife for their king and apparently hadn't planned beyond the wedding.

With a heavy sigh that I *hoped* Levana hadn't heard because I didn't want to come off like a brat, I continued aimlessly wandering down the corridors with her following a few feet behind me. Despite the weirdness of being watched, it was comforting to know that if I got lost, at least Levana would be able to guide me back to my room. It wasn't that the palace was particularly large, but it was *confusing*. The corridors were all well lit with that strange silvery light, and there were no windows to be found.

There was a faint gust of wind that caught in the fabric of my dress, and I followed that direction in search of fresh air, eventually coming out in a covered walkway that curved into a spiral, going down, down, down to the bottom to a dark, circular courtyard. *The whole palace was a spiral,* I realized, leaning out over the balcony and looking at the blackened stone levels above me. The circular shape hadn't been obvious from the portal I'd landed in outside the walls, but I could see it now I was inside.

The dark gray sky above swirled like a churning sea, so much more *active* than the sky at home. There were no clouds, and last night when I'd arrived there had been no moon or stars, but despite that it was still strangely beautiful. In the daylight—or whatever passed as daylight here—it looked sort of like smoke trapped under glass, moving around above us. It would be *strange* not to see sunlight, but I could get used to this too.

I turned my attention down to the courtyard below. It wasn't an overly manicured, landscaped space, and I found that I liked the wild darkness of it. And it was *dark*. Flowers and trees grew from the gray dirt, all in shades of gray and black, almost shadow-like in substance.

It was one thing to see the inside of the palace all in grayscale, but seeing colorless *flowers* was a little unsettling.

I glanced back at Levana, contemplating asking her about it, but she was staring determinedly ahead, semi-pretending I didn't exist. Huh. Who knew I'd miss my surface-level drinking buddy friendships from back home. At least people *spoke* to me there.

With a nervous gulp, I continued down the curving hallway, pausing in front of enormous black double doors decorated with an engraving of a book on each side. I looked behind me, my hands resting on the handle.

"The library," Levana offered quietly.

Since they lived like it was still the 1800s here, getting into reading again seemed like a good option. I pushed open the enormous doors with some effort, wondering why I'd stopped reading when I'd enjoyed it so much as a teenager. Adulthood had made me lazy.

The library wasn't nearly as well lit as the other parts of the palace I'd seen, and I couldn't quite suppress my loud gulp as I edged my way inside. Maybe it was to protect the books? They looked pretty ancient. Black candelabras illuminated the main throughway, but the rows of books that fanned out either side of the main aisle vanished into shadow, and I wasn't quite game for *that* just yet. I stuck close to the main walkway as I paused at the first row, making sure I was standing in the light as I perused the leather spines at the beginning of the row.

It didn't look like I was going to find any YA fantasy here, but I supposed that wasn't a very *queenly* thing to read anyway. If I even was a real queen who was going to do real queen shit. Whatever. Maybe I'd brush up on some geography just in case. I'd been taught about the shadow realm a little before I was booted out for being a horny perversion of a Hunter, and I was curious to see how the maps we had lined up with the actual maps the monsters kept of their own realm.

How did we have maps at all? I wondered to myself. There had been diplomatic visits between Councils to both realms during treaty negotiations, but as far as I knew, I was the only one who'd ever *lived* here. Maybe we'd stolen them.

After checking a few more shelves and getting bored with the entirely nonfiction selection, I headed back out into the corridor with a still silent Levana on my heels. More Shades had appeared while I'd been in the library, hustling about the palace on their business. They didn't hide their outright stares as they passed, though most tipped their chin respectfully and seemed pleased when I returned the gesture. A few looked at me with the same abject terror as the server last night, and I tried to make myself look as nonthreatening as possible.

If only I had an instruction guide.

Or, you know, a husband who was the fucking king who could help me out. Whatever.

"Where are the kitchens?" I asked Levana, still heading down the curved corridor that led to the courtyard.

"Bottom level," Levana replied, looking startled by the question. I supposed visiting the kitchens wasn't a very royal thing to do, but I didn't want to get scurvy so they'd all just have to deal with my peasant-y ways.

A few more awkward head nods later and I was letting myself through swinging double doors to a somewhat medieval-looking kitchen.

"What do you want?" a gruff voice barked, glaring at me over a large stone island with a meat cleaver in his hand, a *whole* carcass laid out in front of him that I decided not to look too closely at.

"This is the *queen*," Levana hissed from behind me. "Watch your tongue."

"She can be the queen outside this room, I'm the king in this kitchen," he grumbled, shooting Levana an irritable glare. I smiled despite myself.

"That sounds fair," I cut in, not wanting Levana to get upset on my behalf. "In here, I'm just Ophelia. What shall I call you, sir?"

"Not 'sir,' that's for certain," he scoffed. I imagined that if he could roll his glowing dark orange eyes, he would. "My name is Calix."

"Call him 'vermin' for his attitude," Levana muttered irritably, flicking her hair off her face in irritation.

"Careful now," I laughed. "The King of the Kitchen may exile you for your cheek."

It was difficult to tell, but I thought I saw Calix's face flicker with amusement. His voice reminded me of a grouchy old fisherman, but on closer inspection, he didn't look aged the way Affra did. His hair was pure black and tied up in a messy knot at the base of his neck, highlighting the twistiness of his black horns, and his muscular forearms spoke of strength and youth.

"You're here about that, I take it," he said, pointing the cleaver somewhat threateningly at my crate of vegetables.

"I am. I don't suppose there's somewhere cold I could store them if I cooked them in advance?" I asked, looking around the kitchen.

"We have ice pits to keep food cold," Calix replied, tipping his chin towards a door on the back wall. "You're not going to demand I prepare them for you?"

"By the night, if the king heard you speak to her like that..." Levana said on an exasperated exhale.

I doubted very much the king would care.

"Not at all. I'm sure you're busy enough without needing to make special meals for me. I'll prepare some vegetables in advance and store them in the ice pit," I said decisively. If nothing else, it was something to fill my time. I'd never had enough free hours in the day to get good at cooking, and now I had nothing but free hours apparently.

With a narrowed-eyed glare, Calix slid a chopping board and knife across the island towards me. The entire kitchen was designed around cooking meat, but I figured I could cook a pot of vegetable stew easily enough, maybe even freeze it in small portions to eat over time. I'd work my way up to something fancier.

With the horrific sounds of Calix butchering meat in the background, I started the monotonous process of washing and chopping vegetables while Levana leaned against the wall, silently watching.

I could thank my Hunter education for this, at least. When we were young, we were forced to participate in our own form of Scouts to prepare us for a life of monster hunting. I hadn't ever particularly enjoyed camping, but I remembered how to make a camp oven stew and the supplies I had access to were pretty similar here.

"Should I help you?" Levana asked, looking torn between guarding the door and swooping in to take over.

"Is this not very new-queen behavior?" I teased.

"Oh, it's fine—" Levana began, but Calix's barked laugh cut her off.

"Not particularly queenly, no. We all assumed you'd be a stuck up Hunter bitch who'd expect us to wait on you hand and foot and remind us of all the Shades you'd killed."

"*Calix!*" Levana hissed.

I nearly sliced off my finger. "No, no, I would never... I *have* never..."

"Yeah, I think we're seeing that," Calix said, his gruff voice sounding thoughtful. "Unless you're a very good actress, there's nothing lethal about you. You're squeamish over meat."

"It's very, uh, squelchy sounding," I replied, my stomach churning slightly. It seemed in poor taste to point out that Shade-killing in the human world didn't involve any kind of flesh since they were in ghost-mode while they were there.

"I'm thoroughly trained in combat and field medicine, and even I struggle with the gore in here," Levana said with a tentative smile. "Calix revels in making everyone around him uncomfortable."

"I don't care to make others *comfortable*—it's not the same thing," Calix countered, shooting Levana a vicious grin.

Were they flirting? It seemed kind of flirty. The kind of flirting you did when someone pissed you off most of the time but you still had sex dreams about them and woke up hating yourself a little bit.

Calix set a small cast iron pot on the counter for me, and I pretended like the concept of cooking on an open flame wasn't terrifying as I filled it with chopped vegetables and set it on the grate.

"Did you cook the food for the feast last night?" I asked Calix, propping my hip against the counter while I waited. "It was very good."

I could have sworn he preened a little. "I did. Barely slept for days getting it all ready."

"And you're here so early? Are there others that work here?"

"They'll be along later," Calix said dismissively. "Gave them the morning off to recover after all the feast preparations. Doing breakfast and lunch just for the royal family is plenty easy enough on my own."

"Oh? How many is that?" I asked, super cool and casual. Calix grinned at me, and Levana let out a strange cough that may have been an attempt to cover up a laugh.

Okay, so my stealth interrogation skills needed work.

"To think we were worried," Calix chuckled. "The royal family consists of you, King Allerick, Prince Damen, and King Allerick's mother, Orabelle."

"Was she at the feast last night?" I asked, giving up the pretense that I was being anything but nosy.

"No," Levana answered. "Orabelle is very... frail. She doesn't leave her rooms."

"Still got a sharp mind though," Calix added. "I'm sure you'll meet her soon enough."

"Are you really?" I asked, arching an eyebrow at him. I was hanging out in the kitchen on my first day as queen, after all.

Calix grinned, moving to the sink to clean his carving knife. "Maybe not soon, but eventually. The king's other siblings choose not to live at court, just Prince Damen."

Curious. Why didn't they want to live here? Allerick had appeared to treat Damen well—the prince certainly hadn't been shy about teasing his older brother, and I hadn't got the impression at all that Allerick would threaten him.

I'd probably just learned more about my husband in an hour in the kitchen than I would have in weeks if he was going to keep ignoring me, I thought wryly.

"Are you going to want that with your dinner?" Calix asked, already clearing his work bench to start on another carcass while I carefully took the vegetables off the heat.

I shook my head, setting the pot down and leaning back as I took the lid off. "I'll eat what everyone else eats at dinner, I can just come here and have my, er, more human food without everyone watching me."

"I'll send it up with your breakfast and lunch," Calix replied easily.

"That's very kind, thank you."

He frowned at me like I'd just offended him and all of his ancestors. "I just don't want you in my kitchen every day."

Levana snorted. "I don't want to accompany the queen to your kitchen every day, so if you could send it up, that would work better for everyone."

They glared at each other from across the kitchen, and while I had firmly set my monster-fucking eyes on the asshole I was married to, the sexual tension in the room made me want to fan my face.

I was definitely going to draw this later. Not Levana and Calix specifically, because I was hoping we'd sort of made friends and it'd be weird to draw kinky pictures of my friends without their knowledge, but I'd draw something inspired by this 'if only you weren't so irritating, I'd fuck you into next week' energy.

Okay, maybe 'friends' was overstating things, but I was feeling marginally less alone after my time in the kitchen. Calix was gruff and rude, but he treated me like I was just a regular person, which was nice. Levana seemed less nervous and wary of me than she had before we got here, which was a huge plus because if she was assigned to shadow me, I wanted her to be comfortable at least.

If I couldn't have friendship, I'd settle for companionship. And maybe on my trips back to the human realm, the Hunters who'd written me off as worthless all those years ago would finally have time for me again, and I'd have friends there as well.

Stay positive, Ophelia. You're going to make the best goddamn lemonade out of these lemons.

CHAPTER 5

I lounged in my chambers before dinner, waiting on the couch for Soren to appear with his report on my wife's movements for the day. I hadn't *solely* avoided her because I wanted to, though that may have factored into it a little. It had been a busy day with a pissed off Council—they'd wanted me to bring Ophelia before them for a formal introduction since I'd already warned them off doing it at the feast last night.

Why *hadn't* I just dragged her in front of them today? It wasn't like she had anywhere else to be.

It was just the thought of them grilling us on whether or not we'd consummated our marriage didn't sit well with me. She'd only arrived here last night, the least they could do was give her a few days to adjust to her new surroundings.

Not that I *cared*, it just seemed... polite.

Fuck, did I care enough to be polite? She was probably here to kill me, or at the very least to spy on me and my court.

"Who put that look on your face?" Damen asked, strolling into my rooms without invitation.

"The Council wanted me to bring our new queen in today for an interrogation," I grumbled before taking a swig of my drink, annoyed at myself now as well as the Councilors. Damen moved to the bar, helping himself to wine. "I'll bring her when I'm ready."

Damen snorted. "Is that the excuse you're running with?"

I shot him a warning glare and he grinned unapologetically back at me. "Perhaps we should look at finding *you* a bride, hm Damen? Perhaps you'd take life more seriously with a wife."

"You wouldn't," Damen shot back, looking appalled. Typical Damen, allergic to commitment of any kind. Any hint of responsibility he'd ever been given, he'd managed to shake off within weeks.

"Perhaps the Council will be dissatisfied with my marriage and demand you take a Hunter bride too, just in case," I teased. To my surprise, Damen's expression turned contemplative.

"So long as I could stop her emitting that awful scent your wife produced last night, I wouldn't mind a pretty little huntress of my own."

"I don't know how they managed to convince *one* woman to move to this world, I doubt they'll convince a second," I scoffed. Perhaps I'd ask my wife at dinner. I supposed that there was no better way to find out what her motives were than to get to know her, as uncomfortable as the notion was.

There was a brief rap of knuckles on the door, and I called Soren in, curious to hear what my new bride did on her first day as the Queen of Shades. Hid away in her rooms, most likely.

"Soren," Damen called jovially, immediately pouring my captain a drink of his own. "Come, come. Give us all the gossip."

Soren ignored my brother, giving his attention to me and inclining his head in a respectful bow, hands clasped in front of him, legs hip-width apart, the constant warrior.

"Queen Ophelia walked around the palace, stopping for a while in the library and examining a few of the books before heading to the kitchens. She spent a couple of hours there preparing the food she brought with her—the vegetables that humans require—and took her lunch there with Calix and Levana. After that, she walked around the courtyard, seemingly very interested in the flowers. She then returned to her rooms in the afternoon to rest before dinner."

"She ate lunch with *Calix*?" Damen repeated, as stunned as I was. Were Calix not such a talented cook, I'd have exiled him from the palace years ago for being a disrespectful prick.

"Levana said he was quite friendly... for Calix's standards." Soren looked like he didn't know what to make of that either. Perhaps I needed to pay Calix a visit. Just because *I* wasn't sleeping with my wife didn't mean anyone else was allowed to get ideas about her.

"She prepared her own food?" I asked, more confused about this little huntress I'd married by the second.

Soren nodded. "And is only intending to eat it at her private meals. She'll eat what we eat when she's in the dining hall."

I didn't miss the glimmer of approval in Soren's eyes that she was making an effort at fitting in, and he'd been the most wary of her yesterday. Apparently, my wife was good at winning people over.

A useful skill for a queen, if she were to stay.

Soren turned his attention to Damen, his gaze turning disapproving. "You'll be pleased to know she wore the hair pin."

"What hair pin?" I asked immediately as my brother grinned.

"A gift for my new sister." Damen shrugged, unrepentant.

"An enormous raven with its wings pinned," Soren added drily. "You couldn't have been less subtle if you'd tried."

"I could have had the raven pinned in the heart," Damen protested with a grin. "I was curious to see if she'd wear it or not. Truly forsake the Hunters, et cetera, et cetera."

"When did you even give it to her?" I demanded. "You can't give my wife gifts. *I* haven't even given her gifts."

"It's not *my* fault you're a terrible husband," Damen laughed, dodging when I took a swipe at him with my claws. "And I gave it to Affra to pass on this morning. A 'welcome to the family and don't get stabbed by Meridia' gift, if you will."

Soren grimaced.

"Don't buy things for *my* wife," I grumbled, downing the rest of my drink in one. "Come on, I should probably walk her to dinner."

"You think?" Damen mumbled from behind me. I'd expected him to toy with a Hunter in our midst like a beast playing with his food—that he was being *nice* to her was a little unsettling. He may have been playing a long game, but Damen didn't usually hide his intentions from me and Soren.

Soren and Damen waited a few feet behind me as I knocked on the door to Ophelia's room. Affra opened it quickly, bowing low enough that I could see my wife standing behind her.

She looked exquisite in black. The dress floated around her like the shadows that hung from my own body, and her lined eyes and painted lips were darker and more sultry than they'd been at our ceremony.

Ophelia was *beautiful*, but it was never her beauty that had been in question.

Affra moved to the side, and my wife perused me as thoroughly as I was perusing her. The sweet smell of her fear didn't hit all at once, rather it seemed to leak from her slowly, perfuming the air around us. I'd taken a step into her room before I even realized what I was doing, drawn in by that scent that grew more potent the closer I got.

Strangely, I didn't relish the idea of her fearing *me*. I took a step back, gesturing for her to follow me. The scent clung to her, but it didn't grow stronger. Moving away from her had eased her panic, which made sense and yet caused some kind of discomfort in my chest.

"Come, wife. We are expected at dinner," I said gruffly. I caught a glimpse of the elaborate hair pin Damen had given her, and was both annoyed and impressed that she was wearing it.

"Of course, *your majesty.*"

Ophelia's polite reply was accompanied by a low curtsy that had Damen glaring at me accusingly.

What did he want from me? Blind trust in a *Hunter*? One who had agreed to upend her life in the sunshine and *marry* me? Nothing about Ophelia was trustworthy.

Ignoring Damen's judgmental gaze, I led the way down the corridor, waiting a moment so Ophelia could walk at my side, careful to keep a couple of inches between us. I had to slow my steps significantly so she could keep up, and I wondered idly how comfortable this palace was for her. Aside from the fact that she would be missing sunlight and color, it was designed for beings much larger than her, and the entire realm was spread out, meant for beings who could shadow walk and cover long distances in seconds.

If I was ever so inclined, I could shadow walk *with* her, but I doubted the occasion would ever arise. *She probably won't stick around for it to come up.*

Two palace staff pulled open the double doors as we arrived at the dining hall and Ophelia sucked in a near-silent breath next to me. I glanced at her, my nose wrinkling as I picked up the faintest sour notes to her scent again. Not as bad as it had been yesterday, but unpleasant nonetheless. And if everyone else in the hall scented it... well, it wouldn't do well for either of our reputations.

"Leave us," I barked at Damen and Soren. My brother looked like he was about to object, but Soren wrapped a hand around his arm and tugged him towards the hall before he could say anything.

It's for her own good, I reminded myself with an internal grimace.

Faster than she could track, I grabbed Ophelia by the waist, spinning her until she was pressed back against the wall by the doors, out of sight of my subjects. I caged her in, my arms braced either side of her head, and called on the shadows to curl around us, creating our own little bubble of privacy.

I was easily a head taller than my dainty wife, and she looked up at me in surprise, her shoulders pressing back against the wall in a way that emphasized the swell of her breasts as her breathing picked up.

Already, the sour scent was being replaced by her sweet fear.

Usually, fear was a craving I only experienced in the human realm, and while it was delicious and satisfying, it was nothing like *this*. I knew if I fed off Ophelia, I'd be full for weeks. And I'd be addicted, of that I was absolutely certain. There was no way I could taste that sweetness and go back to regular human fear after that.

"Mm, much better," I murmured, running one clawed finger down the side of Ophelia's face, pausing at her jaw. She tipped her head back, offering me her throat, and my cock swelled almost painfully at the sight. What a strangely confident little thing she was. Was she so sure she could disable me that she'd willingly give me the most vulnerable part of her body?

Testing her limits, I scraped my claws lightly down the column of her throat, pausing to press against that delicious pulse that thudded beneath my fingers. Watching to see if she'd take a swipe at me, I flattened my palm against her, wrapping each finger around her neck with deliberate slowness. Not enough to cut off her breathing—I wasn't about to kill my wife—but I was curious to see what she'd do.

Ophelia's scent *exploded*, like a bomb of sugar had gone off around us. It was the right reaction to having a monster's claws around her throat, yet it somehow *wasn't*. She was trembling. She smelled afraid. Her breath was coming in short, sharp pants. Her pupils had dilated.

All the signs of fear were there. Why didn't she *seem* afraid?

A good actress, I decided. That had to be it. Hunters began training to kill Shades when they were just children. Perhaps she couldn't suppress her body's physical fear reaction, but she'd undoubtedly learned how to keep it from showing on her face.

Ophelia made a noise in her throat I could have almost mistaken for a lusty moan, her small dainty hands rising to wrap around my wrist, though she didn't make any attempt to pull my hand away. She was so *warm*. Had she been this warm yesterday? The heat of her hands seemed to sink through to my bones.

Focus.

"Remember this feeling," I rasped, the rough timbre of my voice surprising even myself as I leaned down to speak in her ear, my lips brushing the shell with each word. "Whatever you were thinking as we were about to enter the dining hall, wipe it from your mind. *This* is how I want you to feel, to smell, throughout dinner. Do you understand me, wife?"

I caressed the soft skin of her throat with the pad of my thumb, and Ophelia somehow grew more pliant beneath me.

"I understand your instructions," she breathed. "You, I don't understand at all."

"How feisty you are whilst pinned to the wall by a monster," I murmured, trying to understand this unusual creature I'd married. Fearful and defiant, all at once. She was certainly intriguing.

"How talkative you are whilst pinning your prey to the wall," Ophelia breathed, those dark eyes flashing dangerously at me. Almost in... annoyance? Human eyes were so much more expressive than ours, I didn't know how to interpret the wealth of emotions that seemed to pass through hers in the span of a few seconds.

"It's like you *want* to be eaten," I grumbled, releasing her throat and taking a step back, the shadows around us falling away.

Ophelia paused for a moment, smoothing her clawless hands over her dress and tucking her hair behind her ears. "You can stop trying to intimidate me, *your majesty*. I know your kind don't eat people."

She moved towards the double doors, and I had no choice but to follow with the eyes of my subjects watching.

Of course I'm trying to intimidate you. What do you think all of that was for?

Fortunately—or perhaps unfortunately—Ophelia was seated between myself and Damen at dinner, and he conversed enough for all three of us. The intimate round table from last night had been replaced with the usual long table that faced out towards the rest of the hall. Most evenings, it was just Damen and I sitting up here. My mother was too fragile to join us, and while Soren had an open invitation, he usually preferred to stand guard during the evening meal and eat later.

"So," Damen began, pulling a platter of shredded beef towards him and offering it to Ophelia, "are you missing sunlight yet?"

"I wouldn't say I'm missing it," she replied carefully, taking a small sampling of meat. She'd only selected a small amount from each platter, and it annoyed me that I was even a little concerned that she wasn't eating enough. "It's only been a day, and usually I'd be cooped up in a windowless office anyway. It's more that it's strange to look up and not see the sun in the sky."

"What did you do in your windowless office all day?" Damen asked. I was glad he did before I could.

"Boring marketing stuff," Ophelia said absently, flicking her hand. "Writing newsletters and trying to make engineering software sound cool and sexy."

Damen's eyes met mine over her head. Neither of us knew much about the human world, but that didn't *sound* like how a highly accomplished huntress would spend her days.

"Your parents must have been sad for you to move out of their home," I commented mildly, helping myself to a stack of ribs.

Ophelia cut me a glance out of the corner of her eye, noticeably more comfortable talking to my brother than she was to me. *Irksome.*

"I moved out of their home years ago. Of course, I'm a little less accessible to them now, but it's been a long time since I lived under their roof."

None of this sounded like what I had expected Ophelia's life in the human realm to be like. As far as I recalled, Hunters lived in communities. We had our own scouts who tracked them for that exact purpose, ensuring that Shades never fed too close to Hunter grounds.

I'd expected Ophelia to be some kind of high-ranking huntress, assuming the Hunters would have sent their best. To send us a *threat*, to remind us that this was a treaty based on both sides making concessions.

But maybe...

Maybe Ophelia wasn't so much a threat as a *sacrifice.*

I opened my mouth to ask, but movement out of the corner caught my eye. Damen groaned, not even trying to hide his dread as Meridia approached the high table, hips swishing in what she likely assumed was a tempting way.

The shadows covering her body dissolved to all but wisps as she approached, and Ophelia stiffened beside me, her scent souring.

Had it been just yesterday that I'd been concerned about what that change in scent had meant for *Meridia*? Well, maybe not her specifically, because she was a demon sent here to drive me fucking insane, but I'd been worried about what that scent heralded for my subjects.

Today, I was bothered by it for an entirely different reason. An annoying reason that I didn't *want* to feel. Even if Ophelia had been sent here as a sacrifice, that didn't mean I should soften my feelings towards her. I had a whole realm to consider, not just her. She didn't have any loyalty to *my* people, and I couldn't forget that.

That didn't mean Meridia could fuck with her though.

I angled my body towards my wife, leaning one elbow on the table and turning my back on Meridia as she stopped in front of the table. Ophelia's dark eyes shot to mine, her breath hitching as I leaned into her space.

"Didn't we talk about this, wife?" I purred, scraping my claws over her throat. Damen had the good sense to look away, concentrating on his meal.

Ophelia tipped her head back, lips parting softly. Curious little thing. "Perhaps I need a reminder, *husband*."

Meridia made the faintest noise of discontent, one that Ophelia's less sensitive ears likely wouldn't pick up, which was good. Only *I* was allowed to be discontent with my wife.

I cupped Ophelia's neck, leaning in close to inhale her increasingly sweet scent. She held herself completely still as I scraped my sharp teeth over the shell of her ear, the pulse in her neck thudding wildly. *Sweeter and sweeter and sweeter,* I couldn't help myself. I dipped my head and my tongue darted out to taste the inviting skin at the base of her neck. I groaned before I could stop myself, licking a long stripe up the column of her throat.

Ophelia tasted better than the finest wine, the most potent human fear. She was exquisite, *dangerously* so. If Shades had known how delicious Hunter fear was, I doubted we'd have ever run from them no matter how many silver weapons they were carrying.

Her hand landed on my thigh, and I frowned as I realized she was clinging on. Pulling me *closer*. Why did she never respond the way I expected her to? The way any normal being would when they were afraid? What kind of elaborate trick was this?

Meridia cleared her throat impatiently, and I reminded myself that stabbing her in the heart in front of my entire court would not be a good look.

I pulled my head back, but as I was still leaning towards her chair to grip her neck, I'd inadvertently lowered my head below hers. I hadn't meant to put myself in such a position—it was a sign of great respect to bow my head to her even a little—and I didn't think she realized the significance.

My court would.

However I felt about the treaty, it *had* been made with my people's best interests in mind. *This is a good performance*, I told myself. *This is the right thing to do for my people.*

It didn't feel like I was doing it for them as I yanked my gaze away, removing my hand from Ophelia's neck but tugging her chair towards me with a loud screech. I stretched my arm over her shoulders, toying with a loose piece of hair as I slowly turned my attention to Meridia.

Soren had left his station near the door, standing at the base of the stairs that led to the dais, the worry on his face clear at whatever his sister was going to say.

"Your majesties," Meridia cooed, using the infuriating voice she put on when she was trying to play down her own power and dominance. "I wanted to congratulate you on your... nuptials."

"Did you now?" I drawled, scratching Ophelia's scalp with my claws, loosening her updo. My odd little wife hummed, a strangely contented sound. I had no idea what to do with her, so I kept scratching for lack of a better idea.

"Of course," Meridia replied smoothly, her posture stiffening slightly. "And to offer my services to our new queen."

"How magnanimous of you," Damen remarked, leaning forward and bracing his forearm on the table. He tilted his head to the side, and I knew he was cataloging Meridia's every movement—Damen wasn't so good at getting under someone's skin by *accident*. He watched and noted and remembered, then twisted every weakness to his advantage. "How easily you've given up your own ambitions after proclaiming loudly for years that being queen was all you ever desired."

Meridia flashed him an insincere smile. "The position is taken, what would you have me do?"

"Remember who you're speaking to," I rumbled in warning, making Meridia drop her gaze to the floor. Obnoxious trickster or otherwise, he was still the Crown Prince.

Next to me, Ophelia seemed to be holding her breath. Did she think I'd accept Meridia's offer? I wasn't *that* cruel.

"Your offer of assistance is noted, but unnecessary," I told Meridia. "You have your own job to focus on."

Her hand flexed at her side, but she gave no other indication that she was unhappy. Meridia was one of the scouts assigned to keep an eye on the Hunter communities, and I didn't trust this treaty enough to dismiss those positions yet.

"The offer stands if you change your mind," she replied stiffly. I felt the moment her attention moved fully to Ophelia, as did my wife. Our eyes didn't give as much away as a human's, but there was no mistaking that Meridia was staring right at her, and Ophelia's grip on my thigh tightened in response. Had her hand been there the whole time?

"Thank you for your *generous* offer," Ophelia said before I could speak, her voice appropriately aloof. *Huh.* I hadn't expected her to say anything to Meridia directly. The dismissal in her voice was clear, and Meridia had no choice but to give us a curt bow before backing away from the table.

"Look at you go, Queen Ophelia," Damen murmured approvingly. I shot him a warning look over her head that he ignored completely.

"I wouldn't be much of a queen if I couldn't speak for myself," Ophelia replied, swallowing thickly. She seemed to notice at that moment that she had a death grip on my thigh, looking surprised to find her hand there before snatching it back. I took my time untangling my claws from her hair, relishing that fearful little catch in her breath at my proximity. She'd even kept the unpleasant smell away this time, though it was creeping in now.

It wasn't the same as yesterday, not the *sour* repulsive stench that had made my stomach heave. This was something different, but still uncomfortably wrong. Sharp and unpleasant.

"And what kind of queen do you intend to be?" I asked, the words escaping before I could stop them.

Ophelia looked up at me, and I tried to ascertain what the look on her face meant. It was a little strange to be looking at human features when they weren't contorted in terror. What did it *mean* when her eyes narrowed like that? Why did she tilt her head to the side in a way that highlighted her vulnerable throat? Her plush lips were pressed forward, drawing my focus to her mouth, but I didn't know what that was sign of either.

Not knowing was unnerving, even though I was unquestionably the bigger threat when we were in this realm. I should have no reason to be unnerved by *her*.

She should be unnerved by *me*.

"Well, I don't suppose it particularly matters what I want or intended," Ophelia replied eventually, speaking slowly as though she was choosing her words with great care. "I'd hoped I would have something to do to fill my days, some kind of activity or job or something, but I'm under no illusions about what I am."

"And what are you?" I pressed.

"A hostage. A prisoner. A prize." Ophelia shrugged as her words sunk into me more effectively than any claws ever could. "I'm a bargaining chip, though I won't pretend there aren't advantages for me. No one *forced* me to come here."

I should say something cruel. Tell her she was right, that she was nothing and no one, and never to forget that, but I didn't need the warning look Damen was burning into the side of my head to keep those barbs to myself.

Ophelia didn't need me to remind her that both councils who'd arranged this union thought of her more as a symbol than a person, so I didn't.

No, she'd known that before I had.

That lingering sense of *wrongness* haunted me all the way through dinner.

OPHELIA

CHAPTER 6

Remember to be horny, I told myself as I climbed off my chair after dinner to stand between my new husband and my brother-in-law. Usually, that wasn't a hardship in Allerick's company, but I'd thoroughly brought down the mood with my honest assessment of my position here and he'd been even quieter and more brooding than usual throughout the rest of the meal.

Fortunately, the memory of him looming over me, his claws scraping against my scalp, was going to live in my brain forever, so maintaining a baseline level of horniness was pretty straightforward. I wasn't entirely sure *why* Allerick was so intent on getting me wound up when he obviously had no intention to follow through, but I was putting it down to a sensitive nose thing and calling it a day. I knew that I didn't *always* smell good to them, and this was the one scent he and every other Shade seemed to approve of.

It wasn't like it was hard. Allerick was all my filthiest monster fantasies come to life, and there was something quite *safe* about lusting after him. Probably the fact that it clearly wasn't going to go anywhere? I definitely didn't think he was looking at me the way I was looking at him. The second I was feeling even a little achy between the thighs, he'd back off, looking at me like he wasn't sure what to do with me.

I have some suggestions! Ask me!

Supposedly, we'd need to do the deed at least once to get the consummation aspect out of the way, but I wasn't even sure that was going to happen. We could always just *lie*. My Council was well aware I wasn't a virgin before coming here, there was no gross invasive examining procedure that would give them that proof, it didn't exist.

"You did good," Damen said quietly, an approving note in his voice as we made our way down the dais. Apparently, Damen had gotten all the friendly genes in the family, because Allerick was in peak silent mode, his enormous frame dominating the aisle that ran between the long tables to the main doors. I followed in his wake, forcing my chin up and shoulders back, determined not to look like I was chasing him even though I kind of was.

I'd come into this assuming my new husband and I would be allies in this bizarre situation together, but Allerick seemed determined to treat me as the enemy. I'd basically given him the perfect opening at dinner to assure me that I was more than what I'd assumed I was, and he'd said nothing.

Soren joined us the moment we were in the hallway, his posture less self-assured than when I'd last seen him. *He was embarrassed*, I realized. Embarrassed by his sister's conversation with us? It hadn't been *that* bad. Even though their eyes were hard to read, I knew she'd been eye fucking my husband—not great—and obviously saw me as shit beneath her shoes, but as far as confrontations went, it could have been worse.

I'd *heard* worse from my fellow Hunters after I'd been kicked out. If Meridia wanted to mean girl me, she was going to have to up her game.

"Soren, escort the queen back to her room," Allerick ordered, not bothering to turn around.

"Wait," I protested. This was my second night here, and while I didn't want to pressure Allerick, the consummation issue was hanging over both of our heads. "Shouldn't we talk—"

"No, we should not," Allerick said, cutting me off before striding down the hallway without a second look. Damen hesitated, giving me what might have been an apologetic look before jogging after his brother, leaving me standing in the corridor like a gaping idiot.

What was his *problem*? I thought we'd made progress at dinner. He kept me in a constant state of horniness because he found the smell pleasant—weird, but okay—and we'd made civilized small talk, and got to know each other a little better. But apparently that meant nothing, since we were back to where we'd been last night when he'd abandoned me on our wedding night.

As tempting as it was to scream in frustration, I forced myself to inhale deeply and let out a slow breath, closing my eyes for a moment. He'd obviously just been performing for the sake of the court. The horniness was probably just a flex on his part, to show off how hot his idiot little huntress wife got for him. Fine. A little embarrassing, but fine.

I'd given my vow to the Hunters Council that I'd make it work, that I'd uphold the treaty and promote peace between our kinds. Allerick might be an uncooperative prick, but I wasn't about to go back on my word.

Feeling marginally calmer, I turned back to face Soren with my most serene expression in place. He eyed me suspiciously.

"I'm ready to return to my rooms now," I told him, clasping my hands in front of me demurely and keeping my head up, doing my best regal face. I could have sworn his mouth twitched.

"As you wish, *your majesty*," he replied, inclining his head and gesturing down the corridor, the opposite way from where Allerick and Damen had disappeared to.

We walked in silence for a few minutes, Soren leading the way, but I was already feeling my royal facade slipping. I wasn't cut out for holding my tongue and pretending I was unaffected.

"What do queens *usually* do around here?" I asked eventually, not quite able to keep the bitterness out of my tone.

Soren flashed me a look over his shoulder that I could have sworn was judgmental. "A queen, singular, would rule the way King Allerick rules. There has never been a consort in living memory. Those who rule do not marry."

I realized suddenly that Calix had referred to Allerick's mother as just 'Orabelle,' with no formal title.

"But what about heirs?" I asked, genuinely puzzled for a moment before my embarrassment overtook it. I hadn't been asking for myself, I wasn't even entirely sure Allerick and I were compatible in that way.

"It is perfectly possible to make heirs without a marriage agreement in place," Soren replied, sounding almost cheerful for him at my discomfort, the dick. "The King and the Crown Prince are half-brothers. My sister and I are also half-siblings. If there's a family title to be inherited, the strongest rather than the oldest inherits it."

"The strongest as in who has the biggest muscles?" I asked, imagining a Shade arm-wrestling match.

"No," Soren replied flatly. "Who has the strongest... magic, for want of a better word. Manipulating shadows is a skill every Shade has, but the extent to which we can do that depends on the well of power we have to draw from. There is no doubt in my mind that King Allerick is the most powerful Shade of his generation."

I could believe that. "Is your position hereditary?"

"No. I was selected by King Allerick."

Soren's tone didn't invite more conversation, and I fell into silence as I followed him back through the brightly lit halls. Did that mean Allerick would take lovers? It sort of sounded like that was the norm here, and I suddenly felt embarrassingly naïve for not assuming that would be the case.

He was the *king*. Of course he had lovers. He'd probably been with one last night. Maybe a whole harem of them for all I knew. My throat grew uncomfortably tight, and I blamed it on my wounded pride because I refused to accept there was any other reason for me to be *sad* about it. I didn't even know Allerick. He hadn't chosen to marry *me*. Why should I care what he did?

Soren stopped, spinning so suddenly that I stumbled back in alarm. I didn't think he was going to hurt me, but he was a lot bigger than I was, he moved like the shadows themselves, and we were all alone in this quiet part of the castle.

"Stop doing that!" he hissed, retching slightly.

"Doing what? I'm not *doing* anything," I replied, bewildered.

"You're making a horrible smell again," Soren groaned, burying his nose dramatically in the crook of his elbow. "Come on, we need to get you back to your room before someone else notices and panics about it. It's not even the same awful smell as yesterday, you emit multiple unpleasant scents."

"It's not like I'm *trying* to do it," I grumbled, widening the gap between us as I followed Soren at a quicker pace. I discreetly lifted my arm, attempting to sniff myself and figure out what it was that was causing him such consternation.

I smelled fine. It was a *them* thing.

It made sense to me that Allerick could smell my wetness, but I didn't understand where the 'bad' scents were coming from that bothered them so much.

Unless they could smell emotion somehow? Maybe they don't like the scent of my negative feelings?

That didn't make sense. I mean, yes, they wore clothes made of shadows and fed off human fear and *theoretically* anything was possible, but I was still pretty sure my moods didn't smell like anything.

I wondered if my husband was in bed at this very moment with a sweet-smelling Shade, fucking them senseless, and some of my sadness morphed into rage as we approached the guards who watched over the royal wing of the palace. *Fuck Allerick and his bullshit attitude. I'd been nothing but polite to him. I'd made an effort. He could have given me a chance to have an actual conversation like Calix and Levana had, and he'd see that I was a perfectly acceptable stranger wife.*

He could have done a lot worse as far as Hunters went. My sister would have probably smothered him in his sleep by now, like the well-trained killing machine that she was.

Soren pulled his arm away from his nose, opening his mouth like he was about to explain, but then turned to look at me again with his face scrunched in confusion.

"That is... not *as* unpleasant."

"I'm so relieved," I said drily, sweeping past him and the guards for my room. I just wanted a bath and to get this heavy pin out of my hair. Maybe unwind with some drawing before bed. I already knew who my pictures would be of, even though he was an asshole and didn't deserve my lust.

It's just art, I told myself, letting myself into my room and shutting the door with a thud behind me. Affra immediately sprang into action, scuttling towards me to help me get ready for bed with an embarrasingly sympathetic look on her face.

So what if I draw pictures of him. So what if I fantasize about him when I go to sleep? Those things were for *me*.

But if he thought he was going to get even a whiff of my lust for his own benefit while he was out fucking whoever he pleased, leaving a litter of children in his wake, King Allerick had another thing coming.

The gardens behind the circular palace seemed to stretch as far as the eye could see—an endless expanse of black and gray, meticulously maintained, with wide, deserted paths cutting through sections of planting.

The garden was just as dark and gray as the one inside the courtyard, and it was making me feel a little... morose. At some point, I'd need to get some more items from the human realm, and I was already planning on buying some colorful paints while I was there.

I didn't hate the shadow realm, but I needed a little brightness in my life.

Was it too early to take a trip back to the human realm? Probably. I was supposed to always reenter at the Hunters Council portal, and I was sure they'd wonder why I'd only lasted a couple of days before needing to return home.

It felt very eighteenth century to be taking a turn around the garden, but I didn't have anything else to do. Calix had sent a side of vegetable stew up with my breakfast and there was plenty more prepared, so I had no need to visit the kitchen. The library held some appeal, but in a world that was already dark and quiet, the library was even darker and even quieter. I liked the *idea* of spending time there, but the cloak of silence was too oppressive for me to follow through.

I glanced behind me at Levana, who was following my footsteps just a few feet back, ever vigilant she scanned the garden for threats. The palace didn't seem like the kind of place where conflict was a common occurrence—there were no high walls around the garden, no battlements, and the guards I'd seen appeared mostly unarmed. The obsessive shadowing of my footsteps was specifically an Ophelia thing, apparently.

"What does it feel like when you feed?" I asked her, hoping my casual tone would hide the fact that I'd been wondering about this my entire life.

Levana did a double take, everything about her posture wary. "Why do you ask, your majesty?"

Honestly, the 'your majesty' felt a little sarcastic. While Levana was a lot friendlier than the Shade I was unfortunately married to, she was clearly looking at me as an outsider, assessing whether I had nefarious reasons for asking.

"I'm curious. I've basically been shipped here to live forever, and all I know about you is what I've been taught from the Hunter perspective. I'm sure you have some incorrect preconceptions about me, so it would make sense that I have some about you."

Levana hesitated for a moment, and it irrationally hurt that she clearly didn't trust me. It made sense—I was *technically* a Hunter—but I'd also been barred from Hunter business for a decade. Maybe a naïve part of me had hoped I'd fit in here in a way I'd never fit in with my own people. If Allerick's behavior towards me hadn't demonstrated how hopeless that dream was, Levana's certainly did.

"Okay, it makes sense for you to learn more about where you live," Levana said, like she was talking herself into it. *Comforting.* "Feeding feels... good, I guess. Satisfying. Necessary."

"Do you crave fear? What happens when you haven't had it for a while?"

"It feels wrong to be telling you this," Levana muttered. "It's a form of sustenance for us. Yes, we crave it in that we're hungry, and our survival instincts kick in before we starve to death."

Well, that was a lot less ominous than what I'd been raised to believe. Growing up, the Hunters had made it sound like Shades were mindless beasts who fed indiscriminately on every human they encountered. The Councilors had backtracked on that significantly when the treaty was announced, insisting that they weren't entirely mindless, and they could choose where and when to feed.

"That makes sense to me," I replied, sensing Levana's gaze on me as she waited for a response. "When I'm hungry or thirsty or tired, I take action to remedy that."

Besides, it wasn't like Shades killed humans. What would be the point in that? The humans were only useful to them while they were alive.

Levana was quiet, but some of the tension in her posture eased. "Do Hunters really tattoo marks on their back for every Shade they kill?"

"What?" I laughed. "No, definitely not. That makes them sound a lot more... badass than they are. Most of the Hunters I know are accountants or teachers or something by day. Just very sensible. Dull, even. They're encouraged to blend in, not stand out. You haven't encountered one?"

"I likely wouldn't be standing here with you if I had," Levana said quietly and my amusement dissipated instantly. No wonder my husband abandoned me at every opportunity. My people had killed so many of his own, and even for the Shades who'd been kind to me like Levana, Calix and Damen, my presence here was probably a painful reminder of that.

"I'm sorry. It probably isn't worth much, but I'm sorry all the same."

"But you never..." Levana began, clearing her throat. "Right?"

"No," I said immediately, shaking my head. "I've never been hunting, never even owned a weapon. I didn't make the cut, something I've never been more grateful for than at this moment," I added, rubbing my temples.

"Is that why the Hunters Council suggested you come here?"

"No." I snorted a laugh. "I was told that they asked a lot of women before me, but none of them were willing to come."

I could tell Levana had more questions, but she was trying to figure out the least offensive way to ask them—even with her difficult to read features, the 'why you' was written all over them.

Why me, indeed.

At first, I thought it was because no one else would go and I was a last resort option. That's what they'd hinted at, but they'd never actually told me who'd said no. My older sister, Astrid, had been weird as hell about the whole thing, talking about the treaty as little as possible in the few times I'd seen her, but she'd insisted that she was never an option for this.

Maybe... maybe it wasn't that she'd chosen *not* to be an option. Maybe it was that the Council had never considered her one. Maybe they'd never considered any of the other successful, young Hunter women options.

Astrid hadn't seemed thrilled for me that I'd been selected for this role. At best, she'd been resigned. Perhaps even a little remorseful.

"I'm ready to go back inside now," I said quietly.

I'd spent the better part of the afternoon feeling sorry for myself, which wasn't how I liked to spend my time. After I'd been kicked out of the Hunters, I'd gone too far in the toxic positivity direction, and I was trying to let myself be okay with my own negative feelings even if I didn't *want* to have them.

After a little bit of sulking over a lunch taken in my room, I'd manifested my anger in the form of a particularly X-rated drawing of a Shade who wasn't *not* Allerick rigging up a naked, dripping Hunter lover who wasn't *not* me with ropes made of shadows on the four-poster bed.

I'd hidden it away along with all my other drawings in the top drawer of my dresser before bathing and dressing for dinner.

I was prepared this time. I knew what to expect.

And no matter how seductive Allerick's voice was, or how gently he squeezed my throat while sucking down my scent like he needed it to survive, I was going to stand my ground.

He didn't get to have horny Ophelia. Rude kings who probably had a harem of monster side chicks didn't get to have horny wives.

That seemed like solid life advice to stand by.

Schooling my features into my most impassive expression, I stood back as Affra opened the door and then strode out with all the aloof confidence I imagined a jilted queen would have.

"Queen Ophelia," Allerick greeted me with a mocking bow. For all his assholery, he couldn't quite suppress the way he ran his gaze appreciatively down my body.

Do not react, I instructed my vagina. *We're not doing that anymore.*

I'd known exactly what I was doing when I'd slipped on this blood red velvet cocktail dress and dark heels that tied around my ankles. The dress was strapless, and Affra had pulled my hair back into a low bun at my request to show off my neck. While the Council had provided me with a decently fancy "queen" wardrobe, they hadn't included any fancy jewelry which was a shame. I could have done with some vicious-looking earrings to help set the mood.

For me, not for him. I was in a vicious kind of mood.

"You look..." Allerick swallowed thickly.

"Shall we go?" I asked, already turning towards the hallway. If he finished that sentence, my stupid pheromones would be all *'ooh yes, sexy monster husband! Tell me more about how attractive you find me! Let me do the scent dance of my people!'*

"Did you have a good day?" Damen asked, rescuing us all from awkwardness. Allerick looked momentarily stunned as I set off in the general direction of the dining hall with all three of them trailing behind me, and I felt a small swell of victory.

"Levana took me to the gardens." It was probably an unnecessary answer since I had no doubt Levana was reporting back on my movements.

"Were the gardens to your liking?" Allerick asked, taking me off guard with his sudden willingness to converse. *He must really like this dress.*

"Yes," I replied, glancing at him out of the corner of my eye but refusing to get caught up in his intimidating beauty. *Not today, Satan. I'll spend this entire dinner thinking about the day I moved into my old apartment and realized no one had unclogged the shower drain in fifteen years if I have to.*

I'd prepared a mental list of my least sexy thoughts in advance.

"Good," Allerick grunted, delightfully confused.

We paused outside the doors of the dining hall again, ready to make our dramatic entrance, and I breathed through the slight fluttering of nerves before they could take hold. Most everyone I'd bumped into in the halls had been respectful but distant. A few had glared, but that was to be expected. Dinner last night was fine. Meridia was intimidating, but Damen and Allerick seemed more than happy to tell her where to go, and Soren had looked ready to intervene if she'd gone too far. I was probably safer now than I had been just strolling through the gardens with only Levana for company.

"Do you need another reminder?" Allerick asked in a low voice as he stood next to me. I absolutely didn't imagine the rough purr to his words, the seductive tone he was choosing to take with his question instead of barking at me like he was more than capable of.

"No thanks," I replied breezily, keeping my eyes trained straight ahead as the doors swung open. From behind me, I could have sworn I heard Damen snort.

All eyes were on us as we made our way down the aisle, Allerick occasionally acknowledging someone as we passed. It may have just been wishful thinking, but the looks I was getting seemed less *intense* than they had been so far. Like the novelty of my presence was already wearing off.

As we did yesterday, the moment Allerick and I were seated, everyone else took their seats too. Shades emerged from the wings with loaded platters of meat, walking down the aisles as tendrils of shadow floated the dishes into the center of the tables.

"Did you get your vegetable fix today?" Damen teased, pushing an enormous pile of lamb shanks—maybe?—towards me.

"I did," I replied, smiling to myself as I served a small portion of meat onto my plate. "Though I'm already sick of stew. Perhaps I'll grab some tinned vegetables as well next time," I added, more to myself than anything. I could eat them fresh for a few days then have tinned ones until I had a chance to restock instead of having the same stew day after day.

"You can go to the human realm and get them whenever you like," Allerick said in an irritated voice, dragging an enormous piece of steak onto his plate. Apparently, he wasn't a fan of my new aloof attitude. "So long as you return for dinner, there's no reason you can't spend your days there."

Oof, that hurt. *Be more obvious that you want me gone, why don't you?* My nails dug into my palms hard enough to sting, but focusing on that helped distract me from the gut punch of his words. Damen made a slight hissing noise, leaning away from me, and I guessed I was making whatever gross smell they hated once again.

I breathed through the rush of disappointment, taking a stab at meditating my brain into a more neutral space. Aside from the fact that I didn't want to be broadcasting whatever I was feeling with my scent—if that's what was happening—I really didn't want to lose any control of my emotions in front of this room full of Shades. Even the ones who sort of liked me weren't about to forget that I was a Hunter, and that came with suspicion.

As infuriating as Allerick was, I could understand why the sudden changes in my scent from pleasant to unpleasant were alarming for him.

He leaned into my space like he was going to repeat his little party trick from last night, but whatever he saw on my face made him pause before his claws could touch me.

"Stop that," he commanded.

"She has stopped," Damen mumbled, sounding baffled. Whatever, I wasn't about to engage when I was so effectively disassociating.

"Not *that*," Allerick snapped. "The other thing you're doing, Ophelia. Stop it."

He leaned in closer, not touching me but letting me hear the quiet click of his teeth in my ear a hair's breadth from my skin, his warm breath ghosting over my cheek. Everything about him was still kryptonite for me, but it was remarkably easy to *not* get horny when you imagined your husband fucking his way through the entire court behind your back.

It was remarkably easy not to feel *anything*, if I really focused on it.

"Whatever you're doing," Allerick growled. "That is enough. You *will* fear me."

I gave him my blandest smile. "Whatever you say, your majesty."

CHAPTER 7

It was a complete coincidence that I happened to leave my rooms at the same time my wife did. If her schedule was much the same each day for the past week and I had made a note of what time she left for her daily palace wandering, that was beside the point.

Total coincidence.

"Hello, wife," I said in a low voice the moment she was in the corridor. She jumped slightly, not expecting me to be there, and I tilted my head to the side as I watched her collect herself right in front of me.

A week. It had been a whole week of this.

Of Ophelia inhaling deeply, closing her eyes for a moment, before exhaling slowly. She'd straighten her shoulders, smooth her hands over whatever dark-colored outfit she had on that day, fix a resolved look on her face, then look me in the eye and give me absolutely nothing.

Not a whiff of fear. Not a glimmer of curiosity in her eyes. At best, I got a carefully bland smile to accompany her carefully bland words.

And I *hated* it.

"Good morning, your majesty," she replied politely, inclining her head. Nothing else. No attempts at conversation, no signs of fear or interest or *anything*.

"And where are you off to today?" I asked conversationally, already knowing the answer.

"The kitchen first, then the gardens, if Levana is happy to accompany me."

"Levana works for you, not the other way around," I said, a little sharper than I intended.

Ophelia's mask of polite disinterest broke for just the briefest moment, a sad smile teasing at her mouth before she collected herself. "Yes, well, it isn't the most exciting assignment for her and I try to make it as pleasant as possible, given the circumstances. Did you need anything, your majesty?"

She's a spy. She's a Hunter. She's an assassin, I repeated weakly in my head. It was just that she didn't *seem* like any of those things. She didn't even really seem like a Hunter, though obviously she was or she wouldn't have been able to cross through this realm.

Mostly, Ophelia seemed sad and lonely, and it did something to my chest to think that I had played a part in that. I didn't want to be responsible for her pain, especially if she was an innocent in all this.

Which she wasn't.

She's a spy. She's a Hunter. She's an assassin.

I couldn't let myself be fooled by those sad brown eyes, no matter how much they called to me, pulling me in and insisting I look closer.

"No. I don't need anything." I swallowed thickly, my voice sounding strangely hoarse. "Don't let me hold you up."

Ophelia gave me a strange look, already turning away to head down the hallway where Levana would meet her.

"You're the king, your majesty. You could never hold me up. My time is at your leisure."

And you're the queen.

"Maybe she needs a doctor?" Damen suggested quietly as we watched Ophelia wander through the garden. Occasionally, she said a couple of words to Levana, who stood two feet back, but other than that, she just... walked. Observed. Did the bland face and made bland smells.

Maybe Damen was onto something. Perhaps she was ill.

"Or maybe she's planning your death?" my brother suggested, not sounding as distraught about that as I'd like.

"That seems unlikely," Soren volunteered, standing behind us and dutifully watching our backs. "She was able to get closer to you... before this, er, *change* in behavior. With this sudden aloofness, there's more physical distance between you."

That was true. She'd need to put a silver blade in my heart to kill me, and she was careful to sit further apart from me at meals and steered completely clear of me at any other time.

Damen hummed in agreement. "Obviously, the risk that she was some kind of assassin sent here with nefarious intentions was worth considering, but I don't think she is. Maybe the Hunters Council really does want the treaty to work and sent Queen Ophelia as a genuine act of good faith. The life she described in the human realm was very..."

"Mundane?" I suggested, frowning at her silhouette as she moved further away from where we stood at the base of the palace walls.

"Mundane," Damen agreed with a decisive nod. "I don't think the Hunters sent their most accomplished assassin into the shadows to lie in wait for her moment to strike. I think they sent you a bride they'd *miss* the least."

A low growl rumbled out of my chest, and my brother turned slowly to give me a disbelieving look. "Oh, you're *offended* now? You don't like how the *Hunters* treated your wife? Where have you been this whole time?"

Stalking her like a psychopath.

"Keep your mouth shut. King's orders," I grunted. Damen snorted.

"Maybe all this time away from the human realm is bad for her," Soren suggested quietly. "Perhaps she needs sunlight. Or more vegetables."

That idea... had merit. I already knew she'd gone to the kitchen this morning to check on the food supplies she had left, and Calix had bluntly informed me earlier that she was running low. He'd said it in an almost disapproving way too, like he held me personally responsible for starving her.

The treaty allowed for Ophelia to come and go as she pleased, and originally, I hadn't cared whether she'd gone to the human realm or not. But if the Hunters disliked Ophelia enough to send her here as a sacrifice, I wasn't sure I liked the idea of her going alone so much anymore.

She's probably a spy. It makes sense for you to accompany her to make sure she isn't passing on sensitive information, I told myself decisively, ignoring that it probably made *me* a spy to follow her with the intention of watching her interactions.

"I will accompany her back to the human realm," I declared, crossing my arms over my chest. Soren made an alarmed noise of protest. "As Captain of the Guard, I assume you'll want to come with us."

Both Soren and I were due a trip to the human realm to feed anyway, we'd just be doing it with Ophelia along for the trip.

"I would prefer that," Soren said, choosing his words carefully. Damen had no such compunctions when it came to speaking his mind.

"First, I know there's a treaty, but that seems like a profoundly idiotic idea, considering what a prize you would be for any Hunter. Second, you've grown fat and lazy as king and won't be able to defend yourself if they attack. Third, Ophelia won't want you escorting her like a prisoner anyway, so all of this is moot," Damen listed, holding up his fingers as he ticked off his points.

I sucker punched him in the gut, his back slamming the stone wall behind him with a thud as he doubled over.

"She doesn't get a choice in me escorting her. And I am perfectly capable of defending myself."

"That... cheap shot... doesn't count," Damen wheezed, grinning up at me, still clutching his middle. "And you talk a big game, but if your wife tells you to go fuck yourself, we all know you wouldn't push." He gasped in a breath of air, rubbing his midsection. "I am looking forward to this grumpy and suspicious era of Allerick being over."

I strode away from him without responding, intending to catch Ophelia in the hallway.

It wasn't an *era*. I was the king, I had to be suspicious. It was absurd that Damen was making out like I was being unreasonable here.

The entry hall was well lit, but the orbs were tied to my power so I extinguished the one that illuminated the corner next to the sweeping spiral staircase and let the shadows envelop me rather than make small talk with anyone.

Ophelia appeared a few minutes later, her cheeks pinker than usual. *From the cold perhaps?* She did look a little chilly. I frowned at Levana although she couldn't see me. She shouldn't be taking the queen out to catch her death in the cold.

"We're going to the human realm before dinner," I announced, stepping out of the shadows and letting the light behind me flare back to life. "Assuming you are from the same city that the Hunters Council headquarters are in, it will be dark there by that time."

There was a beat of silence where Ophelia just stared at me with wide eyes.

"Are you... were you just standing in the corner waiting for me?" Ophelia asked, her brow creasing. Levana immediately dropped her gaze to the floor, and I had the sneaking suspicion that she was trying to hide a smile.

"No," I replied defensively.

"You absolutely were. How did you make it all dark?" She leaned around me, squinting like she could find a mechanism to douse the lights. It was the most animated I'd seen her all week, even if it was at my expense.

"That's irrelevant. You're missing the point. We're going to the human realm later."

"*We?*" Ophelia repeated, slim eyebrows arching in disbelief as she straightened.

"Yes. *We.*"

"The other day, you told me to go spend my days there alone if I wanted, now you want to come with me? With zero explanation?" she asked, throwing her hands up in exasperation. My lips twitched in spite of myself. I'd take this irritation over the blank nothingness she'd given me recently.

"Having reflected on the matter further, I don't think you going into the human realm alone is safe. You are the Queen of Shades after all."

"Was that an admission that you were wrong?" Ophelia asked mildly.

"It's an admission that I prefer you not dead."

"Just the words every new bride wants to hear from her husband," Ophelia replied drily, fanning her face with a hand in a dramatic fashion. "Well, if that's all, *your majesty*, I'm going to change into something more... human."

My gaze drifted down her front, taking in the dark plum dress that molded closely to her curves, down to the impractical silky flats she always wore on her feet during the day. "Pity."

Ophelia sucked in a breath, and there it was. That sweet, delectable fear I'd missed so much. She'd been trying to ignore my blatant attraction to her, the attraction that terrified her so much, and this was the first time in a week that she'd let her fear slip.

She seemed to realize almost immediately, letting out the most adorable growl of frustration I'd ever heard before whirling around and storming up the stairs, Levana rushing to follow her.

I stood for a moment, grinning to myself at my success, so pleased I didn't care that she'd turned her back on me. She hadn't even bowed.

Fire. I'd take her fire over her indifference any day.

Affra brought Ophelia to meet me at the portal in front of the temple where we'd been married. Seeing Ophelia in her "human" clothes seemed strange after seeing her in the gowns she'd deemed appropriate for life here. She was wearing thin black pants that *clung* to her legs like they were part of them, a knitted gray sweater that fell just below her hips, and black boots.

"What are those?" I asked, glaring at her legs.

She furrowed her brow before following my gaze, plucking at the offending garment in question with her fingers. "These? These are leggings."

"They don't hide much."

Affra gave me a look that might have been disapproval as she shuffled away, leaving us to it. Soren stood at my back, a silent sentry.

"You do know the only thing between me and an eyeful of your little monster right now is some shadows, right?" Ophelia asked in disbelief. Behind me, Soren sounded like he was choking. "And don't get all 'it's not little' on me. You're more creative than that."

Huh. Just the promise of a trip back to the human realm had emboldened her.

"I think there may have been a compliment in there," I replied lightly, striding past Ophelia to the portal. While Shades could materialize at any location in the human realm, we could only leave and return through one of five monitored portals. It was a way of checking that no Shade was feeding too much, but mostly it was used to confirm when a Shade failed to return home after a trip to the human realm.

Never again, I vowed. That was why the treaty was in place. I would never again have to spend hours sifting through the portal records, only to tell someone's family that their loved one was presumed dead.

Ophelia didn't look surprised to see the perfectly round obsidian, the size of a boulder, having already passed unaccompanied through this portal to travel to our wedding.

"Oh, and we'll discuss that smart mouth of yours later," I told Ophelia mildly.

She blinked at me. "Ah, yes. When we do all that talking we spend so much time doing. That sounds just like us."

Soren wasn't quite able to stifle his laugh at her renewed sass this time, and I raised an imperious eyebrow at him as I held out my hand and let a coil of shadows unfurl, seeping into the stone. At my side, Soren did the same, and Ophelia moved closer almost subconsciously, staring in fascination.

"Do I need to cut myself this time?" she asked, holding up her hand to reveal a faint scar on her finger. Something about it bothered me.

"No. My shadows will carry you. Only if you are traveling without a Shade do you need to use your blood to activate the portal. Where are we going, wife?"

I told myself that it was only because of her surprised reaction to the pet name each time I used it that I continued to call her 'wife.' It was absolutely not a term of endearment.

"Um, well the Hunters Council instructed me to portal directly to them if I needed anything—"

"Absolutely not," Soren interjected, horrified. "King Allerick is too much of a prize to take him to the heart of the Hunters, treaty or otherwise."

"So little faith in me," I sighed, though I wasn't exactly thrilled with the idea of going to visit the Hunters Council either. "We aren't restricted by traveling between portals, and as my bride, you don't answer to the Hunters anymore. Simply tell us where you want to go, and we'll go there."

"Oh, well then let's go to my sister's house," Ophelia replied, rattling off an address in Denver that I knew wasn't too far from the Hunters Council building. "Astrid is a high-ranking Hunter too, just so you know, but she won't hurt you. She's the one they sent to talk me into this whole marriage thing."

There was a lot to discuss there, but Ophelia was already reaching for the black obsidian stone, looking impatiently back at us. I supposed that if I'd been in an entirely foreign realm for a week, I'd be missing my family too. Soren and I joined her, him pressing close to my side, shoulder-to-shoulder, as I visualized where we were going. At the last minute I wrapped an arm around Ophelia's waist, dragging her through with me.

The shadows swallowed us up, but so long as I kept putting one foot in front of the other and visualizing our destination, that's where we'd end up. While Ophelia had to maintain contact with me since I was guiding this journey, I was surprised when she grabbed my forearm and held it tightly in place around her waist.

Did she not like going through the portal?

Suddenly, the idea that she'd traveled to our realm all alone, hefting a case of her things along with her, sat uncomfortably with me.

I was going soft in my old age.

With some dread, I waited for the sweet smell of her fear to hit, enjoying the scent but disliking the idea of anything except me frightening Ophelia. It never came though. Ophelia may be gripping me like she'd never let go, but she diligently set one foot in front of the other, her breaths coming out in that same measured pattern she'd been using all week to regulate her fear response.

Within minutes, we emerged into the darkness of an alleyway that the scouts used frequently as a portal-in point to monitor the Hunters Council.

Ophelia immediately melted through my grip since a Shade's form was incorporeal in this realm. Here, the shadows covered us like cloaks, hiding our faces and bodies entirely from view, and parting only when we wanted to inspire fear. We were nightmares, reapers, bogeymen, shadow monsters.

Humans around the world called us by different names, but they all recognized the threat that we were.

'Do not disappear completely,' I ordered Soren, not offering any explanation for why. Not *having* an explanation for why, except that it might be unsettling for Ophelia if we vanished entirely into the darkness.

Soren said nothing, but I could *feel* his judgment drilling into the side of my head.

Ophelia squinted as her eyes adjusted to the darkness, looking between us. "You two look *identical*. That is... unsettling."

I reached out, not quite touching her face with my shadowy claws, letting her know who was who. I couldn't speak to her in this form, and it was oddly distressing.

There was a spark of recognition in her eyes, and a delightful pink blush rose on her cheeks, but Ophelia shut her emotions down almost the moment they appeared.

"You're very handsy tonight, *Soren*," she said loftily, her hair whipping through my phantom hand as she turned away, waiting for us to follow. My sassy little wife knew full well I wasn't *Soren*. I metaphorically patted myself on the back for suggesting this trip—it was the most animated Ophelia had been in days. "Alright, let's go walk down dark and empty streets, like I've been warned *not* to do my entire life."

I had half expected her to disappear onto a well-lit path and for us to watch her from afar. That she was willing to stick to areas we could traverse was a surprise, despite her snarky attitude.

'*That is very trusting of her.*' Soren's voice echoed in my head, his tone curious. '*There are plenty of things other than Shades for humans to fear in the dark. She is relying on us to keep her safe.*'

'*Good,*' I replied curtly, floating after her. She should know that if any human tried to hurt my queen, I'd suck the fear out of their body until they were a mindless husk of a being without hesitation.

Ophelia walked briskly, arms wrapped around her waist to keep herself warm in the fall chill. Occasionally, she'd stop and get her bearings, but she seemed familiar enough with this part of the city and eventually led us to a block of condos, shifting to the well-lit path while we drifted through the shadowed gardens. With an uneasy look around her, Ophelia knocked on the door of a ground-level apartment, stepping back on the stoop to wait while Soren and I moved to either side of her, out of the way of the light shining through the panes on the door.

'*It goes against every instinct I have to go into the home of a Hunter, let alone accompany my king into one,*' Soren observed, sounding resigned.

'*I don't think Ophelia would be comfortable with her sister murdering us.*'

'*With all due respect, Allerick, you have no basis to think that whatsoever.*'

Were I in my corporeal form, I would have laughed. He was right, I didn't. Just because I had some kind of unexplained compunction to keep Ophelia safe didn't mean she felt the same way for me.

95

Ophelia's sister opened the door, the family resemblance immediately apparent. Her sister had darker hair that she wore shorter, the same dark brown eyes and angular features as my wife, and none of Ophelia's softness. Seeing them face-to-face, mirroring one another, I wondered how I'd ever thought Ophelia was some kind of hardened assassin.

Her sister had 'hardened assassin' written all over her.

"What the actual *fuck* are you doing here, Lia?" her sister asked flatly, her eyes immediately cataloging Soren and my presence.

Lia. Cute.

"I just came to grab some of my things and raid your pantry," Ophelia replied breezily, swanning past her sister. "Can we turn the overhead lights off so my escorts can come inside?"

"You've really got this queen thing down pat, huh?" her sister grumbled, glaring at us for a moment. "You're not supposed to be here, and it goes against every instinct in my body to have Shades in my house. Don't make me regret it."

Despite the somewhat hostile welcome, she did leave the door open for us before going around and switching the lamps on and overhead lights off. We moved inside when the house was appropriately shadowy, sticking close to the wall while Ophelia rummaged through her sister's faintly lit kitchen. The apartment was small—all bright white and glass, the opposite of what my palace was like.

Had Ophelia lived somewhere like this? Did she miss it?

"Is my other bag still in your closet?" Ophelia asked her sister absentmindedly. "Oh! Introductions. This is my sister, Astrid. Or Atti, if we're going to go by nicknames we hate."

Astrid rolled her eyes. "So, who are your friends, *Lia*?"

Ophelia squinted between us over the kitchen island. "That one is my husband, King Allerick," she said, pointing at Soren. Her lips tipped up slightly in mischief before she flattened them again. "I mean, I'm pretty sure it is—hard to tell without the crown and the scowl. The other one is Soren, chief bodyguard."

'She's a lot chattier in this realm,' Soren observed drily. I grunted in agreement, torn between being glad she was displaying some personality after suppressing it for a week, and being annoyed that it was coming at my expense.

"You know you're not supposed to be here, Lia," Astrid said, her voice softening. "The Council wanted you to arrive via *their* portal any time you traveled between realms."

"Isn't this why we have the whole treaty thing?" Ophelia asked, waving her hand dismissively. "How is it supposed to work if there isn't some level of trust between our kinds? The Shades can portal wherever they like so long as they hunt in approved areas. It seems unnecessary that only *I* should be restricted to one portal. Anyway, to be continued—I need to grab my bag," she added, already making her way around the kitchen towards one of the doors that led off the living room.

Soren wasn't wrong, Ophelia was a lot chattier here, though it was more like nervous babbling than anything. It hadn't escaped my notice that she and her sister hadn't embraced each other or expressed any kind of affection.

"You better be treating my sister well," Astrid warned, crossing her arms and glaring between us as Ophelia vanished into the other room. "Lia may have been born a Hunter, but her hands are clean. She's never done anything to your kind. If I find out you've been punishing her for her birthright, I'll come to the shadow realm myself. My hands are not so clean."

'I don't think this one has read the treaty,' I communicated to Soren, more amused than anything. *'Stand down, she's protecting her sister and I don't want this to escalate.'*

'*That was a direct threat,*' Soren argued, the shadows around him shifting restlessly, watching Astrid closely.

Some of the ire leeched out of Astrid's expression, her posture deflating a little. "Lia is good. She's kind. You have no idea what the Hunters Council is like," she muttered so quietly I wasn't sure if she meant us to hear or not.

She was right, we didn't. But hearing that slight admission of discontent from what appeared to be one of their most accomplished members gave me pause for thought.

"Don't hulk out on my sister, Soren," Ophelia said airily, proving she knew exactly who was who as she lugged a canvas bag with her as she exited the bedroom. "She didn't mean to threaten the king and suggest violating the terms of the treaty."

Twin patches of red appeared on Astrid's cheeks. "Yes, I did."

"Well, don't. I'm a queen. I could... do something about that. Probably. Don't test me," Ophelia replied, tilting her head to the side as if she were trying to decide if it was a bluff or not. She shrugged to herself, stopping in the kitchen to unzip the bag and fill it with whatever she was raiding from her sister's kitchen.

"You don't have jurisdiction over me, but it's good to know you have such confidence in your new role," Astrid scoffed. "What do you even *do* all day? What's the point of having royals if you have a Council that does everything?"

It wasn't an entirely unreasonable question, but Shades respected strength, and I was the strongest. It was my well of power that fueled the portals between realms and the wards that guarded areas of the kingdom. It was my power that kept the dungeons secure and the realm safe from within. I'd been challenged enough for the position to be confident in the fact that I was the best candidate for it. While the Council handled the day-to-day business of running a kingdom, they couldn't do it without my power keeping the realm afloat.

"I do stuff," Ophelia said absently, pulling out a jar of something, shaking it slightly. The green cylinders inside sloshed inside the disgusting looking liquid, and Soren all but shuddered next to me.

'What is that?' he asked. *'It looks rotten.'*

"Don't even think about it," Astrid warned, glaring at my wife. I moved without thinking, going to put myself between her and Ophelia, but the light in the kitchen stopped me at the same time as Soren hissed a warning to stop.

Ophelia blinked at me, her dark eyes wide with surprise. *Idiot. Even if she did require your protection, you don't want her. You don't* like *her.*

"You don't think my sister is going to attack me, do you? I appreciate you're trying to avoid a diplomatic incident, but I'm pretty confident that I'm safe with Astrid," Ophelia said, the corners of her mouth twitching. What did that mean? Was that a happy response? An angry one?

At least she'd assumed there was some bland, entirely impersonal reason that I'd reacted. Which it was. Obviously.

Of course I didn't want my *queen* to be harmed in any way. That was both logical and noble of me.

'Diplomatic incident,' Soren repeated in my head, sounding suspiciously amused.

Ophelia gave her sister a teasing look as she shook the revolting jar, not dissimilar to how Damen and I were together. "Astrid's addicted to pickles. That's why she's so salty."

"You're hilarious," Astrid said flatly. "Don't take my pickles, you don't even like them."

"They are disgusting," Ophelia agreed. "I'm taking all your canned vegetables though, and these apples. Could you grab some paints for me for my next visit?"

"I thought you were more of a sketcher," Astrid replied, pulling a device out of her pocket that I hoped was to take note of my wife's request.

'Sketcher?'

'*She draws pictures*,' I replied quickly, in case Soren started panicking about nonexistent security threats.

"I'm branching out," Ophelia said primly, zipping up the bag and hefting it over her shoulder. It irked me for some reason that I couldn't carry it for her in this form.

Astrid snorted. "Because you have nothing to do all day, but sure. I'll find you some painting stuff. Should I tell Mom and Dad you stopped by?"

Ophelia was already making her way around the kitchen counter, the objects in her bag clinking together as she moved. It never occurred to me that Ophelia's parents *wouldn't* be made aware of her visit. My mother and I had an excellent relationship.

To my surprise, Ophelia grimaced. "They probably wouldn't like that I came here rather than the Council building."

"They definitely wouldn't," Astrid agreed, her voice quiet.

"I don't want to put you in a difficult position—"

"It's fine," Astrid said quickly. "It's not a difficult position. I never liked that they said all of your visits had to go via the Council portal. You may live in the shadow realm, but this is still your home."

I found that I didn't like that idea at all.

"Thanks, Atti. I'm sure I'll be back for a visit soon."

The sisters exchanged strained smiles, but made no move to embrace each other before Ophelia headed for the front door. The moment she was in the shadows, I was at her side.

In case she tried to run, I told myself unconvincingly.

"Well, I hope you enjoyed that thrilling look into my regular life," Ophelia said drily, keeping her voice low. "Ready to go back to the palace, your majesty?"

It had certainly been enlightening. I had more questions than ever for my mysterious wife, and I intended to get some answers. It occurred to me that humans had stores they could visit to purchase goods from and Ophelia hadn't suggested going to one of those. Did she not have the funds to do so? Or had she not wanted to visit such a well-lit space where we couldn't follow?

I supposed I could ask her back at the palace, but first, we needed to feed.

I darted in front of her, annoyed I couldn't just speak to catch her attention. While she couldn't touch *me* in this form, I could make her feel faint sensations if I touched *her*. Unpleasant ones, designed to elicit a fear response.

You like her fear, I reminded myself. *You find her scent most pleasant when she is afraid.*

I might even go so far as to say I'd *missed* her fear since she'd done whatever it was she'd been doing to repress it.

Soren floated back a few feet as I dragged my shadow-like claws down Ophelia's face. It never hurt them, we weren't solid enough for that, but I knew it felt like icy dread raking over their skin, making their fine hairs stand up on end and their natural instincts scream at them to either freeze or flee.

Ophelia did the former, standing stock still in place. I took my time, inhaling deeply as that glorious sweet smell permeated the air. Her lips parted, and I ran my thumb over her lower one, tempted beyond measure to lean forward and suck that delicious fear right out of her, knowing it would sustain me better than any regular human ever would.

Was that...

Did she try to lick my claw?

No, surely not. I must have imagined it.

"You're hungry," Ophelia breathed, tipping her head back and better exposing that beautiful neck to me. "Too bad you can't feed on my fear."

Because of that irritating term in the treaty, yes. It *was* a shame. Though probably for the best because nothing would satisfy me afterwards if I tasted Ophelia, that much I was certain of.

Ophelia's *fear*.

Not her.

It sounded weak even in my own head.

"Come on then," Ophelia sighed. "Let's get this over and done with."

OPHELIA

CHAPTER 8

I took a seat on a park bench, hoping no humans approached me while I was sitting here looking like the world's easiest target in the middle of the freaking night so Allerick and Soren could have their meal.

Okay, I was being dramatic. It was probably nine pm at the latest, but sitting in the dark in public all alone—or alone to the human eye at least—was Bad Personal Safety 101.

Soren went ahead to look for his dinner while Allerick hovered behind me, his claws occasionally running over my hair or neck like he was reminding me he was there.

He was acting odd today. Maybe my whole refuse-to-get-horny act had really bothered him? Too bad I'd gone and ruined it now. I'd gotten too excited at the concept of coming back to the human realm and experiencing a bit of my old life that I'd forgotten to be aloof.

I sighed internally as Allerick's hand ghosted over my shoulder again. Was it normal to get all hot and bothered over shadowy monster claws? No, but I already knew I wasn't normal.

If I was normal, I wouldn't be so goddamn *jealous* over the fact that Allerick was about to feed on someone else. If I could work up one iota of fear, I'd be shamelessly begging for him to feed from me instead, and I really didn't need to embarrass myself any further. I was already failing in my attempts to not smell like an eager beaver. Like my beaver was *literally* eager.

Remember that he's probably going to return to his many, many lovers the moment we're in the shadow realm. Remember that he's likely only showing any interest in you now because you've been ignoring him and he's sulky about it.

A jogger rounded the corner, a young man with his headphones in, probably thinking that this was a nice part of town and a safe neighborhood to go running in the dark.

It sort of was. From memory, this was a pretty low *crime* area. Just not a low *monster* area. He was a big guy too, probably not someone used to tiptoeing through life, constantly watching over his shoulder.

Soren appeared in front of the runner with a dramatic flourish, releasing the shadows enough that just his outline and his orange eyes were visible. Just enough to pass as a trick of the light, enough to make the poor human do a double take, wondering if he was seeing things.

I didn't *love* watching as Soren moved in closer, his form flickering and eyes glowing, the human frozen to the spot as recognition hit that it *wasn't* just a trick of the light—or was it? Maybe it was his own mind playing tricks on him?—but I didn't feel an overwhelming urge to intervene either. Maybe because I knew from talking to Levana that feeding was about sustenance, not pleasure.

I really was a terrible Hunter.

Soren leaned into the man's face and though it was dark and I couldn't see clearly from where I was, I didn't need fancy heightened Shade senses to know that he was terrified and Soren was basically sucking that fear out of his mouth and drinking it down.

The shadows around Soren's form grew darker as he gained strength or power, or whatever it was that fueled them, and within seconds it was over. The human stumbled back, dazed and confused, his memory only supplying the haziest details of what he'd seen. Enough to spur him into action as he *sprinted* down the path towards the streetlights. He'd remember his fear well enough to not jog here in the dark again, that was for sure.

To me, that was why we *needed* Shades. Humans had a tendency to feel invincible, like whatever bad things happened in the world would always happen to someone else. Sure, one in every four car accidents was caused by texting and driving, but everyone who'd used their phones behind the wheel assumed it couldn't possibly happen to *them*.

A healthy dose of fear is what kept us alive, and the Shades ensured that we got one.

Did that mean I wanted to watch Allerick administer that dose of fear to someone else?

No, I did not. Maybe a small part of me worried that it *would* make me afraid of him, seeing what he was capable of in action. Or maybe I was just a jealous little psycho. Or both.

I sighed dramatically, crossing one leg over the other as Soren floated back to us, doing my best to look bored and impatient.

Soren paused in front of me and I tipped my head up to watch him as he and Allerick had some kind of silent conversation over my head. Despite the fact that I couldn't see their faces underneath the shadowy hoods, it looked sort of... heated? Soren was waving his shadowy arms, his head turning this way then that way. Allerick's claws scraped against my scalp and my vagina jumped for joy while my brain pointed out he was scratching me like I was a cat.

That's probably how he saw me. A silly little pet Hunter to show off and cage away as he saw fit. Meanwhile, I was over here imagining fanning those shadows that always hid his crotch away and spreading myself out like a buffet.

It was *very* inconvenient that my hormones were more active than my brain cells, but such was life. I knew I was a bit of a horny disaster when I wasn't actively meditating it away.

Soren threw his hands up in exasperation, though I couldn't actually *see* his hands, just flappy shadow cloak sleeves, and did what might have been a dramatic spin before heading towards a darker section of the park.

"What is happening?" I muttered, twisting to look up at Allerick. "Did he just *flounce*?"

Soren seemed to be *more* expressive in his shadowy ghost form than he was in his solid one. Allerick pointed emphatically in the direction Soren had gone, and I could have sworn his body language was a little bit irritable.

"Whatever," I sighed, dragging the heavy bag over my shoulder and stomping after Soren. "This lack of talking thing is a real double-edged sword."

Soren vanished into the overhanging branches of a tree, and despite my brain reminding me that walking into dark places wasn't the brightest idea, I felt safe enough with Soren and Allerick to follow. The moment we were all safely ensconced in darkness, Allerick's arm enveloped my shoulders, dragging me into the in-between. It was a weird place that regular humans couldn't go, not that they would want to. There was nothing to *see*, not even anything to hear. It was just swirling darkness, and shadows that seemed to crawl up my body like they were trying to devour me whole.

When I'd walked through it alone, I'd had to concentrate on my destination and walk as best I could in a straight line to ensure I got to the right portal, but without asking, I knew Allerick was doing all the hard navigational work and I was just being swept along for the ride.

The moment we were in the shadows, Soren and Allerick's forms solidified either side of me, and someone took my heavy bag in what may have been a gentlemanly gesture.

Maybe we'd bonded on our little excursion to the human realm? That'd be nice.

Except the moment we were free of the portal and back in the gray lands of the shadow realm, Allerick wrapped his hand around my upper arm and turned me towards him, stopping me from going any further.

Guess we hadn't made any progress after all.

"Why did you come here?" he asked, the demand in his voice taking me off guard.

"What?"

"Why did you come here? Why did you agree to the marriage? Did you have a choice?"

Soren easily lifted my bag over his shoulder, dismissing himself with a nod to Allerick before heading back towards the palace.

"You're not a high-ranking huntress," Allerick continued. "You didn't volunteer for this role. You had a life in the human realm. Why did you come here?"

"There is no one reason," I replied carefully. I'd expected him to be a little curious about my life before, but the intensity of his questions was throwing me off. "I did have a choice, though the advantages of agreeing were highlighted a lot."

"What were the advantages?" he ground out. Not for the first time, I wished I understood his expressions better. He sounded almost *angry*. Maybe after meeting Astrid, he was annoyed he'd gotten the dud sister.

"I was never initiated as a Hunter when I turned eighteen. I didn't get any of the bonuses that other Hunters get like free housing and a paid-for college education."

"Your motives were... financial?" he asked, sounding suspicious. Or perhaps just confused. Shades did have a currency, but their society seemed to be less financially motivated than in the human realm.

"That was part of it." I looked down, suddenly finding the ground very interesting. *Oh yeah, and they kicked me out of Hunters youth group for the crime of committing my inappropriate monster fantasies to paper, and I was literally the only person willing to come here.*

"What else?" Allerick prompted.

"Why do you want to chat now?" I asked, exasperated. "You never want to chat."

"I'm in a chatty mood."

"I prefer you silent and brooding," I muttered, knowing full well he could hear me. "I was hoping this would be a better fit for me, okay? I don't regret not hunting, the opposite in fact. But knowing that there was more to our world, knowing what was out there... It was hard to live among regular humans like I was ordered to and pretend that I was one of them."

"They would have never given you a place among them? Never trained you as a Hunter?"

"No. They would have never made me a Hunter, and I'm glad for it. Can we go inside now?"

Maybe I preferred it when Allerick ignored me. Being the focus of his full attention was a little disarming. He was so *intense*.

"So eager to get away from me," Allerick purred, dipping down so his breath skittered over my neck.

No. No more horny smell for you.

I hadn't been particularly successful at suppressing it tonight, but I was determined to get back on track now. *Remember, he's probably banging other Shades. He is possibly attracted to your sister.*

"I have no idea what you're talking about," I replied airily, boldly turning my back on him to head back to the palace. "I don't even know who you are, you're never around."

He snorted, easily falling into step next to me. "I'm busy. Ruling a secret shadow realm and all. You know how it is."

My mouth fell open, and I knew I was looking up at him with an expression akin to horror, because who *was* this guy? Did he get body snatched or something while we traveled between realms?

"Was that a joke? Are you telling jokes now? Did you forget to hate me for a minute?"

"What makes you think I hate you? Hunters are so dramatic," Allerick drawled and if his eyes weren't all a solid unmoving color, he would have probably rolled them. "Come along, wife. We are expected at the feast in half an hour, and I expect you'll want to put your 'queen' outfit on."

Annoyingly, he wasn't wrong. While it had been nice to chill in leggings for a while, I absolutely wasn't going to dinner like this. I had a reputation to maintain.

I didn't know what kind of reputation, but *some* kind. Hopefully. I didn't know why it mattered to me, I'd never had any aspirations about having a reputation or leaving a legacy before, but since I'd arrived here it was something that mattered to me. I didn't want to just drift through this place, *existing* but not really living the way I had in my faux-human life.

I stomped back towards the palace with Allerick easily keeping pace, his stupidly long legs having no trouble despite the fact that I was attempting to angrily power walk away from him.

Why am I even annoyed?

Hadn't I *wanted* him to stop ignoring me? And now the moment he had, I didn't know what to do about it. Possibly because I hadn't expected him to be all relaxed and jokey, and it was kind of unsettling.

"You don't have to sprint, you know. Dinner isn't *that* soon," he commented. I threw him an irritated look over my shoulder, but didn't reply because then he'd realize how out of breath I was and I didn't want to give him any more ammunition.

Fortunately, Affra was already at the door to my room waiting for me, and I walked past her with as much dignity as I could muster while she bowed to Allerick.

"I'll see you soon, wife," Allerick called, chuckling to himself as he went into his own room. The moment Affra closed the door behind her, I collapsed on my bed face first and groaned into the mattress.

This was meant to be a simple, straightforward trip to grab some vegetables and the rest of my clothes, and it had turned into a whole *thing*.

"Would you like to get ready for dinner, Queen Ophelia?" Affra asked, sounding far too amused. "Captain Soren dropped off the things you brought back, if you were wanting to wear something from there."

"Oh, no. All the queen-looking clothes are what I brought with me when I first arrived, that's just some stuff I couldn't fit that my sister had been keeping for me," I explained, rolling over and climbing off the bed. "And more food. Wait, am I supposed to be calling him *Captain* Soren?"

Affra laughed softly. "You are the queen. I imagine you can call him whatever you like. Captain Soren is not shy about making his displeasure known, he would have told you if he had any objections."

All the same, I didn't want him to feel like he *couldn't* correct me because I'd been given this title I didn't really require.

I freshened up before changing into a silky navy dress that had short sleeves and ended above my knees. All of the clothes the Hunters Council had provided for me were pretty modest—this one seemed almost scandalous in comparison. The way Affra's eyes widened in surprise when I pulled it on didn't help.

"Is it too much?" I asked, sitting down at the vanity so she could pin my hair up with the enormous raven pin Damen had given me.

Prince Damen.

"You look very beautiful, Queen Ophelia. And very human with all of that skin on show."

"That seems bad. I should change," I mumbled, attempting to talk and not stab myself in the eye with my mascara wand at the same time.

Affra hummed, carefully twisting tendrils of hair back with her claws. "I am not royalty, and my opinion is worth very little, but I am old and I have seen many things."

"I think your opinion is worth a lot," I cut in, a little sharper than I meant to. Affra had been wonderful to me, and I hated the idea of her thinking she was somehow less than.

"You are very kind, my queen." *Oof.* The 'my' in front of 'queen' really made the title hit differently. It sounded *reverent*, rather than sarcastic. "My opinion is that you are a marvel—a Hunter among Shades, a human body in the realm of shadows. Everything that you are—*as you are*—is magnificent, Queen Ophelia. You don't need to mold yourself into being anything else."

She delivered all of this so factually, nimble claws still working efficiently to secure the pin in place. I exhaled heavily, breathing past the sudden tight feeling in my throat.

"That's really lovely, Affra, thank you."

I wasn't entirely sure I agreed, but I appreciated the sentiment. Dressed and ready, I had no excuses when there was a rap of knuckles on the door a few moments later.

"I will take your food to the kitchen now," Affra said gently, all but shooing me towards the door, probably wary about keeping Allerick waiting. "Remember, just as you are."

I nodded, giving her a tight smile. Being around Affra made me wonder what it would have been like to have a caring maternal figure in my life growing up. Certainly, no one in my family had ever encouraged me to be just as I was.

Who I was had *horrified* them.

Affra pulled the door open, and I was unsurprised to find not only Allerick, but Damen and Soren flanking him. I inclined my head formally at my husband, wanting to get back to the safe ground we'd been on before our trip into the human realm.

It was difficult to tell, but I could have sworn he frowned.

"Let's go!" Damen crowed, bouncing on the balls of his feet. "A traveling troupe of performers have come from the other side of the realm, and they're going to put on a show after the meal. I don't want to miss it."

"The meal hasn't begun yet, so that's an unlikely risk," Allerick drawled, staring at me while responding to his brother.

"Well, I don't want to be responsible for us being late," I replied, starting down the corridor. "Thank you for bringing my bag up, Captain Soren."

Damen snorted loudly. "Oh, he's *Captain* Soren now, is he? Here was me thinking you'd make progress on your excursion, and you seem to have gone backwards if anything—"

There was a loud *oof*, and when I glanced back Allerick was pulling his arm back into his side like he'd just elbowed his brother in the gut.

It was oddly endearing. Maybe because it seemed like such a boyish, human thing to do?

"You shouldn't antagonize him, Damen," Soren said mildly. "He didn't feed on our trip."

"Is that so?" Damen asked. "How intriguing. What possible explanation could there be for that?"

"You two are gossipy old toads," Allerick muttered. *Fascinating.* I supposed they'd always been quite informal when it was just them, but their banter was even more relaxed than usual, almost like they were showing me another side of them.

You are reading too much into this.

There was no hesitation in me as we approached the double doors to the dining hall. After a week of evening meals in front of an audience, I wasn't so much used to it as the court was used to me. Though I definitely got more than my fair share tonight as I made my way up the aisle with Allerick walking close enough that our arms brushed against one another.

I was totally burning this dress. Affra was wrong, no one here needed to be reminded that I was the humanest human to ever human.

Soren broke off from our little group to stand guard, while Allerick and I walked up the stairs to the dais with Damen at our backs. I surveyed the room for a moment as we all paused behind our chairs, noting the ostentatious shadow outfits of the troupe at the back of the room before we all took our seats and platters of food began to appear.

"What kind of performance will they put on?" I asked Damen. Allerick made a discontented sound low in his chest, a growl that was more animal than human, and I jumped slightly in surprise. I wasn't afraid of him per se, but he usually seemed pretty happy to sit and eat his meal at dinner while I asked Damen any questions I had.

Damen grinned, all savage teeth, looking around me to peer at his brother. "Testy, testy. Perhaps you should have fed today, like you were supposed to." He turned his attention to me, seemingly happier than ever at Allerick's annoyed grunt. "The troupe will do some kind of skit they've made up, something meant to make the audience laugh. Usually, it's at the king's expense."

I glanced at Allerick, trying to ascertain how he felt about that. Yesterday, I wouldn't have thought of him as good-natured in the slightest, but he'd been in a teasing mood when we arrived back at the portal so perhaps I'd read him wrong.

He didn't *seem* any more agitated than usual, and I took that as a sign not to panic. If he wasn't worried, I didn't need to be worried. Right?

Because if they'd historically made jokes about the king, it wasn't a leap to think they'd make jokes about the *queen,* and there was a lot to make jokes about. Oh my god, I was basically the dream subject of ire for a Shade comedian. Were they going to insinuate I was some kind of wicked huntress assassin turned wannabe queen? Point out my blunt teeth and fingers? Laugh about my apparently distinctive range of scents?

I forced myself to take a deep even breath as I felt the urge to hyperventilate creeping up, my heart pounding double time in my chest. As discretely as I could, I wiped my now sweaty palms on the expensive satin of my dress, glad that the table hid from the movement from the courtiers, and hoping against all odds that Allerick and Damen hadn't spotted the nervous tell.

You should have just stayed at Astrid's house. You could have fought them off in their noncorporeal forms if they'd tried to shadow walk with you, I chastised internally, letting the regret flow through me.

For the first time since I'd arrived in the shadow realm, I truly wanted to go back to my lonely little human existence.

CHAPTER 9

It wasn't unusual for Ophelia to eat what I considered to be an insufficient portion of food at dinner. She always sampled a little of everything, and didn't seem to be overly picky, but she just never ate *enough*.

Tonight though, she absolutely wasn't eating enough. She had barely even tried—her hands were on her lap under the table, and she was rubbing her thighs so frequently I was beginning to wonder if she was nursing some kind of injury.

Despite her best attempts, her gaze kept catching on the troupe at the back of the room, and while she wasn't quite producing that *awful* scent— thank the goddesses—there was a sour note to her usually *pleasant* smell that made me wonder if the *awful* smell wasn't too far away.

"Do you not like watching performances?" I asked as the tables were cleared away and space was made at the front of the room below the dais.

"I like them just fine," Ophelia murmured, folding her hands in her lap and twisting her fingers in what appeared to be a nervous gesture, not unlike the way my mother fidgeted with her claws.

Strange. I would have expected the smell of nerves to be a more muted version of her sugary fear.

"Your majesties!" the lead performer called out, sweeping into a dramatic bow. On his head was a garish, oversized version of the crown I wore on mine—a prop I'd seen them pull out in performances many times before. "It is an honor for us to perform for you on this fine evening. We are grateful for your hospitality and your dedication to the arts, long may it continue. Enjoy the show!"

The court roared and cheered, and I gestured the go-ahead for the troupe to proceed, chancing a glance at Ophelia. She was wearing that stiff smile I had come to despise over the past week, looking perfectly put-together. Damen looked at me over her head, the barest flicker of concern on his face before his usual arrogant grin replaced it.

Fortunately, we were far enough away that it was unlikely anyone else would pick up the emotions Ophelia was broadcasting with her scent.

"I am King Mallerick!" the actor boomed, making the court laugh. He puffed out his chest, surveying the room regally. "It is an honor to have you here today, on this most auspicious occasion. My wedding!"

I tensed immediately, the laughter in the room becoming slightly more muted as the court's attention shifted to me.

That I was the target of their jesting was no surprise, but I had naively assumed that Ophelia would be left out of it. Perhaps the court had thought so too, because the already quiet laughter descended into an uncomfortable quiet, only broken by the sounds of Shades whispering to each other and shifting nervously in their seats.

"Are you marrying yourself, King Mallerick?" Ophelia asked mildly, when the tense silence continued for a beat too long. "You are looking awfully lonely up there."

Both the actor and the court relaxed at her teasing words, but I didn't.

Another performer shuffled through a side door, hunched over dramatically with three wisps of shadow flailing from the top of their head like Garren's ugly hair.

"The bride is here! The huntress has arrived!" the performer croaked, bowing obsequiously in what was an admirable impression of Garren. Damen snorted.

To hell with the distance Ophelia was trying to keep between us. Not when the 'bride' was about to make their entrance. I silently moved my chair closer to hers and draped an arm over the back of her chair, doing my best approximation of a relaxed pose despite the apprehension I was feeling. Ophelia turned that blank, pleasant smile on me for a moment—a gesture for the audience's benefit—but her strange eyes shone with something that may have been genuine gratitude.

Only five performers made up the troupe, and two attempted to keep out of sight as they sang a slower, more dramatic version of the awful dirge Ophelia had been forced to walk up the aisle to.

What would she have chosen if she'd been allowed to plan her own wedding? I wondered idly, suddenly troubled at the idea that the entire thing had been planned by elderly Councilors with no input from the bride.

The doors at the back of the room swung open with a bang, and one of the female performers entered, hunching into herself and glancing around the room as though she was terrified of being eaten by the seas of monsters she was wading into. The shadows around her had been arranged in the approximation of Ophelia's form-fitting wedding dress, though it was a mocking impression— too tight in the bust, and dramatically long at the back.

At some point, my hand had found my wife's shoulder and I quickly loosened my grip before I hurt her.

Ophelia laughed good-naturedly, and even though the sound was forced to my ears, the pat on my thigh under the table was real. She was telling me to stand down. Curious little thing.

The performers stopped singing and stood to the side, their mannerisms and way they'd arranged their shadows a clear nod to Soren and Damen.

The real Soren stood near the dais practically radiating disapproval, while Damen laughed loudly, putting the rest of the audience at ease.

"How delicious Queen Bophelia smells!" King Mallerick pronounced, strutting around like a peacock. "Look at you all, salivating over her scent. Fools! Her fear is all mine to devour. I shall subsist on it and be the most well-fed Shade in the entire realm."

"Erm, King Mallerick," Fake Soren said in a hesitant, nasally voice that was nothing like the real Shade's. Damen burst out laughing again. "The treaty says you're not allowed to feed on your new bride."

"Then what is the point?" King Mallerick yelled. "Send her back!"

"I'll take her," the actor playing Garren panted, dropping to all fours and attempting to lick Queen Bophelia's thighs.

She screamed dramatically, swooning into King Mallerick's arms as he landed a fake kick on the priest's jaw. The actor's mouth exploded in shadows that seemed to drip like blood, a long shadow tongue lolling obscenely out of his mouth.

"A new priest!" King Mallerick called, gripping his bride greedily to him. "If I cannot feed on her, no one can. Bophelia is mine!"

It irked me that their assessment wasn't entirely wrong. I had wanted to keep Ophelia all to myself the moment I'd seen her.

The shadows around the priest figure on the ground morphed and the actor sprang back up, mimicking Weylin's posture and looking determinedly away from Bophelia like he didn't want to risk his tongue too.

"What ever happened to that first priest from our wedding?" Ophelia whispered, leaning right in to speak as close to my ear as she could with the height difference between us.

"He's fine."

Probably. Shades healed quickly. I'd ask Cyr to check on him tomorrow if I remembered.

"Let us perform the ceremony!" Fake Weylin said with a flourish. "King Mallerick, will you put down your wife for the vows?"

"Never! My wife's delicious fear is all my own, and I will not share even a whiff with you!" King Mallerick declared as Bophelia scrambled up his body, wrapping her legs around his waist and arms around his neck, looking around the room with wide eyes.

Ophelia watched with a bemused smile. "Did I really look so afraid?"

You *were* so afraid, I almost corrected. We could all smell it, that was why the court was laughing at the performers.

"Of course, King Mallerick. Do you take Bophelia the Huntress to be your bride?"

"Yes! Bophelia is mine!"

I sighed, scratching Ophelia's bare arm lightly with my claws, more for my own stress management than anything else. These shows were so tedious.

"Bophelia the Huntress, do you take Mallerick, King of the Shades, to be your husband?"

Bophelia's teeth clattered together noisily, her entire body shaking dramatically. "Ye...Yes. I do." She hiccuped loudly before burying her face in Mallerick's shoulder, sobbing as Mallerick roared in triumph.

"Mine!" stupid Mallerick shouted again.

"I don't sound like that," I muttered.

"The 'mine' is more implied with you," Damen laughed. Ophelia shook under my arm, and it took me a moment to realize she was laughing too.

"Now I will take my bride and seal the terms of the treaty in my bed!" Mallerick shouted, throwing Bophelia over his shoulder and smacking her on the ass. "Goodbye, subjects! Feast without us while I have a feast of my own!"

Mallerick marched down the aisle with Bophelia over his shoulder, waving jovially at the cheering crowd as he went.

Beside me, Ophelia snorted. "I wish."

"What was that?" I asked, twisting in my chair to look at her.

"*Wished*," Ophelia said quickly. "Past tense. At the time. Not now."

"You did?" Was she trying to put me off by saying she didn't want me *now*? I was stunned she'd wanted me *then*.

"No. I don't know. Stop talking, we have to clap now," she hissed, cheeks flushing a pretty shade of vibrant red. "Or stomp. Whatever."

I hummed in agreement, stomping my feet unenthusiastically while the court hollered their approval. The performers all gathered in the space they'd cleared in front of the dais, dropping to one knee in front of us as a show of respect after their show at our expense.

"Very good," I said drily. "Thank you for entertaining us this evening. I'm sure Prince Damen will be able to find a suitable reward for your time."

Damen was already moving down the steps to greet them, accustomed to me throwing meet-and-greet style tasks at him. He was very little help most of the time, and had almost no responsibilities around here, but this he absolutely had to do.

I was not about to make courteous small talk with the actors who'd mocked me and my wife, even if the jests were all in good fun.

"Are you grumpy?" Ophelia teased, taking it all in her stride surprisingly well. That was what she did though, wasn't it? She'd been immensely good at absorbing anything and everything that had come her way.

"These performances are bad for my ego," I replied, which was true, though I was more grumpy because Ophelia had become a target of their teasing, and because I hadn't fed.

I should have fed.

Ophelia had looked so miserable at the prospect, that I couldn't bring myself to feed in front of her.

"Oh right. I forgot how much you're hurting for ego," she said wryly.

"Was that a joke? Are you telling jokes now?" I asked, throwing her words from earlier back at her.

Ophelia pressed her lips together, rolling them in which *fascinated* me. The things she could do with a mouthful of harmless little teeth.

"I tell jokes all the time," she replied primly. "In the human realm, I am *very* funny."

Compared to Astrid, I could absolutely believe that.

"King Allerick, Queen Ophelia," Maddox, one of my Councilors, said as he approached the table, bowing low. "I am sorry, my king. There has been an incident that requires your immediate attention."

When wasn't there?

I made eye contact with Soren who nodded in understanding that I wanted him to escort Ophelia back to her rooms.

"Until tomorrow, wife," I told her, missing the heat of her body next to me as I pulled my arm away and stood up. I was probably just touch starved. Shades were sexual creatures, and I hadn't been with anyone since my marriage was brokered.

Nor would I be with anyone again, unless my wife set aside her fear of me for long enough to consummate our union. Perhaps this union was in name only, but I had made a commitment and I intended to respect that.

And I'd respect Ophelia by keeping my hands to myself and not causing her any more distress than I already did.

After a long night meeting with the Council before traveling to one of the smaller regions to put down a small scale rebellion against the peace treaty with the Hunters, I'd been too exhausted to check in on my sleeping queen, and had gone straight to bed. I woke irritable, feeling as though I'd been cheated of my nightly routine.

After yesterday, something in my attitude towards Ophelia had changed. Seeing her around her sister, the way she was treated as barely a Hunter at all, after she'd watched Soren feed and said nothing... Then when we'd come back here and she'd sat through that horrendous performance and smiled and teased the performers like they weren't blatantly mocking her...

She wasn't who I thought she was. Which meant it was time for me to do some more research, because I didn't like that I'd been wrong. It... sat uneasily with me.

I bathed before quickly eating the now-cold breakfast Cyr had left out for me, contemplating wearing my uncomfortable crown today but ultimately deciding against it. It served as an impressive visual reminder when I had to go confront the idiots who acted like the peace treaty was a life sentence, but I didn't need it. Last night's rebellion had been better organized than usual, and it would require more of my attention today. A surprisingly young female had been leading the charge, attempting to manipulate one of the portals so they could pass through it and feed without leaving a traceable record.

It was idiotic, really. The portals predated any of us, and had magic of their own. They wouldn't be tricked or strong-armed into doing the bidding of a few discontented Shades who refused to compromise.

Unable to delay any longer, I dragged myself back to the Council Chamber with Soren silently at my side, resenting my duties for the first time. Soren was up-to-date on what had occurred, and he'd been at my side when we confronted the rebels, yet even he didn't truly understand the burden of responsibility that came with my role.

"King Allerick," Maddox greeted me as the Councilors bowed. "We found the Shade who attempted to start the uprising. She's in the dungeon awaiting trial."

"Good," I said, dropping into my seat and barely resisting the urge to lie my head on the table. She'd done an impressive job evading us last night while we rounded up the others. "Soren can deal with her, I'm more interested in the *why*."

"There are Shades who feel the treaty is not in our best interests," Raina, one of the other Councilors, hedged.

"I gathered that. How terrible it is for us to not be killed," I deadpanned. Were there sacrifices on our part? Of course. But the benefits far outweighed the disadvantages.

"Quite," Raina agreed, amused. "We always knew there'd be some opposition, your majesty. We'll continue to catch them as they arise and deal with them accordingly. The Shades will see the benefits of the treaty in action, this small dissenting movement has no legs."

I nodded, inclined to agree with Raina's position, although I was still wary. Most Shades just wanted to feed safely, they didn't care if we were following a few rules the Hunters had set out for us to do so. I didn't even think they particularly cared about the marriage agreement side of things. The performance last night was usually a good indication of how regular folk felt about an issue, and there hadn't been any *animosity* towards Ophelia.

They'd laughed at how afraid she was and how covetous I was over her fear, but there were far worse things they could have said. I wouldn't have let them live, but they could have tried.

"King Allerick, we had hoped you'd bring the queen to this meeting for an introduction," Teague, one of the newest councilors, said nervously. Judging by the expressions on the others' faces, Teague had been today's nominated sacrifice to ask after her.

"I'll request her presence at the next meeting," I sighed. "Though I hope you'll all remember that Queen Ophelia is new to our world and everything in it. I won't have you interrogating my wife, Councilors," I added in a deceptively calm voice that all of them knew not to fall for.

"Of course not," Teague replied hastily. "This meeting is merely a formality."

"Of course. Soren, are you ready to go downstairs?"

Soren nodded, still standing at attention next to the door. I didn't intend to get too involved—it would lend too much credibility to the dissenters' claim if the king paid it any attention. There were plenty of dark corners for me to blend into while I watched Soren work though.

Judging by the shadows floating off him like smoke, he was more than ready to get his hands dirty.

Hopefully, this would be the one and only time we were forced to deal with a rebel who couldn't see the value of a treaty that kept the lives of everyone in this realm safe.

"I give up," Soren growled, storming out of the dungeon and slamming the soundproof stone door shut behind him. "She's too terrified to say anything useful."

"I drew the same conclusion," I replied, releasing the shadows that had hidden me in the dungeon while I watched Soren question Kirsa. "Who is a bigger threat than me? She should be terrified of the king's wrath."

"Perhaps this group is better organized than we initially gave them credit for," Soren admitted, tapping his foot impatiently on the floor as he always did when he was stressed. "It may be worth assigning more resources to tracking them."

I made a noise of discontent, leading Soren up the winding staircase to the upper levels. Assigning more resources meant taking them away from somewhere else, and I already knew what he was going to suggest.

"Allerick, perhaps it's time to reduce the guard presence around the palace. Aside from the fact that Ophelia doesn't appear to present any kind of threat, between Levana and I, she's always covered anyway. She's made no attempt to evade Levana—I would go so far as to say she's done the opposite. She seeks Levana out rather than going somewhere alone," Soren pointed out.

We'd agreed that adding extra guards was the right decision before Ophelia arrived for the wedding, assuming that she was sent here as some kind of dangerous plant. Unless Ophelia was a *very* good actress, it seemed those extra precautions had been unnecessary.

Could she even throw a silver dagger? It didn't sound like she'd received that kind of training.

"Fine. Drop the palace guard back to normal numbers and assign the others to track this group of malcontents. Levana stays here though. I don't want Ophelia's main guard changing unless absolutely necessary."

Soren nodded, looking relieved that I didn't put up a fight. "I'll go do that right away, shall I escort you—"

"Don't even finish that sentence," I grumbled, throwing him a warning look. I was the most fearsome creature in this realm, I didn't need to be escorted through my own palace.

Soren gave me a glare back, reminding me silently that I hadn't fed last night and wasn't at full strength, which I ignored. After Ophelia was asleep, I'd go to the human realm and feed. I could easily last another few hours.

I headed in the direction of one of the sitting rooms where I usually took lunch, but Meridia emerged from around a corner, sauntering towards me with just slips of shadows covering her intimate areas.

For fuck's sake.

"Your majesty," she purred, bowing low. The shadows shifted, revealing her nipples, and I directed my gaze to the ceiling immediately.

"How can I help you, Meridia?"

"My, that's a loaded question," she laughed, an entirely false sound. "I just wanted to check on you after that performance last night. Such an unflattering depiction of you, I wouldn't have been surprised if you'd thrown the actors in the dungeon for the offense."

"We don't throw people in the dungeon for unflattering performances here," I replied smoothly, grateful every day that Meridia wasn't queen. "Was that all?"

"Your poor wife probably wishes you did. I can't imagine how *humiliated* she was, especially sitting there alone when it was all said and done. Though I'm sure you know better than I do how she feels," Meridia added lightly. "I'll leave you to your day, I know how important your duties are."

She inclined her head, backing up a few steps before turning and disappearing from my sight.

Wretched she-demon.

Her words had found their mark, and despite myself, I found I was drawn towards Ophelia's rooms, where she usually returned soon to relax before dinner. I had no idea *why* I was drawn there—Ophelia certainly wouldn't share with me how she was feeling even if I had thought to ask—though I supposed there was something about her presence that gave me some comfort. Maybe it was just that she was a physical sign that the treaty was in place and that my people could feed safely. It was probably that.

Ophelia was living, breathing proof of what we had accomplished. That was all.

The guards bowed their heads as I passed, and I nodded at them in return, knowing before I got to the end of the wing that Ophelia wasn't here yet. I could hear Affra snoring quietly as I passed her door, and I expected Cyr would be out running errands.

There was no one around.

If there was anything suspicious in those drawings, now would be the time for me to find out. I'd checked in on Ophelia every night before she fell asleep, and she was *always* drawing, but the angle meant I'd never seen the pictures.

There would be no better insight into Ophelia's mind than whatever was on that paper, I was sure of it.

I let myself into her room, inhaling the smell of Ophelia's fear that lingered on the sheets. Why did she feel afraid in here? Perhaps she didn't like being on her own, or didn't like that this room was darker than the others in the palace.

But then she'd been twisting her hands nervously last night and hadn't smelled even the slightest bit sweet.

That sense that I was missing something continued to haunt me.

Time to find out what that elusive missing thing is...

I headed straight for the large dresser, commending my foresight in having this piece of furniture commissioned, and pulling open the wide, shallow top drawer where Ophelia kept her leather-bound sketch book and a holder containing her supplies.

It's not an invasion of privacy. You're the king. It's your job to investigate unknowns that may or may not be threats.

Careful not to damage the leather with my claws, I uplifted the leather book and carried it to the bed, sitting on the edge and lying the book down so I could untie the fiddly leather straps. I knew from watching Ophelia that each drawing was on a loose sheaf of paper, and I didn't want to risk mixing them up.

With the string undone, I lifted the front flaps so the piece of leather laid flat on the bed, and sucked in a breath at the startlingly realistic image on top of the pile. Forgetting entirely that I was trying to keep them in order, I sifted through them one by one, laying them out on the mattress around me.

All the blood in my body seemed to rush to my cock at once, leaving me lightheaded.

I had been so very wrong about my wife.

OPHELIA

CHAPTER 10

I'd spent longer than I intended in the kitchen, attempting to preserve half the apples that I'd taken from Astrid's house. I knew my sister well enough to know that next time I visited, there'd be a box of canned fruit and vegetables, as well as a bunch of other snacks that didn't require freezing waiting there for me. Astrid was many things—emotionally unavailable, ambitious, basically the ideal little Hunter robot—but above all, she was organized. She would have taken note of my food requirements and planned accordingly for my next supply run.

It had been weird seeing her last night. Astrid and I had always been very *different* kids even before I'd been quietly shuffled out of the way and began living a more regular human life. While she'd been the one to approach me with the marriage idea, I assumed that was because the Council thought I'd be more agreeable if it came from her. I'd never once considered that maybe Astrid was looking out for me, but last night, it seemed like she was looking out for me a little. She'd even talked some shit to Allerick and Soren, which had been both bold and inadvisable.

Maybe I'd been too hard on Astrid all these years. I hadn't exactly fought very hard to maintain our relationship either, and she had her reputation to worry about.

I'd make more effort with her, I resolved to myself. Especially if she was going to let me use her place as an alternative to dropping in at the Council HQ. The more I reflected on that, the more it annoyed me that they'd demanded I check in with them on each trip home. Was I not a citizen of the human realm now I'd married? Why couldn't I go where I pleased? I may have agreed to this marriage, but it had still been *their* idea and I didn't see why I should be punished for it.

"You are very stompy today," Levana remarked, sounding faintly amused. "Did your trip to the human realm not go well, Queen Ophelia? Or was it the performance that bothered you?"

"The performance was fine," I replied, flicking my hand dismissively. I mean, it bothered me a little that everyone had this impression of me as a frightened little mouse, but I didn't want to turn it into a huge deal. "And the trip home was uneventful. I got the food I needed and a few clothes I'd been storing at my sister's house."

Levana hesitated and I glanced back at her, giving her what I hoped was an encouraging smile. She'd gotten more comfortable with me over the past week, and I felt like we were almost at 'friend' status.

We were going to get there, I was determined. I would wear her down and make her love me. I was going to grow all over Levana like shadow fungus. I was pretty sure I was already there with Affra, she basically fussed over me like a grandmother who didn't get to spend enough time with their grandchildren and overcompensated whenever she did.

Despite marrying the king and living in the castle, my life here wasn't exactly a fairy tale, but I'd still grown rather fond of it. I was going to do my best to hold on to it.

"It's just that I heard a rumor that the king didn't feed on your trip," Levana whispered, glancing around uncomfortably.

"Oh! Um, well no, he didn't. Is that bad?" I asked. I hadn't questioned Allerick on why he'd opted not to feed or why Soren had floated off in a huff. I doubted he would have told me anyway, despite his chattier than usual mood last night.

"The king can't leave the realm as often to feed because—" Levana suddenly cut herself off, and it stung to know that she didn't trust me even though I sort of got it. I was new here, and from Hunter stock at that. "Well, he just can't leave as often. He should have fed last night while he was in the human realm."

Huh. I didn't question him not being able to leave as often—he was the king and he had king stuff to do—but I couldn't understand why he hadn't fed. I hadn't been agitating for us to leave, and while that park was pretty deserted, we could have gone literally anywhere with their shadow traveling abilities. They could have found another area on the Hunter-approved list.

"I don't know what to tell you," I said honestly. "Soren fed, and I didn't, like, scream or get all disgusted if that's what you're worried about."

"No, I wasn't implying that at all, Queen Ophelia," Levana said hurriedly, evidently worried she'd offended me. "It's none of my business, I shouldn't even be asking. I guess I was worried something had happened."

I frowned to myself, not saying anything further because we were now within hearing range of Verner and Andrus—the two guards who stood at the wing to the king and queen's quarters. Soren had definitely seemed agitated by Allerick's decision, so maybe something *had* happened, but I just hadn't seen it.

"I will see you at dinner, Queen Ophelia," Levana said quietly, giving me a short bow as I passed the point where the guards remained.

"See you at dinner!" I called back, still mulling over her words. Damn it, I'd been planning on finishing my drawing inspired by the ghostly Shade forms I'd seen last night, but now my brain had taken off on a completely different tangent.

I opened my door, knowing Affra would be taking her afternoon nap, and closed it behind me without paying much attention. Only as I turned to face the room did I realize I wasn't alone.

"What is this?" Allerick purred, sitting on the edge of my bed, sifting through sheafs of paper. Drawings. *My* drawings.

My mouth went dry. I was frozen in place in front of the closed door while my husband sat on my bed looking at *my* drawings.

"You weren't meant to see those," I said in lieu of a better answer. One that I didn't have.

"No?" He gave me a slow smile that revealed a row of vicious teeth, and my belly swooped for an entirely different reason. "But I'm in some of them. And the ones I'm not in... well, you hadn't met me yet."

"It could be anyone," I argued weakly. The images were all shades of gray, done in charcoal. The pale gray I'd used implied Allerick's distinctive ice-blue eyes, but I was frankly willing to argue that it was anyone *but* him at this point.

The crown was an unfortunate giveaway. Maybe he wouldn't notice.

"You're a pretty little liar," Allerick said in a deep voice that traveled directly to my clit. "You'd better hope they're of me. If you've been drawing other Shades fucking *my* wife, wearing *my* crown,"—*shit*—"then I'm going to have to kill some of my own subjects, Queen Ophelia."

"As if you aren't off fucking your subjects every night," I scoffed, even as my idiot vagina was being all *I'm ready for you now, oh big strong predator. Take me.'*

Allerick did a double take. "I haven't taken a lover since this marriage was brokered. I won't take one. We are *married*, Ophelia. Did you think this was a flexible arrangement?" His voice dropped into a furious growl at the end that seemed to rumble through every erogenous zone I had.

"No, *I* have never thought that. I thought *you* thought that," I rasped, pressing my thighs together because my panties were feeling *damp*. Like weirdly damp.

"Never." Allerick groaned. "You have no idea how delicious your fear is to me, wife. I need to lick the pretty pussy you're hiding under those ladylike clothes. Does your cunt taste as sweet as your fear smells?"

Yes! Holy fuck, *yes*. What had taken him so long?

Now we'd gotten that pesky issue of him not screwing other people out of the way, my body didn't understand why I wasn't impaled on his dick yet.

"Wait," I said, frowning as my mind caught up. "My *fear*? I'm not afraid."

Allerick stilled. "Yes, you are."

I snorted at the ridiculousness of him trying to argue this with me. "*No*, I'm not. Not even a little."

The King of the Shades reeled back like I'd slapped him. "Then what are you feeling right now? What is making you smell like that?"

"I. Am. *Horny.*"

I punctuated each frustrated word with a step towards him, kicking off my flats as I went.

He didn't quite frown, but there was no mistaking the confusion in his body language.

"No." He shook his head. "It's not that. You smelled like this at our wedding."

"I was horny at our wedding!"

Oh my god, *everyone* thought I was afraid. There had been a whole skit laughing about how *scared* they thought I was at my wedding!

If I wasn't so sexually frustrated, I might feel sorry for my adorably confused husband. He looked at me before returning that ice blue gaze to my explicit drawings, *finally* putting the pieces together.

His wife had elaborate monster fucking fantasies, and he was a monster who hadn't been fucking me.

Fear. I almost snorted at the thought. Idiot.

"Are you telling me," Allerick said slowly, carefully collecting up my drawings and setting them on the nightstand, "that you have been wet and wanting since our wedding, wife?"

I paused, the deep commanding nature of his voice reminding me that while we may be husband and wife, we were also predator and prey.

My panties grew embarrassingly wet in response, and I was starting to get concerned about the low absorbency capabilities of lace. Had my period started? Surely not, I'd just had it.

If anything, I'd be ovulating.

Allerick inhaled deeply, breathing out on a groan that made my thighs tremble. "Come to me, wife."

It wasn't even a question that I'd go—I'd been waiting for this moment since I met him—but I could see the question in Allerick's body language.

The choice was mine.

How sweet, this monstrous king of mine.

I took a step forward, unfastening the line of small buttons that went down the front of my dress as I went. It was a suitably conservative dark gray silk, fitted at the top with elbow-length sleeves, and floaty to where it fell just above my knees.

Regal-ish. That's what I'd been going for.

The scarlet lace lingerie I was wearing underneath was anything but.

The silk fabric of my dress pooled at my feet as I stepped between Allerick's knees, and I felt the heat of his gaze as it ran down my body. A sound burst out of Allerick that stilled us both—a rumbling almost purr-like noise that made my muscles go weak and my pussy *gush*. As soon as the noise started, it stopped and I missed it instantly, but I didn't have time to mourn it because Allerick was *on* me.

Strong hands wrapped around my waist, claws lightly scraping my skin without breaking it. I landed with an *oomph* on my back on the mattress, already reaching for my underwear to push the embarrassingly wet garment off, but Allerick beat me to it. His head dipped between my thighs, and I was forced to drop my knees flat to accommodate his horns. There was a puff of hot breath over my mons before I felt the unmistakably sharp edge of those teeth.

"What are you—"

My question ended in a gasp of surprise as his fangs ripped through the lace of my panties. It wasn't a suave, practiced movement—it was more like my underwear personally offended him and he wanted to destroy them for their insolence. His claws sliced through the elastic either side of my hips and I sucked in a breath at the sudden disappearance of the friction.

Allerick loomed over me, looking every inch a feral monster with the crimson fabric of my panties caught between his teeth like blood dripping from a beast's maw.

Another absurd gush of arousal flooded the sheets and my face heated in response.

"I don't know why I'm so wet," I mumbled, very unsexy concerns about mattress protectors popping into my head.

Allerick yanked my panties out of his mouth, shamelessly pressing them to his nose before tossing them aside. "I know why, little queen. I've seen your pretty drawings, and you have no idea what is hidden beneath these shadows." His grin was smug as he gestured towards his still covered cock. "Your body knows though. Your body is trying to prepare you."

Well then.

"Show me," I demanded, but Allerick just chuckled darkly, lowering his face between my thighs again, his horns pressing against my flesh.

"Later."

I wanted to argue, but Allerick's long tongue was *prying* me open, moving like no human tongue could move as it explored every inch of me. I almost wept at the sensation as that wicked tongue brushed against my clit. I was no virgin to, well, basically anything, but this felt like no oral I'd ever received before. Experiencing intimacy with Allerick would be like doing everything for the first time again.

"You're so silky," Allerick groaned, his voice sibilant with his long tongue still extended. "Silky and *sweet.*"

His delightfully thick tongue burrowed into my cunt, making me forget how to breathe for a moment.

I'd had dicks inside me that didn't feel this good, I thought hazily. Rough. I felt silky to Allerick because his tongue was so rough.

Delightful.

Every part of him seemed designed just for me. It made me want to see his cock even more. After he finished what he was doing.

He pulled his tongue free with an embarrassingly wet slurp, licking his lips before returning his attention to my clit. As his claws pressed against my spread thighs, I realized he couldn't use his fingers to stimulate me, not without turning my insides to confetti. Briefly, I worried that it wasn't going to be enough to get me over the edge, but Allerick's tongue seemed to pulse around my clit and I became completely undone.

My husband's hands held me in place as I thrashed beneath him, attempting to kick his face away as the pleasure bordered on too much, but he didn't let up. One crushing orgasm rolled into another, and Allerick's attentions grew more languid, easing me back to this dimension after my mind had departed it completely.

"Please, please…" I panted, reaching for Allerick.

"No more?" he assumed ruefully.

I blinked at him.

"Show me your cock," I corrected. "Definitely more, are you joking right now?"

It was his turn to blink in surprise. "My wife is insatiable," he muttered approvingly, more to himself than anything. *He had no idea.* "Tell me if it gets to be too much."

I was about to inform him there was no risk of *that* happening when he moved up to kneel on the mattress and dropped the shadows that preserved his modesty.

My mouth went dry. All the fluid in my body had traveled south on an urgent lubrication mission.

"Ophelia," he rumbled, that strange purring sound flaring back to life. It was even better than the reverent sound of my name on his lips. "Truly, nothing frightens you."

"I have almost no sense of self-preservation," I murmured, rolling onto my front and crawling towards his magnificent cock like a moth drawn to a flame. "It's so…"

"Monstrous?" Allerick suggested wryly, lazily fisting his shaft.

"Glorious," I breathed, my fingers tracing the thick bulge at the base of his cock. He sighed happily, seemingly content to let me explore. "What is this?"

His grin was all smug arrogance. "My knot. Once I am buried to the hilt in that pretty pussy, it will expand, locking us together so not one drop of my cum escapes."

Swoop. My belly dropped all the way to my toes.

"Does my wife like the idea of being bred?" he asked lazily, swiping a drop of precum from his tip with a knuckle and offering it to my lips. I licked my tongue over it greedily, closing my eyes at the unexpectedly sweet taste.

Yes. Yes, I liked that idea very much. I was on birth control, but I could happily ignore the fact for now to let this delicious fantasy play out.

Allerick laughed quietly, lying on the bed next to me, his enormous frame dominating the space, and his impressive cock standing at attention.

"If you want my seed, come and get it," he said, gesturing at his dick magnanimously, ever the insouciant royal.

Cute.

I climbed over him, feeling the burn in my inner thighs as I straddled his hips and rubbed my drenched pussy over his length.

"You may be the king of this realm and used to demanding every little thing you want," I purred, rocking my hips slowly. "But I am your queen. You will put in work for *me.*"

With sexual boldness that was surprising even for me, I climbed up his body, smirking when his tongue flicked out to tease my clit as I crawled over his face before settling on my back against the cushions with my legs spread.

"I will gladly put in work for you, your majesty," Allerick said with a dark smile, shoving my legs wide and settling himself between them, bracing his weight on his arms either side of me.

He was so *warm.* The body heat radiated off him even with the small distance between us, and the warmth made my already relaxed muscles feel even more languid. Perhaps I should be embarrassed by my nudity in front of him, but he didn't look at me like he found my pale, clawless human body revolting at all.

"Are you ready for me?" Allerick drawled, dropping his hips to rub his *enormous* dick teasingly over my clit.

"Are you ready for *me*?" I scoffed. I was going to wear this Shade out, that was for goddamn sure. I had plans and fantasies I wanted to fulfill.

Allerick smirked, reaching between us to line his cock up at my entrance then oh so slowly pushing forward. I sucked in a surprised breath at the intrusion, at the fullness of him. Not even my biggest dildo could have prepared me for the stretch of Allerick's cock and *oh my god, we hadn't even got to the knot yet.*

"Relax," Allerick growled, exposing his vicious teeth. "You will relax for me, wife. Your cunt will stretch for me, for my knot, and I will fucking *breed* you. Understand?"

"I understand," I gasped, grabbing the back of my knees and pulling them up towards my chest, opening myself up for him and saying a silent prayer that my birth control held up against monster sperm, as tempting as his words were. "You're so *deep*, oh my god."

The stretch I'd been prepared for. I hadn't been prepared for feeling like my insides were rearranging themselves to accommodate Allerick's cock. Like he was permanently imprinting himself on my body, shaping it to his will.

I didn't even mind. My mind and body were in agreement—it was Allerick or no one after this.

The veins in his forearms stood out against his leathery skin as he picked up his pace, thrusting deeply but taking his time, lips peeled back to reveal his fangs, eyes occasionally scrunching shut like the pleasure was as overwhelmingly good for him as it was for me, which couldn't possibly be true.

"Your knot," I gasped, arching my back. "I want it."

"You'll get it," Allerick replied, looking a little feral in the best kind of way. "Relax. Let me in."

I made a keening noise, my nails digging into the back of my thighs where I still kept my legs up as Allerick began pushing his knot in. "It's so much."

"You can take it," he grunted, slowly rocking his hips forward. "You *will* take it. Let me in, Ophelia."

I forced my body to relax, to concentrate on the many pleasurable sensations that outweighed the strangeness of the thick knot pressing against my entrance.

"My good, sweet little queen," Allerick groaned, pressing all the way forward. I made a noise somewhere between a squeal and a sigh as his knot seemed to *inflate* inside me, locking us tightly together. I could feel him *everywhere*. Despite his intimidating girth and the size of his knot, even though it looked like there was no possible way it would fit, he *felt* made for me.

It was so much sensation that it bordered on overwhelming, and yet it wasn't enough. There was something *missing*. I clawed the sheets, trying to ground myself before I burst into tears and begged him to put his teeth in my neck. I had no idea *why* I wanted that, but I was craving it more than anything.

Insane, I reminded myself. *That is an insane request.*

Though for a moment, I wondered if it was a shared moment of insanity, because I could have sworn Allerick's icy eyes were fixated on my neck before he scrunched them closed, holding his entire body still for a moment until he regained his composure.

"Look at you," Allerick purred, scraping his claws over my belly, his voice gravelly. "No, *look*. Look down."

I blinked, my orgasm haze clearing enough to realize he was actually giving me an instruction, and looked down the line of my body.

Holy belly bulge.

I could physically *see* his cock in me. Or his cock shifting my guts around. Whatever was happening, I was into it. My pussy contracted around Allerick's knot like a vice as another rush of wetness tried to escape, leaking out in the slightest trickle from where we were sealed together.

Allerick grinned viciously, his head tipping up from gazing at my bulging midsection to my breasts before settling on my neck again.

"How long will we stay like this?" I rasped, shifting my hips slightly. Just that slight movement stimulated *everything,* and my mouth fell open on a silent scream as a faint orgasm caught me off guard, slowly unfurling through me.

"Hopefully, a good long while," Allerick replied, suddenly scooping me up and rolling so that he was lying on his back while I shuddered my way through yet another orgasm on top of him. My husband groaned as I clenched around him, claws digging into my hips as his cock flexed as it swelled inside me, flooding my pussy all over again.

"I'm going to bloat up like a balloon if you keep filling me with cum," I whined, not entirely sure if I was protesting or begging for more.

"Good," Allerick rumbled. "Hopefully your belly will still be nice and round by dinner, so everyone can see as well as smell how well you take your husband's knot."

And then he was rocking into me all over again, making my pussy convulse and my brain go blank, and my only coherent thought was that I hoped he was right.

ALLERICK

CHAPTER 11

Home. I'd found home, and it was with my knot buried so deeply in my wife that I didn't know where she ended and I began.

My claws sank into the round cheeks of her ass, not enough to break the skin, but enough to sting and Ophelia moaned tiredly, her head resting on my chest. She shifted oh so slightly in response to that gentle hurt, and that was enough to set off another chain of rolling orgasms that had her pussy clenching my knot almost to the point of pain.

It wasn't pain that I felt though. It was the most glorious, satisfying feeling of my cum filling my wife as the well of power in my chest seemed to swell to almost overflowing. The more she orgasmed, the more she fed my power reserves. That had been an unexpected perk I hadn't seen coming.

"Fuck, fuck, fuck," Ophelia chanted under her breath, blunt nails scraping harmlessly at my skin. "This can't be healthy. This is too many orgasms. I'm going to die of orgasms."

I growled my displeasure, and the vibrations made her gasp. "You will not die of orgasms. I'll get you so addicted to fucking me that you'll die *without* orgasms."

"Mission accomplished," she panted, forehead resting in the middle of my chest, little fists either side of her head as she rode out the final wave. For now.

As soon as her muscles relaxed, I wanted to feel them tightening around me again, squeezing every drop of cum out of my body.

It was not an urge I had *ever* experienced. I'd never knotted anyone before. Our knots had always been something of a genetic anomaly, a weird thing we had to get around because female Shades could only take them with a lot of work and even then, it was more about emotional significance than physical pleasure for the couple. Their anatomy was designed to clamp down and not let go, and there wasn't enough space for a knot to fit.

Ophelia felt more compatible with me than women of my own kind, and I didn't know what that meant because it seemed too convenient to be a coincidence.

"Don't you dare move," Ophelia growled, as intimidating as a kitten. "I'm going to pull a muscle or something if I have another orgasm, let me lie here for a minute and recover."

I resisted the urge to laugh so I didn't jostle her. "Of course, your majesty."

"Don't you sass me right now," she sighed contentedly, nuzzling her head into my pec. "I was so sure I had more sexual stamina than you, and I need to nurse my wounded self-esteem."

"I will keep my sass to myself," I assured her seriously, not pointing out that it was ludicrous to think she could match my stamina. Especially because I was fairly confident that sex with Ophelia was *giving* me strength rather than taking it away.

Goddesses, how had I gotten Ophelia so *wrong*?

She hadn't been afraid of me, she'd been lusting after me. Not even just a mild, cursory sort of interest in what was hiding beneath my shadows either—Ophelia had elaborate Shade-fucking fantasies and she'd committed them all to paper.

My own wrongness about the entire situation was taunting me. She must have thought I was a moron, and while my ego rejected the idea of *anyone* thinking I was a moron, I was particularly opposed to the idea of Ophelia thinking that way.

I wanted her to like me.

Idiotic. The fact that Ophelia had been drawing her version of Shade-fucking fantasies since well before she'd met me attested to that. I was a convenient focus point for those dreams she'd had, a real life example to pin them on, but it wasn't *me* she wanted.

Ophelia's breathing evened out, either asleep or unconscious from the number of orgasms I'd wrung out of her, and I felt my knot deflate without stimulation, slipping free of my wife's heavenly pussy while our combined fluids leaked out of her over my thighs.

I idly toyed with her silky hair with my claws, knowing I needed to wake her up eventually so she could dress for dinner, but not wanting to. Holding her in my arms, having her trust me enough to rest on my chest, it was a gift I didn't know I'd been missing out on.

Perhaps I was just a fetish to her, a curious itch she'd wanted to scratch, but she was stuck with me whether she liked it or not. I could show her that I could be a good husband to her, I would protect her, fuck her senseless, resist the somewhat unsettling urge to sink my teeth into her, and perhaps one day she'd trust me with her heart as well as her body.

Yes. That was a good plan, I thought decisively. *I'll show her there's more to a marriage with me than just my excellent dick.*

Ophelia didn't stir as I unhurriedly detangled her hair with my claws, vaguely contemplating some of the issues that I needed to raise with the Council that I never spent time just *thinking* about because I was always moving from one fire to the next.

Who knew spending the afternoon in bed with my wife could be so productive?

Ophelia made a sleepy sound, rubbing her nose against me as she slowly woke.

"Oh. Oh! Oh my god, did I fall asleep on you?" she asked, head shooting up so quickly that strands of reddish-brown hair fell over her face. I parted them carefully with my claws so I could see her flushed cheeks, admiring how beautifully filthy she looked after being fucked to sleep.

"You did. It was adorable."

That pinkish tinge on her cheeks grew darker and she pressed her thighs tightly together, trying and failing to stop our combined wetness from slipping out. "Adorable? Now there's a word I never thought I'd hear you use. Especially not in relation to me."

"Why not? You have always been adorable. An adorable little queen."

Ophelia rolled her eyes, and the overtly human gesture made me smile. "You know nothing. You thought I was *scared* of you this whole time."

She said it like it was the most ridiculous thing she'd ever heard.

"You do know that would be an entirely rational response," I pointed out drily.

"That's a fair point," Ophelia laughed. Actually laughed at something I'd said. The sound skittered over my skin, sinking into my bones. "Your eyes look *super* bright right now."

The words cut through my cheerful mood like a knife. "Yes, about that..."

Ophelia frowned, propping herself up on her forearms on my chest and staring down at me. It was a submissive position I would never allow myself to be in with anyone else.

"I think I fed from you. I didn't mean to—it seemed to happen subconsciously. I could feel myself growing stronger while we were knotted together. I apologize for that," I said with a grimace, forcing the words out. Apologizing was not something I was accustomed to. "I didn't mean for it to happen, and it's a violation of the terms of the treaty."

Ophelia's frown deepened. "Is it? I only skim read it."

I gave her a disapproving look. "You moved here and married me without reading the document that is the basis for our whole union?"

"No? Of course I didn't do that," Ophelia hedged, her voice rising in pitch. I snorted.

"There's a clause in the treaty that no Shade was to feed on the fear of the Hunter bride who came here."

"You didn't though," Ophelia replied, eyebrows creasing. "I wasn't afraid. If anything, you fed on my *lust*. Just like it's my lust that you like the smell of, not my fear. Maybe Hunters are built differently from regular humans in that way."

I opened my mouth to object before closing it again. She was right. It was her lust that had called to me, that had made me want to taste her. Like the way she fit me, the fact that her desire sustained me felt too convenient to be a coincidence.

I'd never felt as powerful as I did after feeding from her. I felt *invincible*.

"Your drawings," I said slowly. "Were there other Hunters like you? Who drew those kinds of things?"

"Looking for an upgrade already?" Ophelia teased, though there was a hint of vulnerability in her face that I didn't like.

"Of course not. Merely wondering if there's a connection between me being able to feed on your desire and you *having* those kinds of desires."

"Oh." Ophelia's features scrunched up thoughtfully. "That's something to think about. My parents found some drawings—not nearly as explicit as the ones I do now—when I was sixteen, and they took them to the Council who quietly shuffled me into a more human life."

I bit back a growl of disapproval at the way they'd just cast her aside when she was still a child.

"I've always attributed it to me committing an unforgivable sin, I guess, but maybe there's more to it than that. There was no warning, no discussion about it, just an immediate severing of ties. That seems a bit weird in hindsight, right?"

"It does seem like an extreme reaction," I agreed. "The kind of reaction they might have if they'd seen those kinds of drawings and dealt with a similar case before."

"No one I knew, but then families were shuffled around to different regions all the time."

We were both quiet and thoughtful for a few moments. I wouldn't bring this up with the Council yet—I absolutely didn't want them hounding Ophelia for information about her desires—but perhaps Damen could look in the history books to see what we knew about the very first interactions between Shades and Hunters.

"I need to bathe before dinner," Ophelia yawned, stretching above me before rolling off my body. I clamped an arm around her waist, pinning her to my side.

"Don't," I growled, territorial urges I'd never experienced in my life rushing to the surface.

"I am not going to dinner in front of the whole court smelling like cum, that is non-negotiable," Ophelia said sternly. Was she being serious? Why not? It seemed entirely reasonable to me. "Come on, you can bathe with me as a consolation prize."

"Fine," I grumbled. "*For now.* Next time, I'm going to rub my cum into your skin and walk you through the entire palace."

Ophelia gulped, her scent sweetening into that delicious melted sugar I couldn't get enough of. "Okay."

I climbed out of the bed and cloaked my lower half in shadows to preserve my modesty as I rang the bell to call for Affra. Ophelia moved to grab a robe, but I summoned shadows for her as well, draping them around like a form-fitting dress, commanding them to move with her body.

She looked down in wonder, climbing off the bed and heading for the full-length mirror to admire my work. "I thought it would feel like nothing, but I can sort of sense them there even if I can't really *feel* them, if that makes sense," she said, twisting this way and that and watching the shadows move with her.

"It does. They don't weigh anything, but you can feel the traces of my magic on your skin."

Ophelia's hands skimmed over the shadows, disturbing them but not breaking them apart completely because I created them and they remained under my control unless I gifted control to someone else. In Shade relationships, it was a gesture of trust to go out in public cloaked by your partner, knowing that they could expose you at any time.

"Would the court like me more if I went to dinner like this?"

"Who doesn't like you?" I asked sharply, my vision darkening around the edges.

"You, I thought," Ophelia replied with a laugh.

"Well, now you know better," I pointed out as Affra entered the room with a bow. She immediately headed for the bathing chamber without instruction, and I imagined the smell of our joining was fairly overwhelming. While Affra would undoubtedly change the soaked sheets while we were at dinner, my sudden primal instincts objected furiously to that idea.

I wanted my wife to sleep in sheets that were soaked in the scent of us.

"You should wear one of your dresses to dinner," I gritted out, forcing myself to behave like a civilized being instead of the beast I felt like. "You are a rare spot of color in this realm, it seems a shame to blanket you in shadow."

"Who knew you were a low-key romantic," Ophelia teased, squeezing my forearm as she passed me to head to the bathroom. "Oh my god, I'm leaving a trail on the floor, this is so humiliating."

"It is *wonderful*," I corrected, scooping her up anyway and carrying her the rest of the way. While I liked seeing the evidence of our coupling, I didn't want Ophelia to feel embarrassed.

Affra excused herself as we entered, and I stepped into the almost full circular tub with Ophelia still in my arms. She made a distressed noise, clinging on to me a little tighter, and I did my best not to be offended that she would doubt my ability to safely carry her. The stone bath was round and deep, and definitely not designed for more than one Shade, but my Hunter wife was tiny.

"Oh," Ophelia sighed as I lowered us both into the water, keeping her securely on my lap as I sat on the bench, the steaming water rising to my chest. "You are very strong."

"You are very small," I scoffed. "But even if you weren't, I am feeling stronger than usual after feeding from you. Are you feeling any negative side effects?"

"I mean, I'm tired. But I also just had a month's worth of orgasms in a couple of hours, so I'm pretty sure I'd be tired either way," Ophelia replied drowsily, smiling against my chest.

The sweet, unguarded look on her face did something strange to my chest. That happened a lot around Ophelia—strange, inexplicable sensations in my chest that I should probably have examined by a healer.

But then they might fix them, and I wasn't sure I wanted these strange sensations to go away.

After we bathed, Ophelia got ready in a rush, picking out a sapphire blue dress that clung to her curves and hastily pinning her hair up with Affra's help. Perhaps I should have left her to it, but I made myself comfortable in the armchair in the corner of her room and watched, feeling strangely unable to leave. Damen was probably drinking his way through my liquor cabinet, wondering where I was, unless the scent of our afternoon activities had carried through into the corridors.

I hoped it had.

I was attributing the cursed bath as the reason I was struggling to leave. Ophelia smelled a little like me, but nowhere near enough to appease the hungry beast inside me, and it only got worse when she tied her hair back.

That *neck*. The urge to sink my teeth into it while I'd been buried in her dripping cunt had been almost overwhelming, and I had no idea where it had come from. Perhaps it was some kind of Hunter mating ritual rubbing off on me because Shades did not bite their lovers.

The idea was a little horrifying in fact. My teeth were viciously sharp, I wouldn't want to break thick Shade skin with it, let alone Ophelia's paper-thin skin.

That was a lie, I *did* want to break her skin with my teeth. I just knew it was sick and wrong, so I wouldn't.

Under the guise of stretching my legs, I stood up and wandered aimlessly around Ophelia's room while she finished up, swiping my hand over the soaked sheets while she wasn't looking.

"Okay, I'm ready," Ophelia said breathlessly, sliding her feet into her silky flat shoes. "Are we late?"

"I'm the king, I'm never late," I replied, moving to her side and resting my hand on her lower back, hoping the dampness didn't soak through the fabric of her dress and alert her to the bout of insanity I was experiencing.

I did feel better having scent marked her. I might not accidentally kill someone at dinner.

I guided her to the door before offering my arm for Ophelia to take. She did, resting her slim hand in the crook of my elbow, but the wariness in her expression hadn't escaped my notice.

Did she not expect physical contact *outside* of the bedroom? Did she not want it?

Affra pulled the door open before I could start second guessing myself—a horrifying prospect—and Damen and Soren were already standing outside waiting for us.

"Your majesties," Damen said with an obnoxiously low sweeping bow as I led Ophelia out of her room. I gave him a warning look as he straightened and inhaled deeply, daring him to say anything that might make Ophelia feel uncomfortable. He gave me an offended one back, which was probably fair. For all his many flaws, Damen would never disrespect her that way.

"Soren, anything to report?" I asked as they fell into step behind us.

"The additional guards stationed at the palace have been briefed and gone to their new posts."

Ophelia gave me a curious look, but I could tell she wasn't going to ask me any follow up questions. I almost demanded that she did, but I hadn't given her any reason to think I would be responsive to those kinds of requests.

"We had extra guards placed here when you arrived. They've now been dismissed and will be monitoring the situation with the Shades who still have reservations about the treaty," I told her. The longer I talked, the further her eyebrows inched towards her hairline.

"We had extra guards here in case you were sent here to kill us all," Damen supplied helpfully.

"Prudent of you," Ophelia replied lightly. "I don't think you have anything to worry about. One time, a rat got into my apartment and I climbed on top of the dining table and sobbed until my roommates, um, *dealt* with it. When I say I have no killer instincts, I mean it."

"I believe you," I assured her, barely suppressing a smile.

In going through my list of theories as to why Ophelia, of all the Hunters, had been sent here to marry me, that *lack* of killer instinct was one of the top ones. Perhaps they thought she'd be a liability to me—too delicate and fearful for this world. The impression the Hunters Council had given me on their visits here to formalize the treaty was they thought of us as barely literate beasts, so that tracked.

The doors swung open for us to enter the dining hall and my grip tightened on Ophelia almost subconsciously, expecting her to pull away with so many eyes on her. If anything, she leaned in closer, pressing her shoulder against my bicep.

Probably because the mood in here was very strange tonight. The court always watched Ophelia when we entered because she was a curiosity, but there was something more loaded in their gaze that had me on edge.

If anyone had something to say about me lying with my wife, they would quickly live to regret it.

"Don't leave us in suspense," I drawled, not needing to raise my voice because the hall was near silent. "What is it that has you all so enraptured tonight?"

Leonie, one of the prominent Shades at court, stood, clasping something carefully between her hands.

"Your majesty, if I may..." she began, dipping her head.

"Come forward."

Ophelia's hand on my arm loosened, but I quickly grabbed it and gave it a warning squeeze to stay put.

Leonie approached with her head bowed, stopping a respectful distance away and extending her arms, slowly revealing the item she'd been shielding with her hands.

Ophelia sucked in a breath.

It was a flower. But instead of being black or gray as it usually was, an iridescent gold tipped the edges of the petals, fading into black towards the center of the bloom.

I carefully picked it out of Leonie's hand by the short stem, holding it up to admire. *Color*. Something with *color* had grown in the shadow realm.

"Your majesty," Leonie said, dropping to one knee and bowing her head. "This is thanks to you."

It took me a moment to realize that Leonie wasn't speaking to me, but to Ophelia. That the heads bowed at every table were in Ophelia's honor.

It took even longer for her to realize.

"Thanks to *me*?" Ophelia repeated hesitantly. "I didn't do that."

"You brought color with you," Damen explained softly, standing behind us. "Legend says that there was once color in this realm, but it disappeared over the centuries. You are bringing it back."

Ophelia laughed nervously, her harmless nails digging into my muscle. Keeping hold of the flower, I bowed my head to Leonie in thanks and guided my wife up to the high table for dinner, letting the court know to drop the matter for now. I wouldn't have Ophelia uncomfortable because of their overly reverent behavior.

Conversation resumed slowly in the hall as I pulled out my wife's seat before taking my own, setting the flower on the table in front of us where Damen immediately leaned forward to inspect it.

"It's very pretty," he remarked. "I wonder if we'll get some more. You do spend a lot of time in the garden," he added to Ophelia, giving her a teasing grin.

"I still don't think I did that," she protested, shaking her head. "I don't have some kind of magic green thumb or anything. Every houseplant I've ever owned died a slow and miserable death."

"I don't know what a green thumb is, but I don't think you should rule out that this *miracle* has something to do with you, Queen Ophelia," Damen replied, keeping his tone gentle but firm all at once. "And in the absence of any other explanation, that's certainly how the rest of the Shades will see it."

Ophelia looked up, staring at the windows that decorated the upper walls of the dining hall. "I always thought it was strange to have stained-glass windows with no proper *stain* in them. There used to be color here?"

"So legend says," I replied, piling meat onto her plate then mine. "There are a few human items—artifacts—that have made their way into our world somehow. Gems and gold jewelry mostly. They retain their color, I have seen them for myself. I'm not sure I believe that there was ever color in *our* world though. Or I didn't, until now," I added, glancing at the flower.

Ophelia drank some of her water before picking up the flower and setting it in the goblet, running her finger over the gold petal.

"You can't bring items from the human realm here?"

"You've seen our forms there," I pointed out wryly. "We can't touch inanimate objects, we go straight through them. Carrying them back here would be impossible."

She frowned, probably wondering how those artifacts got here in the first place. Perhaps Hunters had sent a delegation once before to try and broker a peace? Back in the human Dark Ages, Shades were plentiful and angry. Records from that time mostly haven't survived, but I was always taught it was a black stain in our history. A lesson in preserving balance, not taking too much, not letting our subjects go unchecked.

"Eat," I prompted, nudging my wife who hadn't yet touched her food. "Did I interrupt you before your lunch today? Have you had your vegetables?"

A slow smile spread across her face, her expression looking a little... bemused?

"I did, but thank you for checking on me, that's very sweet of you."

"I'm not sweet," I countered immediately, worried someone had overheard.

Damen leaned around Ophelia with a knowing grin on his face. "You're the sweetest, big brother."

Little shit.

Damen and I escorted Ophelia back to her room after the feast while Soren sated his curiosity, wandering around the gardens for more evidence of my wife's golden touch.

Ophelia paused outside of her bedroom door, looking suddenly unsure as she glanced between Damen and I.

"Goodnight, wife," I said quietly, stroking her face with my claws.

There was a flash of emotion on her face too quick and too nuanced for me to catch before she gave me a perfectly unaffected smile, already backing towards the door. "Goodnight, your majesty."

I watched her disappear into her room experiencing a faint sensation of... guilt? That couldn't be right.

Frowning to myself, I headed into my rooms with my brother on my heels, making my way directly to the bar. I had experienced a wider range of emotions this afternoon than I had in my entire life.

"You should show her more softness," Damen observed, flopping down onto the couch. "It was very brave of Ophelia to come here all alone, but I get the sense she's quite a gentle soul and you haven't done a great job at showing her kindness so far. What happens between the sheets doesn't count."

I grunted, mostly in annoyance at him giving me relationship advice. I hadn't been unduly cruel to Ophelia, just kept her at a distance until I understood what level of threat she presented. And she was happy enough now, I'd made sure of that this afternoon many times over.

"I'll consider it. In the meantime, I need you to look into something for me," I told my brother, pouring us both a goblet of wine and handing him one.

"Oh?" he teased, eyes sparkling with mirth, an inappropriate comment on the tip of his tongue.

"Tread very carefully," I warned. "I won't have you or anyone else making lewd comments about my wife. What I want you to look into is the earliest history between Hunters and Shades. The very first interactions, anything we have on record."

Damen frowned, sipping slowly on his drink. "I'll see what I can find, but there's a very good chance I won't be able to read them. The original documents are all written in the old language."

Fuck, I hadn't thought about that. The old language was a form of runes that both Damen and I had learned a little of as part of an upper-class education, but neither of us had any real knack for.

"It would be helpful if I knew what I was looking for," Damen pointed out.

"This conversation doesn't leave this room under pain of death," I muttered, topping up my drink before taking a seat on the sofa. "There's a connection between Ophelia and I that feels too neat, too convenient, too perfect to be a coincidence. We *fit* too well for it to be a case of two opposing species being stuck together by chance and getting lucky."

"You mean she can take your—"

"Do *not* finish that sentence," I growled.

"It's pertinent to my task," Damen retorted, smirking. "I'm not asking for the details, but you did specifically mention *fit*."

"Fine. Yes. I knotted her and it was very pleasurable for both of us and caused her no pain," I stated, trying to keep it as factual as possible. "And I fed on her lust at the same time," I added with a grimace.

Damen's eyes went round. "You *fed* on her?"

"Not on purpose! It didn't feel like I was feeding on her. It felt like she was just... feeding me. Unconsciously."

"I had been wondering if that smell you're so attracted to was in fact desire," Damen admitted. I whipped him with a shadow.

"When were you going to tell *me* that?"

"I didn't realize you needed so much help with the opposite sex, big brother," he laughed. Arrogant shithead. "My best guess then is that the awful smell was, in fact, Ophelia's fear. We scared her that first night when we spoke so casually about Meridia's violent nature."

Of course. By the goddesses, I wanted to go back in time and punch myself in the face.

"So if her fear smells repulsive to our kind and her desire" —Damen dodged another whip of shadows— "smells appealing, and you are physically compatible *and* can feed from her... Well, yes. That all does seem too much to be a coincidence. That's without even considering the sudden appearance of a colorful flower in the garden. I'll spend some time in the library tomorrow and see what I can find. *Discreetly,*" he added hurriedly before I could reiterate that point.

"Thank you."

"Allerick, this could change everything, you know," Damen said softly. "What if all this time they've been killing us and we were meant to be united? Is there any coming back from that? Would it even matter if we were linked after everything that's passed?"

I thought of Ophelia, tucked into her oversized bed as she would be by now, rich reddish-brown hair fanning out over her pillow, eyelashes fluttering softly in her sleep, mouth slightly parted.

"Yes. Yes, it would matter. It would be everything."

OPHELIA

CHAPTER 12

I woke up with a pleasant ache between my thighs and faint scratch marks, well, basically everywhere. I'd had the filthiest dreams I'd *ever* had now that my imagination had received the knotting expansion pack, but none of that mattered, not really. Not when Allerick wasn't here. Hadn't been here all night.

He'd fucked me senseless, gently held me in the bath, been kind to me at dinner when I was feeling all overwhelmed with the flower thing, and then... just left? Gone to sleep in his own room?

What the fuck was that about? The breakfast I'd eaten earlier turned to lead in my stomach.

I slammed my hairbrush down a little harder than necessary on the vanity and Affra plucked it out of my hand with a knowing sigh, taking over.

"Are you married, Affra?" I asked, suddenly realizing I didn't know.

"My husband died many moons ago," she replied, shushing me before I could apologize. "Old age comes for all of us. We met when I was young and had stars in my eyes, and he ensnared me with his confidence. He was fifteen years older than me, and I thought he was so wise."

She wheezed a laugh, shaking her head at herself.

"We have two children—daughters—neither of whom are cut out for life at the palace. Not all Shades are as fiercely militant as the king or Captain Soren. Many just like to live in the outer edges of the realm and tend animals, live peaceful, quiet lives. Before I was married, I lived a life of almost silent contemplation at the Itrodaris."

"Itrodaris," I repeated slowly, getting my mouth around the foreign word.

"*The* Itrodaris," Affra corrected. "It's the home of knowledge and learning for the whole realm, and houses the largest book collection that Shades possess. Though the palace's library is none too shabby," she added, grinning just enough to show a flash of fang.

"What did you do there?" I asked, feeling incredibly self-conscious of the fact that she was spending her morning brushing my hair. Was Affra a professor or something? As a scholar, I'd mostly taken a 'Cs get degrees' approach to my education, and my lack of suitability for the role I'd found myself in had never felt more stark.

"I was a translator," Affra replied, her claws scraping ever so slightly at my scalp as she began braiding my hair down one side. "I've always had an interest in languages, both the ones of this realm and of the humans."

"Would you rather be doing that now?" I hedged, hoping the question didn't come across as patronizing.

Affra patted my shoulder reassuringly before returning her attention to my hair. "Not at all, Queen Ophelia. When I left the Itrodaris to marry, I was content to go, knowing that I would never live there again. It was a demanding life that required total devotion—if I returned there now, it would be at the expense of my relationship with my daughters."

It eased my mind somewhat to know that I wasn't dragging Affra away from a job she'd really rather be doing in order to fiddle with my hair and do my laundry, though my inferiority complex was rapidly developing a complex of its own. Intellectually, I knew I hadn't been put in this role for my brains, but I still wanted to feel like I was bringing something to the table aside from the required genes.

"Do you visit your daughters often?"

Affra gave me a funny smile in the reflection of the mirror. "We can't shadow walk within the palace, but once we're beyond the gates, it is easy. All properties have a pitch black "entry room" near the gate so they can be accessed by shadow travel day or night. I visit my children most days, usually when you're in the garden with Levana."

"Oh. Wow, that's convenient. In the human realm, it can take days to travel somewhere to visit family if they've moved far away."

"*Days?*" Affra repeated incredulously. "I'd have never continued to work at the palace if it would take me *days* away from my children."

That was a lovely thought that unfortunately transported me to memories of my own parents, who weren't super high up in the Hunter hierarchy and had zero compunctions about leaving us for days if they were given orders. The Council would send them out to follow leads and chase Shades, working around their regular nine-to-five office jobs since the Shades only came out at night, and Astrid and I were mostly latchkey kids, left to fend for ourselves.

It hadn't been until they kicked me out and spent most of my time around regular humans that I'd even known enough to be resentful about it. Every Hunter kid I knew had the same experience, it never really occurred to me that it didn't *have* to be that way.

Affra carefully bundled my hair up, pulling the raven pin out of the drawer without asking and securing it in my hair. I didn't mind, I was too lost in my own thoughts to care about my hairstyle anyway. Once she was finished, I quickly did my makeup and pulled on a plum-colored dress and flats, a bit bored of the endless array of silky jewel-toned dresses the Hunters Council had provided for me but not game to pull on leggings and an oversized shirt either. Especially not when half the Shades at court had looked at me like I was some kind of heaven-sent miracle over that flower yesterday.

Affra opened the door for me, and I shot her a grateful smile before exiting to find Levana waiting for me in the corridor.

Not Allerick.

Which was totally fine and to be expected, since he was the king and all and probably had important kingly shit to be doing. We'd consummated our union as per the treaty's requirements, I doubted I'd ever see him in my bedroom again.

"Good morning," I greeted Levana, pasting my most unbothered expression on my face.

I was totally bothered.

"Good morning, Queen Ophelia." Levana inclined her head lower than usual, and when she looked up at me it was with a weird expression on her face.

"Oh no, you're not going to be all awkward about that flower, are you?" I groaned, walking through the corridors towards the kitchen for no real reason at all.

"It was a *miracle*. You are a miracle," Levana replied with unsettling certainty.

"Levana, you know better than anyone that I'm not. You watch me wander around aimlessly all day, doing nothing productive. I'm definitely not out there turning flowers gold."

I gave her a withering look over my shoulder and she looked down to hide her smile. "I suppose we will need to agree to disagree on this. Are we doing something different today, Queen Ophelia?" Levana asked. I didn't miss the hint of hopefulness in her voice—she was probably as bored as I was of wandering around the gardens and occasionally stopping in at the kitchen. Even if she did angry-flirt with Calix the entire time we were there.

"I don't have any plans for anything different," I replied, giving her an apologetic smile. It wasn't like Allerick had suggested an alternative activity for me. He hadn't said much of anything really, not with words.

The dull pain between my thighs seemed to almost pulse in response. Things had certainly changed between us since yesterday morning, but to what extent, I wasn't really sure.

Was it just sex? More than sex? Did he actually like me as a person, or was he just acting on the intense physical attraction between us?

Was it just the novelty of fucking a Hunter?

I'd always craved monster sex, maybe he'd always craved Hunter sex. In which case, did I even have a right to be upset about it or would that make me a massive hypocrite?

"Queen Ophelia?" Levana asked gently.

I blinked, finding myself standing still in the middle of the corridor. "I'm sorry, I must have zoned out. Maybe we could explore some different corridors today? Mix it up a little?"

"Of course," Levana agreed, though she still looked a little hesitant.

Instead of heading inwards to the center of the spiral where the courtyard and kitchens were, or out to the main entry hall which led to the dining area and out to the gardens beyond, I picked a different direction and committed, wandering through hall after hall even though they all looked much the same. A couple of times, I thought I might be in one of the halls Allerick had half-dragged me through after our ceremony, and I wondered if I'd end up back at the temple ruins we'd been married in.

Just when I thought that's where we were headed, I rounded the corner and found myself at a dead end. The end of this corridor was wide open, and I was already turning away from it before Levana could warn me away.

"Wait," a reedy feminine voice called out. "Don't run off. Come in here and take tea with me."

My eyes snapped to Levana's, panicking slightly as I tried to decide how best to handle this in a queenly way. Could I say no? It seemed un-queenly to say no.

"*Orabelle*," Levana mouthed, shooing me back towards the open door with wide eyes.

Orabelle. Allerick's mother.

Fuckity fuck, I couldn't exactly ignore her.

Schooling my features into what I hoped was a sort of dignified expression, I held my head high and did my best version of a ladylike glide into Orabelle's room.

The abundance of black and gray flowers that covered almost every surface immediately caught my attention. The design aesthetic for the rest of the palace could best be described as 'spartan,' which was probably why I enjoyed spending time in the gardens so much. The only other place I'd seen flowers in vases was at our wedding ceremony.

"It's difficult for me to get outside these days, so my son ensures the outside is brought to me," Orabelle rasped. "Come. Sit with me, daughter."

Surprised by the title, I wound through the vegetation to the partially obscured armchairs where Orabelle was seated. My first thought was how frail she was. I thought Affra looked small and old, but Orabelle looked like a strong breeze could knock her over. Despite that, she was still incredibly intimidating. Like a dowager empress, regally surveying her domain.

"Hello," I said awkwardly, clasping my hands in front of me and inclining my head the way Shades did as a sign of respect.

"You're the queen," Orabelle said sharply. "The only Shade who outranks you is my son, uncrowned as you are. And if he demands you bow to him, then you send him to me for a refresher lesson on how husbands ought to treat their wives. Sit down, will you? I don't like being towered over."

I dropped into the seat opposite her instantly.

"Has Allerick been demanding you bow to him? I haven't seen as much of him as I usually do since the treaty was signed. He has to spend all his time dealing with idiots who'd prefer risking their lives every time they need to feed rather than work alongside the Hunters."

"Um, no. No, he's never asked me to bow to him," I replied, clearing my throat. He *had* asked me to call him 'your majesty' back at our wedding, but he'd clearly been trying to antagonize me. I hadn't actually called him by just his first name yet to his face, but I doubted he'd care if I did.

"Well that's something," Orabelle grumbled. "Didn't introduce you to his mother though, did he? Little shit."

A laugh bubbled out of me before I could keep it in, and I could have sworn Orabelle looked a little smug.

"How are you finding your new role then, Ophelia?" she asked, not bothering with any of the ceremony which I appreciated.

"Great. The Shades have been very accommodating, the palace is beautiful, and I feel very fortunate that I get to live here and experience this place—"

"By the goddesses, you're bored out of your delicate human skull," Orabelle interjected. "Levana! Is no one lining up meetings with the queen? Requesting her presence at events?"

Levana was half-hidden behind an enormous pot plant, looking more scared of Orabelle than I'd ever seen her look of anything. "The king made it clear that Queen Ophelia was to be given time to adjust to her life and role here first."

"What a load of nonsense," Orabelle scoffed. "You come here, as brave as can be in the face of such change and I doubt you got a particularly warm reception, and now you've brought color back into our realm. You should have Shades lining up outside your receiving room to meet with you."

I glanced at Levana, trying to ascertain whether I had a receiving room or not, but she was determinedly looking anywhere else. I couldn't really be mad at her—Allerick was the king, she had to follow his orders. I was only pretending to be queen.

"Levana, bring me that wooden box on my dresser," Orabelle commanded, infinitely more regal than me. Levana jumped into action, reappearing a moment later with an aged black wooden box and lowering it carefully towards Orabelle's lap. She huffed in impatience, encouraging Levana to get on with it before producing a key from a necklace she was wearing. "Come closer, daughter."

Ignoring the happy skip of my heart at the title, I stood and made my way over to Orabelle, kneeling next to her as she opened the creaky box. My eyes almost bugged out of my skull at what I saw inside.

It was a necklace. A *colorful* necklace. Amethysts the size of pebbles were set in oval-shaped gold links, connected by intricate gold and emerald flat links, and the necklace was held together by a simple old-fashioned ring clasp. Despite the beautiful condition of it, there was no doubt that it was *old*. The links between the amethysts were cut in a curved pattern that reminded me of some kind of ancient culture—Greek or Egyptian or something. Had Hunters from ancient civilizations visited the realm of shadows and left things here? Surely not.

"These items don't lose their color?" I asked, keeping my voice quiet because something about the necklace commanded my respect.

"No, just things *of* this realm. Allerick has always scoffed at the notion, but I believe that this was once a realm of color and life, and something happened to take it all away."

Like a meteor or something?

Orabelle was looking at me like she thought I might have answers, which was kind of flattering because no one in my entire life had ever looked to me as a source of knowledge.

"Well, if you have nothing else to do, then you can stay and take tea with me," Orabelle announced, reaching for a silver bell next to her that I hadn't spotted and ringing it. "I will tell you about the time my idiot son was chased back into the shadow realm as a youth when he tried to feed from a shaman."

164

"So," I began when Levana and I were back in the corridor and safely far enough away from Orabelle's room that we could talk.

Levana made a strangled noise, giving me a look of disbelief.

"What?" I asked.

"We just had tea with *Orabelle*."

"That's... a big deal then, is it?" I hedged.

"Orabelle is the oldest Shade in the realm. Which is probably not old by human standards, but, well, you know," she finished awkwardly.

Shades didn't get to live until old age because Hunters killed them all.

I hesitated for a moment, not wanting to offend anyone. "She looks *really* old."

Levana snorted, and I was glad she didn't appear to be offended even though I'd totally failed in my attempt at tactfulness.

"Orabelle pretty famously refuses to feed properly from the stores. She wants to keep them stocked for the young. It's been a... well, a point of contention, between her and his majesty, the king."

Levana looked a little uncomfortable with that admission, and I knew she didn't like to talk badly about Allerick, or to even give off the impression that she was.

"Thank you for telling me," I told her sincerely, giving her what I hoped was a reassuring smile. "That's awful that Orabelle doesn't feel that

she can take what she needs. Is there no way to collect more from the human realm for the stores?"

"Not safely," Levana admitted. "Especially with the treaty limiting where we can go and putting us under closer scrutiny from the Hunters."

I frowned to myself, wondering if there was something more that could be done. Could treaties be amended? Constitution-style? Could you tack some shit you forgot to include on the end?

"Do you mind if we head to the kitchens? I need more substantial food than tea and jerky," I asked absently, trying to decide if the Hunters would be amenable to negotiations or not.

Honestly, I was trying hard *not* to think too closely about the tea and jerky combination that would haunt my nightmares.

Levana's expression turned smug. "Of course, Queen Ophelia. I can't wait to see the look on Calix's face when I tell him where I spent my morning."

"Is there something there?" I asked with a laugh as we made our way through the palace. "Between you and Calix?"

"No," Levana replied, far too quickly. "Shoot, I can't lie to the queen. Please don't throw me in the Pit. Yes, there was a thing, but it was just a one-night thing."

I laughed again before I could help myself. "You don't need to tell me about your relationships just because I'm the queen. I'm asking as a friend, and you can choose to tell me about it if you *want* to."

"Oh." Levana looked as though she wasn't sure whether or not to believe me, but that was okay. She'd realize we were besties soon enough. "Calix and I were both drunk at a party in the forest a few months ago and apparently both lost our senses for long enough to think sleeping together was a good idea. Apparently, I made an impression on him," she added wryly.

"I can believe that," I assured her with a grin. "He looks at you as though you're all he sees."

Levana scoffed, though she fidgeted with her claws a little bashfully. "He's grumpy and irritating, and it will never happen again."

I hummed noncommittally at those famous last words as we made our way through the halls, my mind drifting back to that necklace Orabelle showed me. It really did look like an old human relic, and yet it was here, when Shades couldn't physically transport things from the human realm to theirs.

Maybe there used to be some kind of trade agreement between Shades and Hunters? The Hunters on the Council had known to come here in order to negotiate the terms of the treaty, maybe that knowledge had never been lost but rather hidden, only available to the select few considered important enough to know about it.

"Queen Ophelia," Levana murmured, suddenly coming to a halt. There was something in her voice that had me looking around, vaguely alarmed. She was technically my bodyguard after all.

"What is it?" I asked, following her gaze to one of the lights on the wall.

"The orb. Don't you see it?"

"Yes?" I replied hesitantly.

Levana's lips twitched. "The color. Don't you think it's glowing a warmer color than usual?"

I frowned, squinting at it. The orbs all around the castle set off a silvery light that really emphasized how colorless this place was, but Levana was right, the stones it was illuminating seemed to be a warmer shade than usual. I lifted my arm, finding my skin slightly less pallid than I was accustomed to under these lights.

"Huh. That's cool."

"*Cool?*" Levana repeated incredulously. "It's another miracle, thanks to you."

I waved it off, uncomfortable with the reverence in her tone, and Levana quieted as we approached the kitchen. The moment we walked through the door and her eyes found Calix's, she had her best uncaring mask on, even though I was pretty sure she'd given him an appreciative once over before he turned around.

"Ah, what brings my two *favorite* females to my kitchen?" Calix asked, his sweet words belied by the *thwack* of his cleaver as he whacked it into the gray carcass I was pretending wasn't there.

"Sarcasm doesn't suit you," Levana clipped.

"Denial doesn't suit you," he muttered. *Ooh, shots fired.* I gave Levana a pointed look as her lips thinned, arms crossed defensively over her chest. "I sent someone to ask where you wanted your lunch, Queen Ophelia, but they couldn't locate you."

"My apologies, we were in Orabelle's room for tea."

Calix paused, the cleaver hovering in midair. "First, you don't need to apologize to me, you're the queen. Second, Orabelle's a cantankerous old wretch who doesn't socialize with anyone, how'd you manage that?"

"The pot calling the kettle cantankerous," Levana mumbled while I made my way through the kitchen to the shelf Calix had set aside for me and grabbing the canned peaches as well as the can opener I'd swiped from my sister's place. I didn't usually have much of a sweet tooth, but the tea and jerky had done me in.

"Was Orabelle nice to you, or did she make threats and warn you to treat her baby boy well?" Calix asked, ignoring Levana's muttered remark.

It was downright weird to think of Allerick as having ever been an infant. He was so huge and serious all the time, I sort of envisioned him emerging into the world fully grown.

"I think she liked me," I replied, opening the can of peaches and pouring them into a bowl so I looked slightly more dignified while I ate them.

"It's a trap," Calix deadpanned, giving my bowl a disapproving look while I fished out one of the forks I'd taken from Astrid's kitchen.

"It's not a trap," Levana shot back, sidling up next to me and peering into the bowl. "It's so bright. You really think this tastes better than jerky?"

"What are you trying to say about my jerky?" Calix cut in, glaring between us.

"Your jerky is fine," I assured him, stabbing a peach. "It's just that jerky and tea is a very weird combination for a human. Want to try?" I asked, holding the fork out to Levana.

She eyed it warily, plucking the piece of fruit between her claws and sliding it off the fork. "I suppose you've tried all of Calix's cooking without complaint."

"Yeah, and my cooking isn't *orange*," Calix said emphatically, watching Levana with alarmed eyes as she brought the peach to her mouth. As though *orange* was the weird food color and not all the black and gray mystery meat.

Levana nibbled tentatively on the peach, and I held my breath, waiting for the moment where she realized how glorious sugar was, but it never came. She darted for the enormous barrel bin, tossing the remaining fruit in the trash and leaning over it to gag dramatically, spitting out the miniscule amount she'd eaten.

"Levana!" Calix shouted, embedding his cleaver in the butcher's block as he ran over to check on her. "Are you ill? Do you need a healer?"

"It's *disgusting*," Levana said dramatically.

"I'll get you some beef as a palate cleanser." Calix was already running across the kitchen like Levana eating a piece of meat was a Code Red situation.

I silently handed her a glass of water, raising an eyebrow at her.

"I'm sorry, Queen Ophelia, but your human food is repulsive," Levana said solemnly, sipping the water gratefully. "It has a sickly flavor, and the texture is too soft to be natural."

"More peaches for me," I replied, shaking my head as I smiled and pulling the bowl towards me. Whatever trade agreement may have existed between Hunters and Shades in the past definitely hadn't included fruit.

ALLERICK

CHAPTER 13

I slept poorly, alone in my bed, and it had put me in a foul mood for the rest of the day. My meetings were over surprisingly fast when I glared at everyone as though I could disintegrate them with my eyes, so that was an unexpected perk.

It was more than just feeling sexually frustrated and craving more of Ophelia, which I was. I was *jittery*. On edge. A feeling I only experienced when...

"Soren," I called, standing up without excusing myself from whatever discussion with two of the Councilors that I hadn't been listening to. "I need to siphon."

Soren blinked at me in surprise, immediately falling into step with me as I left the room. The Councilors said something about rescheduling, but I barely heard them. Just the thought of siphoning had the excess power rising to the surface, ready for me to expel.

The siphons that led to the energy stores were at the front of the palace, near the portal so Shades who gathered extra could deposit it as soon as they were back in the shadow realm. It was uncomfortable to carry around more than we needed, and it was important to keep the stores filled so the Shades who relied on them to feed never went without.

"You didn't feed in the human realm though," Soren muttered. "Why do you need to siphon?"

I looked around, ensuring that we were alone before giving him an even vaguer version of what I'd told Damen, uncomfortable with sharing any details of the intimacy I shared with Ophelia.

"You're sure it's safe for her?" Soren asked. I looked at him and he immediately grimaced. "Sorry, I didn't mean to imply you would do it if it wasn't. I know you would never cause her intentional harm."

He hadn't ruled out *unintentional* harm though.

Like I'd summoned her, Ophelia emerged around a corner with Levana trailing behind her.

"Your majesty," she said in surprise when she spotted me, bobbing her head.

Why had I asked her to call me that? What an asshole.

"Queen Ophelia. Have you had a good morning?" I asked, rolling my neck to try to control the itch of the excessive energy right under my skin.

Her face turned a fascinating shade of red. "Yes, actually. We went for a walk through the palace for something to do and stumbled upon your mother's room and she invited me in for tea, I hope that's okay."

It took me a moment to figure out what she was saying since all the words had come out as one jumbled rush.

"You had tea with my mother?"

"Yes."

"And it was a... pleasant experience?" I hedged. Soren snorted quietly. Lady Orabelle was a hard woman, friendless mostly by choice, and she fastidiously objected to change of any kind.

Ophelia nodded, eyes wide like she hadn't been expecting the question. "It was lovely. She asked me to come back again so she had some company."

My hand flexed of its own accord, the call of the siphoning chamber growing stronger now we were standing so close. And yet, the idea of just sending Ophelia on her way…

She'd befriended my irascible mother and brought color to the flowers. That was two miracles in as many days. Even the lights seemed to glow a little warmer now, though perhaps it was just my imagination.

"Come with me, wife," I requested, extending my arm for her to take.

"Oh, okay." She closed the distance between us and slipped her small hand into the crook of my arm, looking at me expectantly to lead. I could feel Soren's questioning gaze boring into my back, and Levana was making a show of looking down the empty hall with great interest.

"You can tell me no if you have somewhere else to be."

The corners of her mouth tipped up. "I have nowhere else to be. Where are we going, your majesty?"

"I need to siphon," I said, guiding her forward to the long narrow chamber off the entry hall. It was demonstrating some degree of trust to bring her in this room and I knew Soren would be questioning the wisdom of it, but I couldn't even turn around to read his expression because I was so engrossed in Ophelia's.

She looked at the thin glass pipes that lined the walls and disappeared into the stone like she'd never seen anything more impressive.

"This is amazing. What's it for?" Ophelia asked, craning her neck like she could see through the stone wall to where the pipes led.

"Watch," I instructed, guiding her to the nearest pipe and disentangling my arm from hers before positioning myself in front of it.

Drawing forth the excess energy was easy, it was seeking an outlet already. I cupped my hands below the pipe and allowed the glowing ice-white power to pool in my hands before it was sucked up to the ceiling and disappeared from view.

I'd never seen anything like that before. Usually, siphoned power was pale gray in appearance and thin. This was brilliant white and plentiful, filling the pipe entirely for a few seconds. Ophelia whispered something that may have been "wow" under her breath.

Wow, indeed. Soren's eyes were burning into the back of my head.

"It's excess energy," I explained to Ophelia. "The stores feed the elderly, the young and the infirm."

"Ah, right. Levana mentioned there were stores," she replied, before looking at me with wide questioning eyes, that delightful red stealing across her cheeks again. I gave her a slightly feral grin.

"I was well fed last night."

"And you feel okay now?" Ophelia confirmed, glancing at the pipe in concern. "That looked like a lot."

"It was," Soren said mildly, watching her with his arms crossed and head tilted to the side.

She was worried about me? That I'd given too much away? She was the one I'd fed from in the first place.

"I feel fine, though I wouldn't say no to a top up," I told her, inhaling deeply as her sweet scent slowly perfumed the air. "Unfortunately, I have more work to do this afternoon."

"Of course, I'm sure you're very busy," Ophelia replied quickly, though there was that hint of something in her eyes I didn't like again.

"Until dinner, wife."

"Until dinner... your majesty."

My wife was horny.

Each mouthful of her dinner was slow as her gaze lingered openly on me, dark eyes hooded with lust.

I hadn't made any kind of announcement about what Ophelia's sweet, delicious scent *really* meant, but I doubted it would take long for anyone with working senses to figure out. Damen had looked on the verge of laughter since the moment we sat down.

"You shouldn't look at me like that, wife," I growled, my dick throbbing painfully with need.

"Like what?" she asked, the very picture of innocence.

I leaned in close, licking the shell of her ear. "Like you'd rather be eating my cum than your dinner."

Ophelia knocked her goblet, and only Damen's fast reflexes saved her from getting soaked in wine.

"And if I would?"

"You two really need your own table," Damen muttered. Ophelia's face flared red, but before my idiot brother could ruin the mood any further, I stood up, extending my hand to encourage Ophelia to stand with me. She slipped her smaller hand into mine, looking confused as she rose from her chair, the eyes of the entire court on us.

"Entertain yourselves for a while, would you?" I suggested lazily to the court, already dragging Ophelia away. A cheer went up as I led her behind the dais, heading for the door that led to the seldom used throne room.

I could admit that we probably wouldn't have gotten that reception a few days ago, but feelings towards Ophelia had significantly improved since the first flower had been found, and we'd been informed of a second golden bud before dinner. My wife would soon be more popular than me.

"Everyone will know what we're doing!" she hissed, clutching my hand.

"Good."

"Barbarian," Ophelia snorted, though her vice-like grip eased. I *was* a barbarian when it came to her. I wanted everyone to know she was mine—all mine—and that her screams of pleasure were for me alone. I wanted her perfuming arousal whenever she was near me, and to be wearing the sweet scent of her slick whenever she wasn't.

Shamefully, I still wanted her to wear my teeth marks on her neck.

I'd never hungered for anything the way I did for her.

The throne room wasn't overly large and was mostly used as an impressive place for me—or rather, my ancestors—to sit when Shades from around the realm came to make requests of me. It didn't take long for us to cross it, and then I was pulling Ophelia up the stairs to the small platform, dropping into the grandiose stone seat, carved with elaborate depictions of a garden in bloom.

I needed my tongue in her cunt. *Now.* Five minutes ago.

"Don't you dare," Ophelia scolded as I made to tear her dress off her body. She climbed off my lap, standing between my thighs with a warning look in her eyes. "It's obvious enough what we're doing in here without me walking out in a shadow dress because you've ruined my clothes."

I liked that idea *very* much, but I could admit that watching my wife slowly remove her dress held its own kind of appeal. She let the fabric pool on the floor, kicking off her shoes until she was standing there in nothing but a pair of silky black panties and a shy smile.

A smile that turned hungry when I released the shadows preserving my modesty, letting my wife see exactly how much she affected me. Blinking away the lust that had overtaken her expression, Ophelia made a show of bending forward and slowly sliding her panties down her legs, the movement pressing her breasts together. Tease.

With a growl of frustration, I stood, scooping Ophelia off the ground bridal style for a moment before flipping her upside down, her upper thighs balanced on my shoulders and her face level with my cock while she let out a squeal of surprise.

Like she needed to be worried. I'd never drop her. I banded an arm around her waist, easily taking her weight with one arm while my other hand massaging one generous ass cheek, encouraging her to relax as I extended my tongue and swiped over her glistening pussy.

"New rule: you warn me before you flip me upside down," she moaned, using her palms to press up on my thighs and sliding my dick easily into her throat. After a moment, she relaxed enough into my grip to let go of my thighs, wrapping both hands around my burgeoning knot and kneading it with just the right amount of pressure as her head bobbed eagerly on my dick.

I couldn't keep her here too long with all the blood rushing to her head, so I made the most of it, eating her cunt like it was a five-course meal. The sounds we both made were wet and lewd, and I relished every second of it, twisting my head from side to side, licking every inch of her before sliding my tongue into her pussy, giving her a taste of the fucking I was going to give her with my cock.

Ophelia's ankles crossed behind my head and I moved both hands up to span her hips, my claws digging into her ass cheeks enough to leave marks. Her slick was everywhere, running down over her ass as well as down her front, dripping onto the floor. With a gasp, she pulled off my cock, gripping my knot as her orgasm took her, pussy contracting rhythmically around my tongue.

I drank down as much of her slick as I could, needing the taste of her on my tongue every moment of the day. I could feel my energy stores refilling, the magic of her lust feeding me in a more satisfying way than a human's fear ever could.

"Your knot," she whined. "I need your knot."

Carefully, I turned her upright and sat on the throne with her on my lap, giving the blood time to rush down from her head. Despite the dizziness she had to be feeling, Ophelia was already bracing her feet on the throne, her arms clinging around my neck.

"Your *knot*," she demanded, a petulant hiss.

"Anything my wife wants," I purred, keeping one arm around her waist to steady her while using the other to line my cock up with her entrance. I heard the faint splash of slick hitting the seat below us, and I was going to demand it was never cleaned again.

I pressed forward, trusting her grip on my neck as I moved both hands to her ass again, unable to stop squeezing them. She was so *soft* everywhere, it felt like she was made just for me.

"Oh, your majesty," Ophelia sighed, the title coming out a little sarcastically even as my cock pushed forward until my knot was teasing her clit. "You feel so good."

"You feel better," I rumbled. "I want you to ride me."

She nodded, too hazy from her last orgasm to tell me off for being a bossy prick this time. She adjusted her position and I was never so grateful for how wide the throne was until Ophelia's knees landed either side of me, gravity pressing her down on my knot.

Sucking her lower lip into her mouth, Ophelia braced her hands on my shoulders and lifted up as much as she could given how wide her thighs were spread and the height difference between us, dropping down with a roll of her hips.

The smooth expanse of her neck was bared to me and my gums *ached* with the urge to bite her. What the fuck was *wrong* with me? I clenched my teeth shut until the sensation passed, my fangs digging into my gums hard enough to draw blood.

"My queen," I murmured reverently as I got myself back under control, the claws of my thumbs digging into her rounded belly as I lifted her around the waist, helping her move.

Ophelia let out a breathy laugh. "On your *throne* no less."

Our throne, I thought hazily, the ability to form words failing me as Ophelia bore down on my knot, taking all of me. My head fell back against the stone chair with a thud as my wife came with a surprised intake of breath, her walls clenching tight around my expanding knot.

Fuck, fuck, fuck.

I came with a groan as we locked into place, the pressure exquisite. With just the most minute shift of my hips, Ophelia was coming again with a whining cry, nails scraping harmlessly at my shoulders and chest. I'd never been more thankful for my knot as I was with my wife wrapped around me, shuddering uncontrollably as one peak rolled into another, her slick dripping down my balls. So long as she was on my knot, she was trapped, and I had her all to myself for a little longer.

"Will it ever stop being this intense?" Ophelia asked with a breathy laugh. She leaned back, a bead of sweat dripping down her neck and running between the valley of her breasts. Just the slight shift of her weight had her belly contracting, her teeth sinking into her lower lip.

"I don't know," I replied honestly, my voice hoarse as I stared at her distended torso, her body *filled* with me in a way that satisfied me on a deeply primal level. "I didn't expect it to be like this to begin with."

"Neither did I." Ophelia's face scrunched up thoughtfully. "Well, I *hoped* it would be. You saw the drawings. The knot was an unexpected bonus."

I snorted, running my claws lightly up and down her spine. "You don't ever feel like... like you want to bite me. Do you?"

I didn't even want to ask the question, I didn't want to give her any reason to fear me, but the fact that the urge had risen *twice* now was giving me pause.

"Bite *you*?" Ophelia asked, her eyebrows shooting up. "No, never."

I grimaced. Apparently, I was more of a monster than I thought.

"I do get the urge to *be* bitten though," she continued, watching me carefully. "I have since our wedding, every time I see your teeth."

There was a strange swooping sensation in my gut. "Really?"

"I mean, I don't want you to like, rip out my throat, or anything." Ophelia began to laugh, but it quickly turned into a surprised moan as the movement made her shift on my knot. I gritted my teeth as her pussy clenched tightly around me, bathing my cock in her slick.

"Fuck, this is not a good position to have a serious conversation in," Ophelia gasped.

"I disagree," I murmured, leaning forward to swipe up her sweat with my tongue. "I would very much like to have all future discussions with you sitting right here."

"On your throne?" she teased.

"On my throne," I agreed, swirling my tongue around one pert rosy nipple. "While you're on my cock."

"You have a filthy mouth," Ophelia scolded breathily, a shudder rippling through her as she shifted her hips. "We're meant to be discussing our sudden unusual bitey urges."

"What's there to discuss?" I switched my attention to her other nipple. "It is some kind of primal instinct that seems to have surfaced that we will obviously not act on because it would cause you serious harm."

"But what if it didn't? You feeding on me doesn't cause me any harm."

I was beginning to think my wife had zero safety instincts.

"That we know of." I scraped my claws lightly over her ass, kneading the cheeks ever so slightly, enough to leave pretty red stripes on her skin. "It's early days."

"Indeed," Ophelia hummed, squeezing around my knot until I grunted with pleasure, another rush of cum spilling inside her. "For what it's worth, I don't think we should write it off as just an obscure urge and ignore it. When I'm with you..."

"Yes?" I prompted, suddenly desperate to hear the rest of her sentence.

Ophelia hesitated, her fingers flexing nervously against my shoulders. "Well, we just fit so well together, don't we? Unusually well for different species, I guess."

"Yes," I agreed, fighting off a wave of disappointment. What had I expected her to say? That I meant something more to her? *That* was a foolish thought. Until a day ago, I'd treated her as a pest to be avoided, and basically all I'd done since was fuck her senseless.

I was a curiosity to Ophelia, one she'd quickly get over if I mauled her dainty neck with my teeth.

"I think it's worth looking into," she sighed, her muscles trembling in a way that indicated exhaustion rather than pleasure.

"You're tired and you barely ate—"

"There is absolutely nothing you could say to convince me to go back into the dining hall after what we've just been doing," she laughed. "I want a whole shadow blanket covering me from head-to-toe while I sprint back through the palace before everyone finishes their meal."

I gathered her in close, making Ophelia moan when it set off another orgasm, but settling her against my chest to ride it out.

"I'll carry you back to your room myself," I promised. "Shadow blanket and all."

Whatever this was between us, whatever it could or couldn't be, I could take this chance to at least hold her close while she let me.

OPHELIA

CHAPTER 14

I need a nap, I thought to myself, suppressing a yawn as I forced one foot in front of another, making my way to the room where the Council of Shades convened for my formal introduction.

Allerick had been good to his word, cloaking me in shadows and depositing me at the door to my room before the evening meal had finished, but after he'd given me an awkward look and left, sleep had felt impossible to come by.

Why wouldn't he stay with me?

Maybe it was a cultural thing? Maybe Shades didn't share bedrooms? I made a note to ask Levana later, since Allerick was at my side to escort me to the meeting. It felt more than a little weird—for the first time since I'd arrived here, I felt like I actually had an actual diplomatic role here.

One that I was grossly underqualified for despite binging all the episodes of *The Crown* before I came to the shadow realm, but whatever.

Despite trying my best to stay calm and collected, Allerick's attention turned to me as we paused outside the double doors that led to the Council

Chamber. I wasn't sure what had given it away—a change in my scent or the iron grip I had on his arm.

"Ophelia..." he growled.

"No. I am not walking in there smelling like I'm two seconds away from dropping my panties, don't even think about it."

He groaned, swooping me off my feet with alarming ease and burying his nose in the crook of my neck. I gripped his shoulders automatically, and he moved to pin me against the wall but made no further attempt to get me all smelly.

We may not be in love like most newly married couples, but the sex was great and relationships had been built on less.

Probably. Right?

"Sometimes, I think you should run away. Or that I should be good and wise and let you go."

"Why do you think that?" I asked, startled.

"Because you're so pretty and delicate, and I want to do truly debauched things to you. Because every time I see this slim, fragile throat, I want to maul it with my teeth," he rasped, running the tips of his fangs over my skin to punctuate his point.

"Stop it," I hissed, my pussy clenching around nothing. "I don't want to smell horny!"

"You always smell horny around me," Allerick replied, huffing a quiet laugh. The noise was so delicious—it seemed to come from deep in his chest but it also had a rusty quality like he didn't make the sound often, which made it feel all the more special.

"Well tone down your natural sex appeal," I grumbled, swatting his shoulders to get him to put me down. "I am an accomplished, professional queen lady and I can't spend my days walking around with wet panties while I try to do important queen stuff."

"Mm, that would be terrible," Allerick agreed, sounding completely insincere. "Come on then, let's go get this 'important queen stuff' over and done with so I can bury my tongue in your cunt where it belongs."

"King Allerick!"

He huffed that quiet laugh again, gently setting me down and taking my arm to lead me into the rather plain gray room. The walls were stone, lit by the increasingly golden-toned orbs, and there was a long rectangular table made of blackened wood with high-backed chairs either side. It was definitely a place designed for function, not comfort.

"Welcome, your majesties. Queen Ophelia, it's a pleasure to have you with us today. My name is Maddox." The Shade bowed so low to the ground that I was briefly worried he'd topple over, and my face heated at the display of respect. I supposed the Council were the ones who'd arranged this entire union and the treaty between our kinds, it made sense that they'd be more formal with the whole title thing than the other Shades had been.

"Hello—" I began, but Allerick was already tugging me away, giving everyone at the table warning looks as he pulled me into a seat next to him at the head of the table, with Soren positioning himself stalwartly behind us.

Okay then.

A generous read of the situation would be that Allerick was warning them *off* me, but he was more likely warning them not to say anything in front of me. Honestly, I couldn't even entirely blame him for that. I hoped he would see in time that I wasn't like other Hunters, but I could hardly blame him for thinking that now—he had a whole realm to protect.

"My name is Raina," a feminine voice said before she leaned forward so I could see her further down the table. "Welcome. It's an honor to have you among us today. We'd love to learn more about you, Queen Ophelia, will you tell us about yourself?"

183

I opened my mouth before closing it again, because what was there to say about me? I wasn't overly cool or interesting. I was completely underqualified for any kind of leadership position, and I'd only gotten here because I was a horny little hornbag and just talented enough to draw those horny hornbag thoughts onto paper.

"I'm sorry, I'm not sure what to tell you," I admitted with a nervous laugh. "I had a marketing job back in the human realm at a software company. I lived with human roommates. I, um, wasn't involved with the Hunters at all," I added, hoping that would put some minds at ease.

"But you *are* a Hunter," Raina pointed out, not unkindly. Allerick let out a rumbling growl at the reminder that made me jump.

"Well, yes, I was born a Hunter, but I was deemed unsuitable for hunting when I was sixteen and directed to live a more regular human life."

"Why?" Maddox asked, tilting his head to the side.

I'd expected this question, and yet I wasn't entirely sure how to answer it despite obsessing over what to say since the moment I woke up this morning. Allerick knew my big bad secret. He'd seen the drawings, and however much he enjoyed bringing my fantasies to life, he wasn't on my side here. I couldn't expect him to lie to his Council on my behalf.

If I didn't come clean, he probably would discreetly explain it to them the moment I was gone, and I'd really rather conversations about my kinky sexual proclivities happen to my face rather than behind my back.

"My parents found some pictures I'd drawn and they handed them in to the Hunters Council." Allerick stiffened next to me. "I was politely asked to leave after that."

"What kind of drawings?" Maddox pressed.

"None that you need to worry about," Allerick cut in before I could answer. "I've seen them for myself and there is nothing in Ophelia's artwork that warrants security concerns."

So he *wasn't* going to tell them about the drawings?

184

He's probably embarrassed, just like everyone else in your life has ever been about them.

"Of course, your majesty," Maddox agreed quickly. "I didn't mean to overstep. Ophelia's clean record is something to celebrate, and information that we'd like to disseminate throughout the realm. Rumors of her kind and gentle nature are already spreading through the palace."

"They are?" I asked in surprise, wondering who could possibly be spreading them. The only Shades who seemed to actually like me were Levana and Affra, neither of whom struck me as big gossips.

"Oh yes, Queen Ophelia. Calix tells everyone who'll listen about how polite and helpful you are."

Allerick grumbled under his breath, but I couldn't help laughing that surly knife-wielding Calix was the one singing my praises. "That's very kind of him. He's been very generous in sharing his kitchen with me, even though I know he'd much prefer not to."

Raina glanced nervously at Allerick. "Calix also intercepted a Shade attempting to poison Queen Ophelia's food this morning. They're in the dungeon, healing from the almost-lethal injury Calix gave them with his cleaver."

Shadows seemed to rise off Allerick like steam, his entire body rigid with fury next to me. "I will deal with them personally. Did they say anything before Calix attacked?"

"I believe he tried to convince Calix that poisoning Queen Ophelia was a, er, noble undertaking. That it would send a sign to the realm if she just collapsed out of nowhere that the union was not blessed, and it was unnatural for a Hunter to live in this realm." Poor Raina looked ready to slink down her chair and let the ground swallow her whole as she explained this to an increasingly enraged Allerick.

Tentatively, I rested my hand on his forearm and gave him what I hoped was a soothing smile. "They were unsuccessful, Calix saved the day. And I'll stick to canned goods for now—it'll be easy to see if they've been tampered with."

"Someone arrange a reward for Calix," Allerick grunted, staring at my hand still resting on his arm. "Let all Shades know that they are welcome to voice their concerns about the treaty in a peaceful way, I will continue traveling to the regions and explaining the benefits to those who are interested in discussing it civilly."

I schooled my expression to hide my surprise. I hadn't realized that Allerick was visiting smaller areas and talking about the treaty to his subjects personally. The Hunters Council had just sent out a bulletin from what Astrid had told me.

"However," Allerick continued. "Attacks on my wife will not be tolerated. You can let them know that the Pit awaits anyone who tries such a thing."

"Of course," Raina agreed immediately, the other Councilors nodding earnestly.

Before they could say anything else, the door flew open with a bang that made everyone in the room startle—well everyone except Allerick and Soren, who immediately crowded my chair defensively, glaring at the door.

What now? I thought we were going to drink tea and eat jerky, get to know each other a little. I hadn't expected this meeting to be so dramatic.

Meridia sauntered in, casual as you please, her drapey dress of shadows hanging suggestively low over her breasts and rising worryingly high on her thighs. Soren made a quiet sound of frustration as he straightened, still positioned closer to mine and Allerick's chairs than he had been before.

Right, this was his sister. I mean, no judgment, but I'd be cutting Astrid some serious side eye if she showed up to an official meeting wearing a negligee.

"This is a closed meeting," Allerick clipped, draping an arm over my shoulders and hauling me awkwardly closer to him, stopping a split second before I ended up sprawled across his lap.

"Unfortunately, this couldn't wait," Meridia replied, her voice syrupy sweet. "The Council needs to be informed that this marriage isn't valid."

"Why's that?" Allerick drawled, his claws toying with my hair.

"I have it on good authority that this marriage hasn't been consummated," Meridia said smugly, crossing her arms and looking imperiously around the room like this was some big *gotcha!* moment. "They haven't even slept in the same *room* since they were married."

Well, that was true, but someone should really let Meridia know that consummation didn't have to take a whole night in the same bedroom. She should have tried her interfering witch act a couple of days ago.

To my intense surprise, the entire room reacted, not just Allerick. Soren snorted loudly, while the Councilors all shook with laughter. My face flamed beetroot at the implications of *that*.

"I left dinner early last night as I was tired," Raina said, still laughing. "I walked past the throne room and I can assure you personally that the marriage has been consummated."

Kill. Me. Now.

"Your good authority is clearly not that good. The queen's attendant also confirmed that she saw... evidence of their joining," Raina added, giving me apologetic look as I slunk down an inch in my chair. We'd left plenty of evidence of our joining on the throne room floor too. It had been a fucking slip hazard in there by the time we were done.

Were we bad royals? I kind of felt like we were bad royals.

Meridia's smug gaze turned mutinous, and I felt the first stirrings of fear despite my best attempts to suppress the emotion.

"Out," Allerick ordered Meridia, already standing. "We are done here. We'll reconvene tomorrow."

I stumbled slightly as he encouraged me to my feet, guiding me out of a different exit to where Meridia was and leading me into what appeared to be a small study before slamming the door shut behind him, leaving Soren standing outside.

Before I could question him, Allerick lifted me onto a pitch-black desk, uncaring as half of the contents went flying, and dropped to his knees, shoving my dress up over my thighs.

"Is this a good—" My words cut off on a gasp as my husband ripped my lace panties off my body and shoved his head between my legs, his tongue probing at my pussy before I could so much as exhale.

"Your scent," he mumbled, voice muffled in a way that made me want to giggle. "Need to get your good scent back."

There was definitely part of me that thought we should talk about this, but was I really going to argue with him when he was willing to tongue fuck me into a better mood?

No. No, I was not.

Let the tongue fucking commence.

Allerick seemed to be in a leisurely mood though, taking his time, probably in order to make me as aroused as possible, so I drenched the surrounding airspace with sexy pheromones. I leaned back on my elbows, knocking something that was definitely made of glass off the desk, and watched as his horns moved this way and that, his claws digging into my thighs.

Those horns. When we knew each other a little better and I was confident he wouldn't freak out, I was going to take those horns for a drive.

"You're very good at that," I sighed, dropping my knees as far apart as they could go and lifting my hips to meet his movements as Allerick's rough tongue massaged teasingly over my clit from one angle then another. "I would like to come sometime today though."

Allerick pulled back just enough to nip my inner thigh with sharp teeth before returning to eating me out and the slight sting made *everything* clench with need. I had no idea why the idea of him biting me got me so hot, but I wasn't about to fight it. Not the way he was fighting it.

Allerick continued his steady pace, and I relaxed into it, tipping my head back and letting my eyes fall shut. Even if this was just about sex, just about *smell*, I still felt more cherished than I'd ever felt during intimacy with anyone, and I couldn't understand why.

The slow, languid orgasm rolled through me and I exhaled a long moan of satisfaction, melting into it like I was sinking into a warm bath. My entire body felt like a limp noodle, and it was absolutely glorious.

"How do I smell?" I slurred, legs still splayed open with zero self-consciousness.

"Deliciously appealing," Allerick purred, licking the evidence of me off his lips and *my god* there was a lot of evidence. I wasn't sure I was ever going to get used to just how *wet* I got around him. I mean, I needed it. The more lubrication the better when knots were involved.

With a surprising amount of tenderness, Allerick carefully pinched the hem of my dress between his claws and dragged it down over my thighs to cover me up again. I was still sans panties and was contemplating carrying a purse from now on with super absorbent towels in it for cleanup purposes, but at least I was somewhat dignified again.

"So, uh, thanks?" I said, cringing at my own awkwardness as I carefully moved into a sitting position, trying not to disturb the few remaining items on the desk. It was a small, windowless room lit only by one silver orb of light directly above us, and mostly seemed to be a filing space judging by the small square drawers that lined three of the walls.

"You're welcome," Allerick replied, sounding annoyingly amused for a moment before his face grew serious. "You were scared, that's what that scent is."

"Meridia scares me a little," I admitted, trying to be cool about it.

"Anyone else?" he asked darkly, shadows curling ominously around his horns. "Has anyone else scared you?"

"No?"

"You sure? That sounds more like a question than an answer," Allerick pointed out. Something fluttered a few degrees north of where my body usually responded to Allerick. Maybe because sassy Allerick was my favorite Allerick, which was a slippery slope to go down. I did not want to be that idiot who fell in love with the husband who'd never wanted to marry her.

"I'm sure," I replied, forcing some conviction into my voice.

"Er, your majesties," Soren called awkwardly, knocking on the door. "Allerick, I'm sorry but there's some more discontent, out near Illtal. I thought you might want to address it in person."

Allerick grunted in annoyance. "Fine. Let's go now, then I'll return to meet Ophelia for lunch."

I opened my mouth, ready to assure Allerick that I knew he was busy running a realm and he didn't have to eat with me, but he was already issuing instructions to Soren through the door, requesting our meals were brought to the courtyard while lifting me off the desk. He chivvied me out of the study, apparently content to ignore the mess we'd made of the room.

We were totally bad royals.

To really hammer that point home, Soren was waiting for us outside the door, staring at the ceiling with his hands clasped in front of him.

Sorry, I mouthed at him when he finally caught my eye, Allerick already striding ahead. Soren shook his head, the corners of his mouth twitching into what was almost a smile.

Ha! I was going to win him over too, I could tell. This was excellent progress, even if it came at the expense of my dignity.

I was going to make Shade friends, have great sex with my Shade husband, and make a proper life for myself here in the shadow realm, I was sure of it.

We found our rhythm after that morning Council meeting. Allerick resumed attending meetings alone and spending the morning talking up the benefits of the treaty to wary Shades, but he always met me for lunch, and my usual afternoon nap-slash-drawing time had become fuck-my-husband time.

It was supposed to be everything I'd ever wanted, wasn't it? I wasn't struggling to pay my bills, and I was having the kind of sex that most people were too afraid to admit they fantasized about. I'd lived my *dream* life for a week, and yet there was still an unexpected sense of hollowness I couldn't quite fill.

"Queen Ophelia?" Affra asked, her tone indicating it wasn't the first time she'd called my name.

"I'm sorry," I said, blinking rapidly to clear my head. I'd skipped my morning garden walk to get in some drawing time and I hadn't even heard Affra return after getting me ready for the day.

"No need to apologize," she tutted. "Prince Damen has requested that you and the king meet him in the library. The king is on his way here and I thought you might want to clean your hands," she said, a sparkle of amusement in her eyes as she glanced down at my charcoal-stained fingers.

"That's probably a good idea," I replied with a grimace, carefully slipping the drawing behind the others because of everything I'd drawn, this was probably the one I'd be the most uncomfortable with her seeing. With *anyone* seeing. It was an embarrassing glimpse into my tragic, unrequited reality.

I carefully put everything away and slipped into the bathroom to scrub my hands clean and freshen up, fixing my updo that was secured by the heavy raven pin and smoothing out a crease in my plum-colored dress.

As much as I liked being a subtle pop of color in this world, I kind of wished the Hunters Council had set me up with something a little more youthful. Every time I looked in the mirror, I saw a slightly younger, less frowny version of my mother staring back at me.

There was a knock at the door, and I quickly let myself into the corridor before Affra had to go through all the bowing and greeting fuss, almost stepping directly into my husband's chest as he loomed in the doorway.

"Wife."

His head dropped instantly to my neck, inhaling deeply. It didn't escape my notice that he always went to the same spot on my neck, the one where I desperately craved the feel of his teeth.

"Husband," I replied, because I liked the way it made him almost smile when I teased him a little.

"Come, I had some questions I asked Damen to research. Let's go find out if he's got the answers," Allerick instructed, offering me his arm.

We made our way through the quiet halls with Soren and Levana falling into step behind us, shadowing our steps. It was only their presence that was somewhat deterring me from leaping onto my husband and demanding he rip my panties off and fuck me with my dress on against the wall right here.

I thought I'd had an overactive libido and a filthy mind *before*. Allerick's knot had unlocked an insatiable side of me I never knew existed. As much as I *loved* fucking him—and I absolutely did—I was getting a little concerned by just how much fucking we were doing.

We still had responsibilities. Well, he did. And while I had a small exhibitionist streak, I didn't love that everyone knew I was horny all the time. It'd be nice to have an off switch so I could get through dinner without the entire court knowing I was leaking through my panties.

Ugh. Panties. Why was I even wearing them? They were just an obstacle for my husband to get through.

Allerick's purr rumbled to life, sucking all the oxygen from the room and making my legs tremble. He was right there, spinning me back against the wall, caging me in with his enormous frame.

"You are wanting," he growled, his taut muscles letting me know just how wanting he was too.

"Always," I agreed, my hand already passing through the shadows that hid his crotch. He was already hard—unsurprising—and I wrapped my fingers around his shaft, my pinky brushing his knot, forgetting entirely about our surroundings.

"Could you two keep your hands off each other for five seconds?" Damen called, his voice pouring ice water over my raging fire of lust. "I need to show you something."

I snatched my hand back, hiding it behind my back as though that could disguise what we'd been up to, while the shadows I'd disturbed slipped seamlessly back into place.

"This better be good," Allerick growled, baring his teeth. In my lust fog, I hadn't even noticed that the wall he'd pinned me against was right next to the library door.

"Come in and find out," Damen said cheerfully, not letting his brother's moodiness dampen his mood. He disappeared back into the library, and I shot Soren and Levana an apologetic look over my shoulder as I followed. It didn't escape my notice that they were hanging a *lot* further back than usual.

"What is it?" Allerick barked, his hand on my lower back gentle despite his aggravated tone as he guided me to the table Damen had commandeered at the other end of the library.

"It's about you two and your insatiable sexual appetite," Damen replied without an ounce of hesitation. Soren made a strangled noise and I looked behind me, glad to see that Levana was waiting in the hall.

"Tread carefully, brother," Allerick warned.

"Yes, yes, you're very territorial," Damen said with a dismissive wave of his hand. "I think I've found a solution for that."

Allerick and I stopped on one side of the table while Soren walked around it to join Damen. The book waiting for us in the center of the table looked older than dirt, the pages were yellowed and thin, and the ink was so faded, it would be almost impossible to read even if it was in English.

Which it was not.

"What language is this?" I asked quietly, scared to breathe too loudly in case the book disintegrated.

"They're runes," Damen said with a grimace. "An ancient language of Shades. I can't read it, nor do I know anyone who can. However, there are also pictures, so all is not lost."

There was a picture, but it took me a moment to realize what I was looking at.

"Is that..." Allerick began, tilting his head to the side as he examined it. "Is that a Shade biting a Hunter?"

"It could just be a regular human," I pointed out. We looked indistinguishable in real life, let alone in a faded sketch.

"I've never wanted to bite a human," Allerick said with absolute certainty. "I've never wanted to bite anyone except you."

Oh god, it was happening again. The gush of slick bypassed my already ruined panties, wetting the thighs I had pressed tightly closed.

Damen coughed. "Anyway, I can't read it, *but* there are some pictures in this book that appear to depict relationships between Shades and Hunters." He carefully turned the page and I didn't breathe until he was finished. "See?"

This page was also mostly runes, but there was a picture of what was definitely a female Shade with a human-looking man kneeling between her spread thighs. The ink was just as faded on this page, but it did sort of look like there was a mark on his shoulder that may have been made by teeth.

"How can this be possible?" I breathed. "I thought we were the first union of our kinds?"

"I hate to burst your bubble, but I don't think you guys are that special," Damen said with a dramatic sigh. An ominous warning growl rumbled out of Allerick's chest.

"He is very on edge right now," I said mildly, giving Damen a pointed look. Damen grinned while Soren scowled at him, adjusting his stance like he was ready to leap in if necessary.

"Do you think there's a way to translate this?" I asked. "Like some kind of Rosetta Stone for Shades with all the symbols written on it?"

"I'll ask around. Maybe some of the elderly folks on the Council will know." Damen shrugged.

"You don't think there would be any resources on the Hunter side?" Soren suggested. "Some books like this one?"

"Not that I know of. I'm also not entirely sure they would have kept them if those books ever existed," I admitted. "It would be at odds with their kill-Shades-at-all-costs messaging."

Allerick hummed in agreement. "I agree. It seems unlikely. The treaty was a last resort option for the Hunters Council, they didn't *want* to work with us, but the control the treaty gave them over us made it worthwhile for them."

All the Shades in the room seemed to shrug in agreement at that statement—I supposed they'd had plenty of time to think about it while I'd been drawing monster dick pics and wondering if my stranger husband would like me—but something about it wasn't sitting right with me. It wasn't that they were claiming the Hunters were controlling assholes, I knew that firsthand, but something else I couldn't quite put my finger on. Maybe that it seemed *too* tame for a group of assassins. Maybe the Shades wouldn't have agreed to just about anything in order to stop being murdered, but the list of things they'd say no to would have been pretty short.

"I wonder if my mother kept my old notes from when we studied runes," Damen mused, tilting his head to the side and squinting at the symbols on the page.

"You mean your governess?" Allerick snorted.

"Yes, that would be more likely," Damen laughed. "Maybe I'll pay her a visit, I could do with a little trip to the seaside."

There was a seaside? Was the ocean gray?

"Hold on," I said, forcing my brain semi back on the track it was trying to veer off. "Affra."

"Affra?" Allerick asked. He was kind of adorable when he was confused, in a big menacing kind of way.

"Yes, Affra! She said that before she worked at the palace, she used to work at some kind of library? And she translated things? She knows a bunch of human languages."

"The Itrodaris," Damen said instantly, giving me an appraising look though he sounded impressed. "It's a library of sorts, more a temple of learning. She probably had to leave when she got married—that crowd is devoted to the pursuit of knowledge rather than romance. I'll talk to her about it."

"You'll follow up on this, Damen?" Allerick asked. Both he and Soren were looking at Damen with a healthy degree of skepticism, like he couldn't be trusted with this, which didn't seem fair. Damen had learned more than all of us so far about this.

"I've got it under control," Damen shot back, flashing his usual grin though I thought I detected a hint of offense underneath it. "In the meantime, I vote you bite your wife."

I wrapped my arms around Allerick's waist before he launched himself across the table at Damen, damaging the precious book in the process. He relaxed almost instantly in my embrace, and I marveled slightly at the power—or at least the illusion of it—I had over this apex predator.

"I think we should do it," I murmured, staring at the book in the hopes they wouldn't see how red I'd gotten. "It feels instinctive. Every time we ignore the urge, it feels *wrong*. Maybe our bodies know something our collective memories have forgotten."

"Or maybe you'll bleed out on the mattress," Allerick countered.

"Sure, if you rip my throat out by accident." I rolled my eyes before remembering that I was supposed to be acting all royal, especially in his company, and pasted a more agreeable expression on my face. If anything, that seemed to bother Allerick more.

Damen gave Allerick a pointed look, tapping his claw on the wooden table right next to the faded picture in the book. "This is not a coincidence, brother. And if your wife is on board with it, then shouldn't you consider her point of view? I mean, I don't know, I've never been married. It just seems like the kind of thing a good husband would do."

Allerick growled while Damen shrugged, the picture of innocence.

"You're kind of a shit stirrer, huh?" I asked, marveled. I knew Damen had a mischievous side, but I didn't realize what an antagonizing younger brother he was. Not that I wanted the Shades to be human, but it was humanizing nonetheless.

"I have no idea what you're talking about," Damen shot back cheerfully while Soren scoffed, shooting Damen a withering look. "I'm just a thoughtful brother, making sure the king treats you right by getting those teeth in your neck."

ALLERICK

CHAPTER 15

My teeth ached like they had a mind of their own and understood we'd been talking about embedding them in Ophelia's skin. Despite her encouragement, her scent hadn't lied. The idea turned her on, but scared her a little at the same time. If I'd learned one thing recently, it was that I hated Ophelia's fear. It smelled repellant to me, everything in me demanded I make whatever the threat was go away.

Damen was speaking to Ophelia, but I couldn't hear the words he was saying over the ringing in my own ears. Or perhaps the *growling* in my own ears. Was I making that sound out loud? Having Ophelia near so many other Shades who may want to claim her for themselves, to bite her with their teeth, was aggravating me.

It wasn't sustainable to live like this. Every second of my day that was spent away from Ophelia was an exercise in torture.

"Perhaps we should go for a walk," Ophelia said softly, patting the back of my hand. "Get some fresh air."

"Mm, he certainly needs something," Damen chuckled, his amused expression making me contemplate gouging the eyes out of his skull.

I knew I was behaving strangely, but my wife took it all in her stride. She kept her body pressed close to mine, stroking my skin softly as she guided me back towards the corridor. She moved like she was going to lead us down to the courtyard, but that didn't give me nearly enough privacy for what I had in mind so I steered her back through the palace towards the gardens instead.

The sweet scent of her arousal filled the air, and a purr erupted from my chest without thought, my cock swelling so uncomfortably that it took everything in me not to stroke myself while I walked through the palace corridors where anyone could see me.

"You are insatiable," Ophelia teased, her voice breathy with lust.

"You have no idea," I growled. "It's worse being around others. Every dinner is misery. I've never hated my claws before, but now I want to rip them off at each meal so I can bury soft fingers in your cunt while you eat."

Ophelia blushed scarlet, her grip on my arm tightening as she stumbled slightly. "Perhaps we should both be grateful for the claws then. Perhaps the whole court should be grateful for them."

"Perhaps we should start dining in private," I countered. Already, the urge to throw her over my shoulder and march back up to her rooms was riding me, but there were other private places in the palace that we could enjoy and she *had* mentioned wanting fresh air.

There was always too much I wanted to do with my wife, I didn't know where to start. I wanted to do *everything*. I wanted to fuck her tits, her mouth, basically everywhere. I wanted my cum on her face, her body, down her throat. I already knew I wouldn't be able to resist burying my knot in her this time though.

"Where are we going?" Ophelia asked, panting a little to keep up with me. I stopped, frowning at her.

"Would you be opposed to me carrying you through the palace? You have very short legs."

"You like my legs," Ophelia threw back, before looking like she was going to self-correct, perhaps worried she'd spoken too freely with me.

"I do like your legs," I agreed before she could speak. "But they are very short and it takes a very long time to get anywhere."

Her lips twitched. "Well, I think it'd be a little undignified for you to carry me around, so you're just going to have to walk slower."

I grumbled my assent, slowing my pace so she could keep up and tucking her hand into the crook of my elbow. *I* didn't think it would be undignified. What was even the point of being the king if I couldn't say what was dignified and what wasn't?

"Are we going outside?" Ophelia asked as we rounded the corner into the entrance hall.

"Yes," I grunted. I knew Ophelia liked spending time outdoors at least once a day, and I had my own selfish motivations for leading us to the garden.

Levana hung back as I guided Ophelia away from the usual path she took through the gardens, leading her to a high wall a hundred feet away from the palace.

"Oh, I always wondered what was behind here," Ophelia murmured, craning her neck. Lush gray and silver leaves hung over the top of the black wall, hinting at the jungle that grew beyond.

I loosened a coil of shadow to sink into the discreet lock, and the hidden door swung open, making Ophelia gasp.

"What is this?" she asked, pulling out of my grip to rush forwards. So she *could* walk faster when she wanted to.

"It *was* my father's garden. Technically, it's mine I suppose, but I rarely come out here. It's only accessible to me." The door swung shut behind me, and I glimpsed Levana standing at attention outside, her back to the wall.

"We're all alone in here?" Ophelia asked, eyebrows rising.

"We are. You like to spend time outside. I like to spend my time eating your cunt before burying my knot in you. This way, we can do both," I stated factually, already looking around for the most comfortable spot for Ophelia to lie down. Most of the ground was stone paths, and that wouldn't do. I experimentally made some vines from shadows and draped them over a tree branch, pushing a little power into them until they solidified.

"Did you just make me a shadow sex swing?" Ophelia laughed, watching me work with wide eyes. "Whenever I think I've already had all the fantasies there are to be had, you show me new things I hadn't thought of yet."

I was more than a little smug about that.

"Why don't you tell me more about these fantasies you've already had?"

A vivid pink blush stole across my wife's cheeks, a rare spot of color in this gray garden. *Though were those leaves looking a little green?* Faint splashes of color had been showing up all over the realm. "No, no, the swing is good—"

"Indulge me," I purred, closing the distance between us and running my claws down the side of her face before catching them under her chin, lifting her face up so I could better admire her rosy cheeks.

Ophelia chewed on her lower lip for a moment, making blood rush to the spot where her teeth had been. She was so *vibrant*. Lush and beautiful and alive with color.

"I guess I always had this one recurring fantasy," she admitted, her eyes looking at everything except my face despite me still holding her chin in place. "You might not be into it though. Or you might think it's weird—"

"Tell me, wife."

"It's just that if there's no one else here, maybe I could, you know... run."

"Run?" I repeated, tilting my head to the side.

"And you could, I don't know, catch me."

My cock swelled so suddenly, it almost hurt. "Little huntress, are you suggesting I hunt *you*?"

Ophelia's pupils dilated, the pulse in her neck beating wildly. "Yes, please. That would be great if you could... do that."

"Will you be afraid?" I asked, pulling strands of her hair loose from her updo. "I don't like when you're afraid."

"Because I smell gross?"

"That's certainly part of it," I replied, not wanting to admit just how much there was to it.

"I don't think I'll be scared. It's just us here, right? And if you smell my fear you can stop."

"And if you want to stop?" I pressed.

"I mean, I won't. But if I do, I'll say 'raven.' Deal?"

This may be my favorite version of Ophelia—when she was practically salivating for me, pressing her thighs together, her nipples beaded into tight points visible through her dress, yet she was acting like she was entirely calm and in control.

"Raven," I agreed, releasing her hair and taking a step back. "I'll count down from ten." I leaned forward into her space, snapping my teeth slightly. "*Run.*"

She didn't waste any time, spinning her heel and sprinting through the garden far too noisily to evade anyone. I loudly counted down from ten, listening to her take a right and crash through some of the overgrown brush.

I palmed my cock impatiently, forcing myself to take an even breath and not rush as I hit 'zero.' It would be more fun to take my time, to toy with my prey a little before I pounced. On silent feet, I began winding my way through the garden, taking a different route so I could cut Ophelia off further down the path.

She must know that this game played to my basest instincts. Her kind may call themselves 'hunters,' but that didn't mean Shades were the 'hunted.' We stalked our human prey through the shadows, letting their fear build and fester until they were at the perfect level to harvest. Hunting was deep in my bones, as natural to me as feeding.

Perhaps this was why Ophelia had never made it as a Hunter. Aside from her fascination with the intimate parts of monsters that she should have never been fantasizing about, her nature was more prey than predator. She *liked* being prey.

Her heavy footsteps came to a stop, and I heard rustling as she attempted to disguise herself amongst the foliage, her labored breathing giving away her position.

I crept up to where she was peering around a tree trunk at the main path, totally oblivious to my presence behind her. Had she chosen this particular spot on purpose? The ground here was covered in a soft mossy plant that would be comfortable enough for her to lie on, and it was hidden away by tall trees on all sides, making it feel like we were in our own world entirely.

She began to turn as though she was going to look over her shoulder, and I pounced, pressing my front to her back and wrapping a hand over her mouth to capture her scream.

"Caught you," I murmured, my arm wrapping around her front, fingers splaying possessively low over her stomach.

Ophelia moaned against my palm, a hint of sour fear almost immediately drowned out by the sweetness of her arousal.

"Now," I began, shifting my hand from her mouth down to cup her throat, "what shall I do with you now that I have you?"

"Anything you want," Ophelia replied breathily.

"Silly little huntress, you have no idea what you're asking for," I told her, grabbing her wrists and pressing her palms against the tree trunk in front of her. Ophelia caught on quickly, steadying herself and bending forward, looking over her shoulder with hooded eyes.

Without giving her a chance to protest, I raked my claws through the silky fabric of her dress, shredding it into plum-colored ribbons that pooled at her feet. Ophelia gasped, eyes widening in surprise as I repeated the movement with her delicate lace bra and panties, leaving her wearing nothing but the faint red lines from my claws on her skin.

"Pretty," I remarked, walking around behind her, wondering if she'd be comfortable with me tying her up. Perhaps another day, this was all still very new for both of us after all.

Not that Ophelia seemed to be having any difficulty adjusting to our new dynamic. Her hips were raised up and pushed out—not the position of a meek or hesitant lover, that was for sure.

I took my time admiring her in the silvery light of day, enjoying the way it made her squirm before forming a shadowy blindfold that drifted slowly into place over her eyes.

"Okay?" I confirmed.

"Holy fuck, yes," Ophelia replied instantly. "You come with built-in accessories!"

I snorted at her description, moving silently behind her before quietly dropping to my knees and scraping my claws down her inner thighs. She startled briefly at the touch before relaxing into it, spreading her legs wider without encouragement.

Not for the first time, I wondered if it was actually me who Ophelia was interested in, or if this was just a monster-fucking experience to tick off her list. Perhaps part of me had hoped she'd reject the blindfold, wanting to see exactly who it was that was giving her pleasure.

Shaking off the irritating thoughts, I dug my claws into Ophelia's ass cheeks, separating her so I could bury my tongue in her pussy without warning. She let out a squeal of surprise that trailed off as a groan, scrambling for grip against the tree trunk while I pulsed my tongue in her cunt, letting the sweet taste of her dripping slick pool in my mouth.

Heaven.

I wanted to walk around with her taste on my tongue every minute of every day. It was a travesty that I wasn't doing so already.

"Oh my god," Ophelia gasped. "You are... very, very good at that."

I withdrew my tongue slowly, angling my head so I could lavish attention on her clit. Ophelia went up on her tiptoes, trying to find a better angle to ride my face but too short to get where she wanted. I swatted her ass lazily.

"Settle. You'll get what you need."

My pretty wife threw her head back, loose strands of hair cascading down the pale skin of her back. Putting on a show for me. Too bad I didn't have a good view, and I wasn't about to give up my spot between her thighs for anything, not until I felt her clenching around me, drenching me with her scent.

I tightened my grip, enjoying the way her ass filled my hands so nicely, my claws pricking at her skin as I went to work, holding her in place while I devoured her. Ophelia's legs wobbled, and I encouraged her to lean her weight against me, more than able to carry her.

There was no self-consciousness in the way she writhed, nails digging into the bark of the tree as she attempted to fuck herself on my face. Perhaps later, she could. Not when we were playing this game though. Not when she was my prize and I'd so thoroughly won her.

"Bend," I snarled, my voice coming out thick and rough because my fucking *teeth* seemed to be growing, desperate to get to my wife's neck. Ophelia bent further forward, wriggling her hands down the tree trunk to steady herself, pussy gushing slick while I attempted to lick up every drop.

She'd unlocked the beast inside me when she'd asked me to chase her, and there was no wrestling him back now. At least in this position, with her leaning forward and me tongue fucking her like a savage from below, I couldn't get my teeth in her throat where I wanted them.

I had no doubt that the sounds she was making could be heard from the other side of the garden wall as Ophelia completely gave herself over to her orgasm, and I kept her in place, licking her from one release to the next, wanting her thoroughly dominated by the pleasure I'd given her. I'd caught her, and now she was mine to play with. The urge to mark and *keep* was riding me harder than ever, spurred on by her words in the library and the thrill of the chase coursing through me.

Dangerous. This was a very dangerous game.

Even just keeping my grip on her thighs gentle was a struggle when my control was being so thoroughly tested. There were red indentations in her pale skin where my claws had dug into her flesh.

"Why do you sound so weird?" Ophelia asked—or moaned, rather— struggling to keep herself upright. I hadn't even noticed a steady growl of frustration had been rumbling out of my chest. I attempted to stop it, but it was an expression of my frustration that I couldn't seem to quite shake off. My teeth must have scraped a little close to Ophelia's clit for comfort, as she jolted away and as much as I fucking *craved* her, I'd never pin her against her will. I threw myself back on my ass, forcing myself to put some distance between us, my chest heaving like I'd fought the hardest battle of my life.

I *had*. Nothing had ever been more difficult than resisting the urge to bite Ophelia.

I dissolved her blindfold, and Ophelia blinked at the sudden light before focusing her gaze on my face.

"Holy canines, Batman," she whispered, spinning to look at me, her back pressed against the tree and eyes wide. I could feel that my teeth were larger—and sharper—than usual, and I dug my claws into the dirt beneath me, silently chanting 'stay put' in my mind over and over so I didn't chase Ophelia again when she inevitably ran.

Except she wasn't running. Her thighs squeezed together, and her pink tongue darted out to swipe her bottom lip as she stared at my mouth.

"Wow. I mean, your teeth always appear to be designed for mauling creatures great and small, but right now... They're just really *impressive*," she said, her own blunt teeth worrying her bottom lip, eyes hooded. "Like you could really take a chunk out of me if you wanted to."

"Ophelia," I warned, practically salivating at the thought of sinking my fangs into her flesh.

"Allerick," she replied, mimicking my tone.

We both startled, staring at each in other in realization. She'd never called me by just my first name before. I growled possessively, my body lurching forward so fast I nearly ripped my claws off before I forced myself to still.

Instead of running, my perfect, trusting wife sauntered over to me, climbing into my lap, her slick sliding down me as she pressed her hot center over my cock, rocking her hips with a needy moan.

"I'm wrestling with my self-control right now."

"I know," she assured me, leaning forward and running her blunt teeth over the spot in my neck I so desperately wanted to mark on her's. "So am I."

"I don't want to hurt you."

"It hurts when you hold yourself back," she countered, nipping harmlessly at my skin before making the most adorable growl of frustration. "This is a weird and unusual urge, yet we both feel it. We've seen the evidence that it's a *thing*, or it was back in the olden days. I'm okay with it. You need to get okay with it too."

I was *too* okay with it, if anything. I flipped her onto her back, grabbing the back of her head to cushion the impact with my hand, and loomed over her, my teeth bared.

"Bite me," she demanded, tipping her head back to expose her neck, her legs wrapping around my hips so she could continue to grind her cunt on my knot.

I dropped my head to the crook of her neck, my muscles shaking with the effort of keeping myself still as I inhaled her delicious molten sugar scent.

"It's going to hurt."

"You can kiss it better," she murmured, her breath hitching at the first scrape of fangs against her sensitive skin. Her legs tightened around me, hands gripping my biceps, but there was no sourness of fear to be found.

My teeth pressed down, not quite breaking the skin.

Ophelia's scent sweetened.

I reached between us, pressing my cock to her entrance and pushing forward with no resistance.

Ophelia groaned, using her thighs to leverage herself and take me deeper.

Too good. Too perfect. Too irresistible.

My teeth clamped down before I could give her a final warning, and I nearly came at the sudden tang of blood hitting my tongue. Ophelia relaxed in my hold, sighing contentedly like she'd just received a hit of something potent to her system.

Please don't let this be hurting her.

"So good," Ophelia moaned. "Now fuck me."

"So demanding," I teased, my voice muffled as I extracted my teeth and lapped at the mark with my tongue. It was huge and distinctive—dominating the right side of her throat. An unmissable, unmistakable claiming.

Mine.

Ophelia was all fucking mine.

The ferocity of my need to possess her took me off guard as I braced myself on my forearms on either side of her and started savagely thrusting into her, fucking her into the ground. My wife gave as good as she got, nails raking down my arms as she attempted to meet my movements, flattening her feet on the ground for better leverage.

"Legs up," I demanded, barely recognizing my own voice. Ophelia immediately complied, grabbing the back of her knees and hauling them up to her shoulders, opening herself up to me. One hand slid between her legs, roughly rubbing her clit as she chased her release, and it might have been the sexiest thing I'd ever seen.

"Allerick!" she gasped, clenching around me as she came, and as much as the sweet sound of my name on her lips tempted me to follow, I wasn't ready for this to be over yet.

The *beast* wasn't ready for this to be over yet.

I shifted my weight so I was up on my knees, using my now free hands to grab her hips and bouncing her on my cock like she was a vessel for my pleasure and nothing else. The beast in me enjoyed showing off my strength, but it was more that I knew *she* liked it. She liked knowing I was bigger and stronger than she was. Her scent sweetened deliciously whenever I demonstrated the physical differences between us.

Ophelia's gasps and breathy moans grew louder, her movements almost frantic, and her sudden orgasm taking us both by surprise. *Too tight.* My knot swelled, locking us into place like my cock was worried of being pushed out if I didn't come at that exact moment.

Ophelia's legs shook as I filled her up, and I immediately gathered her up to my body and rolled us so that she was draped over me, something settling in me as she slumped so trustingly into my embrace.

This felt *right* in a way that nothing ever had—there was a warm, pleasantly tight feeling in my chest that felt somehow *permanent*. Like I was attached to Ophelia in a way that I didn't yet fully understand.

My tongue found its way to the bite mark, tracing the wound for a moment by instinct before I realized what I was doing and pulled back. Ophelia seemed just as surprised by the gesture as I was.

"Do you feel that? In your chest?" I asked, eager to draw attention away from my strange behavior. Ophelia nodded, looking a little dazed.

For a moment, she reached up, her hand ghosting over my hair before seemingly thinking better of it. Her cheeks flushed the prettiest shade of pink, and I almost reassured her that she could touch me wherever she liked, but she spoke before I had a chance.

"It's weird that it doesn't hurt," she sighed, blinking sleepily up at me. "It just feels *good*. Like I'm all drugged up on happy hormones or something."

She said it like it was a good thing, but the idea of drugging her in any form didn't sit well with me. I couldn't bring myself to regret the connection between us, whatever it was, but I was panicking slightly at the way it had happened.

We'd barely discussed it. What if Ophelia had wanted it in the heat of the moment but regretted it now?

She shivered slightly on top of me, her skin cooling in the breeze despite lying atop my higher body temperature.

"We need to get you inside," I growled, banding my arms around her back, worried that she was going to freeze to death out here. "You're cold."

Ophelia shook with laughter for a moment before her laughs turned into a moan, a languid orgasm taking over, making her limp. With the bite, I hadn't noticed that my power reserves were growing steadily again, Ophelia's lust feeding me more than I probably took in *months* from humans. As soon as I could drag myself away from her, I was going to need to siphon.

"We definitely didn't think this through," she rasped. "This is an awkward position to relax in outside."

I snorted, cloaking us in shadows and manipulating them until they solidified into a makeshift blanket. It wasn't overly warm, but it would be enough to keep the wind off her skin.

How much clothing did human bodies actually require to keep them safe from the elements? I'd shredded Ophelia's clothes with almost no effort, surely it hadn't actually been doing anything to maintain her body heat.

"Thank you for indulging me with the whole chasing thing," Ophelia said quietly, her head resting on my bicep. "Did you like it? I mean, you seemed to, but I just wanted to make sure you weren't uncomfortable..."

Her words soothed something in me—a part of me that worried I was just a means to an end for Ophelia. A convenient way for her to fulfill her fantasies and nothing more.

"I enjoyed it very much," I assured her. "You don't, er, regret the bite? Hunting you brought out my most primal instincts. Perhaps it was unwise of me to agree to it when I was already so on edge—"

"I like the bite," Ophelia interrupted. "It feels comforting."

Good thing her head was still resting on my chest so she couldn't see my smug grin. "And I wasn't too rough?"

"You could be rougher, I wouldn't mind," she replied, a teasing lilt to her voice. I didn't think I *could* be rougher. I liked the idea of hunting Ophelia, catching her, pinning her down and demonstrating my strength, but the idea of actually *hurting* her was abhorrent.

I ran my claws down her side, lingering at the soft dip at her waist and enjoying the light shudder that morphed into a gentle orgasm, her squeezing cunt draining my balls dry.

"You probably think it's crazy that I used to be envious of the regular humans who were stalked through the night by Shades," Ophelia laughed breathily. "I've always had weird thoughts like that. We used to have lessons about Shades and what was expected of us as future Hunters—"

Murder, I thought wryly.

"—and I'd be daydreaming about trying to befriend the Shades the whole time." I could hear the smile in her voice, and I quickly hid my responding one in her hair.

Was Ophelia unique? Or had she just hidden her proclivities more poorly than her peers?

"I don't think you're crazy. Young Shades are always curious about the human realm, perhaps even a little idealistic about what their experiences there will be like. It's something that is trained out of them for their own safety."

"That's sad," Ophelia breathed, lazily drawing circles on my inner arm with a finger. I did my best to hold still, wanting my knot to soften as quickly as possible so I could get her inside where it was warm. "Though with the treaty in place, maybe it won't have to be like that anymore, right? Maybe they can keep some of that idealism now."

"Not in our lifetimes," I murmured, hating to dash her optimism but not wanting her to get her hopes up. The treaty was a ceasefire, but there was no love lost between Shades and Hunters.

"Speaking of," Ophelia said cautiously. "I've been meaning to ask, how old are you?"

"Worried you're impaled on a thousand-year-old monster?" I teased.

Ophelia's cunt clenched around me, her breath hitching. "Don't say impaled."

"Why? You like it," I replied with a grin, forcing myself not to move. "I am thirty years old. Our life spans are not so different from yours, though we reproduce much less prolifically."

Nowadays, at least. From our records, there used to be far more Shades.

"You're a very young king," Ophelia observed quietly.

"I was crowned five years ago. My father was killed while feeding in the human realm." That was enough to make my knot soften, and I carefully pulled free, my wife sucking in a gasp of surprise at the loss of contact.

"I'm so sorry, Allerick."

She meant it too. Her big brown eyes were filled with remorse, a faint sheen over them as if she might cry for my pain.

"It wasn't your doing," I replied wryly, helping her upright. "That's what it is to be a Shade. We're apex predators here, but we need to travel to the human realm to feed, and in your domain, we're all but helpless prey. If there had been no connection between us, no attraction, I still would have respected our marriage as a critical element of the treaty which I will do everything in my power to preserve to keep my people safe."

"I will too," Ophelia agreed quietly. "Do whatever I can to preserve the treaty. I don't want Shades to die either."

"I believe you, Queen Ophelia."

I covered my own body with my usual cloak of shadows before manipulating the blanket I'd made into a garment for her. My chest swelled with pride at the way she admired the makeshift dress—it was a big moment, although Ophelia didn't realize it. She was wearing *my* shadows in public, soaked in my scent, wearing my mark on her neck.

Though just like after our coupling in the throne room, no one but Levana would see because I fully intended for her to go ahead of us and clear the way. As much as I liked the idea of parading my wife through the palace dressed in shadows and dripping with cum, I didn't think she'd be as fond of the idea and I didn't want to embarrass her.

Ophelia gathered up the scraps of clothing, giving me a withering look as she balled the material up.

"I'm leaking," she complained with a sigh, using the material to wipe her inner thighs.

"Well, I could always carry you back to minimize the mess," I pointed out, the now-sated beast inside me eager to carry his prize back through the palace.

"I swear you planned this all along," Ophelia muttered, reaching for me automatically. There was that strange sensation in my chest again.

I picked her up easily, and she tucked some of the fabric between her legs, hidden by shadows, grumbling good-naturedly the entire time before wrapping her arms around my neck.

"Are you sure you can carry me all the way back?" Ophelia asked doubtfully as we moved towards the gate.

I snorted. "Remember, you're in my realm and I'm the apex predator here, little queen. Besides, you walk so slowly. The sooner we are back in your room, the sooner I can knot you again."

OPHELIA

CHAPTER 16

I'm going to be too boneless to walk down to dinner, I thought hazily, flexing my toes to make sure I could still move them. The moment we'd gotten back to my rooms, Allerick had thrown me down on the bed and fucked me like a Shade possessed, as though he hadn't just come a million times in the garden.

I felt a little ridiculous now, ever assuming my stamina could match his. He was on a whole different level.

As much as the bite had enhanced this gnawing sexual hunger we had for one another, I felt the faintest stirrings of control coming back. Beneath the need to solidify whatever this bond was by fucking ourselves unconscious, there was a sense of the comfort and stability it brought. We might actually be able to build a real relationship *not* based purely on sex, if that was something Allerick even wanted.

Allerick's knot softened, and a flood of liquid threatened to rush out of my pussy that I wouldn't be able to control no matter how tightly I clenched my legs together. I'd already tested the limits of my thigh muscles on the way back to the room, determined not to leave a trail of cum behind me wherever Allerick walked.

That plan had failed spectacularly.

Levana had gone ahead and cleared the halls for us since we didn't want to encounter anyone on our way back. Or rather, I didn't. I got the feeling that Allerick wouldn't have minded so much if *everyone* in the court had seen the mess he'd made of me in the private garden, and I was pretty sure it had something to do with the tingling bite mark that sat pride of place on my throat. Levana had stared at it with the biggest, rounded eyes I had ever seen on a Shade for half a moment before she'd trained her gaze diligently at the ground to await Allerick's instructions.

Note to self: see if Allerick will give Levana a pay rise.

Was that something I could do? Old-fashioned, mistress of the house style? I just wanted to *do* something.

"What are you thinking about?" Allerick asked, his claws running lightly down my back. It was an abnormally casual question that took me entirely off guard.

"Um, just about what I'll be doing tomorrow. And the day after that. And the day after that."

Allerick blinked at me. "And what have you got planned?"

"Meandering around the garden. Eating canned vegetables. Drawing pictures. Maybe I'll grab an instrument on my next trip to the human realm, teach myself to play guitar or something," I added, a touch sarcastically despite my best intentions.

"We have instruments here," Allerick replied. I could practically hear the *whoosh* as the point flew over his head.

"Right, totally." I didn't think Allerick was being intentionally obtuse, he probably assumed I *wanted* to relax all day. Soren had said that consorts weren't really a thing here, and I made a mental note to chat about ideas of things I *could* do when I next took tea with Orabelle.

"Can you get me a towel or something?" I asked my husband, a hint of whine creeping into my voice as I wriggled off his cock and flopped sideways on the bed, clamping my thighs shut.

It was a very dignified and ladylike gesture.

Although Affra seemed almost gleeful, at the... well, whatever the thing between Allerick and I was, but I still felt bad at the amount of laundry she had to do.

"Bossy little queen," Allerick teased, climbing off the bed and heading towards the bathroom. His cock glistened in the almost golden light, still standing at half-mast. Was he ever fully soft? I hadn't seen him that way, but then again, it wasn't like we were ever just relaxing together. Either we were in public and covered up, or he was buried knot-deep in me while I panted all over him and pretended like my insecurities weren't eating me alive.

Allerick returned with a damp washcloth, and I held out my hand expectantly. To my intense surprise, he swatted it gently out of the way, settling himself in between my legs and cleaning me with intense care. I settled back on the bed with a sigh, startling when Allerick's tongue replaced the cloth.

"I prefer you messy," he grumbled, tongue flicking my clit. I nudged his horn with my knee, unable to close my legs with his enormous bulk in the way.

"Stop it, my clit is sex drunk and needs to sleep it off for a bit."

I felt him smile against my inner thigh before bringing the washcloth back and finishing the job. I was less sticky but absolutely still leaking all over the sheets. *I exist in a constant state of leakage now.*

Allerick tossed the washcloth aside, making himself comfortable on the bed again with his back resting on the pillows. It hadn't escaped my notice that he *hadn't* cleaned the evidence of our activities off his cock, and a weird possessive part of me was thrilled about that.

"Come here," he demanded lazily, patting the mattress next to him.

"In a minute." I rolled onto my front and rested my head on my arms, lying further down the bed and just out of his reach. These moments after sex were the only time we were alone together without our mouths being otherwise occupied, and I wanted to make the most of it. *Talk* a little, even.

I'd learned more about him after our brief chat in the garden than I had in all the formal dinners we'd sat next to each other, and against my better judgment, I really *liked* Allerick. I knew it would probably never amount to anything more than what we had right now—it was clear he still saw me as an outsider and he didn't *really* trust me with Shade business—but maybe we could still find some common ground.

I wanted him to trust me. Or at the very least, not see me as an enemy in waiting.

"I suppose you'll need to go do some work soon?" I asked, my voice muffled as I laid down on my front, waiting for sensation to return to my body.

"Why do you say that?" Allerick asked, his tone a little sharper than I expected for what I'd thought was quite an innocent question.

"Because of all the drama with the Shades who don't like the treaty?" I hedged. "And not to overstep or anything, but it seemed like there would be some consequences for Meridia making that big claim about our marriage in front of Council like that with no evidence."

Allerick grunted in agreement. "It affects you, you're not overstepping, Ophelia. She's been suspended from her scouting duties that she usually carries out in the human realm, and Damen has been keeping an eye on her though she's mostly been holed up at her mother's house in the country ever since. He's dealt with Meridia many times over the years in her attempts to get to me."

"If she wasn't so unhinged, I'd almost feel sorry for her," I said. "She obviously likes you a lot."

Allerick snorted, and I smiled against my arm at how remarkably human and un-king-like the noise was. Maybe I was rubbing off on him. "She doesn't *like* me at all. She has no romantic interest in me whatsoever outside of *marrying* me."

"That seems like a pretty big romantic interest," I replied before I could think better of it. *Shit*. Was he going to think I was talking about us? I felt like there was a burgeoning romantic element to our union, but I wasn't sure that Allerick felt the same way.

"It isn't," Allerick scoffed.

Okay, I guess not then.

"Before all the flirting and borderline painful attempts at seduction, Meridia challenged me."

"Challenged you?" I propped myself up on my forearms to look at his face. I couldn't read his expressions as well as a human's yet, but the more I watched, the more I saw.

"My position is only hereditary to a point," he explained. "If someone were stronger than me, they could challenge me for it."

"Let me guess, no one is stronger than you?" I teased, embarrassed at myself for finding his arrogance such a turn-on. I'd always had a weakness for red flags though.

Allerick smirked. "Damen and Soren have never challenged me, but I doubt either of them would win, especially since I've been feeding from you—the stores have never looked so healthy, I have that much to spare. Neither of them has an interest in my role, regardless. Damen wouldn't cope with the responsibility, and Soren has always had the heart of a soldier. Mostly, challenges came from lower-ranking families, sending their strongest to win a place at court. Even if they lose the challenge—which they always did— sometimes they impress wealthy families and benefit from it."

"Is that what happened in Meridia's case?"

"No," Allerick replied, sounding amused. "Meridia and Soren grew up at court with their mother, though they have different fathers. Meridia had plenty of opportunities available to her without challenging me. She *wanted* power and prestige. I suppose I can respect that."

"Was this a long time ago?"

Allerick grimaced. "She was only fifteen. I was eighteen, and the Crown Prince. She stood up in the dining hall after the evening meal to challenge me for my birthright. I thought Soren might die of shame."

"He wasn't worried for his sister?" I asked wryly. Astrid was a certified badass—she was ambidextrous and could throw eighty knives in under a minute—but I'd still worry if she tried something like that.

"We were friends, he knew he didn't need to worry. Whenever someone significantly weaker tried to challenge me, I'd humor them in a fight for a while then pin them until they lost consciousness. I don't beat on those who can't defend themselves."

My easily-impressed heart skipped a beat, as though it was super admirable that my husband didn't beat the crap out of people who were weaker than him.

You need higher standards, I scolded internally.

"Is that what you did to Meridia?"

Allerick hummed in agreement. "I let her show off for a bit, then put her to sleep. She wasn't a bad fighter—she'd been training since childhood—and that's why she's one of our more accomplished scouts now. She didn't speak to me for a few years after I beat her in the challenge, then suddenly she was all over me. It was... uncomfortable, to say the least."

I was absolutely jealous, but it was a weird kind of jealous. Maybe because I knew from Allerick's tone that he wasn't interested in Meridia at all, and I didn't think there was any risk of him actually pursuing something with her. It was more like a possessive kind of jealousy—like I didn't want anyone so much as *looking* at *my* husband.

I opened my mouth to ask him another question, but Allerick's warning growl cut me off, making another embarrassing gush of wetness slip from between my thighs.

"I'm sick of talking about other people. When we're in this bed, it's just us," he rumbled, rolling onto his front and crawling towards me.

"Allerick," I groaned. "I'm still all sticky."

"That's how I like you," he countered, moving behind me and all but shoving my hips into the air. I scrambled to balance on my knees, ass up with my breasts pressed into the mattress. "Are you sore?"

His tongue licked languidly up my inner thigh, and he hummed like he'd never tasted anything sweeter.

"I'm a good sore," I assured him. Even if I was a bad sore, I wasn't sure I had the self-control to say no to him. It hadn't escaped my attention that he'd not only changed the subject, but basically rejected the very concept of chatting in bed. Which was the only time we were alone together.

Cool, cool, cool.

I'd have time to be upset about that later though because Allerick's claws were digging into my thighs as he spread me wide, his tongue swirling teasingly at my entrance, and I decided that if I had to settle for what I could get, then there were worse things to endure than this.

ALLERICK

CHAPTER 17

Ophelia was fast asleep by the time I'd finished rutting her into the mattress, my knot finally deflating fully after what felt like hours snugly inside her warm, wet cunt. The tang of her blood lingered on my tongue, reminding me of how thoroughly I'd lost my mind with the urge to bite her. With the way she'd *encouraged* me. I couldn't bring myself to regret it though—not when Ophelia had looked so satisfied, a smile playing around her mouth even in sleep.

I had no idea how my wife felt about me, how I even wanted her to feel about me, but she had given me a gift. I knew that much from the strange tether that now connected us, sitting like a comfortable weight in my chest. The bite mark on her neck was healing remarkably fast, but her body was still mostly human and needed more rest than mine did, so I ignored the temptation to rouse her awake with my tongue again and forced down the undoubtedly loud purr—a strange new phenomenon that Ophelia had inspired—that threatened to rumble out of my chest at the sight of the mark. *Mine.* That's what that mark meant.

I may never be able to claim her heart, I didn't have the first clue how, but Ophelia was still mine. I'd marked her, inside and out.

She may not know it, but she'd marked me too. Not with sharp teeth and claws, but with her *presence*. Not to mention her delectable scent, that I made sure to have on me at all times.

One of these days, Damen was going to say something about it and I'd have to punch him in the face.

Silently, I climbed off the bed, dragging the quilt we'd disturbed over Ophelia's naked back before backing towards the door. The tether between us pulled taut as I moved, like it didn't want me to leave her, and that would be a strange adjustment. Could Ophelia feel it too? She rolled over, her arm reaching towards me in sleep and my resolve took a solid knock.

Would she regret what we'd done once she realized she'd supernaturally tied herself to a monster? If she didn't now, she would on her first trip back to the human realm when she had to look her sister in the eye with that mark on her neck.

It doesn't matter what her sister thinks, I told myself. Ophelia had not only agreed to the mark, but *begged* for it. I hadn't forced anything on her that she didn't want.

I draped shadows over my body before quietly letting myself into the corridor. We'd missed the evening meal, though I was confident Damen had covered for us. Probably by alluding to exactly what we'd been doing.

A shiver of unease ran through me at that thought. Not that I had any objections to my subjects knowing that I found my wife desirable and acted on those desires, but I didn't want to make Ophelia a target if any of them took issue with that idea.

There were plenty of whispers prior to our wedding, pitying me for having to consummate a union with a Hunter, like the concept was the most repulsive thing they'd ever heard.

I'd never found my wife repulsive. Intimacy with Ophelia was no hardship at all.

Affra was heading down the corridor towards her own room, but she halted as I raised my hand.

"The queen didn't eat dinner. Could you have a selection of things ready for her in her room if she wakes during the night?"

"Of course, your majesty," Affra agreed, bowing her head. "Enough for both of you?"

"No, I'll be in my own rooms," I told her, already walking away. I could have sworn I saw the hint of disapproval on her face before I closed my door.

Should I have stayed?

No, surely not. I'd never stayed before, it would be strange to start now. Besides, Ophelia hadn't asked me to stay. Surely she would have asked if she wanted me to sleep next to her.

Still, I couldn't deny that once I was in my own room, my bed looked particularly cold and uninviting. The bond, or whatever it was, that tethered Ophelia and I together felt unnaturally taut now that I was away from her, and it was with some discomfort that I climbed under the dark covers of my own bed.

Tomorrow, we'd have to face everyone and explain the connection between us probably. I'd at least have to tell Damen and Soren about it, but even if I could put off the Council for a few days, the enormous teeth marks embedded high on Ophelia's neck would raise questions.

She could always cover it up with clothing, but I wasn't entirely confident I wouldn't shred anything she wore that hid my mark. Biting her hadn't *eased* the possessiveness, it had just redirected it. No, that wasn't quite right. The possessiveness did feel more manageable now. Maybe I'd be able to get through the day without wanting to claw someone's face off just because they glanced at my wife.

By the goddesses, I hoped this was more than just a monster-fucking fetish for Ophelia, because it was fast becoming everything to me.

For what seemed like hours, I tossed and turned uncomfortably in my sheets, feeling unsettled. With a growl, I threw the blankets back and sat up, annoyed that the night was so still and quiet when I felt so restless.

Felt so wrong. There was a sense of wrongness that wouldn't let up, and I needed to fix it right-fucking-now.

What was it?

I was the king, for fuck's sake. If I wasn't solving problems, what was the point of me? There was a restive feeling under my skin, and I realized with a sigh at my own idiocy that the agitation was likely just my need to siphon.

I'd barely spent any time *not* feeding from Ophelia this afternoon, no wonder I was fit to burst with unspent power. Satisfied that I had a plan and a resolution to my problem, I stood and cloaked myself, striding confidently out into the hallway before faltering in front of Ophelia's door.

The connection in my chest felt more settled at just this small improved distance. Perhaps sleeping in separate rooms would no longer work, though I'd probably terrify her if I stormed in now demanding changes. *Tomorrow.* I'd propose the idea of her moving into my larger, better furnished room. She could still keep hers as an area to draw and relax if she felt more comfortable there. Perhaps take up playing an instrument like she's suggested.

Another good plan, I reassured myself with a curt nod at Ophelia's door. The night guards bowed as I passed them, but I didn't stop to pause on my way to the siphoning chamber. I should have done this earlier—it felt almost criminal to be carrying around this much extra power. This would be weeks, perhaps months, of work in the human realm for our gatherers to accumulate this much to give to the community.

The rapidly filling stores, the gilded flowers, the golden orbs of light... Ophelia was a miracle for this realm.

Even if she wasn't, she was mine, and she was a miracle to me.

The corridors near my wing of the palace were empty, but the siphoning chamber wasn't. Three Shades who worked as gatherers were shedding the excess they'd collected on their feeding trips in the human realm.

"King Allerick!" one of them gasped, halting their siphoning abruptly to bow.

"Please, carry on," I insisted, gesturing at them to continue while selecting a pipe. "Pretend I'm not here."

They wouldn't. It hadn't taken me long as a child to realize that everyone modified their behavior when I was around, and it had only gotten more extreme when I ascended to the throne, despite my attempts to treat everyone equally. Only Soren and Damen treated me somewhat normally.

And Ophelia. She still censored herself around me sometimes, but not nearly as much as she had in the beginning. Her smiles were genuine now, and she wasn't afraid to tease me. It made my stomach feel... *fluttery* whenever she did.

I rolled my neck a few times as the excess energy hummed below my skin, eager for release. Noting that all the other Shades in the room had gone *very* quiet, I cupped my palms beneath the opening to the pipe and exhaled slowly, channeling the excess power through my body to collect in my hands. As was the case last time, the rush of energy that sped up the pipe to the ceiling was almost blinding in its intensity—a brilliant glowing white that I'd never seen in this chamber before.

There were quiet gasps behind me, but I ignored them to focus on releasing the buildup until my own power levels felt comfortably stable again. Well, far more than merely comfortable—Ophelia made me feel as though I was invincible.

"Incredible," someone whispered. *Roisin*, I thought vaguely. She was the youngest daughter of one of the wealthiest Shades at court, and had pursued a career as a gatherer against her family's wishes.

I turned to face the three of them, unsurprised to see them staring at the last of the glowing energy as it vanished into the store with stricken expressions on their faces.

"Queen Ophelia is a gift to our realm," I said, needing to say something to explain where this sudden abundance of power. "I have never fed on her fear. I would never jeopardize the treaty in any way."

"Long live Queen Ophelia," Roisin murmured, staring at the now quiet pipe. "Long live King Allerick. Our realm will prosper under your union."

That strange feeling started in my chest again, though it wasn't quite the same as the one Ophelia inspired.

This one might have been hope.

Tomorrow, I'd instruct the Council to plan Ophelia's coronation.

OPHELIA

CHAPTER 18

"Queen Ophelia!"

I mumbled something incoherent into the pillow, rolling away from whoever was trying to talk to me when I was so exhausted that my eyeballs felt like they were coated in sandpaper.

"Queen Ophelia, you must wake up, it's important."

Affra. Affra was talking to me. And it was important.

I forced my scratchy eyelids open, coming face to face with absolutely nothing, because the other side of my bed was empty. The sheets felt disgusting with the dried evidence of what we'd been up to yesterday coating both the linen and my skin, and by the way I'd cocooned myself in the entire blanket, it didn't look like I'd shared sleeping space with a certain bitey husband last night.

That hurt more than it probably should.

The mark on my neck tingled, and I brushed my fingers over it as I pushed myself upright.

"Sorry, I'm up, I'm up," I assured Affra, twisting to face her and blinking some of the bleariness out of my eyes. "What is it?"

Affra reached out, pushing my tangled mass of hair away from my face and giving me a sad smile that seemed distinctly maternal. "The treaty has been broken. Representatives from the Hunters Council are here, waiting in the courtyard."

"Does Allerick know?" I gasped, half falling out of bed, not caring that I was very much naked. Okay, maybe caring a little. I darted to the bathroom and out of Affra's sight as quickly as I could.

"He's already there," Affra replied through the door as I freshened up. I paused with the cold damp washcloth pressed against my stomach, attempting to wipe some of the combination of fluids off my skin.

He's already there?

It *stung*. It shouldn't—I wasn't a crowned queen, and I had no official role here—yet I'd never felt more like the king's designated bed buddy than I did at that moment, standing alone in the cold bathroom, wiping his cum off me after he'd fucked me into a stupor before disappearing.

Is that how he thought of me?

My throat felt tight as I quickly washed myself down as best as I could and splashed cold water on my face, hoping it would make me look presentable, but mostly to shake me out of the funk I was in. I'd rather have taken some time to put on makeup like a coat of armor, but I made do with a swipe of lipstick to at least make me somewhat put together.

Affra handed me a stack of clothes through the door, and I pulled on my underwear and a black knee-length dress that wouldn't look out of place at a funeral, but it did seem very Queen of Shades-y.

Even if it felt like that title wasn't really mine. The bite mark on my neck felt as raw and tender as my emotional state, and the ache between my thighs suddenly felt somehow accusatory, like that ache between my thighs and the territorial mark was all I was. The king's *whore*. An interesting plaything. Not a queen. Not a beloved wife. Just a bargaining chip who got horny for monsters.

You're just being insecure. You're feeling a little sensitive after an emotionally draining few days.

It's not a big deal.

That feeling in my chest that connected me to Allerick—the *bond*, or whatever it was—felt stretched tight. I hadn't really had a chance to examine how it felt or what it meant yesterday in between all the orgasms, but there was a sense of strain to it now. Did it mean something? Was I somehow picking up on Allerick's emotions, or was it a reflection of my own stress? Maybe it was distance-related because it didn't matter that he'd walked out on me, I was eager to get back to his side.

Ugh, you are embarrassing, I scolded internally, blinking back a sudden rush of tears before they could fall.

"Levana is here to escort you," Affra said quietly as I emerged from the bathroom, her eyes trained on the mark on my neck, which I doubted even a turtleneck would fully cover, let alone this scoop-necked dress.

"Thank you," I replied hurriedly, stumbling over my feet in my rush to get my shoes on. Had Damen had a chance to give her the book yet? She didn't look particularly shocked by the bite mark.

"Queen Ophelia," Affra called softly as my hand rested on the door handle. "Don't rush. You are the queen. *They* wait for *you*."

"Tell that to the king," I sighed, pulling open the door and stepping out into the hallway. Levana inclined her head, her body rigid with tension. "What do you know?" I asked her, already heading down the hallway.

"Not much, I came here to get you. Just that three representatives from the Hunters Council arrived and claimed that the treaty had been violated last night by a Shade feeding in an unapproved area. They wouldn't say anything else until you arrived."

"They wouldn't?" I asked in surprise. That was kind of nice. Like they saw me as someone whose opinion mattered.

"They want to ensure you're hale and hearty, and not able to be imprisoned or punished for the break in the treaty before they, well, you know," Levana finished, sounding grim.

I didn't know, but I nodded like I did know.

"Surely one feeding in an unapproved area isn't a big enough transgression to throw the treaty away, right?" I asked, power walking through the halls.

I felt Levana's hesitation before she answered. "It could be."

Shit.

Why would a *Shade* break the treaty? I knew there'd been some dissent about it, but it was pretty much all benefits on this end as Allerick had been trying to make clear. Their *lives* were on the line.

I was all but panting for breath when I reached the entrance hall, and my face was probably as red as a tomato, but I didn't want to waste any more time screwing around.

"Queen Ophelia," Damen said, waiting by the front door. "By the goddesses, sister, you look terrible."

"Thanks," I deadpanned, cutting him a glare, even though I melted a little internally at the term of endearment. I'd always wanted a brother, even though I'd always imagined one as basically Astrid but with shorter hair and greater parental approval by virtue of being born with a dick.

"You need to get out there before everyone loses their shit. Hold on. I'll make you look more regal. Maybe cover up the bite while we're at it, so the Hunters don't panic."

Before I could ask him what the hell that entailed, a thin layer of shadows descended over my sweating face. "Did you just make me a veil?"

"I'll remove it whenever you want, but it gives you an air of mystery," Damen replied with a satisfied nod, already pulling the door to the courtyard open.

I had to admit, I did feel more put together and mysterious as I glided down the wide front steps with my shadow veil covering up how red and out of breath I was. I vaguely recognized the three representatives from the Hunters Council, but I couldn't recall their names. They were clearly uncomfortable as hell being in the shadow realm surrounded by Shades in their true forms, that much was obvious.

If this is how Allerick would have looked the first time I'd met him, I'd have probably been terrified too. He was practically vibrating with rage, the elaborate crown making him seem even taller and more imposing than he already was.

"There you are, Ophelia," one of the Councilors said. "Now we can begin."

"*Queen* Ophelia," Allerick snarled, making the Hunter blanch.

"Thank you for waiting for me," I said in my most dignified voice, coming to a halt next to my husband. Movement out of the corner of my eye caught my attention, and I glanced down to see the bottom of a... shadow cape? I frowned at Damen through the veil, only to find his gaze trained on Allerick, a smile playing around his mouth.

"They wouldn't speak until you were here," Allerick growled. Right. He hadn't waited for me, hadn't even *told* me what happened. As always, the things that shouldn't have surprised or disappointed me did both.

"Last night, the treaty was violated when a Shade fed on a human in an unapproved location," another Councilor said.

"It's a new system, I'm sure it was an innocent mistake," I said gently. Perhaps I was overstepping, perhaps I had no idea what I was doing, but Allerick definitely looked like he was going to *escalate* rather than *deescalate*, and that wouldn't benefit anyone.

"Unfortunately that is very unlikely to be the case, *Queen* Ophelia, given that the feeding happened not twenty feet away from the Council headquarters. This was a message."

"What time did this occur?" Allerick asked in a low voice, shadows rising off him like steam. He looked like he'd ascended from the bowels of Hades and was ready to drag everyone back there with him.

"Just past eleven pm," the one who had been silent so far replied, his voice quivering. Judging by the wrinkled noses of the Shades around us, at least one of the Hunters was emitting some serious fear pheromones.

"Fine. We will investigate on our end who was in the human realm at that time and narrow it down from there. Whoever it was will face the harshest punishment possible. Both sides will reaffirm to their people the importance and value of the treaty, and the Shade who violated it will be made an example of."

Allerick's solution sounded entirely reasonable to me—well, depending on what that harsh punishment entailed—but all three Councilors shook their heads.

"The treaty is null and void," the first one said. "As per the terms, 'Shades will not feed in unapproved zones.' The three-mile radius around every Hunters Council building around the world is an unapproved zone, a fact that is explicitly stated in the treaty."

"So that's it? You're just going to go back to *killing* them because of one erroneous feeding?" I asked in disbelief.

"The terms of the treaty were clear. Our hands are tied."

"That is a copout," I spat. "Most of the power brokers are standing right here. If you wanted to make it work, you could."

Damen made a noise of approval behind me, but I barely registered it. Not when Allerick turned to look at me with the most unreadable expression I'd ever seen on his face. He looked at me like he'd never even seen me before, and it was incredibly unsettling.

Where did we stand? Did he regret the bite, and that's why he left as soon as I was asleep? Had he not bothered to tell me about the treaty being broken because he didn't think I needed to know, or had he just not *cared* enough to tell me?

"I will go and see who was in the human realm at the time of the feeding. Whether or not the treaty is in place now, it was in place *then*, and I will not let that transgression slide," Allerick told the Councilors coolly.

He turned to face me, that inscrutable look still on his face. "I will leave you to proceed as you see fit, Queen Ophelia."

Proceed with what as I saw fit?

With a final scathing look at the Hunters, Allerick left, striding purposefully back towards the palace, Soren hot on his heels.

I turned to Damen, who was hovering nervously like he wasn't sure whether to stay or go. Levana was still sticking close by, practically vibrating with tension.

"Unveil me," I whispered to Damen, giving him a watery smile. "You should go with him."

The veil of shadows slipped away as Damen retreated, the concern he was feeling written all over his face, leaving me alone with the three Councilors and Levana. There were other Shades nearby—members of their Council as well as guards—but all seemed to be giving us a wide berth.

The shadows around my ankles didn't disappear, and I realized with a start that Damen must not have created them. Was the cape from Allerick?

One of the Hunters gasped as I turned back to face them, their horrified gaze trained on my neck. "What has he done to you? He has *mauled* you."

"No, that's not what happened at all—" I began, my face heating as I raised my fingers immediately to the bite.

"You weren't supposed to come to any harm here. Even without the unauthorized feeding, the treaty is broken. Congratulations, Miss Bishop. You can come home now."

I opened my mouth, then closed it again. Home? I was already home.

"Come, Ophelia, let's get out of this hell hole. Your parents will be eager to see you," another one said, no room for argument in their tone.

I highly doubted that. I looked at Levana for backup, but the hopelessness in her eyes made my stomach drop. Was this really it? Is this what Allerick had meant by 'proceed as I saw fit'? He wanted me to leave however I liked?

There was no hatred or mistrust in her expression, but already I could see the Shade guards around the courtyard shifting uneasily, unsure whether they were meant to come to my defense or not.

As I looked around, I made eye contact with the guard positioned behind the Hunters, closest to the obsidian portal. There was no uncertainty in his eyes, no indecision. He had the same look of hatred that Meridia had when she looked at me, and his claws flexed menacingly at his sides as though he was envisioning what it would feel like to rake them clean through my flesh.

I didn't need confirmation from Levana or anyone else that I was stinking up the courtyard with my fear. Was this what a future here in the shadow realm would look like for me now? Without the treaty's protection, without Allerick's protection, I was a walking target for that small but vocal group of Shades who'd never wanted the truce in the first place. A symbol of hope turned into a symbol of abject failure.

A reminder of everything that could have been but wasn't. Even the Shades who'd come to like me would eventually resent me for that.

"The wound looks fresh," one of the Hunters was muttering to another. "Perhaps with immediate medical attention, we could mitigate the scarring before her mother sees it."

I should have kept the veil on, though while it had hidden what I was feeling, I didn't *want* to hide.

This was me. Ophelia Bishop, failed Hunter and former Queen of Shades. Seemingly abandoned by my husband, to make my way out of his palace however I pleased because the treaty was over and he had no use for me anymore. It wasn't much, but that was me.

The three members of the Hunters Council were standing there, staring at me expectantly, to say something, to go with them—probably with a grateful smile on my face, full of stories about how awful my time had been here.

I didn't feel grateful.

I felt like there was an icepick pressing into my chest and yanking downwards, slicing me from heart to gut. Everything was raw and exposed and it *hurt*.

It hurt to think I'd been wrong. I'd naively assumed—*hoped*— that the feelings I'd developed for Allerick had been reciprocated, but he'd never given me any indication of that, had he? He was possessive over me, fiercely attracted to me, but that wasn't *love*, and I'd been stupid to mistake one for the other.

I'd put us both in an awkward position by staying. Either he'd be forced to get rid of me later, or he'd need to expend time and energy keeping me safe from those who wished me harm because he was an honorable Shade and it was the right thing to do.

"Well, I just need to get my things I suppose," I said hoarsely, forcing the words out of my mouth. *Rip the bandaid off. It'll hurt less if you just get it over and done with now.*

"We'll accompany you—"

"No, thank you," I interrupted, uncomfortable with the idea of leading a delegation of Hunters into my home. My *former* home. "I'll be perfectly safe. You can wait here for me, or return through the portal and I'll follow alone."

"Are you sure it's safe? The treaty isn't in place to protect you any longer."

"Queen Ophelia will always be safe within these walls," Levana said in a hard voice, sidling up next to me. "She is my queen, and my friend. I will keep her safe with my *life*."

The vehemence in her voice combined with the undeniable aggressiveness in her posture made them reel back, and my throat tightened painfully as I held back the tears.

Now I was feeling grateful.

"Let's go," I told her, resting my hand on her forearm. "I'll be quick."

Levana stuck close to my side as we made our way back to the palace, her posture stiff and defensive. Ready to attack her *own* people to protect me.

Fortunately, she didn't have to. We passed Verner and Andrus standing guard in the corridor as usual, and while they looked unsure, they didn't make any move to stop us from passing.

The glare Levana shot them may have helped with that.

"I always knew we'd be friends someday," I told her quietly, willing the tears not to come, knowing she'd smell them if they did. "And I'm going to miss you so much."

"Then *stay*," Levana said somberly. "Fuck the treaty. Your home is here. We don't want you to go."

"Allerick—"

"I'll defend you from anyone, even your husband's stupidity," she muttered, making me bark out a startled laugh.

"Isn't that like... treason, or something? Are you allowed to say that?" I asked, opening the door to my bedroom for the last time, selfishly grateful Affra wasn't here so I didn't have to say another painful goodbye.

"It's probably treason," Levana conceded. "But since you're abandoning us, who's going to tell? King Allerick is a fair and good ruler. It's a shame he's too distracted by your pretty face to realize what a fair and good ruler you'd be too."

I snorted, though it sounded more like a hiccup with the tears I was trying to repress, and dragged my suitcase over from where it had been sitting empty against the wall, throwing it open on the bed and pulling clothes out of the drawers.

Angling myself between Levana and the dresser, I carefully pulled open the top drawer, staring down at my folder of drawings and case of supplies.

236

I was almost tempted to leave them here—this is where they belonged, and the way I'd drawn Allerick would be agony to look at in the future. He was so unapologetically untamed, and that was the thing that had always pulled my romantic tastes in a more monstrous direction. I wanted to feel wild and untamed too. I wanted to let go of my inhibitions and fuck and fight and feast, and let my baser instincts reign instead of being polite and quiet and agreeable.

But life hadn't worked out that way. Not in the long term.

I carefully gathered up the pictures, leaving one as a goodbye gift to my husband, and placing the rest of them with my supplies gently in the case before moving to the vanity to empty that too.

My fingers stilled over the enormous raven hair pin that Damen had given me on my first day here. It had been a gift for the queen, and perhaps I was selfish to pick it up and put it in my bag anyway, but I wanted something to keep. A memory from the best time in my life.

If only I had a wedding ring, I thought wryly. It'd be more discreet than an enormous pinned raven on the back of my head.

"Wear it," Levana said quietly, as I tried to sneakily wrap it in my silk robe, feeling a little like I was stealing even though it had been a gift.

"What?" I asked, my voice unnaturally loud.

"You should wear the hair pin, not pack it. It's silver."

I gaped at Levana. "Damen gave me a *weapon*? That's a bold move. What if I'd used it on his brother?"

"Well you didn't even realize what it was, so apparently that was never a risk," Levana pointed out drily. "I don't know why he gave you a Shade-killing weapon, but I'm glad he did now. You're going to be unprotected back in the human realm."

"Shades are less dangerous to me there," I sighed, hating the reminder that even if I *did* see Allerick again, it'd be a incorporeal floating version of him that couldn't speak. I *hoped* he didn't visit. It'd be like seeing a ghost.

"All the same," Levana muttered. "Wear the pin."

"It's a pinned raven," I pointed out, carefully sliding the heavy raven into one pocket of my dress and the pointed silver pin in the other, grateful for the thick fabric of the dress that mostly hid the weird lumps. "I can't waltz back into the Hunters Council HQ wearing a pinned raven on my head."

Levana made a grumbling sound of disagreement as I chucked the last few things into the suitcase and zipped it up, wincing at the sound. It was so loud and so unnatural in this cool stone room. So *final*.

I'd left all the stuff I'd taken from Astrid's and the duffel bag I brought it in. On the off-chance the Hunters wanted to search my things, they'd have questions about when I'd acquired the other stuff since I hadn't traveled back via their portal like I was supposed to.

Was that a violation of the treaty? Had I violated it first?

I decided to leave the duffel bag where it was—a bit of irritation from Allerick at having to dispose of it was better than putting Astrid at risk with the Hunters. Maybe one day my leggings and oversized sweaters would become relics here like the necklace Orabelle had. Weirdly, that thought gave me comfort. Like a piece of me would remain in this realm I'd come to think of as home, even after I was gone.

Levana materialized at my side before I could attempt to drag the heavy case off the bed, carefully taking the handle without snagging her claws on the fabric. I knew her well enough now to know that she'd said her piece and she wasn't going to try to convince me to change my mind, even as the disapproval fairly radiated off her.

"Calix is going to be furious," she said under her breath as we made our way down the corridors. I waved an awkward goodbye at Verner and Andrus, who gave me what I could have sworn was a sympathetic look in return.

"He'll probably be relieved to have his kitchen back."

Levana snorted. Not that she'd ever been super deferential when I was all officially the queen, but she'd absolutely dropped the facade now. "Absolutely not. He likes almost no one and respects even fewer. But he likes and respects you, and he'd been telling everyone who'd listen how good you were going to be for the shadow realm."

Don't cry, don't cry, don't cry.

"And don't even get me started on Orabelle. The king may need to avoid his mother for the foreseeable future—"

We turned a corner and both stopped suddenly at the sight that awaited us in the entry hall.

Shades.

The palace staff lined the walls, standing in silence with their heads bowed. Bowed in *respect*. For me. This time, I couldn't push back the tears that sprung forward, running silently down my cheeks as I forced myself to put one foot in front of the other.

Levana's steps dragged at my side like she wanted to prolong this moment, probably hoping that the silent support of so many would change my mind. I wasn't a crowned queen though, and without a treaty in place to force Allerick to be tied to me, this had only been a matter of time anyway. I'd rather leave with some of my dignity intact than be forced to sit through a politely uncomfortable talk with my husband about how he didn't want me anymore.

The shame would kill me.

He'd told me that even if he hadn't been attracted to me, he would have respected our marriage to make the treaty work. There was no treaty now. He'd never said anything about respecting our marriage *without* that incentive.

The three Councilors relaxed slightly as I reappeared in the courtyard, awkwardly looking away when they spotted my tears.

"Queen Ophelia," a soft voice said from behind me. I scrunched my eyes shut, knowing I would see the pain in her eyes if I turned around and not wanting to. Not wanting to say goodbye to the Shade who'd been like a grandmother to me from the moment I arrived.

"Affra," I sobbed, turning to face her. "I'm so sorry."

"For running away without saying goodbye? You should be, my dear. But that's not what I wanted to tell you. I translated part of the book." My breath hitched. "You belong here. This was once a world of light and color, but the Hunters—the *Hunted*—left and took it with them. You are one of them. You are *claimed*. You belong here with your mate."

That certainly sounded like me—I'd always wanted to be hunted. I'd relished the feel of Allerick's possessive gaze on me, stalking me through the garden, his teeth sinking into my throat...

"It doesn't matter, it's too late for that now," I whispered for Affra's ears only. "There's no treaty between our kinds now, and... and he doesn't want me. Not the way I want him."

Not the way I loved him.

Affra reached out, carefully keeping her claws free as she swiped a stray tear off my cheek. "I disagree, but I'm sure we'll see which one of us is right soon enough. A Shade broke this treaty on purpose. Make sure you wear that hair pin, my queen."

I gave her a watery smile, reaching up to give her wrist a quick squeeze before turning away and heading for the portal, snagging my suitcase from a frowning Levana on the way. She nodded gravely, and I nodded back, recognizing that she wasn't a hugger and especially not with so many guards watching on.

The tears wouldn't stop coming, but I held my head high, refusing to be cowed. The time I'd spent here was the best of my life. I'd felt a sense of belonging, of friendship, of *home* for the first time in my life. I'd fallen in love. I'd also had my heart ripped clean out of my chest, and while I wished I hadn't, at least I felt something because I knew that a life in the human realm would be an endless horizon of nothingness.

Goodbye, King Allerick.

ALLERICK

CHAPTER 19

I moved faster than I ever had in my life through the spiraling corridors, down, down down to the securest area below the courtyard that only a select few approved Shades could reach.

My shadows reached for the obsidian lock, pressing into the stone to demand entry, and the heavy door swung open with a quiet click.

Regret was weighing heavily on me. There had been protests and displays of discontent with the treaty for weeks—I'd been leaving the palace to deal with them most days. Diplomatically, as the Council and I had agreed. I'd treated my subjects like the intelligent, reasonable beings I believed they were and explained the advantages that a peace treaty brought us, and for the most part it had worked. Yes, Shades still chafed at the restrictions, at the concept of Hunters knowing where we were feeding and when, but they understood that the safety and security it brought us, especially the most vulnerable among us, were worth the limitations.

Perhaps I'd been too focused on getting back to the palace to meet Ophelia for lunch each day. I should have come down harder on the dissenters, made more of an effort to find out who was feeding them these paranoid worst-case scenarios to rile them up and made an example out of them instead.

Marriage had made me soft.

"Who would do this?" I muttered, mostly to myself. "It's so reckless. What is there to gain other than causing chaos?"

"Maybe the chaos is the point," the youngest Councilor, Teague, murmured as he joined me in the small room. Soren positioned himself as close to me as possible, knowing that I needed extra protection to make myself vulnerable in this way.

Above us were five obsidian stones embedded in the stone ceiling—one in the center, and four surrounding. They were sister stones to each of the five portals, and the most-frequently used and largest palace portal was in the center.

I could sift through the signatures left by the blood required to use the portal and narrow it down based on timing, though it was an imprecise science and I didn't have every Shade's signature memorized. If it was someone unfamiliar to me, I'd need to go hunt them down.

"Allerick," Damen said, his voice unusually serious as he weaved through the old Councilors huddled in the corner of the room. "I don't think you should be here."

"I'm the only one who can do this."

This power to identify each Shade in the realm belonged to the monarch alone. It was lucky that I'd put the crown on before leaving my rooms, as I needed the blooded obsidian that marked me as ruler for the connection to work.

"I know, I know, but I'm worried about Ophelia," Damen replied.

"Levana is with her, as are plenty of other guards." I frowned, wondering if all the guards stationed around the courtyard were enough for three Hunters. In the human realm, we were defenseless, but here we had the advantage by a long shot. "I would have never left her alone if I thought she was at risk."

"What? I don't think they're going to *hurt* her. I think they're going to convince her to leave."

I scoffed, turning my attention away from him to focus on the threads of magical signatures and converting time zones in my head. "Ophelia wouldn't leave, this is her home. I left her in charge of the Councilors. I expect they'll want to hang around until we can provide some answers."

"You *hope* that," Damen corrected quietly. He was right, I did hope that. I hoped that the Hunters would not be so unforgiving as to throw the entire treaty out over one infraction. If I could figure out who was responsible for this and make an example of punishing them, surely that would be enough to undo the damage?

I had to believe it was. I had to believe that all the work we'd done in securing this arrangement to keep my kind safe wasn't for nothing.

With a long exhale to try clear my head, I closed my eyes and raised my arms, drawing the faint traces of shadow signatures into me, portal by portal. Immediately, I narrowed it down to those who were in the human realm at the time, which still gave me twenty or so options.

Some I recognized. Scouts who worked for me, a couple of members of the court. I rattled off their names, listening as Teague scratched them down on paper. They were options and we'd be foolish to rule them out, and yet...

"What aren't you saying?" Damen asked quietly, always more astute at reading me than anyone else.

"Meridia was in the human realm at that time," I sighed, hating the way Soren tensed beside me. For all her many flaws, Soren loved his sister and had always tried to save her from her worst impulses.

"It was probably an accident," Soren muttered. "It had to be an accident. Maybe she'd gone too long between feedings and lost control in an area she shouldn't have."

It was a bullshit explanation and we both knew it, but it hadn't escaped my attention that his immediate reaction was to assume she was guilty. Had

things with her been more serious than I'd initially realized? I knew she didn't like Ophelia, but I'd stupidly attributed that to jealousy.

"Go find her and we'll see," Damen ordered Soren, stepping up in a way he rarely did.

I felt Soren depart, but stayed focused on my task as Damen took his spot, guarding my back while I was vulnerable, memorizing the signatures I was unfamiliar with so I could track them down.

"We all know it was Meridia," Damen said gently. "We shouldn't waste time here trying to find a tentative alternative because we *hope* for Soren's sake that it wasn't her."

I ignored him to continue what I was doing, devoting my attention entirely to my task. While it seemed likely that it was in fact Meridia at fault, I wanted to be confident that I'd done my research so I could find the others if I needed to.

The moment I had them in my mind, I released the shadows back to the portals above me, blinking my eyes against the light. Damen was already staring intently at me with an unsettling degree of intensity.

"You're acting strange," I told him honestly.

"You always tell me to be more involved. I'm being involved," Damen replied as though it was obvious. "Besides, you need me here to handle things so you can be with Ophelia."

"I will meet Ophelia for lunch as I always do, possibly with the representatives from the Hunters Council if she's kept them here. Perhaps I'll invite them to her coronation to try and get the treaty back on stable ground. Come, let's see if we can catch up with Soren, so we can provide the Hunters with a suitable resolution."

"Her coronation? I think you're being too optimistic. This was a declaration of war, Allerick," Damen said, his voice unusually solemn. "You and the Councilors have tried to reason with the idiots who refuse to understand what we stood to gain from the treaty, but this act was a direct rebellion against your rule. I know as well as you do that it's hard to come down strongly on Meridia, we watched her grow up and she's Soren's sister, but this cannot stand."

I wasn't accustomed to taking advice from Damen—he was within his rights to give it, he just never did. And he wasn't wrong. The Shade who'd tried to poison Ophelia had been thrown in the Pit, but all the other rebels and dissenters had walked free, partly to keep relations between them and us stable. I looked to the Councilors who were huddled in the corner, watching us carefully.

"*If* Meridia was responsible, then I intend to banish her to the Pit," I announced, watching their reactions. The Pit was a hole filled with perpetual brightness that no one could shadow walk out of. It was our worst prison, and only used for the worst of infractions. "In breaking the treaty, every Shade has been put at risk. It is a heavy crime worth of a heavy punishment. Speak freely, Councilors."

Raina stepped forward, looking a decade older than she had the last time I'd seen her. "None of us relish the idea of punishing our own, especially when it may look like we're valuing the truce with the Hunters more than our own people..."

"We are," I said bluntly. "But it is *for* our own people that we value the truce."

"Indeed," Maddox said solemnly. "You have our support, King Allerick."

"Good. Let's find Soren and get this over with."

Damen and I followed a series of messages from various guards until we found ourselves materializing in the dark entry room on the outskirts of Soren and Meridia's mother's country home. They held a family seat in this region, Illtal, but it wasn't the most prestigious of areas, and it looked like the house was rarely used judging by the crumbling state of the stone facade and the overgrown vegetation.

There had been unrest in this region about the treaty before. I should have known.

We made our way to the front garden and for a moment, there was no sound at all except for the rustling leaves and quiet chirping of birds, and I was beginning to think we'd been given the wrong information. Then glass shattered loudly from inside, and I knew with a heavy heart that we hadn't. That Meridia was inside with Soren, and it wasn't going well.

"Come on," I grumbled, rushing for the front door with Damen on my heels. I yanked it open, darting to the left as a glass vase flew at my head, narrowly avoiding Damen.

"Settle down, Meridia," I growled. The situation would be worse if Soren hadn't already partially restrained her with his shadows, but Meridia was strong and had almost shaken them off while throwing everything within reach at her brother. Fortunately, none of it appeared to be made of silver.

"I'm sorry," Soren panted. "She tried to run the moment I got here."

"Not exactly the actions of an innocent Shade," I said mildly, my own shadows creeping along the floor too fast for Meridia to register, winding around her ankles to keep her in place before wrapping around her middle, pinning her arms at her sides. The candelabra she'd just swiped fell from her grasp, hitting the floor with a thud.

"I am innocent!" she hissed, writhing to get free of my binds before frowning down at them in confusion. She hadn't expected me to be able to restrain her so easily, that much was obvious, but I was at full strength after feeding on my wife's lust and I felt fucking *invincible*.

Even if I hadn't fed, I felt like nothing could have stopped me at this moment. Meridia was a threat to my people, a threat to my *wife*, and I couldn't let that stand.

"The truth this time," I commanded, a length of my shadows solidifying as it wrapped around her neck. It wasn't tight enough to do any damage, but served as a reminder of what I *could* do, if I wanted to.

"Don't threaten me with a good time, your majesty," Meridia purred, switching tact immediately and pasting a disturbingly sultry look on her face.

"For fuck's sake, Meridia, enough," Soren spat. "Have you not humiliated yourself enough?"

"You are the humiliating one here," she shot back, glaring at her brother. "You could have been anything, anyone, and you chose to be the king's lap dog. You are an embarrassment to our entire family line."

"Yes, I'm sure the entire family will be embarrassed of *Soren* when you are rotting in the Pit," Damen snorted. Soren's jaw tightened slightly, but I could see the resignation in his gaze.

"Did you feed on a human directly outside the Hunters Council building, yes or no?" I asked impatiently, flexing the length of shadow rope around her neck.

Meridia tilted her chin up stubbornly. "Yes."

"Why?" all three of us pressed.

"They suggested it. They also informed me that they weren't going to say anything to you for another twenty-four hours, the fucking traitors," she muttered, like she was the leader who'd been betrayed here.

"You're working with them," I said flatly, a hollow sensation forming in my chest. Had the Hunters been toying with me all along? Had the treaty been a ruse right from the beginning?

"Some of them. Some of the Hunters are visionaries like me. I don't care if you throw me in the Pit. In fact, you should. See how long it takes for my supporters to come and get me out. I'll reward the one who successfully does it richly when *I* am queen. With the help of the Hunters, the rebellion against your rule has already begun." She looked awfully smug for someone who was bound and outnumbered.

I made a show of looking around the room. "Where are those supporters now? Hiding amongst the broken glass on the floor?"

Meridia's gaze darkened. "They will come for me."

247

"Perhaps," I acknowledged. "They'll find themselves in there with you when they do. Let's go, I have work to do. You may have ruined everything, but I'm going to fix it. I will not let this treaty fall apart because of you."

Meridia had said *some* Hunters, not *all*. Maybe there was still a chance we could make this work.

"A treaty makes us look *weak*," Meridia spat, fighting fruitlessly against the bonds holding her in place. "You should have married *me*. We could have been *great* together."

I snorted. "You'd have killed me in my sleep the first opportunity you got, you power-hungry psychopath."

I flicked out another whip to wrap around her mouth before she could respond. I didn't need to listen to any more of her poison before dragging her out behind me to the dark entry room outside the property, Soren and Damen flanking me. While there would undoubtedly need to be a trial, I just wanted her secured in the Pit for the meantime until the Council and I could discuss her fate, then I wanted to get back to my wife.

What was Ophelia thinking right now? Had I left her with the very Hunters who'd been working with Meridia?

Surely not. They hadn't followed the timeline Meridia had agreed with them on, that probably meant they weren't her co-conspirators.

Regardless, seeing those Hunters here, in our domain, had rattled Ophelia, though she didn't like me to know when she was upset about something. I was confident she'd be talking to the Hunters representatives now, calming the situation as she had a knack for doing, and hopefully making them more amenable to overlooking this infraction and dealing with their own dissenters. After they'd gone, I'd ask Affra to draw her a relaxing bath. Forcing down the rage that had been dominating my mind since the Hunters had shown up, I searched for the tether that connected me to Ophelia.

Strange.

Where was she? The tether between us felt strained. Unnaturally so. I'd traveled further than usual today to track Meridia down, that was probably it. Maybe this connection between us didn't like for us to be so physically apart. *I* didn't like it.

The next time I traveled in my lands, I would be taking my wife with me. Ideally with a crown on her head and a baby in her belly. That visual had my heart flopping strangely sideways in my chest.

"How did she even communicate with them?" Damen muttered to himself as we shadow walked.

"Like this, I imagine," I replied grimly. "My guess is a one-sided conversation happened in the human realm and then she walked the Hunters into the in-between so she could engage. There would be no record of that in the portals."

I dragged Meridia through the darkness, emerging at the entry room a few hundred feet away from the Pit. It was the one spot of darkness that allowed us to transport to and from the prison, but aside from that it was a blinding beacon of light that could be seen for miles.

Meridia winced at the overwhelming light while I hid my own discomfort, marching her along the brightly lit path that led to the circular pit with crisscross silver bars over the top to stop anyone climbing out, though the guards who patrolled the outer ring would catch them if they did.

"Your majesty!" one of them said in alarm, stumbling over themselves in their rush to get to me, bowing as they went.

"This traitor needs to be securely held until a public trial can be organized." A public trial that was very much a formality, because I was not letting this traitorous cowardly excuse for a Shade out in my realm ever again. "She has already claimed that she is expecting outside assistance to free her, I want your most diligent Shades watching her at all times."

"Of course, your majesty," the guard agreed, taking the binds that I severed from myself and gifted to him to control.

"Let me escort her," Soren said hoarsely, stepping out from behind me, his hard gaze trained on his sister.

"I want to make sure that she gets to the cell myself," I growled. I didn't *think* Soren had any lingering compassion for his sister after the stunt she pulled, but I wasn't about to take any unnecessary risks.

"You may need to rethink that idea," Damen remarked mildly. I turned to see what he was talking about and finding Levana jogging down the pathway from the entry room, her gaze trained at the floor.

"Where is Ophelia?" I asked sharply.

"I'm sorry, your majesty. She left with the Hunters," Levana replied quietly.

The ground dropped out from underneath me, my breath seizing in my lungs. *No.* No, that wasn't possible. She wouldn't leave.

"*Why?*"

"The Hunters were very adamant that the treaty was void, and she wasn't sure if you'd want her to stay without it," Levana hedged, looking immensely uncomfortable with this conversation. I imagined there was more to it—Ophelia saw Levana as a friend and had probably spoken freely with her—but I was glad Levana appeared to be concerned for my wife's wellbeing first and foremost.

"King or not, brother or not," Damen said in a voice barely above a whisper, leaning in close to my ear. "You are a fucking idiot if you don't fight for her."

He clapped me hard on the shoulder, the disapproval clear on his face. Had Damen not told me to make more of an effort with Ophelia? That showing her kindness between the sheets wasn't enough?

I pulled myself out of his grip, striding towards the entry room and letting the shadows carry me back to the portal outside the palace without a second look behind me. Meridia was Damen and Soren's problem now.

There was no evidence of her or the Hunters who'd visited anywhere. The chaos of the morning had vanished like it had never been, just the regular guards standing stoically in place.

Gone. She was actually gone. My heart was tearing into two inside my chest, ripping brutally in different directions. My breath sawed out of me, louder and raspier than normal. Maybe I was dying. Maybe Ophelia had condemned me to death when she walked out of my life. She'd been my sunshine, and she'd taken it with her.

I deserved it. Damen was right. I should have done more. Should have reassured her somehow, communicated with her in a way that didn't involve burying my cock inside her.

Unless she'd wanted to go. Maybe I really was just an experiment for her. An exercise in monster fucking that she'd wanted to get out of her system.

I walked through the palace in a daze, my feet taking me to her door automatically. Except it wasn't *her* door because she'd gone. Walked out of my life as though what we'd shared was nothing.

The door creaked as I pushed it open, stepping inside the lifeless space. It still smelled like Ophelia, like *us*, and I flexed my hands at my side, forcing myself not to go rip the bedding off and store it somewhere no one else would find.

Thank the goddesses Affra wasn't here to witness my rapid descent into madness.

I paced around the room, noting the bag she'd left behind before making myself look in the one drawer I *wanted* to look in but dreaded all at the same time.

Blowing out a breath, I slowly pulled open the top drawer of the dresser. There was no rattle of drawing supplies like there had been last time, but my heart jumped when I found one piece of paper in the middle of the drawer. Just one.

I lifted it carefully, holding it up to the light to make out what I was seeing. Ophelia's normal pictures showed two figures in the center surrounded by lots of white space, but not this one. She'd drawn to almost the very outer edges of the page, and it was darker than usual, so it took me a moment to realize that it was a close-up depiction rather than a full body one.

It was *us*. She'd drawn herself with her cheek resting against my chest, my chin atop her head. Our eyes were closed, but there was a small smile playing at her mouth, and my hand was gripping her upper arm possessively, claws snagging the material of her dress. She'd drawn us *cuddling*. Surely this meant I was more to her than just an assigned husband she was conveniently attracted to?

How could she possibly think I wouldn't want her here? The shadow realm was her home, her kingdom. She was my *everything*.

Why hadn't I just told her all of that before?

"Your majesty," Affra said quietly, standing in the doorway to Ophelia's room. I turned to face her, clutching the drawing close. "I translated the book. I have some news about you and your mate."

OPHELIA

CHAPTER 20

We stepped through the portal that landed outside the Hunters Council when the world was just waking up. I blinked rapidly at the sudden blinding gold light, squinting through the rays of sun to the dusky sky above streaked in pink. *Color.* There was so much color here.

And it was beautiful, it was. But the sky didn't swirl like smoke and the stillness of it seemed more like lifelessness after spending my days under the gray sky of the shadow realm. And the gold...

I would never be able to see the color again without thinking about the gold tipped flowers in the courtyard. The way the orbs had glowed a little warmer each day. I'd done that. The warmth had been me.

Maybe Allerick would want me back just for that alone, but I didn't like the idea of just being a lamp for the shadow realm, even though it had meant so much to me that I'd brought them *something*.

I glanced at the ground behind me, knowing my cape of shadows wouldn't have survived the in-between, but feeling bereft at the loss of it anyway. *At least I still have the bite mark.* That was something tangible, something I could look at and know that the whole experience had been real. That, and the faint tether in my chest. It was a little piece of Allerick I could always carry with me, and I selfishly hoped he was carrying a little of me with him too.

One of the Councilors—Ben? Bob? something like that—turned to speak to me, but the sound of Astrid calling my name as she exited the Council building drew all of our attention.

It wasn't unlike my sister to work overnight in her role at the Council, but Astrid looked like she hadn't slept in *days*. The dark circles beneath her eyes looked like bruises, and her complexion was pallid.

"There you are, Ophelia. Time to go." My sister grabbed my elbow none-too-gently, tugging me towards the parking lot.

"Astrid, wait—" Blake—or was it Bill?—started. "Ophelia needs to attend a debrief—"

"And she will, but not right now, Bradley." *Ah, that's it. Bradley.* "Right now, she needs to rest. I'm not hiding her, for god's sake. You know where my apartment is."

She didn't wait around for him to answer, all but dragging me to her Jeep and yanking my bag away to throw in the trunk.

"Get in," Astrid ordered quietly. "It was a setup. I don't know who to trust. We're getting the fuck out of here."

Mutely, I climbed into the passenger seat, fastening my seat belt with shaking hands. *A setup?*

Did that mean the Shade who'd fed here was *working with* a Hunter? Maybe multiple ones?

My stomach turned at the idea of them back in the shadow realm, at the risk they posed to the Shades there that I cared about. *Allerick is strong. Stronger than ever before from feeding on me. Whatever it is, he can handle it.*

"Are we going back to your apartment?" I asked as Astrid got in the front seat and immediately threw the car into drive, wasting no time getting on the road.

Astrid grimaced. "Yes. I'm buying us a little time, though it won't be much. If the Councilors *weren't* in on it, then running from them is a death sentence in itself. Fuck, I don't even know which way is up or who to trust anymore."

I'd never seen Astrid like this.

"Mom and Dad?"

"Out of town, but gleeful about the treaty being broken," Astrid replied, looking grim. "That doesn't necessarily mean they were involved, but I'm exercising caution."

No, it didn't necessarily mean that. Honestly, I was shocked that *Astrid* wasn't gleeful about it being broken, she'd never been a huge fan of it in the first place. Then again, her reservations had been more about its effectiveness and unfortunately, it seemed she was right to have doubted it since it had only taken weeks to fall apart.

"We're going to my apartment because your husband has been there before and will know where to find you," Astrid said in a softer voice. "I didn't tell anyone that they visited there."

"I don't want to see him," I replied stubbornly.

"Did he hurt you? I have a new silver dagger under my pillow that I've been saving for a rainy day," Astrid said, her eyes taking on that slightly unhinged look that always appeared when she was ready for the hunt.

"No, you psycho, don't *stab* him. He didn't hurt me. He was wonderful actually." The tether in my chest seemed to fray a little more, and I swallowed past the thick lump in my throat. "I love him."

Astrid blinked. Where I was all romanticism and daydreams, Astrid had always been hard edges and ambition. If she'd ever been in love before, I didn't know about it.

"Okay. Then you have to go back," she said eventually, like it was obvious.

"I love him, I don't know that he loves me. If that emotion even exists for him. When Bill—"

"Bradley."

"—whatever came to collect me, Allerick didn't exactly put up a fight. He was furious about the treaty being violated and immediately went to find the Shade who did it."

Astrid glanced at me out of the corner of her eye. "He's the king, Ophelia. He has subjects to rule and order to maintain. He can't just drop everything to coddle you all the time."

"I didn't want him to *coddle* me," I shot back indignantly.

"Sounds like you did." Astrid shrugged. "You're assuming he didn't care enough to ask you to stay, but maybe he cared so much that he just *assumed* you would stay, that he didn't *need* to ask you."

I chewed on my lower lip, second guessing my decision and more than a little panicky about it. Should I have stayed? Would Allerick be upset that I'd left? Would he assume it was because *I* didn't care? The thought made my stomach turn.

The drawing. I'd left him the drawing. He had to know how much I cared about him.

Even if he *did* want me to stay, I'd just be in the way while there was no treaty in place guaranteeing my safety.

"Look, Lia—" Astrid began, before cursing quietly as a gunmetal gray SUV pulled out in front of us, forcing Astrid to brake. "Fuck, fuck, fuck. That's a Council vehicle. *Shit!* Are they trying to kill us now?"

Our entire lives, Astrid had been the calm, decisive one while I'd been mostly content to wander along in her footsteps, lost in my daydreams of different worlds and interesting people. But Astrid was panicking, and maybe after faking the whole queen thing for a while, some of it had actually stuck because I wasn't. I wasn't going to hide behind my badass big sister and just hope for the best.

"Stick to your story," I breathed, trying to keep my mouth as still as possible as both cars came to a halt. "You're worried about what I've been through. You wanted to bring me back to your apartment to recover from my ordeal before the Council debrief. Be your usual moody self or they'll suspect something."

"I'm not moody." She looked genuinely affronted, like she wasn't the snarkiest person I'd ever met. "What are you going to do?"

"Cry, sniffle, maybe whimper a little, and ultimately go back to headquarters with them."

"*Ophelia*," Astrid hissed. A female Councilor had already exited the vehicle and was making her way over to us.

"They don't want me dead, they want information. I'd put money on it. I can learn more from the inside," I countered, my voice barely above a whisper. I encouraged all the tears I'd been holding in to fall, scrounging up my face so I looked as pathetic as possible. "You can't get stuck in there with me. You need to be at your apartment so Allerick or Soren can find you."

I wanted to say more, but the Councilors were already at the window, and Astrid plastered her signature scowl in place as she rolled it down.

I didn't know what I would have said anyway, what message I would have asked her to pass on to Allerick for me. There was nothing sufficient that I could relay in a secondhand message, not when the words I wanted to say had to come solely from me.

"You could have killed us," Astrid snapped, glaring at the Councilor. I recognized her now—Moriah. She'd been at the hearing where I'd been kicked out of the community. Her severe black bob was a little more silver nowadays, and the frown lines more pronounced, but those brown eyes were as calculating now as they were all those years ago.

"My apologies," Moriah said smoothly. "I confess, I was a little worried you wouldn't stop. That you were running away from us." She laughed, and it was the least genuine sound I'd ever heard.

"Ah yes, running away to my own apartment," Astrid replied drily, rolling her eyes. "A devious plan if ever there was one."

I hiccuped quietly as I made a show of rubbing my tears on my sleeve. Moriah crouched down to look at me through Astrid's window, her expression full of pity.

"Ophelia, you poor dear, I'm sure these past few weeks have been awful for you—you must be exhausted."

"She is," Astrid clipped. "Which is why I'm bringing her to my apartment."

"A kind sisterly gesture that I can certainly appreciate, but will need to refuse. Ophelia isn't just your sister any longer, Astrid. She is—or was—the Queen of the Shades. She has obligations that require her presence at Council headquarters."

I wanted to laugh at the contradiction, but it would have ruined my act. If I was Queen of the Shades, then why did I owe the Hunters Council a damn thing?

Astrid opened her mouth to argue, but I rested a hand on her forearm and leaned over to speak to Moriah. "It's fine, I understand. I don't want to cause any trouble."

"Of course you don't," Moriah cooed. I squeezed Astrid's arm lightly before she punched a Councilor in the face.

"Can my sister visit me?" I asked, adding an extra sniffle for dramatic effect.

"Absolutely. Perhaps tomorrow, when we've had time to do a proper debrief."

"And what am I meant to do until then?" Astrid asked.

"Go home?" Moriah suggested sweetly. "Contrary to whatever you may think, the Hunters are perfectly capable of functioning without you, Astrid."

"You sure about that? I took my first night off in weeks last night and the treaty was broken," Astrid replied sweetly, making Moriah scowl.

I unclipped my seat belt before Astrid could really hit her stride, smoothing my thick black dress down as I climbed out of the car, discreetly checking my hair pin weapon was still in my pocket, but leaving my suitcase in Astrid's car. I'd been so upset I hadn't even realized until now how weirdly out of place I looked being back here—Astrid was wearing ripped jeans, a black tank with an album cover on it, and a bomber jacket, and I looked like the poor man's Jackie O.

If you can't join 'em, beat 'em.

Or something like that.

I channeled my best queen-like energy, holding my head high and pushing my shoulders back as I walked purposefully towards the SUV that had nearly run us off the road. If Allerick was here...

If Allerick was here, he'd be able to smell how afraid I was. I was a marketing coordinator who'd got average grades at college and spent my free time lost in the fantasies I liked to commit to paper. I wasn't skilled in diplomacy, I would be no one's first choice of ambassador, and yet here I was.

Not that the Hunters wanted that from me.

No. They wanted a spy. A *rat*.

Did they really think I'd do that for them? I slid into the backseat of Moriah's car like she was my chauffeur rather than my jailer, and gave her a bland smile in the rearview mirror as I buckled myself in and folded my hands in my lap.

The Hunters had been happy to throw me aside until I was useful to them. If this position had never come up, they'd have never spoken to me again. I'd shown up in the shadow realm as the barely tolerated wife of the king, and I'd still found kindness among so many of the Shades, even when Allerick himself hadn't been so keen on me. Damen had been welcoming right from the beginning, even when he was suspicious of me. Levana had asked me questions, answered mine, and warmed up to me until we'd built a genuine friendship that had been painful to walk away from. Calix had never treated me like I was inferior to the Shades.

"You must be *so* relieved to be back," Moriah said emphatically, pulling the car back onto the road and heading back the way we came while I watched Astrid's vehicle grow smaller in the distance. "I can't even imagine how awful it's been for you."

I remembered the palace staff lining the walls to the entry hall, heads bowed in silence as I passed. Affra wiping away my tears outside the portal, telling me I belonged. And Allerick.

God, Allerick.

The way he was growly and rough and protective, even when he hadn't liked me very much. The way he'd fuck me like a toy whilst worshipping me like a queen, exactly the way I liked it. The way he'd held on to me so tightly even when he seemed confused about what that meant and how to process it.

The bite mark on my neck felt like it was tingling in response.

I glanced up, realizing that Moriah was waiting for a response, looking slightly nervous as though I might start sobbing hysterically all over the cream leather interior of her fancy car.

"The shadow realm was nothing like here, that's for sure."

Moriah showed me to a 'guest suite' inside the Council building that I'd never heard of before. A takeout bag from a local restaurant was sitting on the small table, and Moriah had suggested I eat and rest for a few hours while the various Councilors assembled. She'd also left a small bag of clean clothes, since the Council already had all my measurements from outfitting my 'queen' wardrobe.

I took a moment after she'd gone to walk around the room, examining my prison. And it *was* a prison. They could give it whatever fancy name they liked and fill it with more duck egg blue cushions and fluffy beige throws than a celebrity influencer's bedroom, but a locked door and no windows was a motherfucking prison in my books.

Worried that I was being watched, I decided to do as I was asked and play along for now. I took a seat at the small table and pulled out the cream cheese bagel and cinnamon donut holes they'd brought for me, savoring the sweetness after eating nothing but meat and vegetables for a while, but also finding it surprisingly sickly. *I wonder what Levana would think of these?*

Sufficiently fed, I shut myself in the bathroom and explored each nook and cranny of the small space for cameras, deciding it was probably safe. It wasn't the fanciest bathroom, but there was a tub with a curtain around it that looked pretty heavenly. Underneath my funeral garb outfit, I was still pretty thoroughly caked in monster cum, and while a perverse part of me wanted to keep it that way, I really wanted to feel clean.

Deciding I didn't want to be caught lounging in the bath if the Hunters showed up— and I sort of expected them to because this whole experience had been an experience in keeping me off-balance right from the beginning—I opted for a quick but thorough shower and pulled on a clean black dress before lying on the bed fully clothed for a power nap.

It didn't take them long. I'd been napping fitfully for about an hour when there was a knock on the door, and I jumped up as quickly as I could, smoothing out my dress and shoving my feet back into my flats.

"Come in," I called, doing my best to keep my voice even.

I wasn't surprised when it was Moriah who appeared, dressed now in a suit but retaining the same plastic smile as she had earlier. "Ophelia, I hope you've had a chance to relax. If you'd like to follow me, the Council will see you now."

Lovely.

"Unfortunately, your parents are on a cruise this week, making the most of their time off," Moriah said, doing her best version of a sympathetic smile. I wasn't the smartest person, but I thought I was pretty good at reading people for the most part—it was a side effect of being constantly underestimated. I wasn't picking up *malicious* intentions from Moriah, not necessarily. It felt more opportunistic than anything.

"I'm glad they're taking a vacation," I replied, figuring it was best to make polite small talk and seem as ignorant as possible. "Though of course I'm disappointed not to see them."

"I think they expected you to visit more often," Moriah said lightly. "When you didn't come back for so long, they ended up just taking the trip."

It took everything in me not to roll my eyes. For years, I'd seen my parents exclusively on holidays, and only when I couldn't feasibly find somewhere else to be and they felt too awkward to not invite me. Maybe the Hunters Council finally finding a role for me had given them some sense of pride in me again, but given what that role was, I highly doubted it.

Most of the Councilors ignored me as Moriah and I entered the room, and I quietly took the seat she indicated, across from her and between two portly men I only vaguely recognized. As a kid, I hadn't had much cause to spend time with the Councilors, and even when I was preparing to leave for the shadow realm, it had mostly been with just Astrid for assistance. In hindsight, she'd been quite aggressive about it, like she didn't trust anyone except herself to prepare me.

"Well," Bradley announced, clapping his hands. He hadn't seemed very impressive when Astrid was cutting him down earlier, but it appeared that he was the leader of sorts in this room. "Now that we're all here, let's begin. What an exciting night it was! Here we were, thinking it'd take *months* for them to break the treaty."

Everyone but me laughed, while I looked around in alarm.

"I'll admit, they made it easier than we thought they would," Moriah said with a girlish giggle. "We were fortunate to find a Shade so willing to make a play for power. And Ophelia! For those of you who don't know, this is Ophelia Bishop. She was our sweet, willing huntress bride, responsible for meeting one of their more barbaric demands in the treaty."

"You must have suffered greatly," Bradley said, giving me a grave, pitying look.

Gross.

I had a lot of follow up questions about the 'play for power' comment, but I had a feeling they were only speaking so freely in front of me because they believed I was Team Hunter. I didn't want to ruin that illusion while it was convenient to me, but I physically couldn't bring myself to talk badly of the Shades or the shadow realm.

"I'm fine," I replied with a watery smile, pretending this was all totally no big deal and I hadn't absolutely made the biggest mistake of my life coming back here. "Of course I'm grateful to be home, but I was treated well. No complaints."

The disbelieving looks were honestly insulting.

"They *mauled* you." Practically all of them were glaring daggers at the bite mark on my neck and I barely resisted the urge to cover it with my hand. I wasn't ashamed of it, despite whatever uninformed opinions they had about it.

"Did anyone terrorize you? Feed your fear?" someone else asked. "That was explicitly forbidden under the terms of the treaty, though it's clear they had no qualms about breaking it.

"I barely felt fear the entire time I was there," I replied a little sharply. *Get in character. Act relieved.* "They took the treaty very seriously. That's why I was so surprised to hear it was violated."

More stupid titters from people who thought they were being clever.

"You've done so well, Ophelia," Moriah sighed, her expression almost maternal in a twisted kind of way. "I knew you would—you were my first choice for the role. I told Astrid as much, but she insisted on asking all the other outcasts first. She's grown too big for her boots, that one. Someone needs to remind her of her place," Moriah added with a scowl.

Was being Queen of Shades prestigious enough to get away with punching a Councilor in the face?

"What is it that I've done well at?" I enquired politely, doing my best bland face—the one Allerick hated so much.

263

Oh, Allerick. What was he doing right now? Was he thinking about me as obsessively as I was thinking about him?

Had he thought about me at all?

"You softened them up. Made them forget how much they despise us. That guile you have—it can't be faked. You were exactly the right choice to send in as a bride."

Some of the others murmured in agreement, and the two on either side of me chuckled to each other over my head like I wasn't sitting right there.

I thought they'd asked regular eligible huntresses and all had refused, but no. They'd asked 'outcasts' as Moriah had so eloquently put it. There were more people out there like me, and the Council had seen them—us—as convenient sacrifices. Willing, eager, biddable.

Lonely, probably. I know I'd been lonely.

A slimy feeling radiated out from the center of my body, coating every inch of me. A potent combination of shame that I'd been an unknowing participant in their scheme, as well as humiliation at my own naivety.

No wonder Allerick had been so suspicious of me when I'd first arrived in the shadow realm. He was smarter than I was.

I was a plant. A hopeful little idiot on a mission I'd known nothing about.

"Why?" I asked hoarsely before clearing my throat. "What was the point of all this? Of me?"

"Negotiating power," Bradley replied with a smile that was all teeth. "That the Shades would break the treaty was inevitable—they're barely more than beasts. They've experienced some level of security over the past few weeks, and they'll be eager to have it back, whatever the cost."

"They're used to having a few conditions on them when they feed now, what are a few more?" Moriah agreed. "We thought this would happen sooner, which was why we needed to recruit an unhappy Shade to speed things up. I imagine she's having a very bad day now the news has come out," Moriah added with a laugh.

She. It was totally Meridia. Meridia was a scout too—she monitored this area specifically and would have been in the perfect position to encounter a Hunter willing to talk.

"What kind of extra conditions?" I asked, dreading the answer.

"Prescribed feedings, for one," the man next to me muttered. "We'll decide exactly which humans they can feed on. Set them up at the prisons or something."

For a moment, I couldn't respond. Words stuck painfully in my throat and the whole situation felt incredibly far away, like I was watching in slow motion from underwater. It was all too surreal—too *cruel*—for me to comprehend.

"Who are you to decide that?" I asked quietly, appalled.

"The Hunters Council," he shot back snidely. "Don't forget whose side you actually belong on, Ophelia."

Oh, I hadn't. I knew *exactly* whose side I belonged on.

I said nothing for the rest of the meeting while they discussed the logistics of approaching the Shades and how best to keep them on the back foot, desperate for peace and willing to agree to sign over all their freedoms in the process. I absorbed as much as I could, noticing that the less attention they paid to me, the more freely they spoke. The more *contemptuous* they were. For what? They acted like the Shades were the ones who'd been murdering their families for centuries.

"Let's call it a day," Moriah said, tapping the end of her pen twice on the table. "We'll reconvene tomorrow to get things in motion, no point rushing it now. Let's leave them to sweat for another twenty-four hours."

They all laughed like that was the funniest thing they'd ever heard, and I forced myself to paste a tight smile on my face, hoping my breakfast stayed in my stomach in the process.

"Shall I call Astrid to pick me up?" I asked Moriah politely as everyone stood, chatting among themselves. I already knew the answer. There was no way on this good green earth that they were going to let me walk out of here.

Moriah's answering smile was serpentine. "For your own security, it would be best that you stay here for the interim. We'd hate for a Shade to get ideas about dragging you back into the shadow realm, and you weren't trained in exterminating them the way most Hunters are."

"You're right," I said flatly, holding eye contact. *And I'm grateful for that every day.* "But I also have lived as part of the human world for so long that I'm not accustomed to sleeping in a brightly lit room."

Moriah's lips pursed, an internal debate silently playing out over her face. "We can dim the lights in your room."

"As dark as possible, please. And could I have some additional blankets? It's a lot colder here." I gave her an insincere smile before making my way back through the rabbit warren of fluorescent-lit halls to my prison room, a staff member on my heels the entire time, asking if I needed directions or assistance.

What I *needed* was a dark enough space for a certain Shade to visit me on the off-chance that he'd visited Astrid, knew where I was, and even wanted to see me again. Even if he didn't, surely he'd want to see if I had information about the treaty negotiations? However he felt about me personally, Allerick would still do his best to protect his kingdom.

I'll find a way. Please don't give up on us. I'll regret giving up on us every day of my life.

ALLERICK

CHAPTER 21

The moment Soren and I were in the human realm under the cover of darkness, my physical form dissipated but the tether in my chest strengthened. It was a trade-off I was happy to make.

Unfortunately, we couldn't knock on doors in this form, though we could pass through them which was going to be an uncomfortable surprise for Ophelia's sister, and my wife if she was here, but I got the distinct sensation she wasn't.

'Let me go first,' Soren said, as close to an order as he'd ever given me. *'If the sister reacts poorly and throws a silver dagger, better me than you.'*

'I beg to differ,' I replied, rushing past him and sliding through the door panel while Soren protested furiously behind me. What kind of king would I be if I used my subjects as shields? Not a worthy one, that much was certain.

Astrid's home was dimly lit by lamps, as though she'd left it shadowy on purpose. *She had*, I realized as Astrid made a noise of surprise, startling on the couch where she'd been watching the door. Soren appeared next to me, as tense as a bow as he scanned her for any sign of weapons.

Astrid held up her empty hands, though she was visibly shaking. "I'm not armed. I am fucking *pissed* though, what took you so long?"

I hesitantly gestured at the night sky outside.

"I've kept my house pitch black all day waiting for you assholes to show up," she snapped. "The Council have my sister. They are insisting she stay at headquarters to debrief, whatever that means. Something isn't right. I think they *wanted* the treaty to be broken. The Council won't let me visit Ophelia, and any of your kind would be killed on sight."

It was more than tempting to take the risk anyway. I didn't like that Ophelia was alone there. What were they planning to do with her? Were they treating her well? Was she safe? Was she scared? I should have never left her side.

Astrid made a noise of discontent. "This isn't going to work. You're going to have to take me back to your realm so we can communicate."

'I don't trust her,' Soren said immediately.

'How surprising,' I replied wryly. *'She's a bigger threat to us here than in our realm.'*

At least in our realm, we had a means of defending ourselves. Here, we were sitting ducks, reliant on our speed alone to avoid whatever silver weapons she had on her person, and I had absolutely no doubt there were many. That Astrid didn't look any happier about it than I felt helped a little.

'We could do what Meridia probably did and stop in the in-between,' Soren countered. *'We still have the visual advantage that way.'*

'I won't put her at such a disadvantage,' I replied immediately. Being alone in pitch black darkness with two Shades would be terrifying for Astrid. *'We can talk right next to the portal, then immediately return her here.'*

'Fine, but I want it noted that I don't like this idea,' Soren grumbled, floating forward with his arms extended while I followed, gesturing for Astrid to turn the lamp off. She gulped audibly, and I could admit that this experience was likely far more frightening for her than it was for us.

With a steadying breath that reminded me so much of her sister it hurt, Astrid flicked off the lamp and plunged the room into darkness that both Soren and I could see perfectly in. He could have just held her hand, so I wasn't entirely sure why he wrapped both arms around her shoulders, but I didn't question. Astrid shuddered in his embrace as I gripped Soren's shoulder and began leading us back through the darkness to the beacon of the portal. The moment our forms solidified in the in-between, Soren picked Astrid clear off the ground, carrying her the rest of the way until we emerged under the night sky of the shadow realm, the orb above the portal illuminating us.

"You can put me down now," Astrid said in a strained voice, blinking up at Soren in alarm. Her scent was a little sour, but not nearly as terrified as she probably should have been, given the circumstances. Soren lowered her to the ground slowly, never taking his eyes off her before taking a step back.

"My wife," I prompted, breaking their staring contest. "Why has the Hunters Council taken her?"

Astrid blinked at me. "It's so strange to hear you speak. And you look so different here..." She shook her head slightly as if to clear it. "My guess is they've taken her to grill her for information. The impression I got is that many Councilors hoped the treaty wouldn't hold. Maybe even actively planned for it to fail."

"We already knew they didn't *expect* it to hold, they think we're beasts," Soren growled, staring intently at Astrid. "However, we were confident enough in our own people that it wasn't a concern for us. Unfortunately, one of our own was idiotic enough to fall for whatever the Hunters offered her."

"You should have known the Hunters would try to tear you apart from within," she shot back, glaring at him.

It was an unusual experience, as king, to be so thoroughly ignored.

"Even if we had accounted for that, one Shade making a play for the throne shouldn't burn all the progress between our kinds to the ground," Soren countered. "The Hunters' expectations are unreasonable."

"They are," Astrid agreed quietly. "I don't think that's an accident. They wanted the treaty to fail. Probably to make you as desperate as you are now."

I was desperate to assure peace and safety for my people, but I was more desperate to get Ophelia back. If we had to go back to feeding the way we had before, constantly watching our backs and risking our lives, we could. In fact, we *would*, rather than concede any more freedom to the Hunters. But before any of that could happen, I wanted Ophelia back at my side where she belonged.

"I know the room where Ophelia will be staying," Astrid continued. "It's in the center of the Council building, which is brightly lit at all times and the lights are controlled from the center of the building."

"So there's no way I can possibly get to her," I muttered, pacing back and forth in front of the portal. The limitations of my form in the human realm had never seemed so pronounced.

Astrid gave me a long searching look, and I was struck again by the differences between her and her sister despite their similar features. Ophelia looked at faces like she was trying to find answers, Astrid looked at faces like she was trying to find weaknesses.

"I can handle the lights, but it'll take out the whole building and everyone will be on high alert."

"I don't like it," Soren said with a grimace. "It would potentially put Ophelia at higher risk."

"Lia was devastated when she came through the portal," Astrid said flatly, staring at me. "Heartbroken, even."

"I didn't send her away, if that's what you think. I didn't ask her to leave. I didn't *want* her to leave."

"Then why did she leave?"

By the goddesses, this was the most uncomfortable conversation I'd ever had in my life.

"Because I didn't tell your sister that she was the first woman I loved, the only woman I'd ever love, and I'll die with the regret of not making my feelings for her clear when I had the chance."

"Oh." Astrid blinked while Soren awkwardly looked everywhere except at me. "I guess men are kind of the same in every realm."

I gave her a droll look, hoping she wasn't seriously comparing me to Hunters. "Is Ophelia completely unreachable where she is? You can't get to her even for a brief conversation?"

Soren visibly exhaled at the change in subject while Astrid frowned. "One of the Councilors, Moriah, has taken charge of Ophelia's 'care', and she's a rabid guard dog and hates me, so no. But if Ophelia is organized, maybe you can—"

"Absolutely not," Soren interjected. "It's far too dangerous."

"I won't be kept from my wife," I warned him in a low voice. "Have Damen on standby in my room, ready to take the crown if I don't return."

"Allerick," Soren whispered, stumbling back as though I'd struck him.

"Tell me what I need to do," I commanded Astrid, putting my life in the hands of one of the Hunters' most accomplished assassins.

I waited until it was midnight before I approached the portal alone. Soren was tasked with guarding Damen in case of an emergency transfer of power, much to his chagrin.

I'd never been to the human realm alone. Since birth, I'd been deemed to be too vital to travel by myself, and most Shades went to feed in pairs for safety, anyway. The guards watched nervously as I approached, already releasing a stream of shadows into the obsidian so I could pass. Astrid had drawn me an elaborate map of the Council Headquarters—a surprising sign of trust to hand over such information—and while I'd memorized it, the moment I was in the in-between, I knew I didn't need it.

The tether in my chest flared brightly, encouraging me forwards, guiding me to where Ophelia was. My guiding star. My mate.

This would only work if she was waiting for me—if she *wanted* to see me—and I had to believe she did otherwise I didn't know what I was going to do. Kidnap her, probably. She would either love that idea or hate it.

I walked through the nothingness, feeling the shape of the building take form above me, lit up as brightly as possible. Even in this half-form—both corporeal and not—the light burned, my body encouraging me to turn away and go back to safety. But the tether in my chest held true, and I closed my eyes against the blinding light and let my instincts guide me forward. As the sense of urgency slowly eased, I squinted at the space I'd found myself in. A spot of darkness in the middle of a sea of light.

Relief flooded me. There was nothing more natural than reaching for that sliver of darkness that my queen had carved out for me. I allowed myself to materialize into it, finding myself floating half inside a pedestal bathtub.

Ophelia had created a cave of sorts inside the bath, using the rail that ran around the top of it to hold the curtain as a structure which she'd layered what looked like every blanket she could find on top of.

And lying in the bathtub, curled up in a ball with her mouth half open, was my beautiful wife. I was loath to wake her, but every second I was here was a risk for both of us. If I managed to find my way here, one of Meridia's loyal Shades might too. I didn't want Ophelia in darkness any longer than she had to be.

I ran my claws through her hair and down the sides of her face, hoping I could gently wake her without terrifying her. Especially when she had that damned silver pin in her hair.

'My Ophelia,' I said, my voice silent to her ears. *'My love. Wake up and please don't stab me. I'm bringing you home, I hope you can forgive me for it.'*

Her brown eyes opened with a start, and she sucked in a startled breath as she stared right at me, her eyes adjusting to the darkness. The pin remained loosely in her hand, and I made a note to get Ophelia some weapons training when we were back home. *If* she returned home.

I backed up, holding my hands in the air so she hopefully knew I meant her no harm. Hopefully she *recognized* me, though it was asking a lot when all Shades appeared much the same in this realm.

Could she feel me through the tether in her chest the way I could feel her?

"Say something," she whispered. "Allerick, speak again."

I reeled back in surprise, half drifting into the curtain before moving forward again into the safety of the dark cocoon she'd made for us. *'You can... hear me?'*

"Yes!" she whisper-shouted, eyes wide. "How is this possible?"

I rubbed my hand over my chest, and Ophelia mirrored the gesture before her fingers drifted up to the bite mark on her neck. We'd barely scratched the surface of whatever this bond between us was, and I hoped we had our whole lives together to figure it out.

As much as I wanted to reach for her and spirit her away, I didn't want to startle her by snatching her away even though that had been my initial plan, assuming that we weren't able to communicate. I was racking my brain for the right words to say to convince her to come back when Ophelia gave me a long look and burst into tears.

Fuck, fuck, fuck. I hadn't accounted for tears. How was I supposed to make the tears stop? My queen should never have cause to cry over *anything*.

"Do you hate me? I'm sorry I left, I thought you didn't want me. Maybe you don't want me. Are you here to tell me you don't want me? But you said you were bringing me back. If you're bringing me back to imprison me for being a traitorous queen who ran away, I understand, but I need to tell you all the things they have planned first." She hiccuped slightly, visibly trying to pull herself together as she roughly rubbed her cheeks with her sleeve.

Unable to stand the distance between us any longer, I drifted forward and cupped her face, hating the fact that I could barely feel her under my hands.

'I love you, Ophelia. I hope you can forgive me for not telling you sooner. I have come here to bring you home, where you belong. You are my queen. The Queen of Shades.'

Her eyes started watering all over again, and I panicked that the idea of coming home with me was not as appealing as I'd assumed it would be.

"I love you, Allerick. I want nothing more than to return home with you." Her tears slid through my fingers as I held her face, creating the faintest sensation against my palms. "But I can't, not yet. They're planning something, and I need to be here to... I don't know. Stop them? Or at least tell you what they're doing so you can stop them?"

'I won't leave you here. It's not safe, Ophelia.'

She was already shaking her head quietly. "You want me to come home and be your queen?"

'My crowned queen. My equal in all things. I want you at my side.'

"And in your bed?" Ophelia asked wryly.

'I want to be knotted to you every second of every day, but I would be selfish to deprive our people of your compassionate leadership. You are kind, empathetic, and loyal. You were born to be a queen, and you have already made me a better king.'

Ophelia blinked, her eyes shining with unshed tears. Fuck, wasn't crying bad? Had my words distressed her? Maybe she didn't want to be queen?

"No one has ever believed in me like that, and I don't want to let you down. I don't want to let *them* down, so you need to let me protect our people," Ophelia whispered with a sad smile, her fingers slipping right through mine when she tried to press her hand against mine. "You would never walk away if you knew the Hunters were planning something and you thought you might be able to stop it. Don't ask it of me."

My urge to protect her warred with my desire to give her what she wanted, to show Ophelia with actions that when I told her I loved her and wanted her as my equal, I meant it.

'*What are they planning?*' I asked, resigned.

Ophelia's voice dropped even lower, her eyes flicking nervously towards the door. "They want to trap you into an agreement where they choose exactly where and when you feed. What humans experience fear. They want to play god," she muttered, looking outraged by the idea.

It was a chilling one. I had no doubt they'd keep us on the brink of starvation whilst using us to terrorize the humans they deemed unworthy. The Hunters had already done such an effective job at decimating our numbers, my chest grew tight at the realization that we might have no choice but to acquiesce or they'd wipe us out entirely.

But was signing us up to an eternity of slavery really a better alternative?

No. No, I couldn't do that to my people.

"Did Astrid send you here?" Ophelia asked, a renewed sense of urgency in her voice.

'*Yes. She's waiting in the shadow realm for you to return.*'

"Is that... wise?" my wife asked, looking vaguely horrified at the thought.

'*Levana is watching over her,*' I assured her.

"I am not comforted," Ophelia muttered. "But you need to bring Astrid back. There are others like me—'outcasts' are how the Council referred to us. Astrid had to contact them when they were searching for a bride for you. If they were willing to live in the shadow realm..."

'*It's a big 'if',*' I said softly, forcing the swell of hope in my chest down.

"I hope you haven't treated Astrid badly. We'll need her powers of persuasion," Ophelia said wryly. Goddesses, this was a long shot. "There's another meeting tomorrow at midday."

Was it too much to ask that they'd have their meetings in the middle of the night in a pitch-black room? How was I supposed to be there for my wife when the fucking *light* kept me away from her?

"Tell me what to say," Ophelia whispered, the fear evident in her voice. "I don't know what I'm doing, Allerick. I don't know how to do this, and I don't want to make promises I can't keep."

'You are the queen, your promises will be kept,' I replied fiercely, wishing more than anything that I could scoop her into my arms and hold her. *'When I told you to proceed as you saw fit, I meant it, Ophelia. I trust your judgment.'*

"Oh. *Oh.* I thought you meant to proceed with packing my stuff how I saw fit. You could have been a little clearer," she added, giving me a pointed look.

'You are my mate, that bite mark on your neck tells the world that. You will never have cause to doubt how I feel for you again,' I promised. I glanced at the door, my enhanced senses picking up movement from the hall. *'They're coming to check on you.'*

"Go," Ophelia whispered, attempting to push me back, her hands slipping right through my chest. "Talk to Astrid."

'I will. I love you. Be safe for me, my little queen.'

OPHELIA

CHAPTER 22

When I woke in the morning in my hastily made bed in my still obnoxiously bright room, I felt like I hadn't slept at all. My neck hurt from my nap in the bathtub, and when I made it back into the main room, the light bothered me too much to sleep properly. Even in my human apartment, I'd only ever slept with a nightlight on, not grocery store-level blinders overhead. No wonder all the Councilors were so grumpy all the time.

I still didn't really have a plan. Seeing Allerick had solidified the decisions I'd already made and given me some serious peace of mind—my husband actually *loved* me—but we had the makings of a strategy rather than an actual strategy *at best*.

Basically, we were depending entirely on my sister, who made a name for herself as the youngest Shade-killer in history, to seriously go to bat for the Shades.

Oh my god, this was a terrible plan.

I was sleep-deprived and they'd fed me some kind of trendy mushroom salad for dinner, and I wasn't thinking straight. That was the only explanation for why I ever thought this was an idea worth suggesting to Allerick.

As much as I wanted to curl up in a ball and sleep some more, I forced myself to get up and quickly dashed to the bathroom to double check I'd put it all back to rights after hastily disassembling my cocoon of darkness in the middle of the night. Happy it looked orderly, I made the bed with extra care before anyone could show up to bring me breakfast. *Please let it be bagels and donut holes and no more healthy food,* I thought to myself, pulling out a simple black pencil skirt and a fitted black knit sweater that seemed appropriately dignified and business-like for today. I wasn't the lost little lamb I'd been just twenty-four hours ago—I was going to go to bat for my realm, whatever that looked like, and I wanted the Hunters to take me seriously.

Don't do anything rash, I reminded myself, shoving down the revulsion I now felt whenever I thought of the Councilors who'd dictated so much of mine and my family's life. I'd seen the underbelly of the beast that was the Hunters Council, and I'd never be able to *unsee* it.

All these years, I'd downplayed their rejection of me as a necessary evil, taking all the blame onto myself for being weird and different, but that guilt hadn't been mine to bear. Being weird and different didn't give them the right to be cruel to me, and it had never been about just me anyway.

I washed my face, lamenting my lack of makeup when I saw how dark the shadows under my eyes were, and slipped on my flats, getting the room perfectly in order in case Moriah showed up here to pretend we were friends again. I was a hot mess on the inside, but I didn't want the enemy seeing that on the outside.

God, I wanted nothing more than to drag the blankets off the bed and hole up in my bathtub fort again, hoping my husband would take the ridiculously large risk of seeing me. Well, no. Not really. I didn't actually want him to put himself in danger, but seeing him had soothed all the aches in my soul that had been paining me since the moment I left. Before that, even. All the insecurities and vulnerabilities I'd felt not knowing whether I actually meant anything to him were gone.

Allerick was honorable, and he never said things he didn't mean. He loved me and he wanted me to rule by his side, and I would never doubt his sincerity again. Was it a perfect relationship? Absolutely not. We had a lot to learn about each other, and that would take time, but it was a solid foundation on which to build something that could last.

"Ophelia," Moriah called in a singsong voice that made me want to hit something. "Join us in the meeting room, would you? A few of us are having breakfast while we wait for the others to arrive. There's coffee," she trilled in what she probably thought was an inviting voice.

Taking a deep steadying breath, I made my way to the door and pulled it open, enjoying the surprise on Moriah's face when she saw me fully dressed and waiting for her.

"Then what are we waiting for?"

I sipped on my coffee in the corner, watching the Hunters Council's Metaphorical Circle Jerk in action.

"There were no reported sightings last night," Moriah was saying, scrolling through her phone. "Globally. It seems the Shades went to ground."

"Or to *shadows*, as it were," one of the older ones guffawed.

"King Allerick runs a tight ship," Moriah remarked, looking to me for confirmation. So much for my plan to remain unnoticed in the corner.

"He'd hardly be the king if he didn't," I pointed out, taking another sip of my coffee.

"Well, except for that Shade who was more than happy to break the treaty at our suggestion," Moriah said, her voice deceptively mild. I called her a few unsavory names in my head. "But even kings have weaknesses. Things that can be... leveraged."

Me, I thought wryly. Allerick had taken a huge risk to come here last night to see me. I was absolutely a weakness, and one I didn't want them exploiting.

"Perhaps we shouldn't have thrown the Shade we were working with under the bus. What was her name? Something starting with M," Bradley mused.

"Too volatile," Moriah disagreed. "Allerick is honorable, I suppose. For a Shade. That makes him easier to manage. But what is his Achilles' heel, Ophelia? You must have noticed something in the time you spent there."

All eyes in the room turned to me, and I had to say *something*.

"Shades *die* without feeding. That is an enormous weakness. Being responsible for the lives of all of his subjects, ensuring *they* can feed, that is a weakness."

"Ophelia is right—well done, Ophelia," Bradley said, giving me a fatherly sort of look that made my skin crawl. "What we need from you is not the king's weaknesses, but the *Shades'* weaknesses. How do they feed? How can we limit their entry point to this realm through portals only? That's the solution. If we control the exit and entry points, we control them. We control this *realm*. Shades can be escorted to feedings— with a silver dagger pointed at their throat the whole time—we could come to some sort of agreement with human authorities for the necessary victims. Call it a corrective program or something, make it very secretive and elite."

Barbaric.

Barbaric and total nonsense. There was no way to restrict where the Shades went once they were through the barriers of their *own* realm. Once they were in the in-between, they could basically go where they liked as I understood it.

"If the silver daggers can affect them in their noncorporeal forms, then I think it's time we start investigating other uses for silver to see if they're effective. Collars perhaps," someone else suggested.

"We need to take out the king," another said, banging his fist on the table hard enough to make me jump. "I say we bring back Meridia—she's volatile but it would only be temporary. We can't implement a new order with the old power structure in place. Ophelia can be trained to fight—she's the only one who they'll trust enough to let close to him."

I was going to puke up my lukewarm black coffee all over this table.

"No."

Okay, that wasn't part of the plan. The plan had been vague and abstract at best, and now it was out the window completely. Worse still, I hadn't seen or heard any indication that Astrid was here, and there were no guarantees that she'd come at all.

But I wasn't about to sit here and say nothing while they suggested murdering my husband. While they suggested that *I* murder my husband.

"I won't hurt him. I would never hurt him. Allerick is my *mate*," I said calmly, standing up and sweeping my gaze over the table of arguing Councilors. I didn't feel strong or confident or impressive—my legs were shaking beneath my skirt and my heart was pounding so loud I swore everyone could hear it.

"Your what?" Moriah asked, stiffly polite.

"He is my mate. We are bound. That's what this means." I pointed at the healing bite mark on my throat. "Our people were once intertwined, did you know that? Hunters lived in the shadow realm and it was full of color and we loved each other—"

Moriah stood, bracing her palms on the table and glaring at me. "You don't know what you're talking about, Ophelia. *Love*," she scoffed. "We were once called the *Hunted*, the Shades would chase our ancestors between realms until they captured and bit them. Do you think it's a good thing that we had no choice? That our people were snatched away from our lives to go breed monsters?"

Okay. Okay, I hadn't known about that part.

"Maybe hundreds of years ago, that was how it went. And that's wrong, I'm not going to argue otherwise. But I'm telling you that things have changed now. We could be living in harmony with Shades, not just this temporary truce, but a true *peace*—"

"Did he talk about breeding you?" Moriah asked flatly. "Did he frighten you? Chase you? Hunt you until you gave in? They are *beasts*, Ophelia. You should be on your knees in gratitude for our ancestors who took us away from that world."

I leveled my best glare on her because *fuck that*. She didn't get to talk about my relationship like that. She didn't get to pass judgment over something she didn't understand, or taint what were beautiful memories of my time with my husband.

"He did both. And I *begged* for them," I replied, holding eye contact until she looked away.

"Allerick—" My voice broke on his name, the ache of missing him growing overwhelming. But talking about him made me feel closer to him, even the strange pull to him in my chest felt more stable. "I love him. I love him, and I care for the Shades I came to know. If you wage war against them, I will fight back."

"If you fight us, you will be imprisoned for your own safety," Bradley said with a pitying look.

The lights flickered for a moment, startling the Councilors and myself. *Please be Astrid. I may be on the verge of imprisonment because I lack impulse control.*

"What's going on?" Moriah asked sharply, right as the lights went out completely and the Councilors began shouting in alarm. I looked around as my eyes slowly adjusted to the darkness, apprehensive but not afraid. Not when the pull in my chest seemed to be growing comfortingly stronger.

Was he here? In the middle of the day? Surely not.

The door behind me swung open with a bang and my sister stormed in with a flashlight pointed at the ground, barely illuminating her, and a veritable *army* at her back, spilling into the hallway behind her. It took me a moment to realize that it wasn't just a group of humans—of *Hunters*—but Shades as well. No wonder she'd cut the lights. I could barely see them—Astrid was being careful to keep the light directed away from them—but there was no mistaking the dark mass of movement behind her.

How convenient for us that the Council rooms were mostly windowless bunkers. Without artificial light, there was no keeping the Shades out.

"I think the fuck not," Astrid announced, looking like an avenging warrior as she glared at the Council. "You don't get to kidnap the Queen of Shades without consequences."

"Astrid," Moriah hissed. "Have you lost your fucking mind? Stand down. Who are these people? Any Hunters in this group will be banished for *life* for this treason."

"We're already banished," one of them scoffed.

"Astrid, *stand down*," Moriah insisted.

"No."

I snorted quietly at Astrid's blunt refusal. She had zero diplomatic finesse, but she was an excellent warrior. I hoped she'd return to the shadow realm with us and stay on our side. I hoped all of these banished Hunters were coming back with us, and that they were kind and open-minded and ready for an adventure.

'Astrid Bishop is a force to be reckoned with,' Allerick said, his voice drifting quietly into my head.

I nodded in agreement as I positioned myself in front of him, knowing immediately which floating dark form was his. I hadn't seen any weapons from the Councilors here, but I wasn't taking any chances with my husband. If they wanted to throw a knife at him, it'd have to go through me first.

'*Ophelia,*' he warned, immediately seeing what I was doing. I wasn't sure how his mindspeak thing worked, but I assumed by how little he was saying and how vague he was being that the other Shades in the room could hear him, and he wasn't going to tell me off in front of an audience.

Cute.

All I wanted was to feel his warm leathery skin beneath my palms, his huff of amused breath over my hair when I said something he didn't expect, I wanted *all* of him. I wanted to be as far away from here as possible.

But that was Ophelia-the-Failed-Hunter talking. I was Ophelia, Queen of Shades now. Snuggles with my husband would have to wait.

"Enough," I said calmly, cutting off Moriah's bitching as she cussed out Astrid. "I say this as Queen of Shades with the full support of my husband, and I suggest you all listen because I'm not going to repeat myself. You know as well as I do that fear is a necessity. Fear is part of the balance, and to remove it would be shortsighted in the extreme, but you think you know best? Fine. The Shades will no longer enter the human realm at all."

"That's not what we meant—" Moriah began. Idly, I wondered if Soren was shitting ghost bricks behind me.

"Too goddamn bad," I snapped, really hoping I wasn't making a colossal mistake here. "You think you hold all the power here, but you don't. You're not going to use the Shades as instruments of torture, and you have no right to decide which humans are worthy or unworthy of experiencing fear. My husband and I have extended an invitation to all Hunters who were set aside like me. All who were deemed too compassionate, or whose morals were considered questionable because they didn't relish the idea of killing Shades. Let them come to the shadow realm and find a home in a place where they are appreciated and cared for, not like here where you just set us aside because we don't fit the prescribed mold you've made for us."

'*You think they'll generate enough for us all to feed from the stores?*' someone asked, and I realized with a jolt that it wasn't just Allerick I could hear. Apparently the bitemark had linked me in to the whole Shade mindspeak network.

'*Yes,*' a voice that was unmistakably Soren's clipped. '*I've seen myself how much the king siphoned after feeding from Queen Ophelia.*'

"If I have to fill them myself for the time being, so be it," I whispered towards the group of Shades, a little more aggressively than I intended. I'd fuck my husband every second of every day rather than put a single one of them at risk.

"Astrid has explained to us how you've lied to us," one of the Hunters standing behind my sister said. "Two of us even went to see the shadow realm for ourselves after she knocked down our door in the middle of the night. We've been made to feel our whole lives like there's something wrong with us when the attraction we have towards Shades is entirely normal."

"It is *not* normal," Bradley snapped, sounding vaguely panicked. Good.

"You better go with them, Astrid," Moriah snarled at my sister. "Because you're dead to us."

"Happily," Astrid shot back, which I'm pretty confident was a lie but I was selfishly glad she was coming back with us anyway.

"When you're ready to beg for our forgiveness, we'll be waiting," I said mildly, backing up a few steps. Astrid flicked off the flashlight, and we melted into the darkness, into the in-between, with Allerick's arm securely banded around me. There were gasps of surprise around us, and I guessed that enough Shades had accompanied us to comfortably guide the Hunters through without the use of a portal to assist us.

I felt Allerick gain solid form in the darkness and I turned into his chest, shaking a little as I pressed my face into his skin, inhaling the scent of him.

Despite our brief reconnection last night, there were still a lot of things we had to say, but none of them were things I felt comfortable saying in front of all these other people, so I clung tight to Allerick and hoped he understood how much I missed him. He clung to me right back.

I blinked at the sudden light as we emerged in the shadow realm, surprised to find the action made tears I hadn't even realized were welling fall down my cheeks.

"My Ophelia," Allerick murmured, his thumb sweeping away a stray tear with heartbreaking care. "Come. Let's go to our room, the rest of this can wait."

"But all these people, and Astrid—"

"I'm fine," my sister said sharply, arms wrapped tightly around her middle. She was standing further back from the crowd, but Soren was watching her like a hawk, which was sort of reassuring for me because I knew he'd look after her, though probably not very reassuring for Astrid. "I'll stay with the Hunters," she insisted.

"Set them up at Elverston House," Allerick instructed Levana and Soren, already pulling me away from the crowd. "It's on the outskirts of the palace grounds, they'll have privacy there until they're more comfortable around us," he added for my benefit.

That sounded good. Everyone would need time to adjust to this new arrangement. I glanced around a little anxiously, wondering if any of the Shades were mad about what I'd said to the Hunters Council, what I'd promised, but palace guards were all waving to me and assuring me it was good to have me back.

They might have even been a little... excited?

I supposed my presence here had brought color back to the realm, maybe the idea of having *more* of me wasn't the worst prospect for them. Especially if they could feed without having to constantly go to the human realm.

Eventually, I was sure that Shades would return to the human realm, with the Hunters' blessing. The Hunters would realize they were being idiots and upsetting the natural balance of things, but until then I'd keep those stores topped up if it was the last thing I did.

"They adore you," Allerick said quietly.

"I adore them," I replied, barely containing my grin. "Well, most of them. Meridia—"

"Is imprisoned, probably for life," Allerick interjected. "There will be a public trial in a few days, but I can't see it going her way. Damen is leading a group of Shades to uncover who her allies were and what role they played."

"Do you think the Hunters who came back with us will be safe here?"

Allerick shot me a disbelieving look. "I will make sure of it. This is a new beginning for us, for this realm. I will do everything in my power to preserve it."

He must have gotten impatient with my short legs as we weren't even in the entry hall before he'd lifted me into his arms and was striding through the corridors like the hounds of hell were on his tail. There was an intensity to him that I'd never seen before—he was a Shade on a mission, mouth turned down and shadows rising off him like smoke.

I leaned my head against his shoulder and stared at him like a creeper, memorizing the planes of his face, the curve of his horns, the glow of his ice-blue eyes. He was even more beautiful than I remembered, and I knew no drawing I could have done in the human realm would have done him justice if I'd never seen him again.

Just the thought made my chest ache.

Allerick strode directly past the guards, carrying me into his room and kicking the door shut behind him. I attempted to wriggle down to the ground, but Allerick's chest rumbled in warning as he carried me over to the bed, sitting on the edge with me on his lap.

"Are you going to carry me everywhere now?" I teased, hoping he would relax a little.

"I'm contemplating it," he replied hoarsely, arranging me in his lap so I was straddling him and running his hands over every inch of me that he could reach. "You *left*, Ophelia."

My heart hurt at the pain in his voice.

"I'll never leave again," I promised before giving him a warning look. "Though we need to work on our communication skills."

Allerick hummed in agreement. "I owe you an apology, little queen. When you were out there in front of the Hunters from the Council, arguing for them to be reasonable and negotiate, I realized how confident and dedicated to my people—our people—you are. I'd already decided the night before to request your coronation. I was with the Councilors before the Hunters showed up to order it done."

"You were?" I asked, feeling my eyebrows shoot up. "That's really sweet, though I would have much preferred to wake up next to you."

"You will," he promised, grip on me tightening slightly. "Every morning for the rest of your life."

Swoosh went my belly.

"We'll work out together what you want your role to look like. How you want your days to go. Whether or not you want children…"

"I do," I replied firmly. "But not quite yet. I'd like you to myself a little longer, is that okay?"

"More than okay," he promised, struggling to repress the purr that had started up at the mention of babies. I ran my hands softly over his body, disturbing the shadows, grateful that he was here and mine and I could touch him all I wanted.

"Can I try something?" I asked, face heating in anticipation even though we'd done a lot filthier than what I was about to suggest.

"Of course."

I leaned forward, deciding to tell him with actions rather than words, and closing the small distance between us to brush my lips softly against his. It definitely wasn't like kissing a human—his lips were less pillowy, more firm and leather-smooth like the rest of him—but I didn't mind. I took my time, exploring the similarities and differences between us, relishing the way that Allerick let me lead. It would probably never happen again, but it was fun to be the one in control for a while.

I pulled back, intending to check in with Allerick that he was okay with this, but he chased me, careful to keep his teeth safely covered. *Well, I guess he's okay with it then.*

Testing the waters, I flicked my tongue at the seam of his mouth, teasing and requesting entry at the same time.

"My teeth—" he growled, both in warning and frustration.

"I'll be careful," I interjected before pressing my lips to his again, encouraging him to open for me. With a sigh like he couldn't deny me anything, he parted his lips, his longer, thicker tongue snaking out to tangle with mine before I could get anywhere near his teeth.

Welp, these panties were done for. There was a quiet, subtle drip on the stone floor that may or not have been the slick that was beginning to gush out of me.

"I want to try something else," I mumbled against his lips, barely able to drag myself away.

"Mmph."

Taking that as permission to experiment since his tongue was back at work exploring mine and I couldn't ask any follow up questions, I slowly slid my hands up over Allerick's neck, taking a moment to toy with his hair before doing something I'd always fantasized about doing.

Grabbing him by the horns. Literally.

Allerick groaned as I wrapped my fingers as much as I could around the base of them, massaging slightly to determine if he had any sensation there or not. Judging by the raspy grunts of desire intermingled with the purr rumbling steadily out of his chest, I guessed he did.

I was contemplating how best to steer his head down to my aching pussy when Allerick's hands disappeared underneath my skirt, claws digging into the globes of my ass as he pulled back, panting heavily.

"That was very enjoyable. Especially the kissing. We should do that more often," Allerick rasped, leaning into my touch as I rubbed his horns. "Preferably while my knot is—"

"Mm, maybe I should keep your mouth busy in other ways. You could tell me all the ways you intend to make up for not crowning me immediately and trusting my obviously excellent judgment," I teased, because I had to make jokes about the whole coronation thing or I'd have a panic attack.

"Oh, I intend to make my intentions for you very clear from this moment forth, my love," he growled. Was it possible to have a love kink? My body had a very visceral response every time he dropped the L-word. "But I have other plans for our mouths right now."

I smiled against his lips, tightening my grip on his horns and reassuring myself that he was here with me. "Yes, your majesty."

EPILOGUE

Queen Ophelia made her way up the aisle like she was a blood princess who'd been doing this her whole life. The sweeping gown of shadows I'd constructed trailed behind her, dark strands floating behind her like ribbons, and it scooped low enough between her breasts—at her insistence—to make my cock ache in front of the goddamn priest and my entire court. *Our* entire court.

Shades and Hunters alike stood to watch their queen make their way towards the altar where I was waiting for her, a beautiful golden crown sitting on a red velvet cushion atop a gray stone plinth. The Hunters who'd come here were still mostly holed up in Elverston House, getting accustomed to life here in the shadow realm, but some tenuous friendships were developing. We were able to escort them back to the human realm whenever they liked to get supplies, though most of them were too fearful of the Hunters Council to make the trip.

Fortunately, Astrid wasn't afraid of anything. She regularly traveled back on supply runs with Soren glued to her side, watching her with an intensity that bordered on obsessive. He was so focused on Astrid, he'd nearly caught a silver dagger to the chest from her father the one time Astrid had tried to visit her parents, pleading for their understanding. It was only Astrid's fast reflexes that had saved him, earning herself an impressive scar along her palm for her efforts.

Ophelia smiled as she waited at the bottom of the steps, her eyes shiny in a way that I knew signified tears, though I was fairly confident these were not the bad kind of tears.

Weylin, the priest who'd married us, hovered nervously next to me. The priests had all been oddly skittish around me since I'd made Garren eat his own tongue. It was fortunate for everyone that they'd taken a shine to Ophelia, otherwise relations between the priesthood and the monarchy would be very strained.

"Be seated," Weylin called to the gathered crowd, who quietly took their seats. My gaze was entirely on Ophelia, who despite her tremulous expression managed to wink at me.

"Queen Ophelia, are you here of your own free will and willing to take the Coronation Oath here today?" Weylin asked.

"I am here freely and willingly."

Weylin nodded. "Then I address my next question to those present today. We have gathered here for the coronation of Queen Ophelia. Do all those present solemnly swear to give your new queen your loyalty and service?"

"We do," the crowd called back in unison, both Shades and Hunters alike. They may be new to our realm, but it hadn't taken the Hunters who'd come here long to get attached to Ophelia. How could they not? She was all sweetness and light when she wasn't a horny mess, and I liked her equally both ways.

"Queen Ophelia, do you promise to guide and govern the realm of Shades in keeping with the laws and customs of our land?" Weylin asked Ophelia.

"I promise," Ophelia said solemnly.

"Do you swear to protect the interests of the Shades and the Hunters who reside here?"

"I do so swear."

"Then take your place at the king's side," Weylin instructed, giving Ophelia a soft smile.

I extended my hand, and Ophelia placed her palm in mine as I guided her up the steps. As we agreed, she lowered herself gracefully to the ground on one knee, and I idly arranged the shadows cloaking her into a sea of blackness that seemed to pour over the stone steps. The gesture of submission was not for my benefit, but to show reverence for the crown, for the role she was undertaking, and the subjects she was bound to serve.

Ophelia's beautiful brown eyes met mine, and there was nothing but happiness and light there. She was the perfect contradiction—all brightness and smiles, with a hidden dirty side. Kind to everyone, but willing and able to stick up for herself and those she cared about. Ophelia was compassionate, intelligent, watchful and strong. She was everything the Queen of Shades should be, and there wasn't a soul in this room who didn't know it.

Carefully, I lifted the golden crown we'd had especially made for her off the cushion. It was solid at the base, with thin arches of gold rising above it, culminating at the tallest point in the center where a large golden star sat.

Because my wife was my guiding star, and I couldn't think of anything more appropriate to be the crowning jewel in her crown.

The entire room seemed to be holding their breath as I lowered it onto her head. Ophelia exhaled tremulously as the weight settled on her, both physically and metaphorically. To be queen was no small responsibility, but it was one I knew Ophelia would be able to bear and with more grace than any who'd come before her.

My mother caught my eye from the front row, and she practically beamed with approval. While I'd had no luck persuading her to feed more from the stores over the past two decades, Ophelia had managed it in just one conversation. She claimed it was because she'd convinced my mother that there was plenty to go around now, and she didn't need to deprive herself any longer to ensure the young ones got enough.

I was pretty sure it was because Ophelia had mentioned the possibility of grandchildren in the future, and that was a compelling enough reason for my mother to take better care of herself.

Either way, I hadn't seen my mother so strong and healthy since I was a kid. She'd even resumed wandering around the palace and garden, inflicting terror on the staff with just her disapproving presence alone. I knew she was counting down the days until the public trial of Meridia and her co-conspirators, all currently being held at the Pit. It had been pushed back to accommodate the coronation because the realm needed something to celebrate, and Ophelia deserved to be celebrated.

My wife slid her hand back into mine, and I helped her up as we both turned to face the crowd. The Shades jumped to their feet, stamping them loudly on the ground as they cheered, and the Hunters clapped politely, looking slightly overwhelmed by the noise.

"King Allerick and Queen Ophelia!" Weylin yelled.

"King Allerick and Queen Ophelia!" they roared back. Ophelia's hand tightened in mine as she startled, immediately glancing upwards to make sure she hadn't disturbed the crown.

"You look beautiful," I murmured, wrapping an arm around her waist and pulling her into my side. I almost groaned at the sensation of touching her bare skin beneath the shadows rather than the fabric I'd become accustomed to when we were in public. "Come on, let's get this feast over and done with. I want to fuck you in nothing but that crown."

"I still can't believe my sister lives here," Ophelia murmured, watching Astrid talk to Soren from our usual position at the high table. I glanced down to where they were standing near a side exit, wondering if I needed to intervene judging by how tense both of them looked.

"Don't worry," Damen laughed, catching my frown. "I just walked past them. There's, er, nothing to be concerned about."

"What do you mean?" my wife asked, twisting away from me to look at my brother. *Stupid feast. Stupid everyone taking her attention away from me.*

Damen gave her an apologetic look. "It's just that Astrid smells quite... sweet."

"No way," Ophelia gasped, leaning forward and making no attempt to hide her open stare. "Astrid is hot for a Shade?"

"Is that so surprising?" I asked. "Given what we've learned about the history of our kinds?"

We'd pored over Affra's translations for hours before disseminating them throughout the realm. From what we'd read, it made sense that the Shades had been so selectively terrible at their history keeping when it came to their relationship with the Hunters.

Or the Hunted, as they had indeed once been.

The Shades centuries ago had seen the Hunted as prey to be caught, not as partners or equals. I hadn't hidden any of this from the Hunters who'd come here, and I'd sworn that we had no interest in emulating the abhorrent actions of our forbearers. Some were still wary, while others were trying to decide on a name for themselves that wasn't Hunter or Hunted, but was representative of who they wanted to be.

"No, logically it's not surprising... Well, yes, it is a little." Ophelia frowned, and I plucked her out of her seat and onto my lap immediately, wanting to wipe the expression off her face. "*Biologically*, it isn't surprising, and some of the Hunters have seemed really open to getting to know the Shades, but this is Astrid. She was on track to be the youngest member of the Hunters Council ever. She holds... records."

I hummed in agreement, hating the reminder of the number of lives Astrid had taken. Only the fact that she'd done so much to help in the end could make me even try to overlook the fact that there was a murderer in our midst, sitting at the table in my court, eating my food and drinking my wine.

My tolerance of her presence here hadn't eased the terror my subjects felt whenever they saw her. There would be no more devoted mate than Soren, but he and Astrid could never be.

Bored of discussing things that weren't me and Ophelia tangled up in bed, I turned my attention to her hair, burrowing my hand beneath the silky strands to grip the back of her neck, while resting the other on her leg, rubbing circles over her knee with my thumb, my shadows concealing my movements.

"Bye," Damen muttered, pushing his chair back hurriedly as Ophelia's slick began perfuming the air around us.

"You are very bad," she said breathily, making no move to stop me. "We are supposed to stay the whole feast."

"Mm, you're the queen, crowned and everything. The feast is over when you say it's over," I murmured, my lips pressed against her shoulder.

Ophelia hesitated, entertaining the idea. "Maybe we could just dip out for a moment, tell everyone to keep enjoying themselves. Oh no, they'd definitely know what we were doing though. It'd be like the throne room all over again."

"I have no objections to repeating our throne room experience. In fact, I might insist upon it." I ran a claw down her inner thigh. "I want to see if you can keep that crown in place while I bend you over the throne and bounce you on my knot."

"Allerick," Ophelia hissed, her scent growing too potent for the rest of the room to ignore. "Oh my god, everyone is staring. Do I stink?"

"You smell delicious," I growled, standing up with her in my arms and not bothering to offer an explanation as I carried her into the throne room, the court cheering loudly behind us.

"My sister is going to be judging me so hard right now," Ophelia laughed, wrapping her arms around my neck and leaning into me as I kicked the heavy door shut and carried her to the dimly lit throne.

"If she's going to spend any amount of time here, she'll have to get used to it. I have no intention of hiding how much I desire my wife."

"I hope you never stop," Ophelia said gently, leaning up to kiss my jaw. "I love you, Allerick."

"I love you, my queen."

THANK YOU

Thank you so much for taking a chance on this book! I've never written anything quite like this before, and I appreciate you giving it a shot when you probably have a TBR list a mile long. Luxuria actually wasn't on my writing schedule for this year, but I couldn't get these characters out of my head, so I went ahead and wrote it down! Hopefully, you enjoyed it.

Book two, Superbia, featuring a certain grumpy Captain of the Guard and a rage-fueled ex-Hunter will be out in 2023.

I have to thank the incredible Steph from Rawls Reads Author Services who did a phenomenal job editing this beast of a book. I already adored her before, but she'll never be rid of me now. Thanks also to Lysanne for being such an incredible beta reader! You are the best. I also need to thank Becky Edits for proofreading.

This book would have never happened without the encouragement of my friends, who fully supported my foray into monster romance. In particular, Ashley Bennett, Rory Miles, T.S. Snow, Rachel, and Lucy. I love you all.

And to you, dear reader! None of this would be possible without you, and I appreciate each and every one of you so much.

Colette R. xx

P.S. To keep up with the latest news and releases, join my Facebook Reader Group or subscribe to my newsletter.

ALSO BY COLETTE

SHADES OF SIN:

Luxuria

Superbia

STATE OF GRACE:

Run Riot

Silver Bullet

Wild Game

Dare Not

Saving Grace

THREE BEARS DUET:

Gilded Mess

Golden Chaos

LITTLE RED DUET:

Scarlet Disaster

Seeing Red

KNOTTY BY NATURE:

(RH omegaverse with T.S. Snow)

Allure Part 1

Allure Part 2

EMPATH FOUND:

The Terrible Gift

The Unwanted Challenge

The Reluctant Keeper

DEADLY DRAGONS:

The (Not) Cursed Dragon

The (Not) Satisfied Dragon

STANDALONE:

Dead of Spring (MF - Hades & Persephone retelling)

Blood Nor Money (RH - vampires)

Fire & Gasoline (MF - wolf shifter fated mates)

www.ingramcontent.com/pod-product-compliance
Lightning Source LLC
LaVergne TN
LVHW040211170325
806091LV00022B/380